SKULL'S VENGEANCE

LINNEA TANNER

BOOK FOUR IN THE CURSE OF CLANSMEN AND KINGS SERIES

Book 4: *Skull's Vengeance*
Curse of Clansmen and Kings Series by Linnea Tanner

Books may be purchased by contacting the publisher or author at:
www.linneatanner.com or
linnea@linneatanner.com

Map: D. N. Frost, maps@DNFrost.com
Editing, design, and distribution by Bublish, Inc.
Publisher: Apollo Raven Publisher, LLC

ISBN: 978-1-7336002-0-0 (paperback)
         978-1-7336002-1-7 (e-book)

1) Historical Fantasy 2) Historical Fiction 3) Fantasy Historical 4) Ancient Rome
5) Ancient Britannia 6) Celtic Myth and Legend 7) Greek and Roman Myth & Legend

First Edition: Printed in the USA

Praise for Linnea Tanner and Her Books From
THE CURSE OF CLANSMEN AND KINGS SERIES

"One of the novel's most ambitious gambits is its richly atmospheric blending of supernatural elements into the broader story. The tale features ghosts, animal familiars, shapeshifters, and all kinds of spiritual communications, and Tanner's skill at interweaving these elements is shown by how seamless the whole process feels. This kind of fidelity to research will please readers familiar with this period of Rome's occupation of Britain (they will likely be hunting for a mention of the legendary British resistance fighter Boudicca, and they won't be disappointed). A strangely evocative, smoothly readable tale about lovers dealing with Britannia's tribes and ancient Rome."—*Kirkus Review*

"Catrin is a very strong female lead despite her very young age, forced to mature early thanks to all the horrible situations she had to live through or witness. Not only her physical prowess but also her mental strength shape her into an admirable heroine, suffering through a range of emotions and letting her weaknesses teach her how to turn them into strengths too."— *International Review of Books*

"Ancient Rome and Britain are the background settings for this epic tale of love, betrayal and political intrigue. The Roman era and the ensuing battles between the clan leaders in Britain during the first century AD do not often appear as the setting for fantasy novels — a pity, since this era is very intriguing. A must read for anyone who enjoys history involving ancient Rome." —*Majanka Verstraete for InD'Tale Magazine*

"Author Linnea Tanner is a master storyteller of historical fantasy. Set in first century Britannia, a fantastical isle, the theme of balancing duty with illicit love, the consuming lust for power, intrigue and Celtic magic provides conflict and twists in this spell-binding story." —*AuthorsReading*

"Imbued with both Roman and Celtic traditions, myths and legends, the story draws a contrastive parallel between the two cultures and civilizations. If the realism of the story is ensured by the constantly changing network of political alliances and backstabbing, its beauty springs from the wonderfully interwoven mythological references and enlightening mystical experiences."—*OnlineBookClub.org*

BOOKS BY LINNEA TANNER

THE CURSE OF CLANSMEN AND KINGS SERIES
Apollo's Raven (Book 1)
Dagger's Destiny (Book 2)
Amulet's Rapture (Book 3)
Skulls' Vengeance (Book 4)

OTHER BOOKS
Two Faces of Janus: A Short Story of Ancient Rome

LIST OF CHARACTERS can be found on page 387 and can be downloaded in a PDF printable form at https://BookHip.com/STLRRBZ

MAP OF BRITANNIA

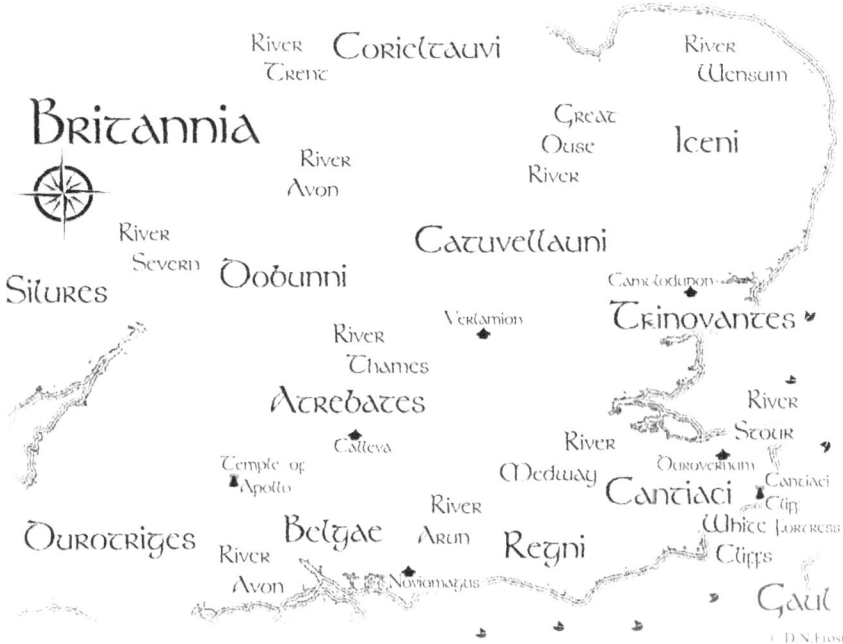

River Trent

Corieltauvi

River Wensum

Britannia

Great Ouse River

Iceni

River Avon

Catuvellauni

River Severn

Dobunni

Silures

Camulodunon

Verlamion

Trinovantes

River Thames

Atrebates

River Stour

Calleva

River Medway

Durovernum

Cantiaci

Cantiaci Clip

Temple of Apollo

Durotriges

Belgae

River Arun

Regni

White Fortress

River Avon

Noviomagus

Cliffs

Gaul

© D.N.Frost

MAP OF GAUL

Britannia

Cliffs
or Dubris

Itius
Portus

Gesoriacum

Meuse
River

Rhine
River

Fretum
Gallicum

Nemetacum

Germania

Durocortorum

Argentoratum

Seine
River

Gaul

Loire
River

Saône
River

Rhône
River

Charente
River

Lugdunum

Italia

Dordogne
River

Valentia

The
Alps

Tolosa

Narbo

Massilia

Pyrenees
Mts.

Garonne
River

Mediterranean Sea

© D.N.Frost

PROLOGUE

White Cliffs in Southeast Britannia, Eve of Samhain, 31 October, 26 AD

Three human skulls hung over King Marrock's stallion, dangling from a rope like ornaments. Feeling as invincible as a god, he rode to the precipice of the sheer cliffs and listened to the roar of the waves crashing below. Yet, the raven soaring overhead chilled him to the bone—an omen he was but mortal and could plunge to his death.

He embraced the warmth of Boudicca, his younger half sister, who sat astride his horse in front of him. A toddler full of mirth, she was a healer who could connect to the souls of the dead.

Whereas their mother accused *him*, also known as Blood Wolf, of being a soulless murderer.

On this eve of Samhain, Marrock knew the souls of the dead freely roamed among the living. He spotted his deadliest assassin, Gawain, searching for the wraith on the emerald hilltop. Gawain had a blue, triangular tattoo of a dagger's blade on his forehead and deadly weapons underneath his black cloak—the royal insignia of the red dragon stitched to the front panel.

For Marrock, the Otherworldly dragon, with its leathery wings and fiery breath, symbolized perpetual power. It was said that where dragons trod, mystic energy flowed. The untamed beast guarded the portal into the Otherworld.

He yearned for the dragon's mystic power—the power to summon forces from the earth's molten underbelly to immolate his rivals.

Gawain pointed to a pile of rocks. "The sheepherder saw the wraith over there," he said in his deep, gravelly voice.

Marrock handed Boudicca to him and then dismounted, pulling the rope of skulls off his horse and draping it over his shoulders. His family's skulls served as a warning to anyone who threatened his sovereignty.

Until now, he had only been able to summon the deadly powers from the skulls of his stepmother and bastard sister; their souls were encased in the bone crowns. The soul of his father, King Amren, still eluded Marrock, even after he had sliced off his father's head. If his father's soul was indeed wandering the hilltop, he would imprison it in the largest empty skull he had.

Then, he would be able to unleash the collective forces from all three souls.

Glancing all around, he could not see his father's ghostly figure in the thickening fog. Boudicca's gleeful giggle roused his attention. He watched her waddle toward a mound of stones and place her tiny hands on the stacked rocks.

"Pa. Pa. Am," she squealed with delight.

Marrock cast a glance at Gawain. "Did the sheepherder see the wraith disappear into those rocks?"

Gawain nodded. "Indeed, I believe so."

Marrock transferred the roped skulls from his shoulders to the grassy ground and looked at Gawain. "Help me remove the rocks so I can see what is underneath."

Gawain joined Marrock in the task of removing the white stones one by one. They inspected each rock for any defect before setting it aside.

Boudicca, mimicking the men, picked up flint pebbles and dropped them on the chalky ground.

After a while, they uncovered the gemstone handle of a dagger; its blade was embedded in a coil-shaped serpent stone. Marrock recognized the jewel-studded dagger as once belonging to his father. Intrigued, he gripped the handle with both hands and strained to pull it out, his muscles aching and his face dripping with sweat from the effort.

Suddenly, to his shock, the hilt turned sizzling hot. He jerked his hands away and inspected the blisters that had formed on his reddened palms. Hearing Boudicca's gleeful babble, he looked down just as she gripped the dagger's handle.

"Pa. Pa. Am," she trilled.

To Marrock's surprise, Boudicca's hands did not burn.

A prickling sensation noosed around his neck as he recalled the original curse cast by his mother just before his father had executed her.

The gods demand that the scales be balanced for the life you take. If you deny my soul's journey to the Otherworld by beheading me, I curse you to the same fate as mine. I prophesy your future queen will beget a daughter who will rise as a raven and join your son, Blood Wolf, and a mighty empire will overtake your kingdom and execute my curse.

King Amren had etched the words of the curse on the dagger's blade using the Roman alphabet with the belief he could thwart the dark prophecy.

Marrock shuddered.

Does my father's soul live in the dagger? Has he come back to exact vengeance on me?

An idea seeded in his mind. With Boudicca's ability to connect with the dead, she might be able to transfer his father's soul from the dagger into his skull.

Smiling, he knelt beside his little half sister and pointed to the dagger. "Do you see Grandpa Amren?"

Boudicca's face lit up. Her shoulder-length, coppery hair swept freely around her face in the stiff ocean breeze as she shrieked, "Pa. Pater Amren!"

Marrock dragged the roped skulls to the serpent stone, setting his father's skull in front of the dagger and the other two skulls on either side of it. He gave his half sister a playful smile. "Do you want to play a game?" he asked.

A broad grin broke out on the little girl's chubby-cheeked face. "Yes. Yes. Game play!"

Marrock took her right hand and spread her tiny fingers apart to grasp the dagger's handle. He then placed her other hand flat on the crown of the largest skull, instructing, "Keep your hands like this as I speak to the gods."

She nodded excitedly, appearing to understand.

Lifting his arms to the windswept clouds, Marrock intoned, "Lost soul, return to the temple of your skull and connect with family souls. Forge the souls into a steel-edged blade of vengeance. Gods of the Otherworld, bequeath me with the power to summon dark forces from three crowns of bone."

Streaks of lightning webbed all around him. Claps of thunder rumbled the ground beneath his leather shoes. As he looked at Boudicca, her blue eyes transformed to a brilliant amber glow. A ball of light discharged from the dagger's handle to her hands. She released her grip and wiggled her fingertips, and strands of light spun in and out of each of the skull's eye sockets. When the skulls glowed a brilliant white, her amber-colored eyes slowly turned blue again.

Marrock had seen the phenomenon before, whenever Boudicca touched anyone who was sick or disfigured. As a newborn, she had miraculously saved their mother from the throes of death in childbirth. Every time she touched his pitted, moon-cratered face, tissue filled in the unsightly gaps. And the strawberry-colored birthmark covering half of his wife's face diminished each time she nursed Boudicca.

Euphoric, Marrock kissed Boudicca on the forehead for her part in trapping King Amren's soul in his skull. His newfound ability to use the skulls as conduits through which dark energy from the Otherworld could flow again emboldened him with a sense of immortality.

But then, his mind grappled with the possibility that three people from his past had the ability to block his heightened power.

First, there was his mother, Rhan, who had escaped death three times, including his own attempt on her life. Rhan's centuries-old coadjutor, Myrddin, could anoint a more powerful ruler to replace him.

And finally, there was Catrin, his other half sister.

A chill iced down his spine as an image of Catrin as a nine-year-old, golden-haired girl came to mind. Though she appeared as innocent and cheerful as Boudicca, she had the vile temperament of a raven. She had summoned Otherworldly ravens to peck out half of his face to thwart his attempt to transform her into a wolf.

The raven from the curse. An evil druidess to match his powers.

Fortunately, he had left her for dead two years earlier, after his final battle to overthrow their father's kingdom. Now, he only had to contend with Rhan and Myrddin.

No one will stop me now! I will forge a great empire to match Rome.

Marrock cast a sinister glance at Gawain and gestured for him to come closer.

"Let us discuss your next assignment," he said as he stroked the stitched emblem of the fiery-red dragon on the assassin's black cloak.

The Raven is not only a messenger from the gods;
it has a darker purpose— collecting the souls of the dead from battlefields.

I

PORTALS TO THE OTHERWORLD

One Year Later . . .

Antonii Villa in Gaul, Eve of Samhain, 31 October, 27 AD

The ground Catrin had disturbed to bury her stillborn baby almost a year ago had grown over and blended into its surroundings. The white blooms on the nearby rosebush had shriveled in autumn's first frost. Only the gravestone that her secret Roman husband, Marcellus, had erected in mid-September acknowledged their child's existence—a symbol of their forbidden love. Though he had freed her, Catrin still felt chained to the past, too paralyzed to move forward. It was as if she had been buried alongside her tiny daughter, who'd been too premature to live.

Dispirited, she again read the message written on the parchment in her hand.

To my beloved Catrin,

Because of you, I dare to dream more than I ever have. Last night, a star shot across the night sky to join another in a brilliant glow—a sign that we are destined to be together. I need you. You are my soul mate, the love of my life. Join me in Rome.

I remain your husband in heart.

Marcellus Antonius

Bitter tears filled Catrin's eyes.

Why should I join him in Rome?

The situation had not changed. Roman law did not recognize marriage vows between a Roman citizen and a foreigner. Marcellus had conceded to his father's demand to marry a twelve-year-old girl from one of the most powerful families in Rome to forge a political alliance. Almost six weeks had passed since Catrin had forsaken him and refused to go to Rome with him so he could attend the banquet to announce his betrothal to the young Roman noblewoman.

She refused to be considered his barbarian mistress from the isle of Britannia. In the eyes of Rome, she was nothing more than a whore whom Marcellus could use and dispose of.

I am the rightful queen of the Cantiaci people.

Marcellus could have ruled as her equal—her king!—if only he had returned with her to her homeland. But he'd refused her. Instead, he had urged her to take more time to reconsider. She could stay at his family's villa in Gaul until she made her final decision. If she chose to leave, he would gift her four horses and a bagful of coins.

"I will take the horses, thank you kindly," she muttered, crunching the parchment in her hands. Though she had made her final decision to return home, one nagging question rumbled in her mind.

How can I raise an army and fulfill my destiny?

Though alone, she still embraced the prophecy of her father, King Amren. In a vision she'd had shortly after the Romans captured and enslaved her, he'd foretold she would overthrow Marrock.

The fulfillment of that prophecy was reinforced when Ferrex, her former fighting mentor—now gladiator—apprised her that warriors from her father's inner circle were regrouping and gathering forces to usurp Marrock and proclaim her as the Cantiaci queen.

But Ferrex had been transported to Rome to fight in their blood sport.

Does anyone else from my homeland know where I am?

At midnight tonight, she knew the Cantiaci kingdom would celebrate the Samhain festival. Portals from the Otherworld would open to the mortal world, allowing the souls of the dead to mingle with the living. Perhaps her father's spirit would show her the next step in her quest to fulfill his prophecy to destroy Marrock.

The deep voice of Falco, the horse trainer, drew Catrin out of her muse. She turned and found a grim frown on his face.

"Servia just told me that a stranger called Trystan came to the villa asking for you," he said. "She told him to go away, thinking he was a thief. He rode off into the nearby woods."

"Did Servia say what he looked like?" Catrin inquired, her spirits lifting upon hearing that her father's former second-in-command had found her.

"Servia only said that he was armed and had demonic eyes that cut through her," Falco answered.

Catrin's lips quirked into a smile, and she looked all around for Trystan. In the evening sun's fading light, she spotted a caped man on horseback at the edge of the forest, where chariot racehorses were corralled. He appeared to be wearing the distinct blue-and-gold plaid braccae of a Cantiaci clansman. Unable to discern his face, she assumed he was Trystan. Nearly three years had passed since she'd last seen him; back then, he had been battling against the Roman legionaries who had aided Marrock's overthrow of their father.

The cloaked horseman raised a bare fist in salute—a signal a Cantiaci warrior often used to request a meeting in secret. The rider kicked his horse into a gallop and disappeared into the dense woods like a shadow.

"Trystan wants to meet me," Catrin mumbled to herself.

Falco looked in the direction of her gaze. "Meet who?"

"The demon Servia sent away," Catrin replied with a thin smile. "Saddle Lugus for me."

Falco raised his thick eyebrows. "For what purpose?"

"To ride, of course," Catrin said with a tinge of sarcasm, offering no further explanation of her plan to meet with the mysterious horseman on the eve when souls freely mingled with mortals.

Falco's eyes widened. "Do you think it's wise to ride alone on the eve of Samhain? Wraiths wander the woods at night. And thieves are always looking for someone to rob."

"Remember, Falco, Marcellus told you to do whatever I asked," Catrin said firmly. "Meet me in the forecourt with my horse."

Falco opened his mouth to protest again, but Catrin shot him a scathing glare. He bowed and headed toward the stables. As he left, she heard him grumble, "If anything happens, Marcellus will flay me alive."

Before leaving the sacred burial site of her daughter, she silently read the monument's inscription: *To the spirit of a little girl who lies in the earth's womb but will bloom again in spring.*

A sob caught in Catrin's throat.

Had Marcellus intended those words for her as well as their daughter, whose light had extinguished before she'd had a chance to shine?

Reluctantly, Catrin left her precious daughter in the earth's dark womb and hastened to the privacy of her bedchamber, which was in the back of the columnated peristyle of the villa. After slipping out of her ankle-length dress, she dressed in a pair of woolen braccae and a tunic. To defend herself against any thieves, she fastened a weapons belt around her waist and sheathed a knife and sword. Outside the chamber, she retrieved a burning torch from a sconce attached to a marble column in the peristyle so she could illuminate her way at night.

Catrin met Falco at the cobblestone entranceway. He was holding the reins of Lugus—a white Arabian-Berber stallion he had trained for her to ride as an *eques* in the gladiatorial games. He took the burning torch from her so she could mount her steed.

"Are you sure about riding tonight?" he asked.

"Yes," she replied, climbing on her horse and taking the torch from Falco's hand. "I'll be back late tonight." Before Falco could utter another word, she kicked Lugus into a gallop.

The full harvest moon peeked through the eastern treetops as she rode to the woods where the cloaked horseman had disappeared. Reaching the site, she halted her horse, anticipating that Trystan would reveal himself once he observed no one had followed her.

A few moments later, the horseman appeared through the trees, holding a burning torch over his head. She glanced all around for any bandits. As she approached the rider, the flaming torch in his hand illuminated his face. At first, she did not recognize the powerfully built man with shoulder-length, gray-streaked hair.

"Trystan?" she asked tentatively.

The man pulled back the cowl of his cloak. His lips turned up into a smirk. "That I am," he said in their native Celtic tongue. "And, if my eyes do not deceive me, you are Catrin. The last time I saw you, you were as skinny as a twig. Look at you now. Built like a warrior."

Catrin gave a wry smile. "And your dark hair was shorn like a Roman's."

"Age changes us all." Trystan grunted as he shifted his weight on his horse. "Follow me to my campsite. We can talk there."

As Catrin rode beside Trystan, both of their torches illuminated the footpath into the darkening woods. Overhead, shadowy branches undulated like serpents in the bone-chilling autumn breeze.

"I thought you fell in battle," Catrin commented.

Trystan looked sideways at her and chuckled. "I'm no ghost, though 'tis the night for it."

Catrin nudged Lugus closer to Trystan's horse. "How did you survive the last battle my mother led?"

"I retreated with other warriors to avoid casualties. Later, we regrouped and rebelled against Marrock. But alas, the gods pissed on us. He captured us and then penned us up like chickens to be butchered."

Catrin chuckled. "So, you obviously escaped."

"Through strange circumstances that you will find hard to believe," Trystan said, reining his horse to a halt. "The people who helped me to escape are at my camp."

Apprehensive, Catrin halted her own horse. "Do I know them?"

Trystan looked down and nervously fiddled with the reins. "Rhan and Myrddin want to ally with us."

Anger struck Catrin's chest like viper's venom. "What? Marrock's mother and her shape-shifting wizard want to join us? What are you thinking? They betrayed my father and murdered everyone in my family."

"At first, I also felt the same way," Trystan said evenly, lifting his eyes to meet Catrin's glare. "That was until Rhan told me Marrock tried to kill her. A most heinous act, matricide. For what Marrock did, Rhan is out for blood vengeance—the same as you and me."

Catrin huffed. "More likely, Rhan wants blood vengeance on me."

"Hear me out," Trystan said firmly. "I believe their intentions are true. They have foretold things about you that have come true."

"What things?"

"Though everyone believed you were dead, Rhan insisted you yet lived. In a vision, she saw you disguised as a boy in the Roman legion. That is why we started searching for you in Gaul."

"Are you so blind that you cannot see through Rhan's trickery?" Catrin admonished, struggling to temper her voice. "She is a dark druidess. She wants me to show her how I can meld my thoughts with my raven guide and travel to the Otherworld. There, Rhan believes she can summon dark forces to destroy not only Marrock but me as well. And Myrddin is her accomplice. He's a centuries-old druid who drops in and out of time to declare the next ruler during times of strife."

"What harm is there in speaking with them?" Trystan asked. "Rhan foresees that you will rise as the raven queen to overthrow Marrock. Furthermore, Myrddin proclaims you as the rightful heir to the Cantiaci kingdom. They have forged alliances with other rulers whose lands have been invaded by Marrock's forces." He sighed. "As you must be aware, many of our warriors fell in the final battle against Marrock. He is a monster who has sold able-bodied warriors from our clan to be gladiators in Rome. We have freed some of them to join our cause, and we are also recruiting mercenaries."

Trystan pointed in the direction of a faint glow filtering through the trees. "Rhan and Myrddin are but a short distance from here. They are at a fire, summoning ancestral souls."

The overhanging branches crackled in a gale of wind—a sign the Otherworld's portals were opening. A sense of foreboding crawled down Catrin's back, warning her to turn back.

"At least speak with them," Trystan pressed stubbornly. "Or go back to the villa as the Roman's harlot."

Angered, Catrin whipped her head toward him. "Be careful with your words, warrior. I am no whore. I am no slave. I am the queen of the Cantiaci!

The Roman is my husband. You witnessed our marriage in Britannia, as you well remember."

"The ceremony was a farce . . . a fertility rite Myrddin performed to make Amren believe he could break Rhan's curse," Trystan retorted.

"I understand Myrddin performed the ritual as a distraction so Marrock could set our village afire and start a war. That is why I do not trust Myrddin and Rhan. Even so, the ceremony bonded Marcellus and me as husband and wife."

"Forgive me, my queen. I meant no disrespect." Trystan paused, carefully considering his next words. "I am asking—no, I am *pleading*—that you speak with Rhan and Myrddin before you decide your next step."

Exasperated, Catrin drew in a sharp breath. Then, she considered Trystan's impassioned plea to meet with two of her most hated enemies. Recalling how her father had respected his second-in-command's advice, she reluctantly conceded and squeezed her legs against her horse's flanks to move toward the campfire's glow.

The night's chill mysteriously transformed into an embracing warmth as they neared a roaring fire with a black cauldron hanging over it. Sitting behind the crimson flames were two obscured figures.

"Welcome, Apollo's Raven," a woman's deep voice intoned. "Come to our fire. Join us in the dance of souls."

Though Catrin hesitated to join them, the fire's radiance mesmerized her, luring her closer to the orange flames. She dismounted and handed the reins to Trystan, who quietly remained with the horses as she sat down on a fallen log near the roaring campfire.

"Drink the magic from the cauldron," the woman offered. "It empowers all who partake with the knowledge of mystical mysteries from the ancient druids."

"I already have that power," Catrin proclaimed, trepidatious that perhaps Rhan had dropped hallucinogenic ingredients into the bubbling mixture. Thick steam flowed over the cauldron's edge and down its metal surface in a thick, greenish fog.

"We know, my love, but you have only had a taste," Rhan replied in a hypnotic voice. "You do not know how to control this dark magic. But we do."

Suddenly light-headed from the smoky fumes emanating from the cauldron, Catrin struggled to maintain her wits. "Once before you said this, when you tried to trick me into revealing how I can travel to the Otherworld."

"Believe me, this is no trick," Rhan said soothingly. "I've seen your father's spirit wander the top of cliffs, near a dagger embedded in a serpent stone. It is the blade on which my curse was etched."

"I sense the curse has altered again, but I can't see how the etched wording has changed on the blade," Myrddin interjected. "You must help us solve the riddle of how the dagger got there."

Catrin inhaled sharply, realizing Myrddin and Rhan had discovered the location of the dagger she had thrust into the stone. The image of her running away from the Romans played in her mind, and her thoughts transformed into words.

"After the final battle, I tried to escape the Romans, but . . . but there was nowhere to go, except jump off the white cliffs. At that moment, I chose to die rather than be captured."

Rhan rose to her feet, walked around the fire, and sat next to Catrin. "But you didn't die, did you?" she said, touching Catrin's arm.

"No. A riderless horse galloped to me, stopping in front of me. My father suddenly appeared and told me not to jump," Catrin disclosed, reliving the supernatural moment in her mind. "I couldn't believe my eyes that Father was there. I knew Marrock had beheaded him. Yet, I felt his essence and his love radiate into me."

Tears swelled in Catrin's eyes as remorse that she had been unable to save her family from Marrock's brutality overwhelmed her. She swallowed down a sob before continuing her story.

"Father told me to lift the cursed dagger toward the sky. To my amazement, sunlight flashed through the dark clouds, almost blinding me. He then ordered, 'Thrust the dagger into the serpent stone that I create.' What I saw next was not a vision. It was real."

Catrin grimaced as she recalled the burning pain she'd felt as she'd held the hilt of the dagger. "The blade turned orange, as if it had been taken out of a furnace. Father's spirit burst apart into gold dust and melted into the blade's etching. Serpents massed together on the ground. The venom dripping from their fangs hardened into stone. Somehow, I was able to push the dagger into the hard rock, like it was butter. And, and . . ."

"And what, my dear?" Rhan pressed.

Catrin's voice cracked. "I was collared by the Romans and put on a warship."

"Did your father say anything else before his spirit melded with the dagger?" Myrddin asked, still sitting across the fire from them.

"Not a word," Catrin said, wiping away the salty tears from the corners of her mouth. "But later, he appeared to me in a vision, when I was wounded and burning with fever on the ship. I recall him saying, 'You must begin a difficult journey in the Roman world.' I begged him not to leave me. The Raven was perched on his shoulder as he proclaimed, 'You must be forged into a battle-hardened warrior on the empire's anvil before you can return home. Only then will you be able to pull the dagger out of the stone and embrace my curse as your destiny.'"

"And what is your destiny?" Rhan asked, scooting closer to Catrin.

"To avenge my father," Catrin declared, not revealing that her father had also told her the gods in the Otherworld would grant her full access to the powers of the ancient druids so she could overcome Marrock and claim the throne.

"Did Amren say anything else in your vision?" Rhan asked.

"'Behold the Raven, the messenger of Apollo. Behold the sun god, your protector.'"

"Is that the Apollo in the altered curse?" Myrddin's voice croaked above the sound of the crackling fire.

Catrin cast a glance at Rhan. "Tell me again how the curse on the dagger blade was altered."

Rhan recounted the altered curse. "The first part of my curse stays the same. 'The gods demand the scales be balanced for the life you take today.

If you deny my soul's journey to the Otherworld by beheading me, I curse you to the same fate as mine.' It is there the curse alters," Rhan continued. "'When the Raven rises out of Apollo's flames with the dark powers of the ancient druids, Blood Wolf will form a pack with the mighty empire and fulfill this curse. The Raven will then cast liquid fire into the serpent stone and forge vengeance on the empire's anvil.'"

"Marcellus must be the Apollo foretold in the curse. It is his family's insignia," Catrin said thoughtfully. "Everything the curse said and what Father foretold has come true. My Roman master, Decimus, believed I was an oracle of Apollo and could foretell his future. For some strange reason, he disguised me as a boy so I could train in the Roman legion. Then, he sold me to fight as a gladiator after he caught Marcellus trying to help me escape. It makes sense that my enslavement by the Romans has forged my desire to seek vengeance on Marrock."

Rhan placed her hand on Catrin's shoulder. "Amren also appeared to me in a vision, when I gave birth to my daughter, Boudicca, and almost died."

Catrin recoiled from Rhan's touch. "Why would the gods spare your daughter but strike mine dead? You shape-shifted into my form so you could seduce Marcellus. With the awful conditions of being transported as a gladiator to Lugdunum, I didn't have the strength to carry my baby to term."

"I understand your hate," Rhan said somberly. "How could someone as good as Boudicca come from me? Yet, I've endured what no mother should suffer. Marrock stole Boudicca after he tried to murder me. He uses my daughter's powers to heal his grotesque face. I want Boudicca back. And for that to happen, I must destroy the monster created in my womb—the same womb that created my blessed daughter. It is my duty as a mother to destroy the evil son I brought into the world and assure the daughter sired in Apollo's flames survives."

"You mean Boudicca, who was sired by Marcellus," Catrin accused bitterly.

Rhan regarded Catrin for a moment. "You seem troubled by this, my love. Who is the Raven in the curse? Is it you? Or is it me? I must admit, Marcellus is a skilled lover. He no doubt practiced his skills on you."

Catrin could feel her eyes blazing at Rhan. "Careful where you step."

Rhan's lips curled into a cruel smile. She leaned over to pick up a ladle near the fire, then stood to stir the boiling, greenish-brown mixture in the cauldron. A thick, orange haze rose from the cauldron as the flames licked at the black vessel. After the steam dissipated, Rhan looked inside the metal pot.

"From which ancestor do you seek advice?" she asked.

"Do you see my father?" Catrin inquired.

"Your father is not yet in the Otherworld," Rhan said in a deep, ominous tone. "His soul is hiding in the dagger, as we well know."

"What about my mother and my older sister, Vala?"

"Their souls are encased in their skulls, from which Marrock summons forces of nature."

Catrin shuddered. Without proper burial, their souls would remain imprisoned in their bone crowns, unable to enter the Otherworld. She wondered if her other sister had suffered the same fate.

"Do you know what happened to Mor?" Catrin ventured.

Rhan continued gazing into the cauldron. "She is not yet in the Otherworld. But wait . . . I see your stillborn daughter. Mother Goddess will suckle her until she can reincarnate as another living being."

Suddenly, Catrin felt as though an invisible force had paralyzed her muscles. Unable to move, she watched Myrddin hobble with the support of a staff topped with a serpent head. The serpent appeared to be swallowing a pearl-white egg. The long-bearded druid halted in front of Catrin and shook his staff until the egg-shaped orb began to glow. He lifted his staff and chanted.

Life springs from chaos
To reincarnate, then be destroyed.
Light rises out of darkness, then sets again.
Each force balances on the circle of life.
Come join us in the dance of souls
Reborn, transformed, and inspired.

Rhan ladled some potion from the cauldron into a cup and drank the murky liquid. "Mmm, so good. So refreshing. Taste, my love."

Catrin took three sips of the bittersweet elixir Rhan offered before immersing her essence inside the cauldron's bubbling brew. Images of various people churned all around her in the boiling mixture: her parents, King Amren and Queen Rhiannon, dressed in regal clothes; her older sisters, Vala and Mor, as little girls; Rhan, Marrock, and a chestnut-haired toddler. Tendrils sprouted in the mixture, interconnecting all the images together as a circular lattice.

Catrin had previously traveled to the deep recesses of her mind with the guidance of the Raven, but it felt different this time.

More foreboding.

2

CAULDRON'S FORESIGHT

Bewildered, Catrin found herself floating inside a concave, bone-white structure. Below her, light filtering through two large openings spun strands of golden light, forming a lattice around her. Indistinguishable voices whispered in her ears. Sensing someone was nearby, she glanced all around but could not see anyone.

Suddenly, an invisible force pressed her against a hard surface, immobilizing her. Panic streaked through her when she realized she could not escape. The voice of her dead father, King Amren, saying, "I've been waiting for you," further struck fear in her.

Uncertain if she'd entered the portal to the Otherworld, Catrin looked up at the ceiling for the multicolored life threads weaving in and out of the tapestry on the Wall of Lives—a transitional barrier between the physical and spiritual worlds where past, present, and future merged into one timeline.

"Am I in the Depths of Possibilities below the Wall of Lives?" she asked her father.

King Amren's deep voice resonated in her mind. "You are in my soul's temple—my prison."

Worried her soul had also been imprisoned, Catrin felt her heart pound erratically within her chest. "Your prison?"

"My skull," King Amren clarified. "This is where Marrock keeps my soul prisoner to use as he pleases. How did you get past his magic to connect with me?"

"After I drank a mixture from Rhan's cauldron, I suddenly found myself here," Catrin explained, although she did not understand how the magic worked.

"Ah . . . a brew of wisdom, knowledge, and inspiration." King Amren added, "Rhan is a cunning and treacherous sorceress. She has a knack for escaping death. A few years ago, when I hid in the dagger, I saw her spirit roaming the white cliffs. I thought she'd died. Obviously, I was wrong."

"Did you hide in the same dagger I thrust into the serpent stone?" Catrin inquired.

"Yes. And the dagger you must pull from the stone to release my soul from the skull. Otherwise . . ." King Amren's voice faded into an ominous whisper.

"Otherwise, what?"

A man's shadow was cast on the dome-shaped ceiling from which her father's voice emanated. "Marrock will drain my essence until I disappear. At first, I fought his attempts to steal my soul's forces. But I no longer have the strength to resist."

The force immobilizing Catrin weakened. Envisioning herself as the Raven, her spiritual guide, she transformed and fluttered to the domed ceiling to be closer to her father's shadow, which was fading quickly.

"Why did Rhan send me here?" she asked.

"So you can access the truths in the depths of your mind . . . a realm few of us explore." A gold corona began glowing around King Amren's shadow, like an eclipsed sun, as he continued, "You asked if we are in the Depths of Possibilities. Perhaps you are, but not me. I am frozen in the past and must relive the day I executed Rhan over and over. The day I forced Marrock to watch me cut off his mother's head. The day I created a monster."

"Do you regret killing Rhan?" Catrin asked, disquieted by her father's merciless act.

"At the time, I believed it was my duty. It was my right as king to condemn all traitors. But now . . ." King Amren sighed heavily, and his voice grew somber. "I loved Rhan so much. She was the air I breathed. Love that strong ignites from the same fire as hate. I opened my heart to her. I shared my fears, my darkest secrets. I would have done anything for her, even die to protect her.

"Yet, when I discovered she'd conspired with other nobles to overthrow me, my love turned to hate. I demanded justice for her betrayal. I sought vengeance against my queen, seeking the power that corrupted my soul. And now, Marrock threatens to destroy the remnants of my soul in exchange for the same power that consumed me."

"If that is what he wants, why does he steal the life forces from my mother's and sister's souls?" Catrin asked.

King Amren chuckled grimly. "What vengeance is more apt than Marrock extinguishing everyone I love?"

Catrin's throat tightened. "What do you want of me?"

The bright light around King Amren's shadow continued to fade as he answered. "Destroy Marrock and free the souls of your mother and sister to reincarnate into other forms. You must unravel your doubts about moving forward. The last time you visited the Depth of Possibilities, before the Romans captured and enslaved you, your future had not yet been set in stone by your past mistakes. But now, the future of our kingdom depends on the choices you make in the present. To see the light to your destiny, you must first behold the darkest depths of your soul. Do you have the courage to do that?"

"I am afraid of what I might see. What I might lose or become," Catrin said, a shudder slicing down her spine.

King Amren blew out a deep breath. "Ah . . . a conundrum. How can you both create life as a mother and destroy it as a warrior? How can the ecstasy of love be swept away in a crashing wave of hate? You need both forces, I believe, to forge the powers needed to draw the dagger out of the stone."

Catrin hesitated, then said, "I once embraced hate, but I almost lost my heart in seeking vengeance against my Roman master, Decimus."

"What stopped you, then?" King Amren probed.

A sob clutched at Catrin's throat. "I would have killed Marcellus, too."

"Did you not forsake him?"

Catrin felt as if her heart were shattering from her conflicted feelings about Marcellus.

"I . . . don't know if I can."

"You still love him, don't you?"

"How can I stop? He is part of my soul," Catrin proclaimed.

"You cannot," King Amren said somberly. "But true love comes with sacrifice."

"What sacrifice?" Catrin asked as the image of a man's face with a blue tattoo of a dagger on his head projected on her father's shadow.

"The Raven will know when you most need the ancient powers of the druids," King Amren's voice whispered as his shadow disappeared.

Before Catrin could ponder where to find the Raven, a reptilian face suddenly came into focus in the same spot her father's shadow had vanished. The creature opened its mouth, revealing jagged teeth. Fire burst from its throat and immolated her raven body.

Catrin knew the creature was a dragon, and she was plunged into timeless oblivion.

3

THE JOURNEY BEGINS

One Day Later . . .

Antonii Villa in Gaul, 1 November, 27 AD

Catrin woke with a start, sensing the heat on her face cooling like an ocean breeze. Opening her eyes, she found herself lying under a towering oak tree. She felt as if her mind were in a fog as she gazed at red leaves twisting and dancing on the ends of twigs above her. A rush of wind made the overhead tree branches moan and crack. Yet, the birds' melodic chirps sounded like sweet songs in her ears. Her head began to pound as she struggled to gain her bearings.

Trystan's face came into focus. "Are you all right?" he asked.

"I think so," she said, feeling dizzy and disoriented. "Where am I?"

"Near the Antonii villa," Trystan replied. "You have been in a deep sleep most of the day."

Feeling woozy, Catrin gingerly pushed herself to a sitting position and leaned against the tree trunk. "That can't be. I was in a dream for just a short time."

Trystan squatted beside her and gaped. "Your eyes are blue again!" he exclaimed.

Catrin shook her head in confusion. "What do you mean?"

"Last night, your eyes glowed like amber gems before you lost consciousness. But they are blue again," Trystan explained.

Slowly recalling what had happened before her vision, Catrin scanned the area for the cauldron but found only cold ashes from a campfire.

"Where are Rhan and Myrddin?" she asked.

"They left at first light," Trystan said, standing up. "Rhan told me to stay with you until you woke. I must admit, though, I was afraid you'd never wake. You were as white as a corpse."

"I had a vision of my father," Catrin said.

Trystan's eyes widened. "What did he say?"

"I should embrace my destiny," Catrin said, offering no further detail of what her father had said as she struggled to interpret the vision.

"You don't plan to go back to Marcellus?" Trystan's brow creased.

Catrin did not answer as she reflected on her father's words. *To see the light to your destiny, you must first behold the darkest depths of your soul. Do you have the courage to do that?* Why did she hesitate to leave the villa to seek her destiny? A sense of foreboding crawled down her back as she sensed the dragon from her vision watching her.

Finally finding the courage to take the next step, she told Trystan, "I want to leave here and begin planning a way to overthrow Marrock."

"I can find some quarters in the city where we can stay," Trystan offered. "But for now, go back to the villa until you receive word from me. If you need to find me sooner, talk to the shopkeeper who sells medicinal herbs just inside the city gate. You will recognize her by the pile of gray hair that coils around her head like a snake. Ask her where to find the butcher of swine."

Catrin chuckled. "You mean my enemy's butcher?"

Trystan's mouth twitched in a smile. "Exactly. Can you find your way back to the villa from here?"

"Of course," Catrin said, noticing her horse was tied to a tree nearby. "Do you have anything for me to eat before I go?"

Trystan handed Catrin some dried meat strips. "From my butcher shop."

"How apt. A warrior turned butcher," Catrin commented with a smile.

Trystan's lips curled up. "Both skilled with a knife, are they not?"

Catrin nodded and devoured the salty pork strips. After she finished eating, she mounted her white stallion and rode with Trystan for the short distance to the cobblestone pathway that led to the villa. There, he left her and galloped away in the opposite direction.

Riding under the fading light of the sunset, Catrin contemplated what sacrifice she would have to make on her quest to destroy the monster Rhan and her father had brought into this world. A sick feeling sunk into the pit of her stomach at the thought that the dragon in her vision was Marrock. Surely, he had sensed her presence.

Was he still there, in the shadows of her mind, waiting to consume her soul?

4

SLAVE CATCHERS

Calleva, Southeast Britannia, 1 November, 27 AD

Thus far, King Marrock's raids had successfully swept across the Atrebates farmlands like a firestorm, all the way to the capital of Calleva—an oppidum with defensive embankments to protect the surrounding inhabitants. Epaticcus, the brother of King Cunobelin, from the northern Catuvellauni tribe, had besieged Calleva earlier in the spring and overthrown its king. The late autumn raids gave Marrock an opportunity to test the strength of Epaticcus's forces to hold their newly conquered kingdom. Furthermore, he wanted to explore how effectively he could conjure the dark forces from his family's three skulls to destroy his enemies in battle.

Marrock's raiding party consisted of seventy heavily armed mercenaries and slave catchers. Also accompanying him was his pack of twenty wolves, trained to chase down any survivors fleeing from the mayhem and sniff out anyone hiding in roundhouses or nearby woods.

Thus far, local farmers, herdsmen, and villagers had given little resistance in their ambushes. They had readily captured noble warriors and commoners to sell in the Roman slave market. The proceeds would pay for more mercenaries in his army to battle adversarial kingdoms across Britannia during the following spring.

After a week of brutal assaults, heavily armed warriors were dispatched by Epaticcus to confront Marrock's forces about two miles from Calleva. The opposing infantrymen lined up at the far end of a harvested wheat field, the dense woods to their backs. The enemy commander, armed with shield and spear, rode in a horse-drawn chariot. As the chariot wheeled up and down the front line of infantrymen, the horn-helmeted commander lifted his weapon to spur war cries from his warriors.

Seeing shadows moving in the forest, Marrock surmised more enemy fighters were hiding there. He whistled for his pack of wolves to scan the area for warriors camouflaged in the woods. The wolves scattered in all directions and formed a circle around the enemy's front line.

Nudging his horse forward, Marrock shouted, "Who has the balls to fight me in single combat? If any of you defeats me, my army will withdraw."

The voice of the commander in the chariot resonated across the field. "We are not afraid to fight your dung eaters!"

Marrock threw his head back to commune with his wolves. Images projecting in his mind from various wolves showed spearmen in chariots, cavalrymen, and foot soldiers concealed in the forest—a battle tactic often used by Epaticcus to lure opposing forces into the thick trees for his fighters to butcher. Also hiding in the woods were commoners—men, women, and older children armed with pitchforks, clubs, and sickles.

The earthy smell in the air signaled an imminent rainstorm lurking overhead. Marrock knew on this day of Samhain, portals from the Otherworld would open, allowing him to summon dark forces from his three skulls. Soon, he would learn how to conjure these powers on any day he chose.

After dismounting, Marrock retrieved from the back of his horse the three skulls that were interconnected by crimson rope threaded in and out of their eye sockets. After setting the skulls on the grassy ground, he lifted his arms to the sky and cried out.

> I call upon ancestral souls
> To open portals to the Otherworld.
> God of thunder, lightning, and storms,
> Thrust your bolts at the earth's womb,
> Stir her anger and crack open her crevasses.
> Goddess of blood, quakes, and war,
> Wreak death, destruction, and mayhem.

For a moment, it was silent. No bird chirps. No raven screeches. No human voices. Then, suddenly, charged energy surged from the skulls into Marrock's fingertips. Dark clouds spiraled above him. Flashes of lightning webbed across the darkening sky. A gust of roaring wind swept back his shoulder-length, auburn hair. The earth rumbled beneath his leather shoes. Then, to his dismay, the charged energy fizzled out.

A streak of panic swept through him as he tried to summon the forces of nature again from the three skulls. Suddenly, Catrin's image flashed in his mind. Sensing her essence, he snapped his head back in shock.

How can this be? She should be dead!

A multicolored aura only he could see rose out of his father's skull. Shaken, he warily knelt and placed his fingertips on top of his father's skull. Sensing Catrin's presence emitting from the bony crown, he knew then that her soul was in the skull. He shuddered at the prospect that she'd possessed their father's skull, as Rhan had at her execution with a mute girl named Agrona. How could this be, though? Catrin had not even been there when he'd struck off their father's head. Or had she?

Enemy war chariots charging out of the dense woods drew Marrock's attention back to the battle. The enemy line split to form gaps, allowing the wheeled vehicles through. The spearmen in the chariots brandished their weapons, while the drivers steered the fast-moving chariots toward the wedged formation of Marrock's forces. To counter the assault, he had to remove Catrin's essence from the skull before he could summon the dark forces.

He recalled his mother saying that Catrin was a soul traveler who could enter the minds of other living entities. Though her physical body was solid, her soul flowed freely like a fluid.

If Catrin has this ability, so must I.

Marrock's soul took the shape of a dragon and flowed into his father's skull. There, he found Catrin's soul in the shape of a raven. He expelled a fiery breath to immolate her essence, then quickly returned to his physical form to focus on the battle.

Seeing a war chariot charging at him, Marrock jumped to his feet and lifted his arms to the heavens. This time, he successfully ignited the full destructive forces of nature from the skulls. The harvested field in front of him cracked like a broken eggshell as the ground rumbled beneath him.

The snaps of wooden wheels catching and breaking in the newly formed fissures echoed across the battlefield. Chariots flipped over, propelling spearmen and drivers onto the ground. Fissures continued to crisscross across the field, all the way to the edge of the thick woods. A cacophony of screams from the opposing warriors as they stumbled and plunged into the widening crevices resonated all around. A bolt of lightning struck down enemy fighters on the far side of the field like hewn trees.

When raindrops began to pelt Marrock's face like shards of ice, he lowered his arms to calm the forces of nature to prevent further destruction of his enemy. He would sell the survivors as slaves to the Romans.

After picking up the roped skulls, he wrapped them around his shoulders and mounted his horse to watch the mayhem. In his mind, he instructed his wolves to leap on anyone fleeing the battle and hold them down.

Marrock's mercenaries and slave catchers gripped the opposing warriors by their hair, neck, or shoulders to yank them out of the earth's cracks like weeds. The clicks of metal collars locking around the captives' necks kept in beat with the heavy rain and thunder.

After most of the surviving enemy had been shackled together, Marrock followed the slave catchers into the woods, where his wolves held down brawny fighters while mercenaries searched for commoners hiding in the trees.

When Marrock heard the raucous shrieks of ravens, a shudder flew down his spine. Several of the creatures were soaring above the battlefield, searching for mangled bodies to feast upon. He recalled his horror when Catrin, as a nine-year-old girl, had summoned ravens from the Otherworld to attack him. The black-feathered demons had sculpted his face with deep gashes as she fought off his attempt to transform her into a she-wolf for his pack. The pain from the grotesque scars agonized him for years, until Boudicca slowly began to heal his face.

Unadulterated hate for Catrin burned in Marrock's chest like a firestorm. If he could not satiate his bloodlust to hump his half sister until she bled, then disembowel and cut off her head, he would choose a female prisoner to torment instead.

Spotting the slave catcher Rufus, who was collaring an adolescent girl, Marrock rode up to him. "Select six girls on the cusp of womanhood for my inspection," he ordered.

The slick-haired slave broker raised an eyebrow. "Why spoil such pretty things? Brutius Antonius will pay top price for maidens to playact as nymphs in the emperor's garden."

Marrock's voice grated with anger. "Should I not indulge in some of the spoils of conquest for payment for dealing with you directly instead of your middleman, Governor Decimus Flavius?"

Rufus lowered his eyes. "I meant no disrespect. I will do as you command."

Marrock reined his horse around to leave but halted and looked at Rufus. "Tell me what Brutius is like."

Rufus gave a crooked smile. "He's like you in many ways."

"Humph. Unlikely." Marrock nudged his horse closer to Rufus. "Tell me, did you confirm Brutius is the brother of Marcellus Antonius?"

"Half brothers," Rufus clarified. "But they are nothing alike."

"You've met them both, then?"

Rufus scratched his chin, his muddy hand leaving a black smear. "I met Marcellus in Gaul. At the time, he was a Roman tribune in the legion. He bribed me for information about a female gladiator I saw fight."

The possibility that Catrin had survived her wounds and reunited with her Roman lover inflamed Marrock again. His mother had assured him she'd erased the memory of Catrin's lover in Britannia.

"What did this female gladiator look like?" Marrock asked.

"As I recall, she was fair-skinned and had golden hair and big blue eyes," Rufus replied. "Why do you ask?"

"That matches the description of my treacherous half sister," Marrock said bitterly. "Let's talk more about this female gladiator when we return to our camp."

5

WARNING

White Cliffs, Coastal Southeast Britannia, 14 November, AD 27

A fortnight later, Marrock returned with his raiding party and captives to the camp on top of the white cliffs overlooking the narrow sea. There, a lighthouse and a palatial villa that Roman architects had designed were in the initial phases of construction. Most of the shackled and collared prisoners were placed alongside a newly constructed stone wall. Though Marrock sometimes visited the Cantiaci capital of Durovernum, where his wife, Ariene, two sons, and Boudicca resided, he preferred the isolation of his partially constructed residence so he could practice his sorcery and sacrifice humans.

As promised, Rufus presented him with six young girls, their hair color ranging from blonde to dark brown. The sallow-skinned slave broker brushed what looked like lice nits from his scalp and wiped mucus dripping from his nostrils with a sleeve. The broker's fecal smell almost overpowered Marrock. Repulsed, he kept his distance from the slave broker as he inspected the six girls. Four of the girls were too scrawny and their hair too dull for Marrock's palette. He gestured for his guard to return the girls he'd rejected to the stockade.

At over six feet, Marrock was a giant among most men. He stepped up to the chestnut-haired girl who was a foot shorter than he was. As he stroked the girl's neck with his massive hand, he delighted in seeing her tremble with fear, and his loins stirred. He forced her chin up with his hand so she would look at him.

"Do you find me handsome?" he asked.

The girl averted her eyes from his hard stare. "Yes, my lord," she whispered.

"Look at me, girl!" Marrock demanded, tightening his fingertips around her jaw. The girl's dark-brown eyes met his stare.

Though Marrock could sense her fear, his appearance did not seem to repulse her. He leaned over and clasped her trembling hand, forcing it to stroke his face. "Smooth, isn't it?" He moaned as he imagined setting her naked body on a wolf pelt and forcing her legs apart as he crawled on top of her.

The girl's plump lips quivered. "Yes, my lord."

Marrock gave a wicked smile. "How would you like to be my she-wolf?"

The girl's acorn-brown eyes grew wider, as if she were cornered by a predator. Marrock chuckled at the chilling effect he had on her, then he turned his attention to the next girl, who had blue-green eyes that reminded him of Catrin's. About twelve years old, she showed the first signs of budding breasts. Even though she had a recalcitrant scowl, her beauty was like a water lily in bloom on the surface of a murky pond. She was toned, unlike the other girl.

"You remind me of my half sister, Catrin," he commented with a smile. "Three years ago, I left her body on the white cliffs to be devoured by ravens."

The girl's eyes grew big, but she still appeared defiant with pinched lips.

"What are you called?" Marrock asked, perturbed he didn't seem to scare her as he did the others.

"Peccia," she said firmly.

Marrock clenched her jaw with his fingertips and squeezed until she winced from the pain. "Peccia, Peccia, I don't like your defiant look," he said with a scowl.

Grimacing, Peccia shut her eyelids, and tears dripped down her face. Marrock grabbed the back of Peccia's head by the hair and licked the salty tears below her eyes. As soon as he pressed his mouth on hers, forcing his tongue into her wet mouth, her teeth clamped down on his tongue. When he tried to pull it out, her sharp teeth bit down and drew blood. Enraged, he pushed her head back as he yanked his tongue through her clenched teeth. He punched her in the stomach.

"You will regret this, bitch!" he raged and spat out blood.

Marrock watched her crumple to her hands and knees, then he kicked her in the belly over and over until she curled into a ball. Unable to breathe, the defiant wench opened her mouth like a fish out of water. He cast a glance at Rufus, recalling their earlier conversation about Catrin's Roman lover.

"Does this wench look like the female gladiator that Tribune Marcellus Antonius asked about?" Marrock asked.

"They have similar features," Rufus replied, his eyes riveted on the moaning girl.

"Do you know where she was taken?"

"To Lugdunum."

"Lugdunum," Marrock repeated under his breath.

The image of ravens circling and attacking him to prevent him from cutting off Catrin's head flashed in Marrock's mind. After the final battle, he had left her motionless body on the top of the white cliffs, afraid the demonic creatures would peck away what remained of his face. He'd assumed she would succumb to her wounds.

What was I thinking? Catrin used the age-old rabbit's trick of playing dead.

Why had he not sensed she was alive the past few years? And why had he found her essence in their father's skull?

A chill sliced down his spine. Was she scheming to destroy him?

Peccia's moans drew Marrock out of his ruminations. The blue tinge of death faded from the captive's face as she frantically gasped for breath. His impulse was to cut her tongue out and choke her to death with it. But the bitch needed to learn a lesson about what it meant to show respect to Blood Wolf—her king.

"Rufus, offer this vixen as a gift to my men," Marrock ordered. "Make sure each of them takes turns riding her until she bleeds and screams for mercy. If she survives, sell her to Brutius to live out her remaining days in a brothel."

"Why not keep her for yourself?" Rufus ventured.

"I only want the girl with the chestnut hair and the big breasts I can suckle," Marrock snarled. "Offer my assassin, Gawain, this spiteful wench first. After he is through with her, tell him to come speak with me."

"As you wish," Rufus said, lowering himself in a bow. He yanked Peccia to her feet by her hair and pushed her out of the chamber.

Marrock, turning his attention to the buxom girl, gripped her arm and forced her to follow him through an open doorway to a dimly lit, stone-walled chamber. Inside, jars of powdered ingredients, pestles and mortars, and ceremonial knives cluttered the shelves on the walls. At the back of the windowless room was a high altar made of three large, oval stones piled upon each other. Beside the altar, on the dirt floor, were the skulls of his family.

The terrified girl began to struggle and sob uncontrollably. Annoyed with her resistance, Marrock bared his teeth. "Stop that whimpering!"

Tears streamed down the girl's freckled face as she pleaded, "My king, please don't hurt me. Let me go back with the others."

Marrock squeezed her arm, and his lips quirked into a smile. "You mistake my intent, girl. I plan to elevate you."

The girl choked down her sobs. "In what way?"

Marrock pointed to the altar, where a yellow-spotted, long-legged spider was weaving its web. "Over there is your throne."

The girl's eyes widened. "It doesn't look like a throne. What about those skulls beside it?"

"It's a throne on which I will work my magic on you. You have a special place in my heart. Trust me. The skulls are harmless," Marrock said ingenuously. "Soon, you will experience a transformation like no other. A new awakening, you could say."

The girl's throat clutched with sobs. "Please, my lord. I . . . I am afraid. The . . . the spider will bite me."

Marrock swept the spider off the top stone with his hand. "There. It is gone," he snapped. Then, he retrieved a wolf-headed pelt from a hook near the altar. He set the pelt on top of the flat stone and smoothed out its reddish-brown fur.

"A fur cloak for my beautiful princess," he proclaimed with pride. "Take off your clothes and sit on it. Stroke its soft fur."

With a shaking hand, the girl took off her short tunic, revealing her hardened nipples, but she hesitated to untie her wraparound skirt.

Smiling, Marrock brushed back the strands of her long hair, then took a knife to cut the belted strap, releasing her skirt. His mouth salivated as his lecherous gaze wandered down her hips to the reddish, coarse hair between her legs that matched the color of the pelted wolf.

Unexpectedly, a gravelly voice in the adjacent chamber calling out, "My king," diverted Marrock's attention.

He snapped his fingers at the trembling girl and ordered, "Sit on the altar and don't move."

In the adjacent chamber, he found his assassin, back turned, looking all around. Turning, Gawain caught sight of Marrock and slightly bowed his head. The blue tattooed knots on the assassin's forehead contrasted sharply with his limewashed, cropped hair and dark eyebrows.

"Rufus said you summoned me," Gawain stated.

"I need your special talents," Marrock said, gesturing for Gawain to come closer. "I did not expect you so soon. Didn't Rufus offer you the fair-haired wench?"

"The foul-smelling shit eater did offer her as a gift," Gawain said, scrunching his nose. "But I have more scruples than to deflower a maiden by force."

Agitated that Gawain had spurned his gift, Marrock gave a nasty scowl. "But you have no scruples when it comes to slicing her throat to the bone?"

Gawain's eyebrows furled together. "You have guards who can do that. Why waste my skills on a helpless girl beaten black-and-blue?"

"Fair point," Marrock muttered, struggling to temper his voice. "I have a more urgent task for you."

"Which is?"

"I want you to assassinate my half sister, Catrin. The wench you spurned looks like her."

Gawain cocked an eyebrow. "I thought she died in battle a few years back."

"So did I, but Rufus revealed she might be alive—a gladiator in Lugdunum, Gaul." Marrock regarded Gawain's deepening grimace as he added, "I want you to leave tomorrow with my best warriors, find Catrin, and bring back her head."

"Why now? Crossing the channel this late in autumn can be dangerous," Gawain grumbled as he readjusted his fur-lined cloak. "What about my mission to kill Rhan and her sorcerer, Myrddin? They continue to elude me."

"True. They are also thorns in my side," Marrock said sharply. "But first, I want you to slit Catrin's throat, then deal with the others likewise."

With his eyes fixed on Marrock, Gawain stroked the longsword at his side. "Is there anything I should be aware of with Catrin?" he asked.

"Don't underestimate her. She is both a skilled sorceress and warrior," Marrock warned. "She was a whore to a Roman called Marcellus Antonius when he was in our capital three summers ago. It is possible she is with him—"

The sound of a loud crash from the adjacent chamber diverted their attention. Gawain, unsheathing his longsword, pivoted toward the open doorway. "What was that?" he rasped.

"It sounds like my prisoner is trying to escape," Marrock whispered, a seed planting in his head on how to convince Gawain to show him more respect as his king. "Do you want to see my powers as a druid before you leave?"

Gawain nodded warily and followed Marrock into the other room. There, the naked, chestnut-haired girl was in front of the altar, holding a ceremonial knife, ready to stab herself in the stomach.

"Give me the weapon," Marrock said calmly, holding out his hand. "I told you I would not harm you, did I not?"

"I don't believe you!" the girl shouted at the top of her lungs.

"Give me the knife," Marrock pressed. "You don't want my butcher"—he motioned to Gawain, who was still holding the sword in his hand—"to gut you like a slaughtered lamb if you do something foolish."

The girl's wide eyes shifted back and forth between Marrock and Gawain. Finally, her shoulders slumped as she reluctantly handed the knife to Marrock. Taking the knife, he swiftly cut the girl's throat. Blood spurted out of her neck as she clutched it and crumpled to the floor.

"Cut off her head," Marrock snapped at Gawain.

The assassin's eyes were frozen on the girl convulsing in the throes of an agonizing death, her gasps bubbling in a pool of blood.

Angered with Gawain's hesitancy, Marrock lashed out. "Did you not hear what I said? Cut off her head!"

Without showing any emotion, Gawain swiftly lowered his blade and cleanly severed the girl's head from her body.

"That's better," Marrock complimented, noting the terror in the girl's glazed eyes. "You see, I must trap her soul in the skull before it escapes to the Otherworld." He gently picked up the girl's headless body from the dirt floor and set it on the wolf-pelted altar, then cupped the severed head in the palms of his hands and set it on the altar next to her body. He carefully positioned the necklace of skulls around the girl's feet.

Marrock said, "Watch closely," and he pulled off his shirt to reveal a blue tattoo of interconnecting human skulls and wolves loping down his back. Observing the assassin's fearful eyes, he gloated, "I derive powers from both my family and my wolves."

Anticipating the thrill of what he was about to do, Marrock could feel blood pump into his throbbing loins as he took off his shoes and untied the leather straps of his breeches to release them to the floor. He flexed his biceps and flaunted his naked, muscular body like a strutting wolf ready to mate.

His mouth agape, Gawain stepped back, as though readying to escape.

Marrock laughed haughtily, knowing his next feat would strike fear into his assassin.

After a lifetime of experience, he had perfected the ability to shift into other forms as effortlessly as snapping one's fingers.

The mass of what I am must equal what I become, he reminded himself.

Without any clothing to impede his movement, he rushed toward the open doorway and abruptly pivoted on his heels. Imagining himself as a massive red wolf, he felt heat blaze into his body like an iron bloom smelting inside a furnace. The pressure in his body intensified until his eyeballs felt ready to burst. He leapt at Gawain, momentarily losing consciousness in the process of forging himself into his wolf form.

Landing on four paws in front of Gawain, Marrock staggered for a moment as his head cleared. Baring his canine fangs, he snarled at Gawain, then padded to the altar and put his front paws on top of the altar. He locked his jaws around the girl's head and crunched it like an egg.

Gobbling the brain matter oozing through the cracked skull initiated the process of absorbing the girl's soul. Crackling, charged light zigzagged in and out of the eye sockets of the interconnected skulls around the altar and enveloped him in a pulsating, white glow. The instant he erased the girl's memories, particles exploded all around him and reformed as strands of multicolored light in a lattice. He slowly inhaled the power from the girl's soul, then exhaled his breath into the girl's nostrils. Her head and body dissolved into the wolf-headed pelt. He took another deep breath and blew the multicolored lattice down on top of the reddish-brown pelt. The wolf's snout gasped for breath, and its paws extended. The furry pelt expanded in all directions to form a she-wolf.

Moments later, the she-wolf jumped off the altar and submissively circled Marrock as he slowly shape-shifted back to his human form. Slightly disoriented from the transition, he stroked the she-wolf's soft fur as he regarded Gawain's gaping mouth.

"Don't forget what you saw here," he growled. "This girl is now a she-wolf in my pack. All her human memories have been erased. She has no autonomy. She is mine. She is a slave whose only purpose is to please me. I am her alpha male. I am her master. I am Blood Wolf—the King of the Britons."

Marrock stepped up to Gawain and bared his teeth to emphasize his mandate. "Remember this. I have absolute power to shape your existence. Go to Lugdunum by the fastest route and find Catrin. Bring me back her head. Or pray for my mercy to leave you intact."

6

DARK PRINCE

Antonii Villa in Gaul, 12 December, 27 AD

The cloud-shrouded sky added to Catrin's gloom as she walked to her daughter's gravesite. Her nerves were on edge from sleepless nights. The image of the reptilian creature she'd seen inside her father's skull had haunted her in reoccurring nightmares. It felt as if a disease were spreading through her mind and eating away at her soul. Were these the effects of Rhan's elixir from the cauldron? Or had the creature put its mark on her before forcing her essence out of their father's skull?

Will I become just like Marrock?

To fulfill her father's directive, she had to find the strength to overcome her grief and fear and pull the dagger out of the serpent stone. Then, her father's curse would transform into her destiny. But first, she must say farewell to her buried daughter.

Reaching the gravesite, Catrin could not breathe from the heart-wrenching grief of leaving her daughter. She crumpled over the gravesite and wept. It felt as if the weight of the earth covering her daughter were suffocating her. She resolved to take control of her destiny instead of giving into the fear that the phantom fire-breathing reptile would steal her soul. She would find Trystan that day to make their next plans.

A woman's voice with a thick accent asking, "Have you changed your mind about going?" drew Catrin out of her melancholic muse. Looking up, she found Servia, the stout Germanian housekeeper, standing in front of her with a tentative smile.

"Marcellus cares for you," Servia continued. "Why not stay till spring?"

Catrin wiped away her tears and rose to her feet, trying to convince herself that she had made the right choice to forsake him. "I must bury my memories and return to Britannia," she said adamantly.

Servia's response, "You are young and can have another baby," did not console Catrin. She glimpsed Falco approaching with her pearl-white stallion, Lugus. She took the reins as he retrieved a purse from his belt. He loosened the drawstrings to reveal the coins inside.

"Marcellus told me to give this to you if you decided to leave," he said. "You can still change your mind, though. I leave tomorrow for Rome."

"I cannot go with you," Catrin replied, stealing another glance at her daughter's gravestone. "I must take another path."

"If that is so, do you want the three horses of your choice that Marcellus promised?" Falco inquired.

Catrin hesitated, not sure if she could stable them at Lugdunum. "Can I retrieve them later?"

Falco patted Lugus's forehead, as if saying goodbye to a good friend. "I'll leave word with the stablemen to give them to you while I'm in Rome."

A lump formed in Catrin's throat from her swelling emotions. "Thank you, my friend, for training Lugus to be one of the best horses in the gladiator games."

Falco's face brightened with a grin. "The city is still abuzz about your fight with the Red Lion. That is how legends are born, you know."

The accolade drew a smile from Catrin. She pictured the bare-chested gladiator with shoulder-length, coppery hair that resembled a lion's mane. Prepared to fight him, she was taken aback when she'd discovered he was Ferrex, her loyal mentor from Britannia. She wondered if he had arrived in Rome to fight in the blood sport there.

Catrin embraced Servia and told her affectionately, "Thank you for your kindness. You were like a mother to me."

"And you, my daughter," Servia said, misty-eyed.

Catrin stepped to the side of Lugus, where Falco gave her a boost with his hands onto the horse's back.

"Take care, Corvus," he told her warmly.

Catrin grinned at Falco, who still called her by her gladiator stage name. Back then, when she was in the arena, the spectators had often chanted, "The raven of death and vengeance!"

"You can call me by my real name," she said.

Falco chuckled. "Old habit, calling you Corvus."

Without another word, Catrin nodded and kicked Lugus into a canter down the dirt road. The air felt crisp on her face as she rode under the overhanging gold- and red-leafed trees to Lugdunum, the capital of the Roman province of Gallia Lugdunensis.

After riding most of the morning, Catrin finally saw the city through the dense trees. The columnar structures were nestled on a hill between two blue-green rivers, unlike the muddy rivers in Britannia. At the top of the hill was a massive amphitheater, where she had combatted on a hot August day. Hearing the clack-clack of wooden wheels on the cobblestone road, she urged Lugus in the direction of the sound. She joined carts and wagons traveling to Lugdunum.

Inside the city gates Catrin found a female shopkeeper with hair coiled on her head like a serpent, matching Trystan's description.

"Do you know where I can find the butcher of swine?" she asked.

The shopkeeper regarded Catrin for a moment. "The butcher, Trystan?"

"That is the one."

The woman pointed up the hill. "His stall is close to the arena, right next to an alley that dead-ends at the fortress wall."

Catrin thanked the shopkeeper and readjusted the belted *gladius* at her side. She mounted Lugus and rode up the steep hill that was lined with a variety of shops. At the top, boisterous celebrants flowing in and out of the amphitheater obstructed Catrin's view of the nearby open storefronts. She finally spotted two tattooed men inspecting a butchered boar hanging from a wooden beam. Recognizing the butcher as Trystan, with his long, gray-streaked hair and the tattooed falcon flying down his arm, she called out to him.

Trystan looked all around until his gaze landed on Catrin. He studied her for a moment, then asked with a smile, "What kind of meat are you looking for?"

Catrin gave him a wry grin. "Raw and bloody."

"Everything here is raw and bloody," Trystan jested, w ping his blood-smeared hands on an apron. He gestured to the other butcher. "This is Gawain—a butcher who recently joined me."

Catrin noted the distinct blue tattoo of a dagger's blade on his forehead and the ice-blue eyes that cut straight through her. The hairs on her arms prickled as she suddenly realized he resembled the image cf the man's face that had projected over her father's shadow in the skull.

Warily, she jumped off Lugus and led the horse by the reins, looking back at Gawain as she trailed Trystan to a stone-walled archway opening into a wooded area. Just beyond, in the privacy of a grove of beech trees, he knelt reverently and bowed his head.

"*Regana*, my queen."

Catrin waved her hand for him to rise. "Where are the other warriors?"

Trystan pointed to a foot trail. "Some of them are camped by the river. I'll take you there to meet them."

"Is your butcher, Gawain, one of our warriors?"

"Yes," Trystan answered, taking the reins of Catrin's horse. "He is a butcher who barely escaped Marrock's tyranny."

"I don't trust him," Catrin remarked as Trystan led her down the steep pathway to the Rhône River.

"Why is that?"

"I've seen him in a vision."

"I'll keep a close eye on him," Trystan said.

At the riverbank, two men were conversing under the overhanging branch of an oak. Catrin studied their features, struggling to remember who they were. One of them had a deep scar running from his shut eyelid to his chin. Red hair spiked the top of his head like a rooster's crest. Tattoos of black knots swirled around his arms, and blue bolts of lightning struck down his bare chest.

Recognizing the battle-axe hanging from his belt, Catrin smiled warmly. "You must be Cynwrig, the Red Executioner."

Cynwrig knelt before Catrin and kissed her hand. "*Cobranoriga*, my raven queen."

She motioned for the one-eyed warrior to rise, then hugged him tightly. "It's good to see you alive, my friend. The last time I saw you, you were fighting off Romans who'd ambushed our village."

"I survived but was left with half a face," Cynwrig said, a bitter tinge in his voice.

"And your wife?" Catrin asked.

Cynwrig spat. "Before the Romans gouged out my eye, they made me watch as they took turns—"

"But she was with child!" Catrin exclaimed, aghast that soldiers would defile a woman almost six months pregnant. The image of her own still-born daughter made her teary-eyed.

Cynwrig's face contorted. "I vowed with my every breath to avenge my murdered wife and unborn child. And to unleash vengeance on the Romans and Marrock, who slaughtered your parents!"

Catrin clasped Cynwrig's arm. "As do I."

The other man interjected, "You don't remember me, do you, Catrin?"

Catrin studied the dark, chestnut-haired man whose eyes appeared green in the sunlight filtering through the trees. Attired in a tunic and toga, with his hair shorn short, he appeared to be Roman. It slowly dawned on her that he was the eldest son of the rival Catuvellauni king, Cunobelin. The last time she'd seen him, almost seven years ago, he'd been a thin, pimple-faced adolescent who had been placed under the guardianship of Catrin's father. Taken aback that the rival prince, Adminius, would be in the company of her father's most trusted guards, she glared at him.

"I know who you are, Adminius. Why are you here?" she asked sharply.

The prince's smile soured. "This is not the warm greeting I expected. We were once betrothed, you know."

Catrin could feel pent-up anger boiling in her chest. "I never agreed to marry you. Besides, you betrayed my father."

"I never betrayed anyone from your family," Adminius said, gesticulating like a Roman noble to emphasize his point. "It was my brother

Caratacus and his followers who joined forces with Marrock, despite my father's order."

Catrin's eyes blazed, but before she could accuse him of lying, Trystan grabbed her arm and forced her to walk with him behind a tree, beyond the prince's hearing.

"Forgive me, my queen, but I must speak plainly," he said fervently. "We need Adminius and his army to defeat Marrock. Most of our warriors have been killed or sold into slavery."

Catrin raised a brow, struggling to temper her voice. "You are asking me to trust people who were once enemies—Rhan, Myrddin, and now Adminius."

Trystan gripped Catrin's arm tighter, the pressure making her arm throb. "If it takes enemies to destroy Marrock, then we must do it. I've been told that Marrock can summon unspeakable powers from the skulls of your family. The monster has wreaked havoc all over Britannia."

Enraged, Catrin jerked away from Trystan and fixed her eyes on him. "And what can he do with these powers?"

"Marrock can make the earth shake, strike his enemy dead with lightning." Trystan regarded Catrin for a moment. "I've been told you also have these powers. Rumors have spread throughout the region that you emitted lightning at the Romans in the stands during your fight with Ferrex. Rhan says you have the powers of the ancient druids."

"Rhan!" Catrin growled. "After I drank the mixture from her cauldron, she left before I awoke. Where is she now?"

"I don't know," Trystan admitted. "She only said that she needed to hide. Marrock's assassins were looking for her. Anyway, we need to ally with our enemies to depose Marrock. Rhan understands how Marrock thinks. She assured me that when it is time, she will be there."

"She will be there? When?" Catrin asked sardonically. "Rhan is a trickster, the same as her son."

"Remember, Marrock almost killed her—his own mother. A most heinous deed," Trystan hissed. "And he stole her young daughter, Boudicca. What matters is Rhan has the same purpose as us."

After further consideration, Catrin decided to heed the advice of the commander whom her father had trusted implicitly. "Father told me to keep my enemies closer than my friends. However, I want to find out Adminius's true intent before I seal an alliance with him."

When they rejoined Adminius and Cynwrig, Catrin asked the dark prince pointedly, "What do you hope to gain by forging an alliance with me?"

"I want you to accept the marital agreement our fathers negotiated," Adminius demanded.

Catrin huffed. "Marry you?"

"Yes. But there is something you should know before making your final decision," Adminius added with a smirk.

Suspicious, Catrin arched an eyebrow. "What is that?"

"Your sister, Mor, is under my protection," Adminius proclaimed.

Stunned, Catrin gasped. "I thought she was dead . . . killed in battle against Marrock. Did she give birth to her child?"

Adminius stole a glance at Trystan, seeking direction on how to answer.

"Tell her everything," Trystan urged.

Adminius took a deep breath. "Caratacus found Mor with serious belly wounds. The healer who treated her injuries said she miscarried. When Mor was brought to our capital as a prisoner, my father banished Caratacus for betraying your father and ordered me to take Mor as my wife."

A heat of anger flushed Catrin's face. "If that is so, why do you demand I marry you, too?"

"She is barren, most likely from the wounds she suffered. Be assured, though, I'll keep her safe as my concubine. That is, if you agree to be my queen and bear my children," Adminius said bluntly.

Though Catrin wanted to slash the dark prince's throat, she tempered her voice to avoid any confrontation that could result in a threat to her sister's life. "If I agree to marry you, how do you plan to aid me?"

Adminius paused and shifted his feet. "I will recruit warriors from my kingdom to serve in your army. Trystan and I spoke with Ferrex the day he fought with you at the games. He suggested we could storm the gladiator schools and free them to join your army as well. But alas, Ferrex was transferred to Rome before we could free him."

The urgency of finding Ferrex in Rome weighed heavily on Catrin's mind. He would be a trustworthy commander to her. And Marcellus was also in Rome. He had promised to support her claim for the Cantiaci throne, even if she didn't agree to stay with him. Why should she not gain support from her Roman husband instead of Adminius? An inconsolable yearning to see her soul mate unexpectedly gripped at her chest.

Adminius's harsh voice broke Catrin out of her thoughts.

"Do you accept my offer?" he demanded.

"Only if you keep Mor safe," Catrin countered.

Adminius's lips curled into a wicked smile. "It is settled, then. Seal our alliance with a kiss."

Catrin swallowed hard and planted a kiss on his slimy lips.

7

SHADOW OF THE RAVEN

Lugdunum, 16 December, 27 AD

At dawn, Catrin buckled her weapons belt around her waist and wrapped a woolen cape around her shoulders. Only a thin curtain separated her sparsely furnished bedchamber from the atrium where the warriors were sleeping. Their loud snoring had stolen her sleep the previous night. At least she didn't have to stay in a makeshift camp outside the city. The coins Marcellus had given her paid for the lease of an austere apartment near the amphitheater.

Hesitant to marry Adminius immediately, she had persuaded him to return to the Catuvellauni capital of Camulodunon. There, during the winter months, he could prepare his warriors and mercenaries for next year's assault on Marrock. She had promised to join Adminius in late spring for their wedding ceremony.

It was a promise she was hesitant to keep.

Ever since Catrin had drunk from Rhan's cauldron, her father's last words dwelled in her mind. *The Raven will know.* How would she ever find her animal guide, the Raven, that had taken the physical form of the scavenger bird? It had flown away from the arena after she'd fought her last gladiatorial match in August over a year ago. It was only through the Raven's mind that she could open the portals to the Otherworld and connect with the spiritual realm. She had lost almost all hope the Raven would return.

Then, yesterday, Catrin had been heartened to learn local shopkeepers were abuzz with stories of a vengeful spirit that had taken residence at the amphitheater. The demonic spirit took the form of a raven to torment unsuspecting Roman nobles with aerial assaults to avenge gladiators slain in the blood sport.

Perhaps this was her long-lost raven that had befriended her as a fledging, when she was first enslaved, and was later showcased with her in the games. Her dead father had promised her in a vision that the Raven would help her learn how to conjure more powers from the ancient druids. With these forces, she could transform her father's curse into her destiny to retake the Cantiaci kingdom.

Pulling back the curtain, Catrin found a handful of warriors asleep on the floor, curled up in blankets near a coal-burning brazier, their only source of warmth during the long winter nights. Trystan and Cynwrig stood guard at the front entrance.

Thick smoke seeping through the floor's cracks from the wood-fired hearth in the shop below made her cough, alerting everyone to her presence. The warriors on the floor bounded to their feet as Trystan and Cynwrig strode through their midst to reach her. Their quick reaction assured Catrin of their alertness to potential danger.

"Up early, my queen," Trystan remarked. "Are you ready to eat?"

"I'll eat later at one of the food vendors," Catrin said, pulling her hair back into a ponytail and binding it with a leather strap. "I'd like Cynwrig to escort me in the city today."

Trystan's eyes shifted to Cynwrig, who then slightly bowed to Catrin. "I serve at your pleasure, my queen. Let me get a dagger and a cloak."

Catrin waited at the entryway until Cynwrig joined her. They descended the stairs to the inner courtyard of the insula, then exited through an archway and walked westward on the main cobblestone road.

The cold, biting air made Catrin shiver. She pulled the cape's cowl over her head and tightened the woolen fabric around her shoulders as they approached the amphitheater. Overhead, clouds cast shadows across the arched, upper tiers of the massive structure, until the sun's brilliance broke through the dark shroud. The gold tones reflecting off the white limestone surface of the building mesmerized Catrin. Relishing the calm moment before the bustle of vendors setting up their storefronts, she quietly sat on a stone bench in front of a cheese shop across the road from the amphitheater. Cynwrig stood next to her, his eyes shifting all around.

The sunrise, marking the beginning of Apollo's journey across the sky, made Catrin reminisce about Marcellus. She sighed ruefully. The horse-drawn chariot emblazoned on his gold signet ring was etched into her mind. Marcellus was her Apollo. She couldn't erase the memory of his radiance as they'd made love near a waterfall, their bodies and souls entwined under a brilliant sunrise. Without him, a profound emptiness still gnawed away in her chest. Her breath caught in her throat as she fought back unwelcome tears.

A nudge on her arm drew Catrin out of her muse. She looked at Cynwrig, who appeared concerned and restless. "Are we waiting for someone?" he asked.

"I'm waiting for the Raven," she replied.

"Your raven?"

"It is my animal guide that took the form of a raven. I showcased it as a gladiator before each fight," Catrin clarified. "It served as a harbinger of impending death for my opponent."

Cynwrig's eyebrow raised. "Surely, a weapon to be used against Marrock?"

Curious at his suggestion, Catrin asked, "Why do you say that?"

"Some of the local townspeople speak of a female gladiator who sent lightning down on her unfaithful lover in the stands," Cynwrig said. "Afterward, a raven arose from the rubble. Trystan said that gladiator was you."

"I sought vengeance against my Roman master, Decimus Flavius," Catrin said in a biting tone.

"Did you kill him?" Cynwrig inquired.

Catrin hesitated to tell him she'd diverted the lightning bolt at the last moment to save Marcellus, who was standing beside Decimus. "No. I failed to do so," she admitted.

Cynwrig's one eye narrowed. "If you have magic to summon lightning, why did you not use it earlier to escape from the Romans?"

"It takes deep rage to unleash these deadly powers," Catrin tried to explain, though she did not completely understand herself. "It's an uncontrollable force that is difficult to rein in. My father's spirit told me the Raven would teach me how to control the magic to destroy Marrock."

"I have no knowledge of such things," Cynwrig said. "But I believe Rhan's prophecy that you will save our people from Marrock's tyranny."

"I hope I meet their expectations," Catrin said, though doubts gnawed at her about defeating her half brother by allying with former enemies who considered her nothing more than a puppet queen they could maneuver.

"You will succeed," Cynwrig said with conviction. He paused and squinted at the amphitheater. "What makes you think the Raven will return here?"

Catrin's lips quirked into a smile. "I've heard rumors that an incorrigible raven swoops down on Roman nobles as they stroll by."

Suddenly, loud shrieks diverted both Catrin's and Cynwrig's attention to a marble statue of a nude Apollo with a cape loosely wrapped around his extended arm. On top of the statue's head was a large raven flapping its iridescent wings. She recognized the Raven in its physical form.

"Corvus. Corvus." The Raven screeched Catrin's gladiator stage name. "Strike now. Strike now."

A chill ran down Catrin's spine. This was the same warning her raven guide had uttered whenever Decimus approached her stark, barred cell, where she was isolated from the male gladiators. She closely watched the Raven swoop over the heads of a couple shopkeepers, then dart up the road and circle above a litter carried by four slaves.

Pressing two fingers to her lips, Catrin gestured for Cynwrig to follow her in the direction of the Raven's flight. They weaved in and out of shoppers in front of storefronts until they spotted the four slaves setting the litter down near stairs that ascended to a temple with a marble altar. The massive altar was flanked by two winged, bronze statues of women holding palms.

A richly dressed noble, attired in a purple-striped, white tunic, stepped out of the litter. Catrin's heart raced when she recognized Governor

Decimus Flavius climbing the steps with armed guards. At the top of the steps was Prince Adminius, a fur-collared cloak draped over his shoulders. It felt as if a sword had been thrust into her back as she watched the two men clasp each other's forearm in greeting.

Disconcerted, Catrin turned to Cynwrig. "That is Governor Decimus Flavius speaking with Adminius. I fear he has betrayed us."

"That is my thought, too," Cynwrig agreed.

"Beside them is my spiritual raven guide in its physical form. You know of my ability to meld my thoughts with the Raven?" Catrin asked.

"Aye, I do."

"So I can hear what Decimus and Adminius are saying, I will connect with the Raven's mind and use its senses to hear their conversation. As I do this, my body will become motionless. It has been a while since I've done this, and it's possible something could go awry when I connect or disconnect with the Raven."

Cynwrig's brow creased. "Like what?"

"Lose consciousness. Possibly have convulsions." She regarded Cynwrig's raised eyebrow above his good eye, then pointed to a lion-faced fountain. "Let us sit over there while I connect with the Raven."

As they both sat down on a bench near the stone lion that spewed water from its mouth, Cynwrig said under his breath, "I'm not sure of this."

Preparing to connect with the Raven, Catrin closed her eyes and felt electric heat surge into her fingertips. A bright light flashed in her mind—a sign she could see through the Raven's eyes. She directed it to mingle with the pigeons that were waddling around Decimus and Adminius as they strolled around the massive temple.

As instructed, the Raven quietly landed amid a flock of pigeons pecking at a dead rat behind the backs of the men. At first distracted by the easy meal, the Raven reluctantly waddled behind the men, struggling to keep up with their stride. The clarity of their conversation faded in and out among the clamor of worshippers at the temple.

A gravelly voice that Catrin recognized as Decimus's began the conversation. "I am glad you could meet me here. I sacrifice a dove to Apollo every day to keep his raven at bay."

"A raven?" Adminius asked incredulously.

"An evil creature your betrothed, Catrin, sends to haunt me," Decimus grumbled.

Catrin inwardly snickered at the image of her raven tormenting Decimus every day. He deserved that, after what she had suffered as his slave.

"That is why . . ." Adminius's voice faded under other nearby voices and shuffling footsteps.

Decimus's gruff voice now grew louder. "Supply me with slaves. In return, I will send Roman soldiers to safeguard your trade routes."

"And help destroy Marrock and acknowledge me as king," Adminius demanded.

"That, too," Decimus agreed. "Tell me about Catrin."

The sound of priests' chants drowned out the conversation for a few moments. Then, Catrin heard the distinct voice of Adminius offering, "I will weaken Catrin's influence."

"How?" Decimus asked.

"By marrying and breeding with her . . ."

The men's mocking laughter chiseled away Catrin's self-restraint. Raw emotions boiled to the surface as she recalled Decimus's snickers as he'd stripped and chained her in front of male gladiators, threatening to have her gang-raped. He'd violated her inner sanctum with sharp fingernails to humiliate her. She'd been nothing more than property for him to debase at his pleasure.

Unadulterated anger overtook Catrin. Her only thought was to strike at Decimus for what he had done to her. Her fury incited the Raven to ambush Decimus in an aerial assault.

Swooping down from behind Decimus, the Raven unleased Catrin's vengeance. Its sharp talons pierced his head, making him cry out in pain. He anxiously looked up for the culprit.

The Raven circled overhead, pulled its wings inward to flip upside down, and dove at Decimus again. In defense, he crouched and covered his head with folded arms to ward off the next attack. Another raven joined in the frenetic aerial dance, pirouetting and coordinating its maneuvers with the first. Other birds—pigeons, wrens, crows—then joined in the aerial attack and swarmed around Decimus and everyone near him like an army of gigantic bees.

Through the Raven's sight, Catrin could see Decimus's fearful eyes as the screeching birds attacked and attacked again. On the final assault, Adminius and the Roman guards waved their arms at the Raven, but it veered up sharply before they could strike it down with their weapons. Adminius and the guards slashed at the other birds with their swords. Several birds dropped like bloody sacrifices on an altar.

It was then that Catrin directed her raven to halt the assault, fearing her feathered guide would meet its doom. With the cessation of the aerial attack, Decimus looked all around, and his stare locked on Catrin's motionless human form. She knew he was aware of her ability to meld with the Raven and would order his guards to apprehend her. For her to escape, though, she had to transmute her senses back into her human form.

But I might lose consciousness.

Seeing Decimus's guards running in her direction, Catrin had no choice but to act.

As she disconnected from the Raven, a force hurtled her through a tunnel of brilliant gold light. In the next instant, she found herself facedown on the cobblestones, sharp pain shooting through her head.

Strong hands turned her over, and Cynwrig's blurred face came into focus. Other blurry figures next to Cynwrig appeared to spin, making her nauseated. Loud shouts rang in her ears.

Cynwrig bent her knees, clasped her wrist, and pulled her up quickly, hoisting her over his hard, muscled shoulder. He wrapped an arm around one of her legs, keeping it in place, and then dashed down the street, her head dangling wildly with each of his steps.

The pressure of blood pumping to her head plunged Catrin into the spiritual realm, on the other side of the Wall of Lives. It was the first time the Raven had transported her there. The fluid tapestry on the wall looked familiar. Life threads of every human wove in and out of the tapestry, then untangled. Her father's dagger, with Rhan's curse emblazoned on its blade, rose out of the multicolored life threads. The radiance of the blade's gold surface almost blinded her.

The weapon's force overcame her, sucking her into a blast furnace and melting her essence with other souls to meld with the metal of her father's blade. Marcellus's red life thread entwined the gold, two-edged blade like bloodred ivy coiling around a gigantic oak. Catrin's iridescent, black life thread tied a knot with Marcellus's thread at a juncture in the future. A crimson thread sprouted out of the knot and moved to and fro across the blade's sharp edge, slowly fraying the delicate fiber.

A piercing shriek jolted Catrin out of the Otherworld and into darkness. A breath clutched in her throat, then another and another—heartbeats drumming inside her head. She felt rock-hard vines squeezing her chest, and a man's voice demanded, "Wake up. Wake up!"

Catrin screamed in terror.

The grip loosened, and she flopped on her back. Breaths whooshed in and out of her lungs until life-sustaining air surged into her brain.

She popped her eyes open and beheld a blurry face beneath a burning lamp.

Then, the Raven's repeating croaks, "Enemies everywhere," resonated in her ears.

Disoriented, she thought she felt soft feathers touch her hand. She squinted at the two figures hovering above her, and the faces of Trystan and Cynwrig slowly came into focus. Looking around, she recognized her bedchamber. Her tongue felt numb, and her words flowed thickly from her mouth.

"Wha . . . what . . . happened?" she asked.

"You had the falling sickness," Cynwrig explained. "You hit your head, and I had to carry you back here."

Once before, Catrin had suffered convulsions after she had melded with the Raven. "Where . . . is my raven?" she asked weakly.

"It is beside you," Cynwrig said. "It refused to leave your side."

Tasting blood from her swollen tongue, Catrin swallowed before painstakingly uttering, "And Decimus?"

Cynwrig and Trystan stole a glance at each other. Trystan finally said, "We need to discuss this later when you are better."

Extremely fatigued, Catrin mostly slept the next couple of days. Her swollen tongue healed slowly, making it difficult for her to eat, swallow, and talk. The Raven never left her side and would nestle its head next to hers, as if trying to warn her of something. The aftereffects of the falling sickness made her leery of connecting with the Raven again.

Yet, the vision of a crimson fiber shooting out of the raven-black knot tied around Marcellus's thread haunted her in nightmares. She often woke with a start, finding the Raven perched on her chest and croaking, "Enemies everywhere. Long night."

Catrin regretted that her rage had incited the Raven to attack Decimus. The plan to build an army may have been jeopardized when Decimus recognized her during the Raven's assault. Or perchance, Adminius's betrayal had already doomed their objective to recruit allies and mercenaries.

Finally, three days after the incident, Trystan voiced his concern that Adminius had not returned to Britannia but had instead stayed in the city to meet with Decimus. He agreed with her that they needed to heed the Raven's warning that enemies were everywhere. They ultimately concurred to escape to another city once the snowstorms eased and she was well enough to ride.

8

THE DRAGON INSIGNIA

Lugdunum, 20 December, 27 AD

On the eve of the winter equinox, the apartment was unbearably cold. To get warm, Catrin wrapped a shawl around her shoulders and closely watched the guard with tattoos of Celtic knots lining his forehead as he filled the brazier with coal. His glacier-blue eyes pierced through her. Unnerved, she felt a chill slice down her spine.

Studying the various faces of the men in the atrium, she counted ten more guards whom Trystan had invited to sleep inside on the frigid, cloudless night. The image of the raven-black life thread tying a knot around Marcellus's red strand on the Wall of Lives flashed in her mind. She knew the vision was a glimpse of her future.

She excused herself to the privacy of her bedchamber, drawing the curtain back to enter. There, waiting on the straw mattress bed was the Raven. She fed it some dried meat strips, then blew out the burning candle and lay on her bedding. The Raven's soft, feathered head nestled against her neck, providing her much-needed warmth and comfort.

Yet, a chill gnawed at her bones. To ward off the air's frigid nip, she cocooned herself in a woolen blanket. The silvery moonlight filtered through the uneven surface of the gray-smoked window in the curtained-off room, casting shadows on the wall.

Falling into restless sleep, she dreamed of her life thread tying a knot around Marcellus's red life strand, but then . . .

Blood unexpectedly spurted out of the knot and splattered all over a blade that was plunging at her throat.

"This is not a dream!" the Raven's deep voice cried out.

With her warrior's instincts awakened, she opened her eyes to find a shadow of a man kneeling beside her. Seeing the dagger in his hand, she quickly blocked his arm and discharged sizzling heat from her fingertips. The sparks of energy forced him to dropped the dagger.

She rolled abruptly to her side to escape, but his strong arm pulled her back as his legs coiled around her hips like a snake. As he reached for the dagger, she cried out to awake the others in the main room and poked her fingers into his eyes.

"Wicked bitch," he snarled in Celtic as he wildly thrust his blade at her. Its metal tip bit into her shoulder, shooting sharp pain down her arm. Fighting for her life, she punched him in the throat.

In the blink of an eye, his body fell hard on hers, forcing the air out of her lungs. She gasped and pushed him off her with a burst of strength. Finally freed of his weight, she staggered to her feet and scanned the floor for the loose dagger or another weapon.

Any weapon!

Another strong hand unexpectedly gripped her injured shoulder from the back. A wave of pain flamed across her chest as she quickly turned to defend herself against the next attacker.

To her relief, Cynwrig's good eye blazed in the silvery illumination of moonlight from the other room.

"Get back! There are two of them!" he roared.

To make room for the ensuing fight, Catrin stepped back into the atrium and watched. The tattooed men swept around Cynwrig in a deadly dance. Each darted back and forth between the silver light of the moon and the darkness.

The assailant, whom Catrin recognized as Gawain, slammed Cynwrig into the wall and wildly thrust his knife. Cynwrig blocked Gawain's forearm twice, then swiftly shot his other arm under the assassin's armpit at the next thrust, gripping his upper arm.

With a loud roar, Cynwrig pushed Gawain back while at the same time curling his leg around the assassin's calf to trip him into the other attacker.

The dagger flew out of Gawain's hand and landed with a clink on the floor. Catrin swooped the weapon up into her hand and plunged the blade into the other assailant's lower back. The man tried to reach around with his hand, but then, his body went limp and crumpled to the floor.

Momentarily relieved, Catrin knew she had hit her target—his kidney.

Suddenly, Gawain blindsided Catrin, knocking her against a column in the atrium. The hard slam punched the air out of her lungs again. She momentarily blacked out, then found herself on the floor.

A man's deep voice barked, "Come to me," and the clamor of shuffling feet and clinking metal grew louder in the atrium.

With the fogginess in her mind clearing, she staggered to her feet and watched two shadowy figures disappear at the back of the atrium.

A burning torch held by Trystan illuminated the carnage in the chamber. A headless body was sprawled on the tile floor near the brazier, his outstretched hands reaching for his severed head. The blue woad tattoo dissolved from his face into a pool of blood.

It was then she felt the throbbing ache in her shoulder. Seeing her blood-soaked tunic, she pressed her hand on her injured shoulder to stop the bleeding.

"Let me see," Cynwrig demanded, pressing the end of his cape against the wound. "Are you hurt anywhere else?"

Light-headed, Catrin said, "No." But then, she began to shake.

Cynwrig assisted her to a sitting position and continued pressing on her wound until her head began to clear.

A few moments later, two guards appeared in the doorway, one of them announcing, "They've escaped."

The reality that guards in their inner circle had attacked them sunk into Catrin's belly like tar. The remaining guards cast suspicious glances at each other.

"Why are assassins in our midst?" Catrin asked sharply, shaken and angered by the betrayal.

Trystan, inspecting a superficial wound on his side, replied, "I take the blame. Gawain tricked me, swearing he and the three men had escaped Marrock after he captured them. They swore their allegiance to me and asked to fight in our army." He knelt over the headless body and fingered what appeared to be a stitched emblem on the cloak. "A dragon. The insignia of Marrock's assassins, I've been told."

A shudder crawled down Catrin's spine. "How could Marrock possibly know I am here? Could Adminius or Decimus be behind this?"

Trystan shrugged. "Not likely. But possible."

Nausea hit Catrin like a crashing wave, and she leaned over to vomit. Feeling wretched, she lay on the floor to settle her stomach and ruminated over what had just happened. How could she trust former enemies who purported to be loyal to her? As far as she knew, the two dead attackers could be associated with any of her former enemies: Marrock, Adminius, Decimus—possibly Rhan and Myrddin. They all had reason to kill her.

To deny her the throne.

Catrin addressed Trystan. "How will I distinguish friend from foe?"

Appearing guilt-ridden, Trystan ordered everyone outside except for Cynwrig and Catrin. They huddled near the coal-heated brazier to warm their hands as they planned their next moves.

Trystan began. "I need to find other allies your father trusted in Britannia. Verica from the Atrebates kingdom is regrouping to win back his territory from Epaticcus—Adminius's uncle. We still need Adminius's aid, no matter what we suspect. He is competing with his brothers to claim the Catuvellauni kingdom after their father dies. Furthermore, his younger brother, Caratacus, has allied with Marrock."

"What about my sister, Mor? How can we ensure her safety with Adminius as you speak with other rulers?" Catrin asked.

"I could travel to the Catuvellauni capitol and insist that Adminius show me Mor before you will agree to marry him."

"What about Myrddin and Rhan?" Cynwrig ventured.

Catrin exhaled slowly, again pondering the meaning of her vision, where she had tied a knot around Marcellus's life thread. His love had been the only stable force in her life up to that point.

"There is only one person I can implicitly trust—my Roman husband," she declared. "I declined his offer to help me overthrow Marrock. A decision I regret. Until we can discern who is ally or enemy, I know he will keep me safe in Rome. And I will hold him to his promise to support me."

Trystan's brow creased. "Do you think that's wise?"

"What other option do I have?" Catrin snapped. "You've failed to protect me, have you not? Besides, all my enemies now know where I am. They view me as nothing more than a hapless fly for them to spin into their political webs."

Trystan and Cynwrig exchanged glances but offered no alternatives.

"I take it from your silence that you agree with me," Catrin said firmly. "I will use the remaining coins Marcellus gave me to pay for lodging and for stabling horses on my journey to Rome. Once there, I will find Marcellus. If possible, I will find a way to free Ferrex and any other gladiators who could serve in my army."

Cynwrig knelt before Catrin. "I beseech you, my raven queen, to take me as your protector," he humbly requested. "Give me a chance to redeem myself for not saving my wife from the Romans."

The one-eyed warrior unsheathed his dagger and held it upright by the blade. The moonstone in the hilt sparkled from the torchlight as he swore, "My raven queen, I pledge my fealty and loyalty. I will defend you and your claim to the throne with my body and soul. If I fail to do so, you can claim my life with this dagger."

Moved by Cynwrig's gesture, Catrin waved for him to rise. "I gladly accept you as my champion. As long as you serve me honorably, you will stand by my side and have a place at my table."

Cynwrig rose and squared his shoulders. "We can leave for Rome at your command."

Catrin beamed. "Tomorrow, then."

"It is settled," Trystan interjected. "I will return to Britannia to convince other rulers to join our cause. I will find Mor, if she is . . ." His voice faded, and he lowered his eyes.

"If she is alive," Catrin finished, voicing his thoughts. "How will we stay in contact?"

"What about your raven?" Trystan asked, gesturing to the Raven pecking at the face of one of the fallen assailants.

"Yes. My raven can stay at the amphitheater and taunt Decimus while I'm gone," Catrin said with a smirk. "We should all return to Lugdunum by early summer and find my raven. I will direct it"—Catrin looked at Trystan—"to take you to me to prepare for war against Marrock."

Trystan bowed slightly. "Then it is settled. We will regroup next summer and strike at the throat of Blood Wolf."

9

SACRIFICE TO JANUS

Antonii Villa in Rome, 9 January, 28 AD

After a brisk morning ride through the countryside outside Rome, Marcellus and his companion, Arius, who was on winter leave from the northern legion in Gaul, returned to the family's villa on Palatine Hill. Although jaunts in the countryside usually lifted his spirits, Marcellus anticipated his father, Senator Lucius Antonius, would confront him about the recent snag in the marital contract between Marcellus and Licinia. Senator Marcus Licinius Crassus Frugi wanted to renegotiate the dowry for his daughter. Much to his parents' chagrin, the banquet to be held for the public announcement of the betrothal had been delayed.

"You must leave your reckless ways," his father had scolded Marcellus earlier that morning, "if you want to rise in Rome."

Later that afternoon, Marcellus and his parents would attend the Feast of Janus—the two-faced god of beginnings, gateways, and transitions. His father had paid a hefty sum to sacrifice a bull to assure the two-faced god's blessing on the political marriage.

On the cobblestone road in front of the entrance, Marcellus inhaled deeply and dismounted the chariot horse that had been trained by Falco. There, the household steward, Linos, and the dark-skinned slave from Ethiopia, Selena, greeted him and Arius.

"Tell the domina her son has returned," Linos directed Selena, then gestured for the stablemen to take the horses.

Handing the reins of his sweat-soaked stallion to a stableman, Marcellus smiled when he saw his mother, Drusilla, exuberantly step through the doorway. His throat tightened when he noticed how similar her gold-blonde wig looked to the color of Catrin's hair. Swallowing down his regret that he would never see his true love again, he embraced his mother and picked her up.

"You look so beautiful today!" he exclaimed.

"Put me down!" she squealed.

After setting her down, Marcellus saw her smile disappear as she studied his face. "I had hoped that dreadful scar would have faded by now."

"Why hide a memento left by Gallic rebels bent on killing me?" Marcellus quipped.

"I just hate to see your face so marred like that," his mother said, touching the ridged edge of the scar with her fingertips.

"Every day, it reminds me of my good fortune to be alive," Marcellus retorted.

Drusilla's eyebrows furrowed. "Don't jest with me about death. Did your stomach wound finally heal?"

Marcellus recalled how Catrin had miraculously pulled out a rusted, metal shard that had caused the abdominal wound to fester for more than a year. "You can hardly see the scar," he said, trying to humor his mother. "Do you want to see it?"

Drusilla scrunched her face. "No. I believe you."

"You remember Arius." Marcellus gestured toward his companion in an effort to divert his mother's attention from his battle wounds. "He will stay with us until after my betrothal is announced."

Drusilla lightly touched Arius's arm. "I grieve your father's death. You are most welcome here. My husband awaits you both in the atrium."

Taking his mother's arm, Marcellus escorted her, with Arius walking alongside them, into the vestibulum, where busts of the immediate family lined the wall. When they entered the atrium, several female and male slaves were bustling to clean the tile floor and the statues near the pool. Artisans were in the final stages of repainting the walls to resemble burgundy masonry blocks bordered by green marble slabs.

Drusilla pointed out some of the renovations made to the pool used to collect rainwater from the opening in the roof. Four white marble columns had recently been installed, one at each corner of the pool. The original tile at the bottom of the pool had been replaced with a spectacular mosaic of a chariot race.

As they walked, Marcellus noticed his mother glower at Selena. The striking Ethiopian slave dropped her eyes and froze like one of the statues as they passed. At the back of the atrium, his father greeted them with a hard frown. He'd rarely smiled since returning to Rome almost a decade ago. With the legal authority of a paterfamilias, he had the power of death over his family. If Marcellus resisted his father's marital arrangements, he would no doubt suffer irreparable repercussions.

Drusilla animatedly waved her hand. "Lucius, look who is here," she trilled. "Our son is here with Arius."

The senator's hooded, brown eyes pierced Marcellus like an eagle searching for its prey. "What took you so long to get here? Nothing can go wrong when we seek Janus's favor for your upcoming marriage."

Marcellus leveled his eyes at his father. "I am well aware of this."

Lucius's brow creased. "We need to talk now, before the sacrifice."

"Can you at least greet our guest?" Drusilla interjected.

"Of course, my apologies." Lucius embraced Arius like a son, a warm gesture seldom extended to Marcellus. "Welcome to our home. I was sorry to hear of your father's death. Rest assured, I will continue my patronage of you and your mother during these difficult times. She asked that I give you a message."

Lucius snapped his fingers at Linos, who stepped toward Arius with a scroll.

"Thank you, Senator Antonius," Arius said, taking the sealed parchment. "I will read this after I settle into my quarters."

"Linos will show you to your room and have slaves help you dress for the Feast of Janus."

After Arius left with the steward, Lucius kissed Drusilla on the forehead. "Why don't you dress for the festival while I speak with Marcellus?"

After his mother reluctantly left, Marcellus was shocked to see his father walk over to Selena, grip her by the arm, and pull her to the locked tablinum, where secret meetings with political allies were often held. After his father unlocked the wooden door to the chamber, Marcellus entered, perplexed by Selena's presence. He noted everything was the same in the room. Three steps ascended to the top of the dais, where a massive stone table and curved-back chairs with brass lion-headed armrests had been set. The walls were painted with panoramic battle scenes between Romans and blue-faced Celtic warriors. In front of the steps were the forbidden busts of Marcellus's grandfather, Iullus Antonius, and great-grandfather, Marcus Antonius, which his father refused to destroy in abidance with Augustus Caesar's decree of *damnatio memoriae.*

Lucius gestured for Selena to stand behind the table on the dais. She lowered her head and tiptoed up the stairs, then remained as still as one of the statues below.

Unsettled by Selena's presence, Marcellus warily watched his father rub the bust of Marcus Antonius—a gesture he often did to soothe himself.

After a few moments of heavy silence, Lucius began. "I've been told by Governor Decimus Flavius that Arius has the potential to rise in the ranks as a military commander. There is no stronger bond than that of someone who holds a debt of gratitude to our family."

Marcellus frowned. "Is that your intent for Arius? To serve you as a trained dog like Decimus?"

Lucius's stare riveted on Marcellus. "Patronage is based on utmost loyalty to me, as you well know. Remember, I rescinded my patronage of Decimus when he broke my trust in Britannia. I only took him back after you convinced me to do so."

"You never told me what happened between the two of you in Britannia," Marcellus said, hoping his father would explain.

Lucius raised an eyebrow. "You still don't remember what happened to you in Britannia?"

"I don't recall anything," Marcellus said, even though he had learned from Catrin that a druidess had erased his memory of the time he was in Britannia. "Decimus never told me why you and he had a falling-out."

Instead of revealing what had happened between the two of them,

Lucius unexpectedly asked, "Are the rumors true that he sponsors gladiators in Gaul?"

Marcellus hesitated to answer. Did his father know of Decimus's fraudulent use of imperial funds to finance his clandestine business? Keeping the illicit dealings a secret was the price Marcellus had paid for Catrin's freedom.

"The rumors are true," he reluctantly admitted.

"Why did you order Decimus to leave our villa in Gaul after I agreed he could reside there?" Lucius asked shortly.

Marcellus tensed. "Did he write you about this?"

"Decimus complained you threw him out, even though we had an agreement that he could stay there," Lucius disclosed. "I don't understand why you did this, especially after you wrote me, exalting him as your commander."

Marcellus hesitated to divulge too much information about Decimus that would jeopardize their fragile agreement. In exchange for Decimus's recommendation for Marcellus to be promoted as a military commander in the Roman legion in northern Gaul, Marcellus had agreed to keep quiet about Decimus's illicit use of imperial funds.

"As a tribune under Decimus's command," Marcellus finally replied, "I respect his military judgment and consider him a mentor. Yet, I did not agree with his use of our villa to negotiate rates for sponsoring gladiators with a lanista. He also used our horses in gladiatorial games without paying us a fee."

"I see," Lucius muttered, stroking his chin as he considered the answer. "Then why did you insist I again become his patron when you knew about his side business?"

"Is this why you called me in here, to question me about Decimus?" Marcellus asked, growing uneasy with where his father's questioning was heading. "If you want to know the truth, at first, I was angry when you banished me to serve under Decimus in godforsaken Gaul. But then, he taught me how to earn the respect of my men by fighting alongside them. Not only did my decisions have consequences for me, but they also had consequences for the soldiers I led. I tried to handle the situation with Decimus and his side business discreetly in order to avoid any further conflict between the two of you."

Lucius sighed and looked at the painted battle on the wall. "Look, son, I do not want any more bad feelings between us before the Feast of Janus. We have our differences, but I want you to understand what drives me. I must live with dark secrets that could negatively impact my family."

Seeing his father's throat clutch with emotion discomfited Marcellus. His father had always ruled over his family like a tyrant—his ambitions taking precedence over any display of his love.

"What dark secrets?" he asked.

Lucius pointed to the painted military battles. "Look around you," he began. "You are in the presence of your noble ancestors—powerful military leaders and politicians. As I remind myself every day, I must fight for my family's legacy, which Augustus Caesar stole from me. You and I are related to both Augustus and Tiberius.

"Your great-grandfather, Marcus Antonius, was a lion who fought alongside Julius Caesar. The Roman people loved him after he defeated Julius Caesar's murderers—Brutus and Cassius. But he fell from grace when he left his Roman wife, Octavia, to marry the Egyptian sorceress, Cleopatra. After his defeat at the Battle of Actium, he ended his life in shame. His name was erased from all records because he chose an Egyptian whore over Rome."

Marcellus winced as he again had to endure his father's rants about their ancestors' ill-begotten fates.

"My father, Iullus, was the second son of Marcus Antonius and his third wife, Fulvia," Lucius continued. "My mother, Claudia Marcella, was the eldest daughter of Octavia and her first husband, Gaius Claudius Marcellus. What greater ancestry is there than this? Even Augustus Caesar held my father in esteem. Yet, almost thirty years ago, my father was condemned to death for committing adultery with Augustus's daughter, Julia. And the emperor forced me to watch my father fall on his sword."

Shaken, Marcellus could see the pain on his father's face. "Why did you not tell me this before?" he asked.

"It is a nightmare I have had to live with." Lucius lifted his eyes, as if reliving that horrible event in his mind. "I remember that day as bright and sunny. I tried to catch a butterfly for Brigata."

"Brigata?"

"A Germanian slave I had deep affection for," Lucius said ruefully.

Marcellus gaped at his father. "Affections for a slave?"

"Confused feelings of a young man," Lucius rasped, then he swallowed hard. "She was another dark secret that could destroy our family."

Marcellus felt his stomach drop. "What do you mean by *another* dark secret?"

Lucius looked away, as if he had inadvertently opened a Pandora's box. "Some secrets can never be shared."

Unnerved, Marcellus scrambled to make sense of what his father had said.

"Forgive my ramblings," Lucius said, breaking the awkward silence, "and let me continue my story about my father. On that fateful day, I had the hubris of a young man. I anticipated Augustus Caesar would grant my ambition to be a praetor in the justice system. But when that butterfly flew out of my hands before meeting him, all of my dreams fluttered away as well. Augustus disclosed that my father had been condemned to death for treason. And worse, I had to show my loyalty by witnessing my father commit suicide instead of being executed in public. I was the only person who could help him do the deed."

Marcellus met his father's misty eyes in a rare, heartfelt moment he had too often been denied. As a young boy, he had been expected to constrain his emotions. "What did you do?"

"Father asked me to help him die with dignity by holding the sword for him. I knew if I attempted to rescue him, everyone in my family would have met his fate. When I saw the tears in his eyes, I refused to help him die. Before falling on his sword, he told me to restore our family's legacy. The only way I could avenge my father's death was to live and to rise out of the ashes of his shame. I voluntarily exiled to Gaul to avoid public execution and to secure the inheritance for my family. It was almost fifteen years before Tiberius allowed me back in Rome. Since then, I've clawed for every political favor and position. I defy the act of *damnatio memoriae* by keeping my grandfather's and father's statues in here to remind me of my promise to my father."

"Why are telling me this now?" Marcellus asked, suspecting his father's confession was meant as a warning for him to follow through with his commitment to marry Licinia.

Lucius's eyes hardened. "Senator Frugi has learned of your past affair with Eliana, the wife of a consul. Your reckless behavior has jeopardized your marriage to his daughter!"

Marcellus felt the crushing weight of his father's words. "I never intended to harm you or our family. I was a young man tempted by an older woman's flattery."

"Flattery!" Lucius hissed. "There are codes of conduct you must follow as a nobleman." He motioned for Selena to join them.

The slave's lips quivered as she descended the steps from the dais to stand beside Lucius. He roughly stroked her neck. Both she and Marcellus cringed in revulsion upon hearing Lucius's offer.

"Release your urges with my slave before you marry," Lucius said, untying and releasing Selena's tunic to reveal her nakedness.

Aghast, Marcellus now understood his mother's hard stare at Selena when they'd first entered the atrium.

Lucius gave a lecherous smile as he fondled one of her breasts. "As a Roman master, you have the right to take her at any time. Romans embrace the war god, Mars, as we plunder the bodies of our conquered. Men abducted Sabine Women to conceive their sons, assuring Roman might. You only need to be discreet around your mother and future wife when you take a hot-blooded slave into your bed."

Selena's face paled and contorted as Lucius's hand freely wandered down her body.

"Enough!" Marcellus snapped, repulsed by his father's blatant behavior. "I have no desire to take this slave. Or any slave! Let her dress and leave us."

Lucius snickered and waved Selena away. Clutching her tunic, her eyes widened like a frightened deer's as she scrambled to a dark corner of the room.

Lucius dragged over a couple of wooden chairs so he and Marcellus could sit down. After settling on his seat, he continued his discourse with Marcellus.

"I will assure Senator Frugi that Eliana was nothing but a fleeting moment for a lusty, virile man. Now that you have led men in battle, you have matured and distinguished yourself as a Roman commander. I will emphasize that we both have the ancestry and influence to rise in Rome. I will flatter him, saying your marriage to Licinia will benefit both our families. Just think of the noble ancestry both families will bring into the marriage. Licinia is descended from Marcus Licinius Crassus and his wife, Scribonia, the granddaughter of Pompeia Magna. Your children with Licinia will be descendants of all the great men in the original triumvir, including Julius Caesar. But you can't risk this marital contract with your womanizing. Do you understand?"

"I understand," Marcellus muttered, struggling to masquerade his resentment that he would be forced to marry a girl just on the cusp of womanhood.

Lucius rose from the chair and gesticulated, as if giving an oratory speech before the senate. "I will make a sacrifice to Janus today to obtain his blessing for a great beginning for our families. And, if needed, I will sacrifice to Jupiter, Hera, Minerva, or whatever other god to assure your marriage takes place. Once I've sealed the nuptial agreement, we will have a splendid feast to publicly announce your betrothal. I expect the most notable patricians in Rome will accept the invitation. Make sure you charm everyone there. Nothing—let me repeat, *nothing*—ill can happen today as I sacrifice to Janus. From now on, you must cut off any entanglements with free women. Roman or barbarian."

Marcellus inhaled sharply at the mention of barbarian women. Did his father know about Catrin? Rising from his chair, he stole a glance at Selena, who was cowering behind the table on the dais. "I understand," he said firmly, considering a way to keep the slave from his father's clutches. "I'd like to keep Selena as a personal slave in my bedchamber until I am married."

Lucius gave a lewd smile at Selena and nodded.

"If you would excuse me, I would like to bathe before the Festival of Janus," Marcellus said to end the conversation.

Lucius walked over to Marcellus and slapped him on the back in a friendly manner. "I am glad we had this time to speak as father and son. I lost that opportunity with my father. Remember, once the butterfly escapes, you cannot catch it again."

The image of orange and red butterflies flashed into Marcellus's mind. He remembered a swarm clustering like fiery blossoms on a hazel tree near where Catrin, who'd been disguised as a boy at the time, had been practicing with her sword in the Roman legion, not too far from where he had been stationed. Feverish from an infection, he'd thought it had been a dream at the time, a hallucination. Was it more than a coincidence that his father had mentioned catching a butterfly for a special slave?

Brigata.

Drawing out of his thoughts, he gestured for Selena, who was visibly shaken, to join him. He shrugged off the possibility that his father would ever have had genuine affection for a slave. The angst on Selena's face was evidence of his cruelty in his sexual forays with her. Her lips were quivering when she cast a nervous glance at him. She undoubtedly anticipated having a similarly loathsome experience with him.

Quietly, Marcellus walked with her out of the chamber, through the atrium, and to the peristyle garden. Before going inside his bedchamber, toward the back, he assured her, "Don't worry. I will never force myself on you."

Selena seemed to relax as they entered the room, which was furnished with a white canopy bed, several tables, and shelves. After she left him to gather supplies for his bath, Marcellus sat down on the bed and felt an emptiness in his heart that only Catrin could fill.

Yet, after his disturbing conversation with his father, he realized she would be in great danger if she ever joined him in Rome. His father would consider their relationship a direct threat to his marriage to Licinia.

Reason told him to forget her.

But how can I live without my true love . . . my soul mate?

IO

BETROTHAL RECEPTION

Rome, 2 March, 28 AD

Marcellus held out his arms for the slave, Selena, as she draped a blue-bordered, white toga over him in preparation for his betrothal reception. The cold, misty day dampened his mood. He had hoped the empty feeling in his chest would have dissipated after his return home. He couldn't sleep, eat, or concentrate. The image of making love to Catrin in the cave behind the waterfall played over and over in his mind. How could he capture the same bliss in the arms of a twelve-year-old girl he hardly knew?

He couldn't.

Had he made a mistake by not returning to Britannia with Catrin? *Why can't I have both my family's name and her?*

Loud footsteps entering the room and his mother's squeal of delight drew Marcellus out of his grim musings.

"You are a sight to behold!" Drusilla trilled.

Marcellus noted her garish, red-haired wig that clashed with her purple stola. Her face was as white as chalk with thick makeup, and her rouged cheeks matched the color of her hair. He dared not burst the bubble of her excitement and thus forced a smile of admiration.

"Mother, you are the epitome of Venus."

Drusilla beamed as she pushed a strand of unruly hair from her forehead. "You think so?"

"Of course, I do. You will . . . appear as a goddess in the crowd," Marcellus flattered her.

"It's so important we look our best tonight," Drusilla said, lightly touching his arm. "I spoke with your future mother-in-law yesterday. She said some of the most notable people close to the emperor will be at the reception. And I can tell your bride-to-be is enthralled by you. You will be surprised at how much Licinia has changed. She is blossoming into an elegant young woman."

The image of Catrin shape-shifting from a white raven into her athletic, womanly form at the waterfall swooped into Marcellus's mind. To distract himself from the image of them making love, he adjusted the toga over his arm and gestured for Selena to leave.

Arius bolted into the bedroom and looked surprised to see Drusilla. He slightly bowed his head to her. "The litters are here to transport us. Lucius has already left."

Drusilla turned up her nose and sashayed out of the room without greeting Arius. Marcellus grimaced, painfully aware his mother now considered Arius beneath their social status after learning about the suicide of his father, who had impoverished his family with gambling losses.

Arius leaned closer to Marcellus. "Your mother dismisses me with one flick of her nose."

Though Marcellus whispered, "Ignore her," Arius's frown deepened with obvious discomfort. His friend remained silent as they walked to the courtyard. There, Linos was assisting Drusilla into a litter carried by four men. Arius and Marcellus rode in the next litter for the short ride to Consul Frugi's residence up on Palatine Hill.

After they reached the courtyard of the expansive villa, a stout steward escorted them into the atrium, where Consul Frugi and his wife, Scribonia, greeted them. Marcellus raised the hand of his future mother-in-law and pressed a kiss to it. "It is an honor to be here."

The consul introduced his daughter, Licinia, who was standing on the other side of him. Marcellus noted her curvaceous figure. With features similar to her mother's, Licinia had almond-shaped brown eyes, voluptuous red lips, and high cheekbones that gave her an exotic look. Dressed in an ankle-length white tunica, she wore a child's crescent-shaped lunula around her neck to ward off the evil eye until she married. She still displayed the awkwardness of a shy girl, as she nervously lowered her gaze to her sandaled feet when Marcellus lightly kissed her fingertips.

"It is a pleasure to see you again, Licinia. Your beauty is only matched by your mother's."

Licinia's childlike giggle further unsettled Marcellus about the prospect of consummating a marriage with someone so young. The consul took the arm of his wife and paraded Marcellus and Drusilla to the center of the atrium, where Lucius and Brutius awaited. In the center of the extravagant atrium, under a large opening in the roof, were four mosaic pools separated by rose-colored tiles. Jade-green marble columns surrounded the pools. Painted murals of lush, rolling hills with blue and yellow wildflowers on the walls added to the festivity. Family busts located at one end of the chamber proclaimed the rich legacy of Consul Frugi and his wife, Scribonia. A waft from fragrant, flower-decorated tables on which trays of food were being served tantalized his nostrils.

The consul and Lucius, standing together, prepared to announce the formal betrothal of Marcellus and Licinia to approximately eighty aristocrats.

Consul Frugi shouted, "May I have your attention?"

The chamber hushed as the consul began. "It is my honor and privilege to announce the betrothal of my only daughter, Licinia, to Marcellus Antonius, son of Senator Lucius Antonius and his wife, Drusilla. In honor of their betrothal, food and wine will be served for your pleasure."

Lucius raised his goblet of wine toward Consul Frugi and offered a toast. "To Marcus Licinius Crassus Frugi and his wife, Scribonia, who honor our family in hosting this marvelous affair. I look forward to joining our families and the alliance this marriage will forge. I invite all of you to meet my son, Marcellus, who recently returned from military service as a tribune in the outer boundaries of Gaul and Germania. Licinia, I am told, is a skilled musician with the lyre."

A reception line formed at the end of the atrium. Marcellus was placed between his mother and father so they could give him a brief background of any guest he met. Consul Frugi stood between his wife and daughter.

Brutius, Marcellus's half brother, began the formalities by escorting Sejanus, Commander of the Praetorian Guard, and his companion, Livilla, to the front of the receiving line, ahead of the other dignitaries. Casting a glare that pierced Marcellus, Brutius gestured to the most influential adviser of Emperor Tiberius.

"Let me introduce my close friend Sejanus, Commander of the Imperial Praetorian Guard responsible for Tiberius's safety. As the emperor now resides in Capri, Sejanus stands in his stead and governs the city. It is also my honor to introduce Livilla, widow of the late Druses Julius Caesar, who tragically died a few years back."

Marcellus slightly bowed to Sejanus, then he kissed Livilla's hand. He had heard rumors that Sejanus had written a letter a few years back to Tiberius with a request to marry Livilla, causing a scandal. It was unthinkable that an equestrian had dared ask the emperor for permission to marry his son's widow. Brutius had somehow risen above the ugly gossip of his cruelty to his former wife and now associated with some of Tiberius's most powerful dignitaries. The eagle-beak nose jutting out between Brutius's bloodshot eyes could sniff out ambition at every turn.

Brutius told Sejanus in a condescending tone, "My half brother, Marcellus, trained with common soldiers in northern Gaul under Legatus Decimus Flavius."

Sejanus smiled thinly. "Interesting. Why did you do that?"

Recognizing how important it was for legionaries to respect Sejanus as a military commander, Marcellus looked him in the eye and answered, "Consistent with the Roman military tradition, you must first know how to obey and endure the hardships of the men you lead before you can command."

Sejanus clasped Marcellus's arm and smiled at Lucius. "Well said, young man. What resistance did you encounter with local tribes?"

"I quelled an unpleasant rebellion in northern Gaul," Marcellus said. "Still, I'd like to return there and take command of the Roman legion."

"Speak to me later about this," Sejanus offered.

"I will," Marcellus said, regarding Brutius's nasty scowl. He could see a glint of jealousy in his half brother's eyes. After his scandalous divorce from the wife he'd abused, Brutius must have been desperate to win back their father's favor by latching onto the second-most powerful politician in Rome.

"May Jupiter favor you with sons in your upcoming marriage," Sejanus said, finishing the conversation and continuing down the receiving line.

Marcellus continued greeting the guests, including Consul Lucius Calpurnius Piso, who shared duties with Consul Frugi. Following Consul Piso was Matron Antonia, whose gray, plaited hair was piled high on her head. As she strode toward Marcellus, he recalled his father saying that Antonia had inherited Marcus Antonius's comely features. Known for her beauty as a young woman, Antonia maintained that reputation by wearing heavy makeup and green eye shadow accentuating deep-set hazel eyes. Elegantly dressed in a blue stola cascading over a white tunic, Antonia emitted radiance like an evening star. She raised her fingers for Marcellus to kiss.

"Greetings, Marcellus. You have such a strong, manly smell. A welcome change from the heavy perfume that most noblemen here wear."

Not sure how to take Antonia's comment, Marcellus gave her a perplexed look, tempted to smell his underarms for any disagreeable odor.

"Don't take offense," Antonia said bluntly with a smirk. "I've heard of your military exploits in Gaul, crushing the rebels. Some say you display my father's traits as a general. Let me warn you. Don't embrace my father's weakness for women. Stay true to your future wife, Licinia. Why don't you arrange a time for me to chat with you and Licinia?"

Marcellus gave a slight nod, wondering how much Antonia knew of his scandalous affair with Eliana and his relationship with Catrin. She would go into a rage if she found out he had married Catrin in Britannia.

Warm sweat beaded on his forehead as he finished meeting everyone. He forced a smile as he watched Matron Antonia mingle on the opposite side of the room from Sejanus and Livilla. After he greeted the last guest in line, he turned to Consul Frugi to excuse himself so he could find Arius, who had mysteriously disappeared.

Before he could say anything, the consul demanded, "Speak with me at the basilica next week to discuss an administrative post I have in mind for you."

"I had planned to return to Gaul," Marcellus replied.

Lucius chimed in, "Marcus and I both agree it would be best if you stay in Rome to advance your career."

Marcellus bit off his angry retort; it was neither the right time nor the right place to argue. He said reluctantly, "I will consider your offer. If you would excuse me, I'd like to mingle with other guests here."

Before he could escape, Drusilla gripped his arm and whispered in his ear. "Before you leave here tonight, give Licinia a kiss in the garden."

Taken aback by his mother's suggestion, Marcellus's mouth dropped. "She is too young. And it is too cold."

Drusilla squeezed his arm. "Just do it!"

"Where is she?" Marcellus glanced around the room.

Drusilla motioned toward the end of the table, where Licinia was standing alone, her eyes downcast.

Marcellus nodded and walked over to Licinia. She gave him a demure smile.

He proffered his arm. "Would you like to stroll through the garden?"

Licinia bit her lip and gave a slight nod.

"Does that mean yes?" Marcellus asked, taking her arm into the crook of his.

Licinia giggled but became silent as he escorted her through the atrium into a garden scented with roses. As the full, orange moon rose over the horizon, its light illuminated the fading red, white, and pink rose blossoms. They ambled across a pebbled path leading to the other end of the garden and away from the guests.

Gazing at the moon, Marcellus commented, "The goddess Diana favors us tonight."

Licinia quietly looked at the sky.

After a few moments of awkward silence, Marcellus asked, "Do you enjoy playing the lyre?"

"I do. Perhaps I can play for you," Licinia said softly.

"I would like that," Marcellus replied. "What else do you like to do?"

"I like to weave alongside my mother."

"Anything else?"

"I sometimes read Greek stories to Matron Antonia," Licinia said, shifting her eyes toward Marcellus, who gave her a warm smile.

"Does she give you good advice?"

"Yes. She tells me I should aspire to be like her mother, Octavia. She was a devoted wife to Marcus Antonius and cared for all of the children he fathered with other women. Antonia told me I must be an obedient wife to you and a loving mother to your children."

Marcellus felt chilled in the evening's fading light. "Good advice, no doubt. Is there anything you hope for?"

Licinia gazed at the moon, as if struggling to find the appropriate answer. "I only want to please you."

Please me? What am I doing here with a child?

Marcellus felt as if his heart were splitting apart between his duty to marry a girl and his love for Catrin.

"Let's get back to the party before anyone misses us," he finally suggested.

The morning after the betrothal reception, Arius and Marcellus rode their horses on the cobblestone Appian Way into the countryside just south of Rome. The tall pine and cypress trees lining the road provided shade from the bright morning sun on the unusually warm, cloudless day. The white stallion had not been ridden in several days and was spirited, ready to gallop. Marcellus kicked the steed's side, and it raced down Appian Way. Marcellus could hear the pounding hoofbeats of Arius's horse behind him. After a short distance, Marcellus reined in his horse at a stone wall, where they dismounted and strode to an abandoned storage house hidden in a cluster of trees. Marcellus sat down against a large cypress tree and invited Arius to join him.

Arius groaned as he sat next to Marcellus, then he remarked, "That was quite a lively celebration last night. Licinia is a beauty."

Marcellus shrugged. "Sweet as a child. I took her into the garden."

Arius's eyes widened. "To do what?"

"My mother suggested I kiss her, but I couldn't do it."

Arius raised an eyebrow. "Why is that?"

"It would be like kissing my younger sister," Marcellus said, suddenly longing to see Catrin again.

"You're still not over Catrin, are you?"

"No," Marcellus reluctantly admitted.

Arius slapped his thigh with enthusiasm. "Why not join me at a party hosted by Claudia later this week? Remember her? How about we share one last fuck before I leave?"

Marcellus frowned. "My father threatened me with my life not to do anything stupid with women. My mother watches over me like a lioness and accuses you of leading me down the wrong path."

Arius looked away. "Perhaps I should stay at Claudia's domus instead of yours. Your mother is ready to strike me like a viper."

"Don't pay any attention to her. You are welcome to stay at my family's villa until you return to Germania."

Arius rose to his feet, stretched his arms, and stared into the distance before turning to Marcellus. "How long has Brutius rubbed his nose in the ass of Sejanus?"

Surprised by the question, Marcellus asked, "Why do you ask?"

Arius looked down at Marcellus. "At the reception, I heard rumblings that Sejanus is gaining more imperial power. I also heard gossip that Sejanus seduced Livilla before Druses died. It was even whispered that they both poisoned him. I'd be careful of Brutius. His sails always turn in the direction of favorable political winds. He's a snake ready to sink his fangs into you. I overheard him tell Adonis, his slave, to watch you closely at the reception."

Marcellus flinched. "I wouldn't put that past Brutius. He has always been jealous of me, particularly now that I am betrothed to Licinia. He tried to embarrass me by telling Sejanus I trained with common soldiers."

"How did Sejanus react to Brutius's comment?"

"Sejanus thought I answered him well. I said a commander needs to understand the hardships of his men to lead them. As for Brutius, he's nothing more than a shriveled cock that needs stroking from someone in power to harden his esteem. Don't worry about me. I'll watch my back."

"Make sure you do. I won't be here to protect you," Arius said, offering a hand to help Marcellus up.

II

BARBARIANS IN ROME

Rome, 15 March (Ides of March), 28 AD

Nothing Marcellus had said about Rome could have prepared Catrin for the massive stone buildings and the people swarming all around her, bumping against her white stallion, Lugus. Riding in front of her was the brawny, one-eyed warrior, Cynwrig, weaving his chestnut mare through the throng of people to open a pathway for her.

Ahead was a massive, arched structure that stretched lengthwise between two hilltops. From inside the structure, an obelisk shot into the heavens like a divine finger pointing to the cloud-covered skies. She knew by the colossal size of the arena that it must be the reputed Circus Maximus, where some of the chariots raced under the sponsorship of the Antonius family.

She had successfully navigated the land routes from Lugdunum to Rome for two months in the dead of winter. Yet, finding Marcellus or the horse trainer, Falco, in a metropolitan city where hordes of spectators poured out of the colonnaded stadium's archways could be an almost impossible feat. This made her pause on her decision to seek aid from Marcellus, wondering whether it was wise. Would he keep his promise to supplicate the powerful Roman politicians to support her claim to the Cantiaci kingdom? Though she vowed only reason would rule her head, the anticipation of seeing Marcellus, with his piercing blue eyes, made her heart pound. Love was an elixir that defied all logic, she had to tell herself again and again. Her dream of his life thread on the Wall of Lives reaching out for hers gave her hope that she could reconnect with Marcellus and again share their journey together. Yet, the thorns of reality that they could never bridge their cultural differences stabbed at her heart. Did she dare risk becoming pregnant again if they reignited their liaison? Besides, why would Marcellus warmly embrace her after she had rejected his invitation to return to Rome—a city where he could not acknowledge her as his wife?

To complicate matters further, she wasn't sure if they had sufficient funds to pay for food, housing, and bribes for a long stay in a foreign city that viewed Cynwrig and her as barbarians. The coin Marcellus had given her in Gaul before he had returned to Rome had been depleted during the arduous journey. Faced with threats of thieves robbing their prized horses, she had to pay exorbitant fees to stable them at night, while she and Cynwrig slept nearby to guard them.

When Catrin finally reached the outermost western gate of the massive stadium, she grew uneasy with the clamor of shoppers mulling around open storefronts and carts lining the narrow roadway. The stench of raw meat hanging from metal hooks competed with the aroma of baked bread. The finely dressed noblemen weaving their way through loin-clothed slaves, who were hammering flat, gray stones into potholes, made maneuvering their horses through the masses cumbersome.

Cynwrig reined his horse to a halt and waited for Catrin to join him. He told her in Celtic, "We need to be on close guard here."

Glancing all around, Catrin was unnerved by the stares directed at them. As she trailed Cynwrig through the throng of shoppers, a powerfully built man abruptly bumped against her horse just as a scrawny boy grabbed for her horse's reins. She ripped the leather straps out of the boy's hands, then felt a hand brush behind her. Jerking her head back, she saw a muscular man extending a knife to cut her belted money purse. She surprised him with a swift blow to his wrist, dislodging his weapon. He immediately ran away, forcing his way through two elderly women and vanishing into the crowd. She looked around but could not spot the boy who had gripped the reins.

Cynwrig's whistle caught Catrin's attention. He gestured for her to follow him northeast to a hilltop. She trailed him through spectators streaming into the stadium's arched entrances. When they began climbing the hillside, away from the massive arena, they entered a residential area of lavish villas where the narrow roads became less congested. The extravagant villas with facades of richly colored red, gold, and green concrete lined each side of the narrow roadway. Higher up, she gazed down at the elliptical structure of the arena and the horse-drawn chariots racing around its track. She recalled Marcellus saying his family villa overlooked the Circus Maximus.

Hoping she could perchance find Marcellus here, she glanced all around and unexpectedly spotted Falco holding the reins of a stallion as black as obsidian in a villa's courtyard. Her spirits lifted at the prospect that the horse trainer from Lugdunum could tell her where to find Marcellus. She gestured for Cynwrig to halt in an alley, where they could hide as they waited for Falco to exit the villa.

"Did the thief who bumped into your horse steal any coins?" Cynwrig asked in a hushed voice.

"He didn't steal anything, but I'm afraid we're running short on funds."

Cynwrig grimaced. "We may need to sell something to get more."

"I won't sell the horses. We can sell one of our weapons instead if we need the money," Catrin suggested.

"That thief was a bad omen," Cynwrig grumbled, spitting a glob of sputum on the cobblestone road. "I hate this city and all of its vermin! We should return home."

"Let's wait a little longer."

Catrin nudged her horse forward to get a better view of the courtyard. She noticed Falco walking toward them with the reins of the black horse in hand. As he passed her, she called out, "Falco."

He looked in her direction, and his mouth dropped. "Why are you here?"

"I'm here to see Marcellus."

Falco frowned. "Does he know you're in Rome?"

"Not yet. We just arrived this morning."

Falco eyed Cynwrig. "Who's the one-eyed warrior with you?"

"Cynwrig," Catrin answered. "He was one of my father's fiercest warriors. He's here to protect me."

"It looks like he's been in too many fights," Falco commented, shaking his head. "Does he speak the Roman tongue?"

"He understands a little," Catrin said, casting a reassuring glance at Cynwrig, who had a confused look on his face.

Falco glanced around the area and then spoke in Celtic. "You'll attract undue attention here. Follow me. I'll stable your horses where Marcellus keeps his chariot horses, near the Circus Maximus. After that, we can talk."

Catrin and Cynwrig trailed Falco as he walked briskly down the hillside road. A short distance from the colosseum, they rode through an archway into a massive stone structure. She was awestruck by the hundreds of horses in a multitude of stables.

"Do these all belong to Marcellus?" she asked.

"No. These are chariot horses from various families," Falco said as he opened the gate to a row of stables.

"Does Marcellus race these horses?" Catrin further inquired, eyeing a placard with the Antonius name.

"Freemen drive his chariots in races. It's considered beneath a nobleman's dignity to do so. Marcellus sometimes helps me train them, though."

Falco gestured to an empty, straw-covered stable, where Catrin unsaddled and unbridled Lugus. Cynwrig and Falco settled their horses in adjacent stalls. After they finished with the horses, Falco said, "Collect your belongings. I'll arrange lodging for you at the Red Chariot Inn near the circus. Can you pay for it?"

"I only have enough coins for a short stay," Catrin remarked.

Falco regarded Catrin for a moment. "I'll give you some extra coins for food and other expenses. Buy a dress so you blend in with the plebs. A woman in legionary breeches is an uncommon sight."

"When will you tell Marcellus I'm here?" Catrin asked.

"Tomorrow morning. You should know that his betrothal has been officially announced."

A lump formed in Catrin's throat from her conflicted emotions, and she was barely able to swallow. "He told me about this before he left Gaul. Did he say anything when I didn't come to Rome with you?"

"No. But he looked dejected." Falco sighed. "Truth be told, I could see that you broke his heart."

Taken aback, Catrin didn't know what to say at first. "In Gaul, I couldn't see a future with him."

"Then why are you here now?" Falco demanded.

"Before he left for Rome, he promised he would help me if I sought him out," Catrin said evenly, struggling to maintain a stone face, even though her stomach was twisting into a knot from the anticipation of seeing Marcellus again.

"As I said, I'll speak with him tomorrow and arrange for him to meet you that afternoon," Falco assured. "Tonight, I'll sleep with the horses after I arrange accommodations for you."

They left the stables and strolled on the cobblestone road to the Circus Maximus. About midway toward the stadium, Falco pointed to a sign shaped like a chariot. "This is the inn where you'll stay. Have Cynwrig stay with you at all times to prevent sordid patrons from approaching you. They'll mistake you for a whore."

"I can take care of myself," Catrin said, fingering the hilt of her *gladius*.

Falco smiled thinly. "No doubt. I know of your reputation as a gladiator. Let's go in, and I'll get you set up in a room on the upper level. Near here is a lion-shaped fountain where you can draw fresh water."

As they entered the tavern, the room silenced, and the stares of drinking men shifted toward them. Cynwrig shouldered through two strapping men, making a pathway for Falco and Catrin. At the back of the room, Catrin stood quietly as Falco negotiated rates for a one-week stay with a rotund innkeeper whose hooded, dark-brown eyes shifted constantly between her and Cynwrig. His jowls puffed like a male frog during mating season. After the bargaining was concluded, the innkeeper escorted them to the back of the room, where there was a doorway to a staircase. The innkeeper illuminated the way with a burning lamp as everyone climbed the wooden steps, which creaked under the weight of their feet. On the second floor was a corridor with rooms lining each side. After they reached the last door at the end of the hallway, the innkeeper inserted a latchkey into the lock and clicked the door open.

Inside the small room, the tavern's ruckus rose through the floor like a thunderstorm, while the cries of a couple in climax in an adjacent room made Catrin wince. The small chamber was sparsely furnished with a straw-filled mattress on slabs of wood, a small table with a ceramic bowl on top, and a few corner shelves.

The innkeeper's jowls jiggled as he pulled back a curtain to reveal an opening in the concrete wall that served as a window overlooking the congested street below.

"This is my best room, as you can see," the innkeeper said with a croaky voice. "You have a bed to sleep on and a view of the city." He cleared his throat. "There's no chamber pot. Use the nearby public latrines to do your business. You can buy food in the tavern or at shops close by."

"This will serve both my and my husband's needs," Catrin said to allay any of the innkeeper's concerns about her servicing other men.

"Are you from Gaul?" the innkeeper asked as he scrutinized Cynwrig's scarred face.

"We're merchants from Britannia," Catrin answered, taking Cynwrig's hand in hers.

The innkeeper's eyes narrowed. "How long have you been married?"

Catrin noted his suspicious stare. "Just recently."

Before the innkeeper could continue the inquisition, Falco gripped the man's arm, led him back into the corridor, and closed the door.

While they waited for Falco to finish his discussion with the innkeeper, Cynwrig sat on the bed and frowned. "Hard as a rock."

"Where do you plan to sleep?" Catrin asked.

"On the floor, near the door, in case someone unexpected crashes through."

A hard knock startled both of them. Cynwrig jumped off the bed and cracked the door open. He peeked around the edge and then allowed Falco in.

Falco handed Catrin a money pouch. "I almost forgot. Money for food and new clothes. I need to get back to the horses before it gets dark to guard them. If Marcellus can't meet you tomorrow, I'll let you know."

Falco then quickly turned on his heels and left the room, leaving Catrin alone with Cynwrig. For several moments, they quietly inspected the room for any trapdoors in the flooring or peepholes in the wall.

Finally settled, Cynwrig poured some water from a jar into the ceramic bowl and splashed water on his face. After wiping his face with his cloak, he turned to Catrin. "What if Marcellus refuses to meet you?"

"He'll meet me," Catrin said firmly, though her stomach was aflutter from trepidation that Marcellus may not come. Uneasy, she looked around the gloomy room and noticed spiderwebs in the corners of the walls.

"I can tell you still have affection for Marcellus," Cynwrig said.

"When did you become a seer?" Catrin jested, disquieted by the comment. "I am here for one purpose. To win Marcellus's alliance in helping me take back my throne."

Cynwrig scrunched his brow, as though he questioned her coming to Rome.

"Do you disagree with my decision to meet with Marcellus?" Catrin snapped.

Cynwrig lowered his head. "I apologize, my queen. I serve at your pleasure. It's just . . ."

"Speak your mind," Catrin urged.

A pained grimace contorted Cynwrig's face. "It would be easier to win Adminius's alliance by marrying him. It is hard for me to be in Rome. I vowed vengeance on all Romans for what they did to my wife, Melana."

"With good reason," Catrin said, and she softly touched Cynwrig's arm. "Tell me what happened at the battle."

Cynwrig's eyes blazed as he recounted, "In the battle at the Cantiaci capital, three Roman soldiers had to restrain me as they forced me to watch as each of them took turns with her. I begged them to have mercy. She was"—Cynwrig swallowed the lump forming in his throat and clenched his hands—"with child. But they didn't understand me. They howled with laughter as they lined up to take their turns. I became enraged and broke free, unsheathing one of their swords. I killed two of them before the others jumped on me like wild dogs. And then . . ." Cynwrig's eyes widened as if reliving the horror.

Catrin broke the heavy silence. "I understand your grief and need for vengeance. I have as much reason to hate the Romans as you do. I hate Marrock for beheading my parents and my oldest sister. I thought he had done the same to my sister, Mor. Her safety now depends on me. That is why I am determined to claim the throne as the rightful queen. I want to spare my people Marrock's tyranny and then conquer any rival kingdom that threatens us. But to do so, I need strong allies—even Romans we may consider enemies."

"Do you still consider Marcellus your husband?" Cynwrig inquired.

Tears welled in Catrin's eyes as conflicting emotions bubbled to the surface. "I swore I would forsake him after what the Romans did to me. Yet, during my fight at the arena in Lugdunum, I diverted the lightning I'd directed at Decimus so I wouldn't kill Marcellus, who'd suddenly appeared at his side. At that instant, I realized our souls had joined, and I would never be whole again if I destroyed him. I can't explain why he has such a strong hold on me."

Cynwrig sighed heavily. "That is how I felt about my wife. I would have died a thousand deaths so she and our child could live. Without her, I am the shadow of the man I once was."

"Do you think you could love another?" Catrin asked, noting Cynwrig's downcast blue-gray eye.

"What woman could love a man with a face like mine?" Cynwrig said with a sad tremor in his voice.

"You can't see each other in the darkness," Catrin commented, "but the light shines brightly on a person's true essence."

Cynwrig smiled. "Have you become a philosopher? I accept my fate never to love again. I now must serve you as your champion, my queen."

"Thank you for your loyalty," Catrin said, moved by the battle-hardened warrior's heartfelt words.

"If it gives you comfort, I thought Marcellus was a brave man.

Stupid—but brave. He risked his life to speak with your father so you would be spared from death for treason."

"Could you accept Marcellus as your king?" Catrin ventured.

Cynwrig hesitated. "My duty is to my queen."

"You didn't answer my question. Would you accept Marcellus as your king?"

Cynwrig took a deep breath. "I have no doubt he loves you, but I wonder how deep that affection runs. Would he sacrifice his Roman heritage for you?"

The image of the waterfall where Catrin had made love with Marcellus cascaded into her mind. "He almost did. In Gaul."

Cynwrig's brow lifted with curiosity. "How is that?"

"He was prepared to desert the legion and return to Britannia with me." Catrin bit her lower lip. "But we were caught before we could escape."

"If that is so, why doesn't he go back to Britannia with you now?"

Catrin exhaled heavily. "I don't know how we can build that bridge again with our different backgrounds."

"Malena and I often spoke of our future together," Cynwrig commented. "I now realize what we had was more precious than riches or glory. If you can't imagine a future with Marcellus, then perhaps you were not meant to cross that bridge."

"Perhaps you are right." Catrin sighed ruefully. "Rome will never recognize our marriage. Still, I believe my people would accept him as king, only if . . ."

"Marcellus turns his back on Rome and his family," Cynwrig said, completing Catrin's thoughts. "Tell me, what will you do if Marcellus refuses to meet you?"

"As I said, he will meet me. We are fated to see each other again. I've dreamed that his life thread is reaching for mine on the Wall of Lives and will soon join mine."

"To what end?" Cynwrig asked, raising an eyebrow.

"That is yet to be determined," Catrin said, an uneasy feeling in the pit of her stomach.

12

RED CHARIOT INN

Rome, 16 March, 28 AD

Marcellus felt as though his heart had leapt against his chest when Falco relayed, "Catrin is here in Rome to see you."

"In Rome," Marcellus repeated, barely able to catch his breath. "When did you see her?"

"Yesterday. Near your home," Falco answered.

"Near here? Did anyone from my family see you talking to her?" Marcellus asked, worried that one of Brutius's spies might have spotted them.

"I directed her away from your home," Falco assured.

Marcellus nervously raked a hand through his hair. "Did she look well?"

"She looked weary from her travel," Falco admitted. "Another warrior—a Briton, I believe—was with her. I gave her some coins to help pay for lodging at the Red Chariot Inn across from the circus. She wants to meet you there at midday."

Marcellus could barely swallow the lump in his throat from the emotions whirling inside of him at the prospect of seeing Catrin again. Since his return to Rome, he had struggled to accept that he may never see her again. Though his parents had welcomed him back and his political future looked bright, he nonetheless was miserable without her, with a constant ache in his chest.

But now, he couldn't believe she had come to Rome. The memory of the burning rage in Catrin's eyes, when he'd last seen her in Gaul, quelled his elation. Did Catrin still blame him for Decimus condemning her as a gladiatrix?

"Did she say anything about me?" Marcellus asked, suddenly uneasy.

Falco regarded Marcellus for a moment, then narrowed his eyes. "As I said, Catrin seemed anxious to meet you. She drew undue attention, though. She was dressed in military braccae and riding Lugus—a prized horse worth stealing. A one-eyed warrior with a scar fracturing half his face was with her. I stabled their horses with yours at the stalls near the circus."

Marcellus reached for his purse, which was tucked beneath his belt, and picked out some gold coins. "How much do I owe you?"

Falco extended the palm of his hand. "Two hundred denarii. Should I make the arrangements for you to meet Catrin?"

"Yes. Yes," Marcellus said, dropping eight gold coins into Falco's hand. "Tell her I'll meet her at noon, when the trumpets announce the chariot races. Don't tell my family about this. I fear Brutius has hired henchmen to spy on me."

"You've been jittery about Brutius since you arrived in Rome. What does he hope to find out about you?" Falco inquired.

Marcellus's brow creased. "No doubt he wants to find me in a provocative situation with another woman to jeopardize my betrothal to Consul Frugi's daughter. Or perhaps he wants to tattle to Prefect Sejanus that I've spoken to one of his political rivals. They are disappearing like sand washed away in a tidal wave."

Falco narrowed his eyes. "On my way here, I saw three strange men whose heads were covered. They were milling around close to your villa. Do you think they are Brutius's spies?"

A chill ran down Marcellus's spine. "Are they still there?"

Falco looked all around. "They're gone."

"Be sure no one follows you after we speak," Marcellus warned.

Falco gave a slight nod and turned on his heels to leave.

Marcellus watched Falco until he disappeared down the road. As Marcellus stepped into the family's villa, he almost collided with Brutius, who was scurrying down the vestibule.

Marcellus grabbed Brutius by the arm. "What's your hurry?"

Brutius yanked away and shot Marcellus a nasty scowl. "I have important matters to attend to."

"Meeting with Sejanus today?" Marcellus asked with a cock of his eyebrow.

"None of your affair. I can say, though, everything I do benefits our family. You, on the other hand, squander the day at blood games and chariot races," Brutius said in a contemptuous tone.

Marcellus grinned. "Consul Frugi has asked me to coordinate gladiator games for the spring festivals."

The corners of Brutius's mouth twisted up. "Indeed. Games of brute violence suit you, while I maneuver my rivals like political pieces in backgammon."

Marcellus blocked Brutius from leaving. "Am I one of those rivals?"

"Everyone is my rival," Brutius said, matching Marcellus's steel-hard stare. "Get out of my way. I'm not one of your lowly soldiers to order around."

Marcellus stepped aside and allowed Brutius to leave. After his half brother strode through the entryway, Marcellus peered around the wooden door and spotted Brutius talking to three men. After they finished conversing, each of them walked away in different directions. Wary that Brutius had ordered one of them to trail him, Marcellus closed the door.

His thoughts then shifted to Catrin. He reflected on why she'd decided to come to Rome, particularly after she had vowed to return immediately to Britannia and overthrow Marrock. With her divine power to alter the future, was she weaving his life thread to join hers on the Wall of Lives?

Deep in thought, he strode down the vestibule and entered the atrium, where he found his mother lighting a candle at the family lararium. She turned to him and asked, "Will you be speaking with Consul Frugi today about your new assignment?"

"No. We had planned to meet tomorrow to clarify my duties," Marcellus reminded his mother.

Drusilla's eyebrows arched. "You remember our dinner with his family tonight, don't you? You can speak with him there."

Marcellus's heart tightened like a fist in his chest. The banquet had completely slipped his mind. "I haven't forgotten, but I must inspect some chariot horses Falco just acquired."

"Be sure you take a bath before the dinner. I don't want you smelling like horse—"

"I'm not a street urchin," Marcellus snapped, but he bit his tongue when he noted the hurt on his mother's face. To make amends, he quickly kissed her forehead and apologized. "I'm sorry, Mother. I shouldn't have spoken to you in that manner."

Drusilla gave a thin smile. "I only want what is best for you. You know how important tonight is. Everything needs to be perfect. It's so rare a political marriage works out, but Scribonia has revealed her daughter is smitten with you. Do you feel the same way about Licinia?"

Marcellus nervously smoothed his hair, realizing that noon was an inopportune time to meet with Catrin. Perhaps if he left immediately, he could find her at the inn, which would give him time to bathe and dress before dinner.

His mother's voice saying, "Did you hear what I said?" drew Marcellus out of his rumination.

"Yes, I heard."

Drusilla pressed for an answer. "How do you feel about Licinia?"

Marcellus shrugged. "What do you want me to say? I hardly know her. She is still . . . just a child."

"New brides must be young to assure their virtue," Drusilla declared sharply.

His mother's blunt remark took Marcellus by surprise. Though his memory of meeting Catrin in Britannia had been erased by a dark druidess, he wondered if she had been as innocent and naïve as Licinia. Catrin was now eighteen years old and worldly beyond her years. She was the same age as Octavian, the previous emperor, when he'd first challenged Marcus Antonius.

"Licinia is only twelve years old," Marcellus finally responded. "I must handle her as gently as a skittish filly."

"Is that how you think of Licinia? A young filly you can ride?" Drusilla asked, sharp disdain in her voice.

Marcellus clasped his mother's shoulders. "Mother, that is not what I meant. I only want what is best for our family."

"If that is so, be on time tonight and in suitable attire. And make good use of your time with Consul Frugi," Drusilla emphasized with a flourish of her hand.

"I will," Marcellus said, not wanting to argue with her. "If you would excuse me, I need to start my day."

Drusilla waved him off and knelt before the family altar to pray.

Marcellus hurried through the atrium, thinking of ways he could juggle all of his commitments. He stepped onto the gravel pathway of the peristyle that led to his bedchamber. Inside the room, he dressed in a simple gray tunic and latched a sheathed dagger to his belt. He wore his commoner's cloak to disguise himself and covered his head with the cowl.

After entering the Red Chariot Inn at midmorning, Marcellus perused the patrons. Several of the men standing at the bar cast him a glance. It unsettled him that Catrin was lodging on the second floor above a den of gamblers, drunkards, and harlots. His first impulse was to search for her upstairs, but he was wary of a wild-haired man swaggering into the tavern. If the man was one of Brutius's spies, he didn't want to risk being discovered with Catrin.

Marcellus seated himself at a small side table with a clear view of the tavern. A young woman he presumed to be a harlot by the spillage of her breasts in a low-cut dress approached him and flashed a grin. He waved her away but then was distracted by a group of young men forcing their way through the packed room to the back wall. There, a plump man was sitting at a table and taking bets on the chariot races. The green team was favored to win the final race that day.

A man's gruff voice saying, "Tribune Antonius," startled Marcellus. Looking sideways, he found a bearded, disheveled man wearing a faded red tunic and the cape of a legionary. He gave the stranger a quizzical look.

"Don't you remember me? Gaius Septimus. I served with you in Gaul."

Repulsed by the man's rank odor, Marcellus scrunched his nose. He vaguely recalled that Gaius had been a foot soldier under his command. "Yes, I remember you. What are you doing in Rome?"

"I recently retired from the legion and am down on my luck," Gaius answered with a grimace.

Marcellus nervously glanced around the room for Catrin, apprehensive that Gaius might recognize her. Assured she was not in the tavern, he pulled a silver coin from his belted money purse and slid it across the tabletop toward Gaius.

"For your service."

"*Gratia*. But I was looking for something long-term . . . like your patronage," Gaius said bluntly. "I can help settle differences with any of your rivals, if you understand my meaning."

Marcellus noted the desperation in the soldier's downcast gray eyes. As a commander, he had vowed loyalty to his men in exchange for their obedience.

"This is not the best place to discuss such matters," Marcellus finally replied. "Take the coin and enjoy yourself at the chariot races. Find me tomorrow at the forum, where the government offices are situated. We can discuss possible terms for my patronage then."

Picking up the coin, Gaius gave a thin smile. "Tomorrow, then."

Marcellus nodded, suddenly finding it odd he would have a chance encounter with one of his foot soldiers from Gaul. He warily watched Gaius get in line to place a bet at the back table.

A sudden nudge of a hand on his back made Marcellus jump. Glancing back, he beheld a one-eyed man with wild, auburn hair flung over an eyelid that appeared to melt into his cheekbone. Marcellus recoiled at the tattooed bolts of lightning flashing down the man's muscular chest.

"My name is Cynwrig. Follow me," the one-eyed man grunted, opening the palm of his hand to reveal the Apollo amulet Marcellus had given Catrin.

Taken unawares, Marcellus stared at the amulet for a moment, his mind scrambling to remember if he had previously met this warrior in

Gaul. Finally, he recalled Falco mentioning that Catrin had a disfigured Briton accompanying her.

"Are you with Catrin?" Marcellus asked, taking the amulet from the scar-faced man.

"Yes. Catrin," Cynwrig said with a thick, Celtic accent.

Marcellus followed Cynwrig through some boisterous patrons to the back of the room, where there was a rickety staircase. The steps creaked as Marcellus climbed the splintered wooden stairs behind Cynwrig. On the second floor, they passed six closed doors to sleeping quarters and halted at the seventh one.

Cynwrig knocked three times and said something in the Celtic tongue. He then inserted a key into the lock until it clicked, opening the door for Marcellus to enter.

Inside the room, Marcellus found Catrin gazing out an open window; the sunlight filtered onto her face. A breath caught in his throat as Marcellus beheld her. She appeared lost in a dream. A single braid of gold-blonde hair hung over her shoulder. She was simply dressed in a loose-fitting, gray tunica that hid her curvature. When Cynwrig closed the door, she turned toward Marcellus, and her eyes brightened.

With emotions rising in his chest like a tidal wave, Marcellus could hardly say the words to greet her. "*Salve*, Catrin."

Catrin bit her lower lip and inhaled sharply. "*Salve*, Marcellus."

Marcellus studied her eyes for any glint of hatred. In the candlelit room, he couldn't discern whether she still harbored resentment toward him. He swallowed the lump forming in his throat, searching for the right words to tell her how much he had missed her. Instead, he decided to move more slowly before expressing his feelings.

"How was your journey?" he inquired.

"It was a difficult journey, but my guard"—Catrin gestured toward Cynwrig—"protected me."

Marcellus shifted his gaze to the one-eyed warrior. "Do you want to introduce him to me?"

"Of course. This is Cynwrig, a warrior who was in my father's inner circle."

Marcellus nodded. "*Gratia* for escorting Catrin to Rome."

With his one eye fixed on Marcellus, Cynwrig grunted something in Celtic. The jagged scar below the warrior's missing eye sent a shudder down Marcellus's spine.

"He prefers not to speak the Roman tongue but understands what you say well enough," Catrin interjected.

"Have we met before?" Marcellus asked Cynwrig directly, sensing some deep-rooted resentment.

Cynwrig nodded. "Axe."

"You competed with him in a battle-axe contest at one of our festivals," Catrin clarified.

Marcellus jerked his head back. "I did?"

Catrin gave a slight chuckle. "Yes, you were drunk."

Becoming uneasy with the one-eyed warrior's piercing stare, Marcellus looked at Catrin. "Could we speak privately?"

Catrin nodded and motioned for Cynwrig to leave, saying something in Celtic. He seemed reluctant to go, fingering the hilt of a sheathed dagger at this side. The tone of her voice sharpened as they continued speaking in Celtic. The one-eyed warrior finally stepped back with a slight bow and turned to depart. After Cynwrig clicked the door shut, Marcellus could hear the warrior's heavy footsteps pacing back and forth in the corridor.

"Cynwrig will stay outside to guard as we speak," Catrin informed him.

Marcellus creased his brow. "He looked as though he wanted to disembowel me with his weapon."

"Romans killed his wife," Catrin explained.

Marcellus suddenly felt awkward, not sure what to say. He nervously raked his hair as she slowly walked over to him. Her brilliant turquoise eyes searched his. At that moment, he felt the weight lift off his chest, replaced with the hope they could salvage their relationship.

"Have your wounds healed?" he asked, softly touching her hand. She lowered her gaze toward his hand but didn't pull away from his touch.

"They have healed, but I feel lost . . . empty."

"Do you still blame me for what happened?" Marcellus asked tentatively.

Catrin took a deep breath. "No. But it's hard to forget all I've suffered."

Marcellus's heart ached from the possibility he could lose her a second time. "Catrin, I regret what happened to you. I live with constant guilt that I should have done more to protect you."

Tears welled in Catrin's eyes as she brought Marcellus's hand to her breast. "No matter how hard I try to hate you, forsake you . . . I can't. You are my husband, and you will always be a part of me. But how can I still be a part of your life if you marry that Roman girl?"

Marcellus hesitated. "I don't know . . . if I can marry her."

Catrin lifted her eyes to meet his. "Has something changed?"

"You are here now," Marcellus said softly, like a whisper in a breeze. "I never thought I would see you again . . . that you could love me again."

"I've always loved you," Catrin assured him. "Every day, I thought about how safe I felt when you slept with me before you left for Rome." Catrin wrapped her arms around his neck. "You freed me. And for that, I am grateful. Yet, I ask myself how could I return to Rome with you if you cannot recognize me as your wife? I would have proclaimed you as my king if you'd only returned with me to my homeland."

Overwhelmed with emotion, Marcellus could hardly breathe. "When I was banished for my affair with Eliana, I believed I had lost my family's trust and heritage. But then, I received accolades for crushing a rebellion in Gaul. My father summoned me back to Rome with the promise I would rise like Apollo in the political climate."

Marcellus's throat tightened, and his voice cracked. "I had everything I could possibly want. My parents embraced me as their favorite son. My future father-in-law offered to elevate my political standing in exchange for marrying his daughter. Even so, I felt empty, lost without you. Every day, I wanted to dissolve into the Wall of Lives you described and relive that moment at the waterfall, when we made love and were happiest."

"I have always loved you," Catrin proclaimed again. "But Rome stands against us. How can we ever get past this?"

"I've struggled with this, trying to think of a way we can be together," Marcellus admitted. "You must understand, my family will never recognize our marriage. If I refuse to marry Licinia, I'm not sure what my father might do. He's vindictive and . . ." Marcellus swallowed as he wondered whether his father could be so heartless as to have them both killed.

"I won't ask you to forsake your family for me," Catrin said, tears spilling down her cheeks. "I don't want you to suffer like I have after the loss of my parents, sister, and stillborn daughter. More than anything, I want to stay with you. But is this possible?"

Marcellus pulled Catrin into his arms. "If Rome won't recognize our marriage, I will stand by you as an ally. I will help you overthrow Marrock. But to move forward, you must tell me what happened that made you change your mind about coming to Rome—in the dead of winter, no less."

Catrin sighed heavily. "My father's second-in-command, Trystan, found me at Lugdunum and declared his fealty to me as his queen. He's building an army with other Cantiaci warriors who survived the conflict with Marrock and the Romans. Do you remember when I told you about how distraught I was when my father negotiated for me to marry Adminius—a prince from the Catuvellauni tribe?"

Marcellus gave her a perplexed look. "I recall this. But why would this change your mind?"

"Adminius was with Trystan in Lugdunum. He pledged to join his forces with ours," Catrin explained. "Later, Adminius told me the price I had to pay for his alliance—marry him and declare him as my king."

Marcellus felt a sharp pang of jealousy rear in his chest. "Did you refuse?"

"I could not refuse," Catrin said, dropping her eyes.

"Why is that?" Marcellus asked, more sharply than he intended.

"Adminius holds my sister, Mor, as hostage," Catrin revealed. "She survived the final battle with the Romans but was captured by the Catuvellauni and forced to marry Adminius. Trystan reinforced to Adminius that I was the rightful queen. Further, a druidess has spread the prophecy that only I can overcome Marrock. Nonetheless, Adminius threatened to harm my sister if I didn't agree to marry him. I realized then that I could not forsake you. That is why I'm here. I don't want to marry that dark prince."

"And I won't let that happen!" Marcellus declared.

Catrin met his eyes. "Then you will help me find a way to rescue Mor and usurp Marrock?"

Marcellus embraced Catrin tightly. "Of course, I will. After all we've been through, I want to rekindle the love and trust we had in each other. You need to understand, though, we are playing a dangerous political game. My father will consider it an affront if I declare we are married and are working together to overthrow Marrock. This is counter to his political ambition to lead the invasion into Britannia with Marrock's aid. He could have us both killed!"

The obstacles they faced whirled in Marcellus's mind as he spoke his thoughts out loud. "The political climate has changed in Rome. Tiberius is unpredictable. His prefect, Sejanus, has taken control of all the emperor's administrative duties in Rome. If I am to appeal your claim to the Cantiaci throne, I'll need to arrange a private meeting with Tiberius through Sejanus. Even at that, I still need the senate's final approval to appoint me as commander of northern Gaul and to transport troops to Britannia."

"This is all possible," Catrin said, her voice rising in hope. "I saw in a vision that our life threads are weaving together once again on the Wall of Lives and that we are destined to be together."

"I have no doubt of that," Marcellus said, though doubts did gnaw at the back of his mind regarding whether he could sway Sejanus to arrange a private meeting with Tiberius. "Let me speak with my great aunt, Matron Antonia. She can influence Tiberius. But I cannot make any promises."

"I trust whatever you do," Catrin said as she softly stroked his face.

"I'll lease a nicer apartment where you can stay safely. That way, we can be alone together." Marcellus held Catrin tighter, the words spilling from his mouth. "I missed you so much."

"I missed you, too," Catrin whispered, tightening her arms around Marcellus's neck to pull herself to his lips. When he hungrily pressed his mouth to hers, their pent-up desires released. She pressed her hip into his hardening groin as he kissed her, taking her breath away. With his lips still locked on hers, he laid her down on the straw bed. He pushed her arms flat, overpowering her with his desire. The sweet taste of her skin as he gently bit the side of her neck made him hunger for more. Her womanly scent intoxicated him, holding the promise that he would relive the bliss of the moment when they'd made love in the cave behind the waterfall. The moment he was happiest. The moment his emotions soared with the roar of the water cascading from the cliffs overhead. The moment that was etched into his memory forever.

Then, suddenly, a loud bang against the door shook Marcellus out of the ecstatic moment. Men's voices from the corridor made the hairs on the back of his neck stand up. He abruptly lifted himself off Catrin and reached for his dagger. He froze, eyes at the door, as the banging of a scuffle in the corridor rumbled outside the door.

I3

UNWELCOME DINNER GUESTS

Rome, 16 March, 28 AD

Marcellus scrambled to the door and pressed his ear against it. For a moment, he could only hear his rapid heartbeats.

Catrin, with a *gladius* in hand, leaned against him and whispered, "Check on Cynwrig."

Marcellus unlatched the door and cracked it open. But then, the door was abruptly thrust wide, and Cynwrig rushed in, latching the door behind him. He spoke animatedly to Catrin in Celtic, frustrating Marcellus.

"What happened out there?" he asked Cynwrig.

"He confronted a man at the top of the steps," Catrin translated. "A fight broke out between them. The man fell down the stairs and escaped."

Marcellus looked at Cynwrig. "Did you recognize him?"

Catrin interpreted as Cynwrig answered in Celtic. "He wore the faded red cloak of a Roman soldier."

"Was he built like a gladiator?" Marcellus asked, wondering if Brutius's slave bodyguard, Adonis, had been tasked to spy on him.

"The man was dirty and smelled like shit," Catrin answered.

The description did not match any of the henchmen associated with Brutius. The image of the foot soldier, Gaius, flashed into Marcellus's mind, but it could have been anyone in the tavern. Realizing he had recklessly risked Catrin's life by meeting her here, guilt struck him like a hammer.

"Until I find out who the man is, you'll need to stay elsewhere," Marcellus warned.

"Where?"

"Look for other inns near the Circus Maximus," he suggested. "I'll go first, then you and Cynwrig leave. Don't say anything to the innkeeper."

"Once we find a place to stay, how can I contact you?" asked Catrin.

"Get in contact with Falco at the stables. Ask him to relay a message to me about where you are staying." Marcellus embraced Catrin and whispered, "Goodbye, my love."

He reluctantly released Catrin and cracked the door open. Seeing no one in the corridor, he covertly padded down the stairs to the back of the tavern. Pulling the cowl of his cape over his head, he scanned the room. Most of the patrons had left, most likely cheering for their favorite chariot team.

He stepped outside the Red Chariot and blended in with a swarm of multinational shoppers buying an assortment of goods and wares at the wooden storefronts. Frequently glancing around, he looked for anyone suspicious tailing him. He saw no one. His head raced with ideas about where Catrin could stay. Leasing a high-end flat or domus would require a loan, and that would likely draw unwanted attention, unless he could trust the lender to keep this secret. He recalled the magistrate who had loaned him money with steep interest a few years back.

Marcellus veered toward the Basilica Julia, where he had previously met the magistrate. At the bottom of the white marble steps to the multi-arched basilica, he halted when he saw Brutius conversing with Praetorian Prefect Sejanus. Marcellus noted that Brutius's head was perked up like a dog, as if waiting for permission to lap up scraps from his master's table.

After a few moments, Brutius and Sejanus departed; Sejanus went to the basilica, and Brutius walked in the opposite direction.

Marcellus waited briefly, then furtively scrambled up the stairs and dashed through an archway into a courtyard. He merged with other patrons headed toward makeshift offices that had been partitioned with wooden walls. When he caught sight of Sejanus waving him over to his office, he felt his rapid heartbeats pound in his chest.

What could the prefect want with me?

Apprehensive of what might have transpired between Brutius and

Sejanus, Marcellus slightly bowed his head and greeted, "*Salve*, Prefect Sejanus. What an auspicious day to see you here."

Sejanus gave a thin smile. "Greetings. What brings you to the basilica?"

Marcellus hesitated, wary of what the praetorian prefect may tell Brutius. "I'm here to speak with Senator Frugi."

Sejanus's gaze scoured over Marcellus's tunic and cloak, as if questioning why he was dressed like a commoner. Unsettled by the prefect's probing eyes, Marcellus blurted, "Forgive my appearance. I just came from the stables."

"Your green chariot team had a poor showing today," Sejanus said brusquely. "I lost good money betting on them."

Marcellus grimaced, unsure where their conversation was heading. "Our family just bought fresh horses from Gaul to replace them. That is why I was there, to inspect the horses."

"I have a good eye for horses. I'd like to see them when I have some free time," Sejanus said in a more cordial tone.

Feeling more relaxed, Marcellus readily agreed. "Of course. I'd be honored to hear your opinion. I heard you were quite a horseman under the command of Tiberius in Germania."

"He valued my advice as his commander of the cavalry. He still values my advice," Sejanus said with an air of arrogance.

"I'm aware of your influence with the princeps." Marcellus smiled nervously, wondering if Sejanus read all the messages given to Tiberius. "Perchance, did you see the letter of recommendation from Legatus Decimus Flavius that I be given command of the legion in northern Gaul?"

Sejanus raised an eyebrow.

"It was sent directly to Tiberius," Marcellus added. "I thought you might have seen it."

"You seem too young for such a position," Sejanus said bluntly.

"I'm nearly twenty-four years old and have military experience as a tribune in Gaul," Marcellus said, noting the skepticism in the prefect's expression.

"Tiberius never said anything about the message from Decimus,"

Sejanus said with a dismissive wave of his hand. "Your brother, Brutius, invited me to dinner hosted by your father and Marcus Frugi tonight."

Marcellus winced. No one had told him Sejanus would be joining them for dinner. There would undoubtedly be tension between Sejanus, Matron Antonia, and Tiberius's mother, Julia Augustus. It was no secret that the two women despised the conniving weasel.

Sejanus regarded Marcellus, then gave him a sly smile. "Licinia has blossomed into quite a young woman."

"She's much too young to marry me," Marcellus blurted. "I would prefer to serve Rome in northern Gaul before we marry. I'd still like to speak with Tiberius about this."

"Tiberius can't be bothered with such trivial requests." Sejanus frowned. "Besides, you should speak directly to your father and future father-in-law about such matters. Brutius told me they have special plans to advance your political career in Rome."

Marcellus jerked his head back. "When did he tell you this?"

Sejanus hesitated. "Just today. That is why I was invited to dinner."

"Is there something I should know?" Marcellus asked, looking wide-eyed at Sejanus.

"Don't tell anyone I've let the horses out of the stables, but there is to be an announcement at dinner. You'll be pleased to know that Senator Frugi will offer you an important position in Rome," Sejanus disclosed.

Taken aback, Marcellus felt his stomach drop. All his hope of going to Gaul was fizzling away. Struggling for composure, he straightened his shoulders as his thoughts turned to Catrin and his need to protect her. "If you would excuse me, I have an appointment with Senator Frugi now."

"Then I'll speak with you at dinner," Sejanus said with a disingenuous smile.

Marcellus slightly nodded. "Dinner tonight. *Avento*."

Sejanus turned and stepped into his office.

Glancing all around, Marcellus made sure no one was watching him. He then rushed past several administrative offices to the end of the courtyard. Breathing hard, he scanned the various tables where Magistrate Titus

Asinius might be situated. He spotted the rotund magistrate counting gold coins on a table. Distinctive gray sideburns stretched down his face to his fleshy jowls. A few strands of hair covered a bald spot on top of his head. Standing beside Asinius was a broad-shouldered man built like a gladiator, whom Marcellus surmised to be the magistrate's bodyguard.

Marcellus cleared his throat to get Asinius's attention. The magistrate looked up and licked his thick lower lip with a lizard-like tongue. "*Salve.* What can I do for you?"

"Do you remember me?" Marcellus asked, not seeing any recognition on the lender's face. "I am Marcellus Antonius."

Asinius jerked his head back and regarded Marcellus. "I believe so. As I recall, you had a thorny issue with a woman. What happened to her?"

"It ended badly," Marcellus grumbled. "Is there somewhere we can talk privately?"

"I can't afford to rent an enclosed office," Asinius grumbled.

Marcellus leaned over and said in a hushed tone, "I need to a rent a flat at one of your insula complexes, but I need utmost secrecy."

Asinius arched an eyebrow. "Your father keeps that tight of a purse string?"

"You could say that. I need a place to stay within the next two days."

"Fortuna favors you." Asinius's tongue flicked out again, like a lizard eagerly grasping for a fly. "I have a nice domus close to a block of insula complexes I own. Do you know the jewelry shopkeeper, Vibius Gallius, on the Capitoline?"

"I do."

"Good. Meet me in two days just before the shop closes. I'll show you the domus."

"I'll be there."

Asinius bowed his head. "*Vale, mi amice.*"

"*Vale,*" Marcellus replied. Then, he rushed out of the basilica to return home.

After Marcellus quickly dressed in a tunic and toga in his bedchamber, he strode through the peristyle garden into the atrium to greet the dinner guests. His parents and Brutius were already there, along with Consul Frugi and his wife, Scribonia. They all turned to Marcellus with surreptitious smiles, as if they were keeping "the horses in the stables," as Sejanus had aptly stated that afternoon. Marcellus felt queasy about what they planned to announce at dinner. Had his father and the consul conjured a scheme to prevent him from returning to the legion in Gaul?

He was startled out of his thoughts when his mother trilled, "Come over here. Let us see our husband-to-be."

"Shh," the others shushed Drusilla, who clasped her mouth with both hands as her face blossomed to a bright red. Consul Frugi waved Marcellus forward.

Joining the group, Marcellus glanced all around the atrium, noting Licinia was not with them. "Where is my betrothed?"

Drusilla blurted, "She will make a grand entrance once all of the guests have arrived."

"And who have we invited?" Marcellus asked, thinking back to his conversation with Sejanus.

"Julia Augustus and Matron Antonia are both coming," Drusilla said gleefully, clapping her hands. "A few other senators and their wives are also coming."

"I invited Sejanus and his escort, Livilla, who is Matron Antonia's daughter" Brutius added with a wicked grin.

The consul snapped his head toward Brutius. "And when did you do that?"

"This afternoon at the forum. He told me he is bringing Livilla," Brutius said in a smug tone. "I thought you would be pleased that he accepted my invitation."

Consul Frugi's face contorted into an anguished grimace. "Julia Augustus detests Sejanus and believes he is beneath us. There is bad blood between Antonia and her daughter. Antonia resents Sejanus for asking Tiberius's permission to marry Livilla."

Marcellus could tell by Brutius's sneer that he had schemed to put everyone in an uncomfortable situation. He shot a burning glare at Brutius.

What a spineless snake you are!

Lucius Antonius stole a glance at Brutius and offered Drusilla his arm. "What is done is done. We can make this work. We'll keep them separated. Marcellus can entertain Antonia, while Brutius will converse with Sejanus and Livilla. Drusilla and Scribonia can speak with Julia Augustus."

Luckily, Matron Antonia was one of the first guests to arrive. A gold palla covered her gray-streaked, plaited hair and draped over her shoulders onto a red-hemmed, white tunic. The heavy lilac perfume overwhelmed Marcellus's nose as she extended her hand for him to kiss.

"*Bonum vesperam.* How lovely you look tonight," Marcellus complimented.

"How you flatter," Antonia said with a coquettish smile. "I was hoping to see you in uniform. Nothing makes an old woman's heart race like seeing a virile man strapped in armor."

Aflush with embarrassment, Marcellus felt warm sweat dampen his face.

"Good color in your cheeks," Antonia remarked, a twinkle in her gray-blue eyes. "Where is my darling Licinia?"

"She will delight us with a surprise before dinner," Marcellus said with a grin. "Please take my arm, and I will show you around."

Luckily, Sejanus and Livilla arrived late, after Senator Frugi had introduced his daughter, Licinia. The guests smiled their approval as Licinia entertained them by strumming melodies on the lyre. The music elicited images in Marcellus's mind of Catrin shape-shifting from a white raven into her womanly form.

After Licinia finished playing, she joined Marcellus and Antonia, the latter of whom hugged her and trilled, "How beautiful! Both Marcellus and you made me think of my younger days with my husband, Druses, and the happy times we had together. It was much too short."

Marcellus felt awkward, noting Licinia's curvaceous body. "Indeed, you played like a muse."

The deep voice of Senator Frugi drew everyone's attention. "We are here to honor Marcellus Antonius tonight for his accolades as a tribune in northern Gaul. Even though he is still only twenty-four years of age, I am pleased to announce the senate has granted an exception and appointed him as quaestor to supervise the public games. The assignment will be the next step in his *cursus honorum*."

Though Marcellus had anticipated that announcement, nothing prepared him for Senator Frugi's next pronouncement.

"As Marcellus is in the position to marry, and Licinia has flowered into womanhood, both Lucius and I agree they should marry early in the summer."

The claps and chatter droned in Marcellus's ears. It felt as if the walls were whirling around him and the floor sweeping from beneath his feet. Over and over, he told himself, *This can't be happening. This can't be happening.*

The guilt that he could not aid Catrin bubbled to the surface. He couldn't fail her again; he had sworn. Then, he saw Licinia's fearful eyes. She also didn't want to marry—not yet.

Do something!

"Licinia is too young," Marcellus protested. "She is but twelve years old!"

"She turned thirteen last week and is ready to do her duty as a wife and bear children," Senator Frugi replied firmly.

Marcellus stubbornly held his ground. "I've not served long enough in the military. Let me go back to Gaul to serve Rome. There will be time to marry afterward."

As Marcellus looked around the room, all the guests' eyes were fixed on him, and their mouths were agape. His father's deadly glower seemed to shout at him, *You are an imbecile!*

Antonia's voice rose above the chatter in the chamber. "I agree with Marcellus. Licinia is too young. I was eighteen years old when I married Druses. I bore him three living children while he nobly served as a general and died for Augustus. What harm is there granting Marcellus's desire to serve in the legion? Allow Licinia to enjoy her youth."

Livilla raged, "You have no right to interfere, Mother! These are decisions made by fathers."

"You have yet to obey me as your mother!" Antonia retorted, whipping the bottom edge of the palla over her shoulder.

Sejanus gripped Livilla by the arm and pulled her into the peristyle. Senator Frugi waved his hands downward, trying to calm the dinner guests, while Marcellus's father pushed through the rattled spectators to escort Antonia and Marcellus toward the back of the atrium, where Drusilla waited to speak with the matron.

Marcellus fought back the urge to yank away from his father's grip as they entered the tablinum with the spectacle of Roman soldiers slaughtering Celtic warriors in battle painted on the walls. Marcellus felt his father's hot breaths on his face as he pushed him against the wall.

Only hard discipline from military training quelled Marcellus's impulse to strike out as his father grated, "I am the paterfamilias. You obey me, boy. Or you will meet a fate far worse than death. When we go back to our guests, I don't want another word out of you."

Marcellus hesitantly nodded. His father's grip loosened, and they returned to the atrium. The guests appeared calmer as they feasted on eel, oysters, figs, bread, and olives. With Antonia, Sejanus, and Livilla gone from the gathering, the dinner conversation focused on the weather and the upcoming games.

Brutius ventured a glance at Marcellus, and his lips twisted up into a sneer.

Marcellus broiled with anger, but he remained coolly silent as his thoughts drifted back and forth between Catrin and Antonia. Until that moment, he hadn't considered that Antonia could be a potential ally who could open the door for him to speak with Tiberius about his aspirations to return to Gaul.

14

TIBERIUS'S MINNOWS

Brutius Antonius Villa, Rome, 17 March, 28 AD

Brutius carefully inspected the young male slaves in the privacy of his countryside villa outside Rome. Most of them appeared to be younger than ten years old. The cherubic boys had features similar to those of Marcellus when he'd been a boy. Dark, curly hair. Glacial-blue eyes. Full, fleshy lips. Exhibiting no blemishes, they would satiate the aging emperor's perverse desires. All powerful noblemen, Brutius conceded, sought such pleasures in secret hideaways. That was their right. No one questioned it. Yet, he had never anticipated winning favors from "the gloomiest man in Rome" by selecting young males who excited the emperor's flagging passions.

Tiberius, the grim harvester of innocents!

Brutius chuckled, then closely inspected the tone of the boys' bodies. They had to be athletic to become good swimmers. Tiberius went to great lengths to train his "minnows" to crawl between his legs while he was submerged in water. The minnows tantalized the "old goat" with their licks and nibbles.

The boys reminded Brutius of the first boy he'd wrestled to the ground and forced to succumb to his desires. The image of the naked, nine-year-old slave, Hector, struggling to get away brought a smile to his face. A reflection of Marcellus, Hector had to do whatever Brutius wanted. After all, he was the master; Hector was his slave. After Hector threatened to tattle about their encounters, Brutius snuffed out the boy's life with a knife at the climactic moment. That was more thrilling than squeezing a newborn pup's muzzle to make it yelp before snapping its neck.

"Have them undress," Brutius ordered, his heart hammering against his chest with the excitement of inspecting them closer.

The foul-smelling slave dealer, Rufus, slicked back his oily hair, which was like black snakeskin on his head. His eyes turned to slits as he commanded, "You heard the dominus. Take off your clothes!"

Bright shades of red blossomed on the boys' faces as they took off their tunics and loincloths. Brutius noted a couple of the boys showed hints of pubic hair. In particular, one slave looked like Marcellus at a younger age.

"I'll keep this slave for myself," Brutius ordered, lifting the boy's square chin. "Such blue eyes. Where are you from?"

The wide-eyed boy didn't answer.

"Do you speak the Roman tongue?" Brutius growled, squeezing the boy's jaw between his fingertips.

"Northern Gaul," Rufus interjected. "He cannot speak our language, but his tongue offers other delights. He is a mongrel pup born to a Gallic prostitute who pleasured Roman soldiers."

"Is that so? All the better," Brutius said with a sneer, imagining all the rough acts he could do to the comely boy. "Was he born near the Roman fort where Marcellus was stationed in northern Gaul?"

"Gesoricum, yes," Rufus answered. "I've heard of your brother's accolades for crushing a rebellion in Gaul."

"Is that so?" Brutius hissed. "He is my half brother. And those accolades are exaggerated!"

Rufus dropped his eyes and softened his voice. "As you say. Do you still want information about Marcellus?"

"Of course. That is part of our bargain, is it not?" Brutius gritted his teeth, jealous that his scandalous half brother had gained their father's favor.

"I only met Marcellus once," Rufus began. "He sought me out at my slave quarters near the Roman fort. He inquired about a female gladiator I had sold."

Brutius's eyebrows perked up. "A woman warrior?"

"As I recall, she was a fair-haired Briton—a fierce warrior captured in battle. A lanista by the name of Verus watched her fight an Ethiopian in an exhibition." Rufus scratched his head and looked at the white specks that came away on his fingertips. "He was called the Black Sphinx, as I recall, and easily defeated her. Verus purchased them both."

"Where does Verus train his gladiators?"

"Lugdunum, Gaul. At an arena recently built there," Rufus said, clawing at red sores on his neck.

"Near our family villa," Brutius muttered, noting the white flecks falling off his scalp—a sign of lice.

"Does that tidbit not at least deserve a gold coin?" Rufus finally asked, breaking Brutius's thoughts.

"It depends on what else you have to offer," Brutius said with a sly grin.

"I also offer young females for the old satyr's garden of Pans and nymphs," Rufus remarked, stifling a chuckle.

Brutius nodded. "Show me."

The slave dealer escorted an assortment of scantily clad girls from a side chamber to join the boys. Though Brutius was seldom aroused by these inferior creatures, he took an interest in a silver-blonde girl on the cusp of womanhood. Rufus unclasped her tunic, letting the woolen fabric fall below her budding breasts. Brutius pinched one of her puffed nipples. The grimace on the girl's pale, white face made him grin with delight.

"What country is she from?" Brutius inquired, relishing the sensation of her trembling from his rough touch.

"A Briton fresh off the boat," Rufus remarked with a broad grin, displaying an assortment of missing teeth.

Brutius groped between the girl's inner thighs, noting the dealer's eyebrows scrunching together with obvious disapproval. "Do I bother you?"

"I'd like to keep these slaves unblemished before the sale," Rufus said sharply.

Brutius pulled his hand away and smelled it. "I'm the one with the coin here."

Rufus frowned.

"Besides," Brutius continued, "Tiberius will do far worse to this slave. He takes his sadistic pleasure from fair-skinned wenches."

"Understood," Rufus muttered, scratching the top of his head.

"I'll take them all," Brutius finally agreed. "As we previously agreed, I will pay double what Governor Decimus Flavius offered. This should make up for the money he owes you for slaves. Of course, you must not say a word to Decimus or my father about my slave business."

"I would like payment now," Rufus demanded.

"Indeed. My Greek attendant, Adonis, can settle—"

A loud knock on the entry door diverted Brutius's attention. Pounding footsteps resonated through the vestibule, and the herculean Adonis—a former gladiator—appeared with a disheveled soldier.

"Dominus, this is legionary Gaius Septimus," Adonis announced.

"*Salve*, Gaius," Brutius greeted. "Please join me in the tablinum, where we can speak privately." He then turned to Adonis and arched an eyebrow. "You can make the final payment Rufus deserves."

Adonis cast a glance at Rufus and gave an insidious smile. "With pleasure. Follow me to the back of the peristyle."

Brutius escorted the disheveled soldier into the tablinum, where the scrolls and tablets with records of Roman patricians crippled with gambling debts were stored. The windowless chamber was starkly furnished with a small table with just enough space to seat two people. The gray walls were notably barren of murals and friezes. Only a single lamp, casting a shadow on the wall, lit the room.

Brutius poured some posca—vinegary wine diluted with water—into a brass cup and offered it to Gaius. The body odor and fecal smell of the unwashed soldier overwhelmed Brutius. Scrunching his nose, he scooted his chair away from the table and sat down across from Gaius. Brutius regarded the soldier's straggly dark hair and brown-smeared hands as Gaius gulped the liquid down.

"Did you speak with Marcellus?" Brutius finally inquired.

Gaius snapped his fingers and stretched out the palm of his hand.

Brutius scowled, wondering if he could trust the greedy soldier. Perhaps

Adonis should dispose of Gaius alongside Rufus in the Tiber River. On further thought, he decided to interrogate Gaius before deciding what to do with the fecal-smelling soldier. He retrieved a small metal box from a shelf behind him, opened the lid to retrieve a silver coin, and dropped it in the soldier's hand.

"As we agreed," he said. "There is more if I find your information of value."

Gaius lifted the coin to the lamplight to inspect it as he spoke. "Yesterday at midday, I tailed Marcellus to an inn called the Red Chariot. I found it odd that he was dressed like a pleb."

"Did you get a chance to speak with him about his patronage?" Brutius asked.

"I did." Gaius paused and poured more posca from the flask into his cup. "I introduced myself and told him I was down on my luck."

"He agreed, then?"

"Yes. I am to discuss terms for his patronage in his office in the forum later today." Gaius's brow creased. "Forgive me for saying so, but I don't feel right about deceiving him."

Brutius raised an eyebrow, again questioning whether he could trust the soldier who had once served under Marcellus. "Is that so? Tell me, was he a commander you respected?"

"I didn't think much of him. He struggled to keep up with the seasoned soldiers during marches and in drills. That all changed, though, after he was caught messing around with Decimus's slave."

Brutius's ears perked up. "Tell me more."

"I wasn't there when Decimus found them," Gaius said, keeping his eyes fixed on Brutius as he took a sip of posca. "But I was told by other soldiers that they saw Marcellus fucking the commander's slave by a waterfall. They had believed the slave to be a boy, but he was missing a cock."

"A gelded slave, then?" Brutius asked, his curiosity piqued that his half brother might taste from other sexual palettes.

"The slave had teats—a woman," Gaius disclosed.

"I thought women were not allowed in camps. Bad luck," Brutius commented.

"Decimus told the soldiers Vibius was his boy slave. Soldiers don't question their commanders. They ignore what they do with their slaves. But I have more to tell." Gaius stretched out his hand again.

Brutius waved a gold coin before the ex-soldier's eyes. "You will get this if I find the information useful."

Gaius smiled and leaned back in his chair. "Some of the soldiers in Gaul were with Decimus when he accompanied your father and Marcellus to Britannia to negotiate more tribute from a British king called Amren. Marcellus was taken as a hostage to assure the safety of the king during tense negotiations."

"Is that so?" Brutius asked, mulling over in his mind why his father had never disclosed this.

"The soldiers said Marcellus attacked a centurion to save Amren's daughter during a hostage exchange when fighting broke out."

"What would make Marcellus do that, I wonder?"

"A good question. One I also asked."

Brutius leaned back in his chair. "And what did you discover?"

"Marcellus was bewitched by Amren's daughter—a beauty who could spin black magic."

"A sorceress!" Brutius chuckled. "Marcellus was always a fool for a wet cunni."

Gaius pushed the lamp to the side and looked Brutius straight in the eyes. "Some of the men who were in Britannia swore Decimus's boy slave was Amren's daughter."

Brutius tapped his fingertips on his chin, considering Gaius's story. He was bothered by his father's reluctance to reveal what had happened to Marcellus in Britannia that had made him lose his memory.

Brutius probed further. "What happened to the slave after they were caught in the act?"

Gaius snapped his fingers. "Vanished. After that, I was ordered to serve under Marcellus to crush a rebellion in northern Gaul."

"For which he received accolades," Brutius said bitterly. "Did you consider Marcellus a brave man?"

"Quite so. Some would say he was reckless when leading men into battle."

"That sounds like Marcellus. Stupid and rash." Brutius's jaw tightened as he dropped a gold coin on the table.

Gaius quickly picked up the coin and smiled. "By the way, I saw something that might interest you when I was at the Red Chariot yesterday."

"Say it," Brutius growled, becoming vexed with how Gaius was goading him for more money.

"Marcellus met a horribly scarred, one-eyed man in the tavern. He had reddish hair and plaid trousers typical of what warriors from Britannia wear. They conversed for a while, then went to the back of the inn. I followed them up the stairs and observed them entering a room toward the back of the corridor. Shortly after, the scarred warrior left the room and waited outside. Even though I thought I was hidden, he spotted me and threw me down the stairs. He pulled a dagger from his baldric with the intent to slash my throat."

An outburst of screams suddenly resonated into the tablinum, giving Brutius a start. Gaius's eyes grew big as he glanced around. "What was that?"

"My personal attendant, Adonis, is making a final payment to Rufus. Remember the slave dealer here when you first entered the atrium? Let me be clear. There are limits to my generosity. Are you still loyal to Marcellus?"

Gaius's voice trembled. "I'm only beholden to you."

"Good man," Brutius growled. "The price for betraying me is steep. Keep an eye on Marcellus and tell me who he meets. Understood?"

Gaius gulped. "Is there any person in particular I should look out for?"

"A woman," Brutius said. "Or someone of note, like a senator."

"I understand . . ." Gaius's voice was drowned out by the crescendo of screams coming from the peristyle garden.

Brutius smirked when he saw fear in the hardened soldier's eyes. He rose and gestured for Gaius to stand.

"Let me escort you out," Brutius offered. "Are you satisfied with your payment?"

"Quite so." Gaius pressed the palms of his hands flat on the table as he stood up. "You needn't show me out. I know the way."

Brutius chuckled inwardly as Gaius scrambled out of the chamber.

15

SEPARATE HEADQUARTERS

Rome, 20 March, 28 AD

For the last two days, the tension had been so thick between Marcellus and his parents that a knife could slice through the air between them. After the embarrassing calamity at the dinner, his father had been uncharacteristically silent after commanding Marcellus to stay home until he could quell the strain with Senator Frugi. The steward, Linos, had informed Marcellus that his father had ordered all messages be withheld from him. Any visitor requesting to see Marcellus would be turned away until further orders.

Marcellus surmised his father did not want him speaking with Matron Antonia about the hurriedly planned marriage. What else could explain his father's stubbornness about not delaying the wedding?

Was this about the negotiated dowry? he wondered.

Whatever his father's reason, he had to escape the paterfamilias's fist of authority. He couldn't risk losing Catrin again. Not now. Not ever. He had to get word to her.

But first, he had to face his father that morning in the tablinum. Until then, he had to wait in his bedchamber until summoned, like a dog.

A woman's quavering voice saying, "Sire, your father has summoned you," drew Marcellus out of his thoughts. Turning to the doorway, he found Selena with her palla-covered head lowered. He sensed something was wrong with her.

"Are you all right?" he asked, concerned.

"Yes," she whispered unconvincingly.

Marcellus waved her in. Selena pulled the palla around the bottom of her face and limped into the chamber.

"Let me see your face," Marcellus said softly.

Selena's chin almost touched her neck as she shook her head.

Disquieted by her refusal, Marcellus gently lifted Selena's chin, seeing that her left eye was swollen almost shut. "Did my father do this?"

"Please. No questions," Selena pleaded.

"Don't be afraid," Marcellus assured her. "I want to help you. Pull the palla away so I can see."

Selena's hand was shaking so hard that Marcellus had to help her take the palla off her head. He was dismayed to see her upper lip was split open. Her neck was swollen with a red indentation, showing that she had been choked with a rope. He knew the perpetrator was his father. In the midst of a bad dream, he had heard his father's voice, followed by cries of pain. This was Selena's reality, a living nightmare. A Roman master could treat his slave as cruelly as he wanted.

Repulsed, Marcellus swallowed the bile in his mouth. "I am so sorry."

Selena gave him a perplexed look. "It's not your fault."

"But it is," Marcellus said, suddenly feeling guilty that his father had unleased his pent-up rage toward him on Selena. He cringed at the thought of what Decimus may have done to Catrin when she was his slave.

"Stay hidden in here until I return," he ordered.

Still shaking, Selena covered her head again with the palla and sat down in the dimly lit corner of the room.

Marcellus huffed with anger as he strode out of his bedchamber and down the columned passage to the back of the atrium. Without knocking, he pushed the heavy wood door open to enter the triclinium. The wall painting of Roman horsemen slashing at Celtic warriors and his father's deadly scowl greeted him.

Marcellus swallowed hard, recognizing he could no longer live in the same residence as his parents. He stared at his father silently and waited for him to initiate the conversation.

Lucius's eyebrows furled together. "Do you hear the laughter from the atrium?"

Not hearing anything, Marcellus remained stone-faced and didn't answer.

"I still hear the laughter of our dinner guests from the other night in my head." Lucius stepped forward and pointed to himself. "They were laughing at me, a jester in a comedy of errors. The most powerful patricians, who despise each other, were invited to honor you. Honor you, not me!"

Marcellus pointed out, "I didn't invite Sejanus—"

"But you started a battle!" Lucius thundered. "You stirred up Antonia by saying Licinia is too young to marry."

"Well, she is!"

"Licinia has been bleeding for six months and is ready to bear your children," Lucius proclaimed with a stomp of his foot. "Antonia butts in like a ram, thinking she can overrule decisions made by Marcus Frugi and me. Gods above! That woman refused to remarry after Druses died, despite Augustus's insistence. Then there is Julia Augustus. She thinks of herself as an almighty empress because she is Tiberius's mother. And you mix Sejanus into the cauldron! Those women hate him! And then you spout out your demands to be in the legion."

"Why can't you consider what I want?" Marcellus protested.

"I am the paterfamilias! You will do what I command."

"And what is that?"

"You will wed Licinia in June."

Marcellus jerked his head back. "Despite what happened at dinner, Marcus Frugi still agrees?"

"Yes. More than ever."

"Then these are my terms if you want me to marry Licinia," Marcellus demanded. "I will no longer live under your roof but will live in my own domus."

"With what funds?"

"My own," Marcellus said. "And I will take Selena as my personal slave."

Lucius's glare pierced Marcellus. "You will what?"

"She will satisfy my needs," Marcellus said, noting his father's bewildered expression. "I still want your blessing to return to the Roman legion. *After* I return from service, I will marry Licinia."

Lucius gripped Marcellus by the arms. "Impudent jackass! Sejanus spoke to me about your request to command the legion in northern Gaul—a request made behind my back. Besides, you are too young for such an honor. As I said, you will stay in Rome and accept the position Marcus Frugi has offered you."

Marcellus removed his father's hands. "For now, I'll take the position through the spring festivals. Still, I'm moving out today and taking Selena with me. Don't try to stop me."

Lucius gave Marcellus an icy stare. "I won't stop you. You can have your fun with Selena as long as you marry Licinia. If you fail to do so, you will regret you ever crossed me!"

"I have no doubt," Marcellus said, fully aware his own father would sacrifice anything—even cut his own son's life short—to rise to the pinnacle of his ambition.

Heart racing, Marcellus rushed out of the room and returned to his bedchamber, where he found Selena waiting for him.

"We must leave now! Get my formal attire and put it in here," he ordered, picking up his leather satchel and handing it to Selena. She gave him a perplexed look.

"I'll explain later," Marcellus told her. He knelt next to the wooden chest where he stored his military armor and weapons. Fumbling through his military equipment, he found his baldric and put it over his shoulders, then wrapped and tightened the belt around his waist, sheathing two daggers, a knife, and a sword.

After Selena finished packing, he gripped the satchel and waved for her to follow him. She scurried behind him, trying to keep up, as he hurried to the atrium and scanned the area to confirm his parents were out of sight. They left the atrium, walked onto the open road, and descended Palatine Hill toward the Circus Maximus. On the way, he explained to Selena what had happened with his father and his plans to rent separate housing where he could hide her. He decided to wait to tell her about Catrin until after he introduced them.

When Marcellus arrived at the chariot horse stable, he cautiously approached Falco and glanced all around for any suspicious-looking people. Falco acknowledged Marcellus with a nod and gave a blue tit bird whistle, a sign for them to meet outside. Marcellus grasped Selena's hand and pulled her outside to a public fountain from which water spurted out of a lion's mouth.

Seeing the fear in Selena's widened, almond-shaped eyes, he assured her, "Trust me, everything will be fine," even though he felt uneasy about where his father's wrath would lead.

Gods forbid he ever discovers Catrin!

A few moments later, Falco finally came out and greeted Marcellus, though he kept his eyes steadfast on Selena.

"Have you seen Catrin?" Marcellus asked.

"I saw her yesterday," Falco replied. "She's growing concerned that it is taking you so long to find a place."

"Let's just say I've been walking on cut glass with my father the last few days." Marcellus fisted his shaking hand to calm himself. "I stormed out of his house today with his favorite slave."

Falco's brow furrowed. "Jupiter's bolts! Does he know I'm helping you?"

Marcellus gave Falco a steely stare that made the horse trainer flinch. "Not unless you tell him. Stay loyal to me on this. Get a message to Catrin that I will meet her early this evening at the Temple of Marcellus. Have her wait at the plaque commemorating Marcus Claudius Marcellus. It's on the side closest to the Temple of Apollo."

"I'll take her there myself to avoid any problems," Falco suggested.

"Good idea." Marcellus took out some coins from his belted purse and handed them to Falco. "Before you see Catrin, buy her a wine-colored palla befitting a noblewoman. Instruct her to wear it so she stands out among the theatergoers. I'll wear a similarly colored cloak. I need to go now and make final arrangements."

"*Apollo custodiat te*," Falco said.

"And may the gods be with you," Marcellus replied, clasping Falco's forearm.

16

THEATER OF MARCELLUS

Rome, 20 March, 28 AD

The theater where Catrin was to meet Marcellus reminded her of the area around the gladiatorial coliseum where she had fought in Lugdunum. Sensing a slight charge in her fingertips, she felt a thread lacing around her fingers. She recalled last night's dream, when she'd visited the Wall of Lives. There, she'd meticulously tied Marcellus's crimson life thread with her raven-black strand, securing it into a knot so they could stay together forever.

Yet, no matter how often she had rewoven Marcellus's thread to extend his life, fate always pulled his thread out of her fingertips to redirect his destiny. And now, she sensed heat radiating into the palm of her right hand and envisioned the dagger she had thrust into the serpent stone on the white hills in her homeland. In her heart, she knew the curse etched on the blade was transforming, and she could not defy her destiny to return home and overthrow Marrock. Her half brother now taunted her in nightmares, carrying the three skulls of her parents and eldest sister in his arms. In the visions, lightning sparked in and out of their eye sockets like serpents as Marrock's facial scars disappeared.

Does Marrock now control my fate?

She lightly rubbed the bronze plate identifying the multi-arched structure as the Theater of Marcellus. A foreboding sense of doom clouded over her as she recalled Marcellus telling her in Britannia that he feared dying young like his namesake. It seemed ominous that Marcellus had asked her to meet him here.

Are we lovers playing roles in a tragic play? she wondered.

Their love was so strong, and Catrin swore that not even the gods could sever their bond—not in this lifetime or the next.

Blasphemy to defy the gods!

Catrin was pulled out of her contemplation when Cynwrig asked, "How can Marcellus spot us in such a large crowd?"

"He'll find us," she assured Cynwrig, although she also felt unsettled that he was so late. The daylight was now fading into dusk.

Did he have a mishap?

Cynwrig raised the eyebrow on the unscarred side of his face. "I don't like the way people are looking at us."

"It's your appearance," Catrin said with a chuckle. "They don't want to meet your fate."

"Is that so? I'm ready to leave this godforsaken city. Too many people gawking at my face," Cynwrig grumbled.

"Let's stay a little longer."

Catrin studied the theatergoers waiting to enter the amphitheater through the archways. Noblemen wearing purple-striped, white togas over full-length tunics escorted bejeweled women. Many of the noble-women modestly covered their heads with pale-colored palla draped down the backs of their heads as veils. Other heavily made-up women flashed brightly colored togas over sheer, knee-length tunics, with long, gold chains hanging loosely down to their waists.

Freed women prostitutes, she surmised.

Suddenly noticing a passerby casting a suspicious glance at her, Catrin felt uneasy about the disparity of her velvety, wine-colored veil draping over the linen tunic of a plebian. She furtively scanned the congested area for Marcellus. She caught sight of a striking, slender woman with ebony skin as dark as Negasi, the Ethiopian gladiator who had befriended and mentored her on fighting with a spear and a sword with deadly purpose in the gladiatorial school in Lugdunum. Next to the sleek woman was a man with the hood of a burgundy cloak covering his head. He slightly favored his right leg as he strode toward her, with the lithe woman at his side. Her heart quickened when she finally recognized Marcellus.

But why was the dark-skinned woman at his side?

Catrin stared straight ahead at the brick theater, remembering Falco's warning to look away when Marcellus approached her because someone from his family had been spying on him. She told Cynwrig in a hushed tone, "Marcellus approaches."

Cynwrig nodded and glanced sideways. Then, Catrin felt a soft touch on her hand, and Marcellus's voice said in a hushed tone, "Follow me."

As Catrin turned to follow Marcellus, another man's voice greeted, "*Bonum vesperam,* Marcellus."

"*Salve,* Senator Frugi and Madame Scribonia," Marcellus replied in a gasp.

Catrin didn't know whether she should leave as a nobleman with silver-streaked, dark hair shifted his eyes between her and Marcellus.

"Are you attending the reading of *The Aeneid* by Virgil?" Senator Frugi asked.

"I've just come from the stables and hadn't planned to do so," Marcellus said, keeping his eyes steadfast on Senator Frugi.

Senator Frugi gave a thin smile. "What a shame. I had hoped to speak with you about managing the upcoming games."

Marcellus's lips quirked into a smile. "Perhaps we could speak at your office tomorrow about this. I'm not appropriately dressed."

"Maybe that is best—more private." Senator Frugi's dark-brown eyes shifted to Catrin. "Introduce me to your female companion."

Marcellus's brow furrowed. "Companion?"

"The lovely woman beside you with the wine-colored veil."

Marcellus looked at Catrin, trying to find the appropriate answer. "Oh, we don't know each other, do we? I thought you were someone I might have known in my youth."

"I thought the same," Catrin said, wondering if Senator Frugi had seen Marcellus familiarly touch her hand.

Senator Frugi's piercing stare unsettled Catrin as he amicably asked, "Are you a patron of the theater?"

"I sometimes come here with my husband. Not tonight, though."

Catrin gestured toward Cynwrig. "I'm here with my bodyguard, who is escorting me to a nearby event."

Senator Frugi regarded Cynwrig. "Is that so?"

Marcellus abruptly interjected. "It looks as though the reading is about to begin,"

"Indeed." Senator Frugi took his wife's arm in his. "We can't be late, can we?"

Scribonia smiled at Marcellus. "It is so good to see you again, Marcellus. Feel free to visit Licinia any time."

Marcellus's voice cracked. "I will."

"Tomorrow, then," Senator Frugi said, finishing the conversation, and he escorted his wife to the closest archway. Before entering the theater, Senator Frugi glanced over his shoulder at Catrin.

Catrin looked away, her heart racing with the realization she had just met Marcellus's future in-laws, a delicate situation she had not expected. Without saying a word to Marcellus, she followed him through the multitude of people gathering around the Temple of Apollo. Questions began gnawing at her on how she could stay with Marcellus in Rome without the wrong person discovering their relationship. Was her earlier foreboding sense of doom a presage of her fate with Marcellus?

They trailed Marcellus up Capitoline Hill, where they stopped at the storefront of a jewelry shop. Marcellus told Catrin and Cynwrig to stay back as he talked with the landlord by the name of Titus Asinius. A heavyset man with jowls that reminded Catrin of a bullfrog came out of the shop with a notably plump woman. Catrin pretended to look at merchandise at a nearby shop while she listened to the conversation.

"Is everything set?" Marcellus asked the thickset man.

"Fortuna favors you. I have a small, furnished domus with a bath and a couple of chambers for house slaves. The owner has left for an assignment to Greece and is not expected back for several months. As part of the bargain, he left his chief housekeeper, Herta, to serve your needs." Asinius gestured toward Selena. "Is this the woman you want kept secret?"

"A favorite slave of my father whom I borrowed to satisfy my needs. How much is the rent?"

Taken aback by Marcellus's comment, Catrin's ears perked up as she turned her head toward Titus. He looked at her for a moment, then licked his lower lip. "Two talents of silver denarii per month."

"That much?" Marcellus grumbled.

Asinius's brow creased. "Do you want the loan or not?"

"You leave me no choice, do you?" Marcellus said, a bite to his voice.

"You always have a choice," Asinius retorted with a smug smile on his face. "The housekeeper, Herta, will show you the domus and serve your household needs. If you would excuse me, I have other arrangements to attend to."

After Asinius went back into the shop, Selena and Marcellus followed Herta up the hill, with Catrin and Cynwrig trailing them. When they reached a domus with a rose-colored facade, Catrin and Cynwrig joined Marcellus and Selena as Herta unlocked the front door with a lion-headed clapper. Appearing confused, Herta scrunched her bushy eyebrows at Marcellus.

"How many stay?" she asked in a thick, Germanic accent.

"There are four of us," Marcellus answered. "Selena is my slave and will attend to my mistress, Catrin. Cynwrig is her bodyguard."

Herta regarded Cynwrig with a grimace, then smiled at Catrin. "Ahh . . . How do I call you?"

"Address her as domina," Marcellus interjected.

"Welcome, domina." Herta smiled and gestured to another chamber leading off the atrium. "Follow me and eat."

Everyone followed Herta into the triclinium, where they reclined on couches to eat. Marcellus introduced Catrin and Cynwrig to Selena. Catrin nodded at Selena, unsettled by the prospect of a slave assisting with her personal needs. Remaining quiet, Catrin heartily ate a mackerel dish prepared in a creamy sauce. She noted the apprehension in Selena's eyes as she watched Cynwrig pluck a large piece of the cooked mackerel with his hand, stuff it in his mouth, and then gulp it down with wine.

To break the tension, Catrin told Selena, "Cynwrig and I are from Britannia. He was a guard in my father's army. Romans disfigured his face when he tried to save his wife during an attack."

Selena looked at Cynwrig. "What happened to your wife?"

Catrin answered for Cynwrig. "He barely speaks the Roman tongue but understands some of the words. Sadly, his wife was killed. He is a loyal warrior who will protect you with his life."

Selena's eyes welled with tears. "I'm so sorry."

Cynwrig asked Catrin in Celtic, "What did you say to her?"

"She is frightened by your looks. I wanted to put her at ease," Catrin explained.

"Ask her why her face is so swollen, then. Did Marcellus beat her?"

Cynwrig's accusation stunned Catrin, and she didn't know how to answer him.

Marcellus touched her hand. "What are you two saying?"

Catrin looked at Marcellus, who had a bewildered look on his face. "I explained to Cynwrig that Selena is a slave from your father's household, but I'm not sure why you brought her here."

Marcellus hesitated. "Let me explain this to you later, when we're alone."

Catrin glanced at Cynwrig. "We will talk about Selena tomorrow, after I have a chance to speak with my husband."

The answer didn't seem to quell Cynwrig's agitation. He glared at his uneaten fish and pulled the head away, then speared a piece of cooked meat to eat.

As Herta took plates from the table, Marcellus asked, "Have you prepared the bath for Catrin and me?"

Herta lowered her eyes and replied meekly, "Yes. I take you there when ready."

Catrin could tell by Marcellus's smoldering eyes that he had intimate intentions for her. Still, her mind filled with questions about what had happened to him the last few days and why Marcellus had implied to Asinius that Selena would meet his sexual needs.

"I'm ready now," Marcellus told Herta, reaching for Catrin's hand and pulling her up from the couch. He lowered his head to kiss Catrin but held back as his eyes shifted toward Cynwrig.

"Help yourself to wine while you wait for Herta to show you to your quarters," he offered. "You can sleep in a room close to the front entrance."

Cynwrig stared.

"You understand?" Marcellus asked.

Cynwrig grunted.

"I guess that means yes."

Cynwrig nodded, narrowing his eyes at Marcellus, then asked Catrin in Celtic, "Do you want me to guard you outside your sleeping quarters?"

"Do what Marcellus says. Stand guard near the entrance," Catrin ordered.

Marcellus grabbed her hand and said in a hushed tone, "That cyclops won't surprise us with a visit?"

Catrin chuckled. "Only if you attack me."

Marcellus glared at Catrin. "That is not funny."

Catrin repressed her smile, sensing Marcellus's tension, and slipped her hand out of his.

Leaving Cynwrig in the triclinium, they followed Herta into the torch-lit, compact garden outside the atrium. The rosebushes displayed green growth, a promise of blooms in May. To the right was a room with a white marble bath that could accommodate up to ten people.

After Herta showed Selena the oils, strigils, and towels, Marcellus un-abashedly removed his clothes with Selena's assistance. As Catrin beheld his nakedness, her face flushed, and she unexpectedly felt shy. She recalled that when they'd first met, he was slender with smooth, scarless skin. But now, his body had filled out with muscle, and his chest and abdomen were covered with scars from battle-inflicted wounds. What would he think of the telltale injuries from her gladiatorial training and the abuse she had suffered as a slave?

Catrin refused Selena's assistance, saying, "I don't need help to undress. Leave us."

Selena lowered her eyes and backed away, then left the sweltering chamber.

Marcellus slowly walked to Catrin, unclasped one of her tunic straps, and pulled the fabric down to fondle her breast as he leaned over and kissed her neck lightly. The touch of his fingertips circling her nipple made Catrin cringe as the image of Decimus chaining her to the wall came to mind. He'd stripped her naked and harshly explored her body with a rough hand. The humiliation had been compounded when he'd forced Negasi to watch.

Marcellus must have sensed her discomfort because he pulled back and gently lifted her chin so she would look into his eyes, which had a glint of violet in the lamplight.

"What is wrong?" he whispered.

Confused about why she had felt repulsed by Marcellus's gentle touch, Catrin covered herself with crossed arms and lashed out, "Why did you bring Selena here? You told the man at the shop that she would satisfy your needs."

Marcellus's eyebrows scrunched together. "And you believed this? It was nothing more than a ploy to draw attention away from you."

Recalling Cynwrig's accusation, Catrin asked bluntly, "Why is she bruised? Did you beat her?"

Marcellus's face turned red with anger. "Is that what you think? It was my father who beat her and took her by force. That is the right of a master, to do what he wants with his slave. She is his property. I could not accept this, so I took her away from him."

Catrin's jaw clenched. "Then why do you proclaim her as your sex slave?"

Marcellus jerked his head back. "My father thinks I stole her to use her as he did. If he thinks that, he won't be so inclined to check our living arrangements."

"It is so wrong—"

"I know what he did is wrong! It grieves me to know you suffered the same as her." Marcellus exhaled and looked away. "For one night, can we not enjoy each together? Leave our troubles behind?"

Not answering, Catrin lifted the fabric of her tunic and clasped the strap. When he looked at her, she could see the pain in his eyes. From beneath his tunic, he pulled out the leather-strapped Apollo amulet and showed it to her.

"I forgot to give this back to you." He placed the amulet around her neck.

Tears welled in Catrin's eyes as she stroked the marble figurine that had been sculpted with Marcellus's facial features. "You gave this to me when we pledged our love for each other in Britannia."

Marcellus pulled her chin up and wiped away the tears. "I wish I could remember the moment you captured my heart. But you must have been special. You still are."

Suddenly feeling ashamed, Catrin confessed, "I cannot erase the memories of what Decimus did to me."

"He never took you by force, did he?"

A sob clutched in her throat. "He shamed me in other ways."

Marcellus gazed into her eyes. "If I could, I would erase those memories from your mind. You are so precious; I often ask myself if I can love a woman too much. You have me under your spell. I would do anything for you."

Catrin regarded Marcellus, whose eyes were reaching out to meet hers. "I know you would. It is so hard to love, to trust again. I have lost so much. My family. My dignity. I could not bear losing anyone else I love."

Marcellus took Catrin's hand in his. "Is that what you're afraid of, losing another child with me?"

Catrin lowered her eyes. "Perhaps."

"We cannot let the wings of happiness flutter away because we are afraid to fly." Marcellus sighed heavily. "We are different people now, but our love is the same. Love will give us the strength to overcome anything we face."

Catrin looked into Marcellus's eyes. "Promise me you will acknowledge and protect any child I bear with you."

Marcellus tightened his fingers around her hand. "Why are you saying such things?"

"I have had troubling visions and foreboding sensations," Catrin revealed. "When I was at the Temple of Marcellus, I sensed a deep loss there."

"Join me in the bath so the water can warm us. There, I will tell you about the tragedy of my namesake."

Marcellus stepped into the bath. He softly moaned with pleasure as he swirled the surface of the water with his hand. His eyes challenged her to do likewise. Catrin finally relented. She allowed her tunic to drop to the marble floor and joined him in the warm water. Marcellus wrapped his arms around her and pulled her back against his chest. He leaned his face next to hers as he told the tragic tale.

"Augustus dedicated the temple to his nephew, my namesake. At one time, he was destined to be Rome's next ruler. But he died of the plague. His mother, Octavia, never recovered from losing him. She fell into a deep depression and isolated herself. She refused to have a portrait created of her son and to have anyone speak his name in her presence."

Marcellus kissed the back of Catrin's neck before continuing. "She attended a reading by the poet Virgil, who gave extracts from his epic poem about Aeneas. He was a hero who escaped Troy's sacking to establish the city that would become Rome. Aeneas visited the underworld, where he met the dead and the shades of the unborn. He noticed a handsome but downcast youth. The spirit of Aeneas's dead father told him it was the future Marcellus."

After a deep breath, Marcellus's voice became somber as he recited the poem.

> Fate shall allow the earth one glimpse of this young man—
> One glimpse, no more.
> Alas, poor youth! If only you could escape your harsh fate!
> Marcellus, you shall be. Give me armfuls of lilies
> That I may scatter their shining blooms and shower these gifts
> At least upon the dear soul, all to no purchase though
> Such kindness be.

Then, Marcellus concluded, "And when Vigil said, 'Marcellus you shall be,' it struck me that I was also that shade of the unborn."

"What meaning does this verse hold for you?" Catrin asked, relaxing within Marcellus's arms.

"I fear I will meet the same fate and die young," Marcellus said ruefully. "Augustus molded his nephew's image into his, but his designated heir's life was cut short before he could continue the Julio legacy. I swear I will not allow this to happen to me. I am my own man and will forge my destiny. I would rather die than let you go."

Moved by Marcellus's words, Catrin turned around, wrapped her arms around his neck, and drew him in for a lingering kiss. Her mind eased as she captured the fleeting wings of happiness, reliving the moment they'd made love at the waterfall in Gaul.

17

LEAVE NOTHING BUT BONES

Rome, 20 March, 28 AD

As Brutius walked with his father to the tablinum, he anticipated a rebuke for having invited Sejanus and Livilla to the dinner in honor of Marcellus. His father's deathly silence signaled his disapproval of Brutius instigating a political cataclysm between the dinner guests.

I would do it again, he thought as he followed his father into the chamber.

Brutius bristled and rolled his eyes at the sight of the wall paintings of Roman soldiers fighting Celtic warriors.

What a farce.

His father had never fought a day in battle. Yet, he displayed gory battles on the walls, as though he were a conqueror. The bloody scene made Brutius inwardly smile at his clever scheme to rise by destroying Marcellus, by cutting away, slice by slice, at his half brother's reputation as a military commander. He would leave nothing behind but the bare bones of his unworthiness to be called a favorite son. There had to be some truth to Gaius Septimius's assertion that Marcellus had been bewitched by a sorceress in Britannia. So typical of him to be manipulated by a woman. What else could explain Marcellus's urgent desire to return to Gaul to serve in the legion?

Brutius noted his father rubbing the bust of Marcus Antonius—a characteristic that demonstrated his frustration. After his father stared at the painting of the Roman battles for a while, he waved for Brutius to join him at a small table.

When they both sat down, Lucius grumbled, "Marcellus and you have caused me nothing but pain. I've been trying to calm the storm between Senator Frugi and Matron Antonia about the timing when Marcellus should marry Licinia. And now this—Marcellus has declared he won't live under my roof and stole away with my favorite slave."

Brutius jerked his head back in surprise. "He took Selena?"

"Yes, Selena," Lucius snapped. "He slipped away with her this morning. I don't know whether it was an idle threat that he would rejoin the legion without my approval. If he doesn't marry Licinia, I could lose everything."

Brutius refrained from smirking. "I told you Marcellus would be the doom of our family. He doesn't honor Roman traditions."

"I know. I know," Lucius groaned. "A substantial dowry is at stake. And worse, Marcellus's actions could splinter my alliance with Marcus Frugi and his support for my election as consul next year."

Brutius thought back to his conversation with Gaius Septimius about how Marcellus had mysteriously met someone at the Red Chariot Inn. "Do you know where he is now?"

Lucius frowned and shook his head.

"Did he take his personal belongings?" Brutius asked.

"Some of his clothing and weapons are gone."

"He might come back for the rest," Brutius ventured. "Meanwhile, I'll ask some of my men to search for him."

"And if you find him, will you bring him back here?" Lucius growled.

Brutius raised an eyebrow. "Is that what you want? Another confrontation?"

Lucius hesitated. "No, but I can't let him defy me."

"Can I speak plainly, then?" Brutius asked.

"Speak your mind."

"For now, be patient. Allow Marcellus to cool down," Brutius advised. "Perhaps there is more behind his actions that I can discover. Is there something more I should know about what happened to him in Britannia? I've heard rumors that he was involved with a woman."

Lucius's eyes widened. "What have you heard?"

"Marcellus seduced a king's daughter," Brutius disclosed, closely watching his father's expression. "He's always been a fool for women."

Brutius noted the hard way his father swallowed.

"It's true," Lucius rasped. "He was held as a hostage under the charge of King Amren's daughter to assure his safety during our tense negotiations with a rival ruler. After about a month, I unexpectedly received a message from Amren's queen. She accused Marcellus of raping their daughter. That crazy bitch threatened to sacrifice Marcellus to her war goddesses unless I released Amren. I'd never held Amren prisoner, but that all changed when she declared war against us."

Lucius paused, lifting his eyes. Brutius, taking advantage of the momentary interlude, asked, "What was the name of their daughter?"

"Her name was Vala, as I recall." Lucius scratched the back of his neck. "Or that might have been the name of Amren's eldest daughter, who we held as hostage."

"Was it Vibius?" Brutius pressed.

"No. That sounds Roman," Lucius said. "What I remember is she was a golden-haired sorceress who put a love spell on Marcellus."

"How do you know that?" Brutius asked, curious that his father's story was consistent with Gaius's.

"During a prisoner exchange of Marcellus for Amren, Marcellus became crazed after a conflict broke out. He attacked one of my centurions to save . . . Catrin, that was her name. He was almost killed in the attempt."

Brutius recalled Marcellus's injuries after his return to Rome. "Then that explains why he had a stomach wound."

"No. That was inflicted after the prisoner exchange," Lucius clarified.

"Later?"

Lucius sighed heavily. "Marcellus returned to Amren's village to negotiate a truce, but he was captured. A druidess cast a spell on Marcellus to erase his memory, and she cut his belly open with a knife. That is when Amren's son, Marrock, rescued Marcellus from the barbaric ritual. I rewarded him for saving Marcellus by joining forces with him to overthrow his father."

"What happened to Catrin?" Brutius inquired, wondering if she and Vibius were one and the same.

"She was killed along with the rest of Amren's family."

"Did you witness this?"

"No. I left the deed to my commander, Decimus Flavius," Lucius answered. "I had hoped to return the next year with a bigger force to invade Britannia, but Emperor Tiberius refused to support me. That is why it is so critical for you to win Sejanus's trust, so he can convince Tiberius to change his mind. Marcus Frugi's alliance is also vital to support my ambition to lead the invasion."

"I am well aware and will do whatever I can to aid you," Brutius said.

"Find Marcellus," Lucius demanded. "Keep an eye on him. Report back what you find out. Do not share our conversation outside this room or you invite danger."

Brutius tingled with delight at the thought of trapping Marcellus like a fly in his political web. "For you, Father, I would do anything."

"I must now speak with Drusilla to reassure her. She is in a fret about Marcellus. You and your slave, Adonis, can spend the night here, if you'd like."

"Thank you for the invitation," Brutius said, smiling. "Perhaps we can talk more about the political situation at breakfast tomorrow."

18

CATRIN'S COMMANDERS

Rome, 21 March, 28 AD

Marcellus watched the rising sun shower golden rays on Catrin as she slept next to him. For more than a year, he had dreamed of holding her in his arms, savoring every touch and taste of her body. He nuzzled her mussed blonde hair and breathed in her womanly aroma, cherishing what seemed an impossible dream, living together as husband and wife. It felt normal, as if their relationship had always been safe and secure.

For now, at least, he tried to reassure himself.

As he reminisced about last night's intimate moment with Catrin, he remembered how he had sensed her reticence whenever he touched her between her thighs. Could he ever recapture the love they'd felt at the waterfall in Gaul, back before Decimus had found them? How could she completely trust him, a Roman, after what Decimus had done to her?

Marcellus forced the images of Decimus's heinous acts against Catrin from his head. He would rather live in the moment, gazing at his goddess. Her face was radiant in the sunlight. He snuggled against her back and kissed her lightly on the neck.

She moaned and turned to face him, rubbing the sleepiness out of her eyes. "Is it morning already?"

"Another glorious day together," Marcellus said with a smile. "I hear Selena outside our chambers fixing breakfast."

"Last night was the first time I have slept so soundly since . . ." Catrin's voice faded, as if a distant memory floated in her mind. "I felt so safe in your arms."

The words eased the doubts gnawing at Marcellus that Catrin did not yet trust him completely. He kissed her on the nose. "It felt good to hold you as my wife. And you will be treated as such here."

"What about your betrothal to Licinia?" Catrin asked, sitting up, the blanket falling from her shoulders.

Marcellus, noticing the scars on her back, ached from the guilt that he had not protected her in Gaul. He sat behind her and fingered the hard-edged scar that extended from her shoulder blade to halfway down her back.

She flinched.

"Does it still hurt?" he asked somberly.

She looked over her shoulder. "No. But I don't want your pity."

Marcellus swallowed hard as he looked into her brilliant turquoise eyes. "I don't pity you. I love you the way you are. You are more beautiful today than when I first beheld you."

Catrin leaned back against his chest. He lightly kissed the nape of her neck as he cupped her breasts with his hands. "Can I touch you like this?"

"Yes," she purred, closing her eyes.

He rubbed the tips of her hardening nipples until she moaned, then pulled her down on the bed. Pressing his lips to hers, he explored the contours of her body, until they were roused out of the moment by Selena's voice saying, "Forgive me, dominus. You asked me to wake and help you dress for your meeting with Matron Antonia."

Turning over, he found Selena staring at them. Though slaves often saw intimate moments of their masters, Marcellus could tell by Catrin's reddened face that she was both embarrassed and irritated.

She squirmed away from his embrace and ordered Selena, "Fix breakfast. I will help Marcellus dress."

Selena lowered her eyes, seeming to sense Catrin's irritation. "As you wish, domina."

After Selena left the chamber, Catrin glared at Marcellus. "I don't want any female slave attending to your personal needs. I will do it."

"But you are my wife and should not be burdened with such duties," Marcellus protested.

Ignoring his response, Catrin rose from the bed and glanced around the room. "Where are my clothes?"

Marcellus pointed to a shelf in the corner. "Over there, where Selena left them last night."

Catrin retrieved a tunic from the pile of clothing and pulled it over her head. "Why are you meeting with Matron Antonia? I thought you were to meet with . . . what's his name?"

Marcellus shook his head, not sure to whom she was referring.

"The richly dressed noble at the theater. Your future father-in-law," she clarified, a slight tinge of bitterness in her voice.

"Senator Frugi, you mean?"

"Yes. Him."

Marcellus regarded Catrin's frown, wondering where her question was leading. "I am to meet first with Matron Antonia and seek her aid in convincing Senator Frugi to postpone my wedding with Licinia. Antonia agrees Licinia is too young to marry. She might be receptive to my request to help me arrange a meeting with Tiberius."

"For what purpose?"

"So he can assign me as a military commander in northern Gaul," Marcellus answered. "That would give me a good excuse to convince my father to postpone the wedding. I could house you in Gaul, close to the encampment."

Catrin paused, as if considering what he had said, then gestured for him to get out of bed. "Will you be wearing your formal attire today?"

Marcellus dangled his legs over the edge of the bed and pointed to a satchel next to his weapons. "I packed a white tunic and red-striped toga before I left my father's home."

Catrin stepped away, knelt next to the satchel, and rummaged through its contents. She retrieved a white tunic and handed it to Marcellus. He rose from the bed and pulled the tunic over his head. He held out his arms for Catrin to drape the toga over his shoulder. She then wrapped the toga around his torso and carefully hung the end of the fabric over his left arm.

"You've done this before?" Marcellus asked, admiring how meticulously the toga lay on his arm.

"I helped dress Decimus for formal occasions in Gaul." Catrin paused and looked at him, like a cat eyeing its prey. "Senator Frugi still wants you to manage the spring games?"

Marcellus cocked an eyebrow at the sudden change in conversation. "I believe he does."

"Does that include gladiatorial contests?" Catrin asked, smoothing the wrinkles of the toga on his arm with her hand.

"And chariot races," Marcellus added.

Catrin bit her lower lip. "If that is so, could you purchase gladiators from the lanista, Verus?"

Marcellus jerked his head back. "Why would I do that? He abused you when you trained with him."

Catrin lightly touched his chest. "He has two gladiators I want in my army."

Marcellus gave her a befuddled look. "Your army?"

"The army my father's second-in-command, Trystan, is helping me form. While I'm in Rome, Trystan is recruiting warriors and forging alliances with other British kings."

The prospect of Catrin fighting and leading men into battle ran a shiver of dread down Marcellus's spine. "Let me fight for you. I can't lose you in battle. Isn't that why I am going to Gaul? To help you overthrow Marrock?"

Catrin's blue-green eyes glinted as she caressed the fabric on his chest. "You are not only my king, Marcellus, but I need your Roman army to help me fight for my throne. Yet, if I am to earn the respect of my people as their queen, it must be me to lead the revolt against Marrock. That is why I am asking you to purchase these gladiators. They will be my military commanders."

Marcellus sighed, noting the fiery determination in Catrin's eyes. Now was not the time, he conceded, to argue with her, especially before his crucial meeting with Matron Antonia. He asked, "What are their names?"

"Negasi and Ferrex."

"Negasi, the Ethiopian? He wanted to rip my head off at the *ludus* where you trained!" Marcellus exclaimed.

"Yes, I know. But he is my most loyal friend and mentor," Catrin said evenly, then added, "You must also free Ferrex. He is known as the Red Lion. He trained me to fight in Britannia."

Marcellus shook his head in disbelief at the demands of his wife, his soul mate whom he wanted to protect. "Help me understand. You want me to accept the position offered by Senator Frugi? To manage the games and stay here with you in Rome?"

"I'll stay here until you can free Negasi and Ferrex," Catrin said. "Besides, it could take some time for you to arrange a meeting with Tiberius and take command of the northern legion in Gaul."

"The longer we stay here, the more likely my family will discover you," Marcellus warned. "My father could have us both killed. Be careful whenever you leave the domus."

"I will. Cynwrig will serve as my bodyguard." Catrin wrapped her arms around Marcellus's neck and pleaded him with her eyes. "You must also be careful."

"Don't worry about me," Marcellus said, returning Catrin's embrace. "This will give us time to reacquaint with each other."

"But what if we're discovered?"

"We'll think of a way to escape then. For now, let us enjoy our time together."

Pulling Catrin closer, Marcellus kissed her fervently, as though it could be their last moment together. Then, he whispered, "I would do anything for you."

19

WEB OF LIES

Matron Antonia's Villa, Rome, 21 March, 28 AD

After knocking the clapper on the front door to Matron Antonia's villa, Marcellus was surprised to see a strapping slave with deep-set, hazel eyes greet him. At first, he thought he had gone to the wrong residence, distracted by mulling over how to convince Matron Antonia to help him.

"How can I help you?" the young slave—who was about Marcellus's age—asked in a distinct, Germanian accent.

"I am Marcellus Antonius. I've scheduled a meeting with Matron Antonia."

"Greetings. The domina expects you," the slave said, gesturing for him to enter.

As Marcellus walked down the corridor, he gazed at the statues of men in military attire, two of which had inscriptions identifying them as Matron Antonia's husband, Nero Claudius Druses, and her son, Germanicus Julius Caesar—both renowned generals who had died in the prime of their lives. He had only visited Matron Antonia's villa a couple of times, when he was fourteen years old, after his father had returned to Rome. She had graciously hosted banquets to introduce his father to some of the most influential politicians in Rome, including Senator Frugi.

As Marcellus entered the opulent atrium, he saw statues of other notable members of Matron Antonia's distinguished family: Octavia Minor (her mother), Emperor Tiberius (her brother-in-law), and Augustus (her uncle). The statue of her father, Marcus Antonius, was notably missing from the prestigious lineup of ancestors—all traces of him erased from the

Roman mind by the act *damnatio memoriae* after Augustus, then known as Octavian, defeated him.

Marcellus followed the Germanian slave around a pool in which a mosaic of a charioteer in a four-horse-drawn quadriga could be seen at the bottom. Toward the back of the chamber, he spotted Matron Antonia speaking with an adolescent boy who was about sixteen years old. She was modestly attired in a white stola and a pale-blue palla draped from the back of her head as a veil.

"Domina, Marcellus Antonius is here to see you," the Germanian slave announced.

Matron Antonia turned and smiled. "What a pleasure to be visited by two young men." She gestured to the young man by her side. "This is Gaius Julius Caesar, the youngest son of Germanicus. The legionaries like to call him Caligula, as do I. He was always so cute tromping around the camp with his father in those little military boots. Such a charmer."

Marcellus gave a slight nod, noting Gaius's sunken brown eyes beneath his broad, furrowed forehead, which made him appear grim. The boy's long neck seemed disproportionate with his thick torso and thin legs.

"It is an honor to meet a son of Germanicus," Marcellus said amiably. "I studied his battle tactics."

Antonia interjected, "Caligula, did you know Marcellus served as tribune under Legatus Decimus Flavius in northern Gaul? He received accolades for quashing a rebellion there."

Gaius seemed distracted by his own thoughts, frowning, as Madame Antonia continued, "Gaius stayed the night at the villa. We had the most interesting chat about his mother's disagreements with Sejanus. But I told him"—she turned her head sideways toward her grandson—"I would speak to Tiberius . . . and Julia Augusta, too, on his mother's behalf."

Gaius stiffened, and his brow creased into a deeper line. "Grandmother, should we be talking about this?"

Matron Antonia waved off his remark. "Nonsense. Everyone knows Sejanus is a thorn in Tiberius's side that should be removed before it festers."

The brash remark took Marcellus by surprise. Matron Antonia was known for her proprietary and deft ability to maneuver secretly through imperial politics. Nonetheless, her candor reassured him she might help him bypass Sejanus to supplicate his case to Tiberius.

"How foolish of me to speak so plainly," Matron Antonia added, a wicked glint in her eye. "But it is no secret Sejanus considers your mother a political detriment."

Marcellus smirked at the realization that the elder noblewoman must have had a reason for openly talking about the threat Sejanus posed to Caligula's mother, Agrippina. "Any secrets revealed in this house are sealed behind my lips."

"Aptly said," Matron Antonia replied with a wry smile. Then, she turned to Caligula. "Run along and tell your mother what we discussed."

Caligula frowned. "We'll talk soon?"

"Certainly," Matron Antonia said with a wave of her hand. "Now give me a kiss."

Caligula kissed her lightly on her cheek. She shifted her eyes toward the Germanian slave and ordered, "Ranulf, show my grandson to the door."

As the two left, Matron Antonia hooked Marcellus's arm into one of hers. "Let's eat."

They entered a smaller room to the side of the atrium, where platters of dried figs, pears, cheeses, and bread had been set. The walls were colorfully decorated with frescoes of painted gardens.

Marcellus sat on a curule and helped himself to dried fruit from the platter set on the oval travertine table. Although Matron Antonia was in her sixties, she still had an elegant beauty—her pale-gray eyes sparkled with mirth as she delicately held a fig by the stem and ate it. After finishing it, she began, "What did you want to speak to me about today?"

"Have you recently spoken with my father?" Marcellus asked, not sure if gossip of his sudden departure from his family's villa had spread.

Matron Antonia's eyebrows perked up. "Lucius hasn't spoken to me since the discord at his dinner party."

Marcellus breathed deeply to gather his resolve to move forward with his request. "As you must be aware, Father and I are sharply divided on my returning to the legion. Furthermore, we argued about when I should marry Licinia. She is still but a girl, not ready . . ." Marcellus cleared his throat, searching for the right words. "For me, you know, the night after our vows."

"You mean copulation?"

Marcellus felt the heat of embarrassment blossom on his face.

Matron Antonia chuckled, obviously relishing his discomfort. "Now tell me, Marcellus, why are you here? To gain my support for delaying the marriage?"

"Yes, if you are so inclined. I would also like you to support me in my ambition to become a military commander, as your husband was."

Matron Antonia sighed, and her eyes lifted, as if capturing a memory. "I was eighteen years old when I married Druses. We grew up in the imperial household like a brother and sister." She gave a wistful smile. "Let me tell you a secret. Although Augustus arranged our marriage, we were already in love and doing it." She winked at Marcellus. "Do you feel the same way about Licinia?"

"I hardly know her." Marcellus said, more candidly than he had intended. He met Matron Antonia's probing gaze. "Don't misunderstand me. I accept my betrothal, but we both know it would be safer for Licinia to birth children when she is older. Until such time, I could serve Rome in the legion. Before I left Gaul, Decimus sent a letter to Tiberius recommending I be assigned in northern Gaul. I suspect Sejanus may have intercepted the letter."

"Why do you think that?"

"I asked Sejanus directly about the letter. He told me Tiberius could not be bothered with such trivial matters."

"Well, then, how can I be of help?"

"I've been told you have direct access to Tiberius," Marcellus said. "Would you arrange a private meeting between the two of us so I can make this request directly?"

Matron Antonia didn't answer, making Marcellus apprehensive that he had overstepped his reach. The matron's eyes shifted toward the entryway of the chamber, where the young Germanian slave was entering with a flagon in his hand. She held out her goblet for him to pour some wine into.

"This is my new steward, Ranulf, from east of the Rhine," Matron Antonia said to Marcellus. "I bought him on a whim. When he was being auctioned, he refused to remove his loincloth for us to view his attributes. He had several scars from lashes on his back. I should have been wary of purchasing a rebellious slave. But the steel-edged determination in his eyes intrigued me, reminded me of my husband and his drive to conquer barbarians such as Ranulf."

Marcellus noted Ranulf's clenched jaw, his stare fixed on the wall as Matron Antonia continued. "As you can see, my comment upsets Ranulf. He is ill-suited for domestic duties and was once a charioteer before he was auctioned on the slaver's block."

Unsettled by the matron's sudden change in the conversation, Marcellus asked, "Why are you telling me this?"

"I thought you might give Ranulf as a gift to your brother, Brutius, to be his personal attendant."

Discomfited by Matron Antonia's sly smile, Marcellus asked, "Why? You just said Ranulf wasn't fit for domestic duties."

"He is fit to be a spy," Matron Antonia said without a flinch. "I've promised Ranulf his freedom if he gathers information about how Sejanus is scheming with Brutius. What is the saying? 'You help me, I help you.'"

Marcellus gasped. "You are speaking of treason."

"No. I am seeking to shine the truth on Sejanus."

Marcellus felt his mouth gape open, unsettled that she might be cornering him into playing in her political game. This was a side of the imperial noblewoman he hadn't anticipated. No wonder foreign dignitaries and senators sought her patronage. She quietly flaunted her political power outside of public view.

"You've placed me in an awkward position," Marcellus finally replied. "As I told you, I've had a falling-out with my father after I refused his order to marry Licinia and—"

"That is what puzzles me." Matron Antonia cut off Marcellus before he could explain his strained relationship with Brutius. "Most men would not give a second thought about bruising the delicate flower of a maiden for political gain."

"I'm not like all other men," Marcellus protested.

Matron Antonia's stare bore into him. "No dark secrets, eh?"

Marcellus swallowed hard, not sure whether the elder stateswoman knew about his prior affair with a married Roman noblewoman or his Celtic wife. He considered leaving before being pulled into Matron Antonia's political web, but he could only get a private meeting with Tiberius through her.

He finally said, "We all have dark secrets."

Matron Antonia's hazel eyes searched his, as if seeking ways to open the door to his soul. "If you want to play the imperial game, you must follow the rules."

"And what are those?"

"I will pledge my patronage as long as you are beholden to me."

Marcellus's throat constricted. "If that is so, I am beholden to you."

"Good. I'm glad we've settled that." Matron Antonia took a sip of wine and waved for Ranulf to leave. "Tell me why your father is blocking you from returning to military service."

"I assume he needs the dowry," Marcellus said. "He must believe his political fortunes will rise with mine if I marry sooner and accept the position offered by Senator Frugi."

"That is understandable. An ambitious father has no regard for his child's happiness if it stands in his way." Matron Antonia picked up a piece of cheese and flicked some bread crumbs off its surface. "If I help you, you must camouflage your intentions like a cuttlefish changing its color to blend in with the sea bottom—undetectable, until it strikes its prey."

Marcellus gave Matron Antonia a confused look.

"Don't openly defy your father," she clarified. "Accept Senator Frugi's position until I can do my magic behind the scenes. Where are you now staying?"

"I'm staying at a friend's home until I find my own apartment,"

Marcellus said, fishing for information on what she knew about his current living arrangements with Catrin.

Antonia tapped her mouth with a fingertip. "Hmm . . . this is a prickly situation for your father. I doubt he will want it widely known that you've left his household. He must believe your estrangement from him could threaten the marital arrangement if Senator Frugi finds out. Your father will most likely put up a facade that everything is fine between the two of you. Don't say anything about your situation to Senator Frugi while I arrange a meeting for you with Tiberius."

"What if Senator Frugi asks me about my outburst at the dinner party that I didn't want to marry Licinia so young?" Marcellus asked, suddenly uneasy about the upcoming meeting with him later that afternoon. "As you are aware, he offered me a position as a quaestor to manage the spring festivities."

"Graciously accept his offer," Matron Antonia advised. "This is an honor seldom bestowed on someone as young as you. If he questions you about marrying Licinia, emphasize that you care about her fragile nature."

"It was my intention to accept the position at our next meeting," Marcellus disclosed.

"That is a good start. I'll speak with his wife about delaying the wedding. Will you help me place Ranulf with Brutius?" Matron Antonia asked.

"It is no secret we despise each other," Marcellus said. "It would be out of character for me to offer him your slave as a gift."

"I surmised as much." Matron Antonia tapped her mouth with her forefinger. "Did you know Brutius proffers boys as sex slaves for Tiberius?"

Marcellus jerked his head back. "No."

"That is one reason Tiberius stays in Capri. To keep this quiet." Matron Antonia grimaced. "I must close my eyes to his vices. I understand his bitterness stems from how Augustus played him like a piece in his political game. Nonetheless, Tiberius recognizes my grandsons as heirs to his empire. And Sejanus's ambitions threaten them."

"What I don't understand is why do you trust me?" Marcellus asked, wary about what Matron Antonia would be willing to do for him or *to* him if she ever discovered his deception about Catrin.

"I understand how imperial politics work and what drives ambitious men. You have a soldier's mind. You are battle-hardened but can sometimes lose sight of the danger lurking beside you, disguised as a friend. You loyally serve without hesitation those you respect. You would die defending someone you love or fighting for a cause you believe in. I cannot say that is true of Sejanus. I've heard rumors he lusts for imperial power."

"You honor me," Marcellus said, humbled by her words. "I hope I can meet your expectations."

"You will," Antonia said resolutely. "When is your meeting with Senator Frugi?"

"Later today," Marcellus replied.

"Then I won't keep you."

Marcellus rushed through the courtyard of the Basilica Julia, warily glancing at the various people of all nationalities waiting in lines, no doubt seeking patronage from noble politicians. But some of these people could be his family's spies, blending into the masses and covertly watching him now.

Heart racing, he halted beside a marble column to catch his breath and to gain his composure. From the corner of his eye, he caught a glimpse of a disheveled soldier. He whipped his head sideways, but the man disappeared into a throng of people.

Keep your wits, he reminded himself.

Despite the risks, Marcellus knew how important it was to Catrin for him to free the gladiators to use in her army. He had to anchor the web of lies spinning in his head to make sure they were consistent with every politician he spoke with. Straightening his shoulders, he strode to the front of the line of supplicants waiting to see Senator Frugi. He presented himself to the Greek attendant, Orvius, a freeman who had once been a personal slave of the senator. A pudgy man, he was eloquently garbed in a gold-striped, burgundy tunic and bejeweled with gemstone rings and a gold necklace hanging around his neck. Gray wisps of hair streaked across the top of his shiny, sunburned head. He squinted at Marcellus, as if he had difficulty focusing.

"*Salve*, Marcellus," Orvius finally greeted in a nasal tone. "Senator Frugi is expecting you."

Grumbles from the people waiting in line filled Marcellus's ears as he followed Orvius into the office chamber with shelves of scrolls on all sides. Sitting behind a bulky, wooden table toward the back was Senator Frugi, reading a parchment. He lifted his eyes when Orvius announced, "Marcellus Antonius is here to see you."

Senator Frugi clicked his fingers for Orvius to leave and momentarily regarded Marcellus. He frowned and again quietly read the parchment. Silence split the room as Marcellus waited for the senator to address him.

Senator Frugi finally rolled the parchment into a scroll and turned in his chair to place it into one of the shelves behind him. A chill pricked at Marcellus's neck when the senator shot him an icy glare.

"I'd offer you a chair, but there are none to spare," the senator began brusquely.

Marcellus met his stare. "I can stand."

Senator Frugi's jaw tightened. "You realize the importance of why you're here? The honor I bestowed upon you at your family's dinner?"

Marcellus paused, carefully considering his next words. "I am deeply grateful for your offering me the position. That is why I'm here, to learn more about it."

The senator's brow creased. "You have nothing more to say regarding your outburst about refusing to marry Licinia?"

Marcellus swallowed, recalling Matron Antonia's advice to focus on Licinia's fragile nature. "I apologize for the misunderstanding. Trust me, I am honored to marry your daughter. The announcement to wed so soon took me by surprise. I thought we'd be married in a couple of years, when she is older and after I have served in the legion."

"And that is the only reason you voiced your objections?"

Worried that the senator was aware of Catrin, Marcellus felt his stomach twist into knots as he answered, "My main concern is for Licinia. She is but an innocent girl with a fragile nature."

The senator scowled and clasped his hands on the table. "What about Eliana?"

Dumbstruck, Marcellus felt his mouth gape open.

"Let me be blunt," Senator Frugi continued. "I question your motives for returning to the legion. It is known you were banished to northern Gaul as recompense for your indiscretion with the wife of a consul. Nasty business. Both she and the baby you sired died in childbirth."

Marcellus shifted his feet to balance himself from the dizzying accusation. "I won't deny what happened. I deeply regret my actions and what happened to Eliana. But I've changed. Serving in the legion taught me the importance of duty and family. That is why I want to return. I want to serve Rome."

"Do you still seek the comfort of other women?"

Does he know about Catrin?

"No. I do not," Marcellus answered firmly, though his stomach was roiling from his lie. "I'm committed to marrying Licinia and will remain faithful to her. I understand the importance of joining our houses."

Senator Frugi coldly stared at Marcellus. "Make no mistake. If you are to be my son-in-law, you will not humiliate me again in public. Is that understood?"

Marcellus felt as if the walls of shelves were collapsing in on him. "Yes. It won't happen again."

"If you have any disagreement with me, you will speak with me privately," Senator Frugi added, emphasizing each word.

Marcellus nodded. "*Ita domine.*"

"I've spoken with your father about my reservations about you. He humbly asked me to give you another chance to demonstrate your loyalty to me. As a good friend of your father, I again offer you the position as a quaestor to organize the spring games, with me as your patron. In return, you must swear your allegiance to me and do whatever I say."

For the second time that day, Marcellus had to promise his fealty to an aristocrat so he could maneuver events in his quest to help Catrin over-throw Marrock. "I pledge my loyalty to you."

"Then it is settled," Senator Frugi said. "I'll speak to your father about our agreement. Still, your actions give me pause about sealing the date of your marriage with Licinia. I need to judge how you best serve me while organizing the games."

"I won't disappoint you," Marcellus said resolutely, suspecting in the back of his mind that bribes and tributes would be required from the sponsors.

"Ahh . . . I see Orvius with someone seeking my patronage," Senator Frugi said, rising from his seat. "Report to me tomorrow morning for fur-ther instructions."

"Thank you, sir, for giving me this opportunity."

"You can take your leave," Senator Frugi growled.

Marcellus's stomach lurched as he quickly exited through the doorway into the basilica's inner court. He recognized the disheveled soldier, Gaius Septimus, standing by a marble column across the way and staring at him. Pretending not to notice him, Marcellus merged with a group of senators ambling down the courtyard, then furtively escaped through one of the archways and scurried down the steps. To make sure he was not followed, he rushed to the stables near the Circus Maximus, where he blended in with the shoppers, and backtracked to the forum before heading to his domus on Capitoline Hill.

20

FLEETING MOMENT

Rome, 21 March, 28 AD

When Marcellus finally returned to the domus at dusk, Catrin could tell by the way his face was drawn down and his shoulders slumped that he was deeply troubled. He hardly spoke or ate the dinner the housekeeper had prepared. Though Catrin was anxious to learn what had happened in his meetings, she waited to ask questions until they were alone in the bath—their retreat from the world.

After dinner, Selena warmed the water in the bath by pouring hot water from pottery buckets, then fragranced the bathwater with lavender oil and lit three candles. After she left, Catrin disrobed, but Marcellus stood there, dazed, his eyes listless. She pulled his tunic up, a gesture to nudge him out of his brooding. After he undressed, she stepped into the tepid, waist-high water and offered Marcellus a massage.

He sat down in front of her and leaned his shoulders against her chest so she could knead his muscles with her fingers. He appeared to relax and moaned, "Mmm . . . that feels so good."

"You're so tense. Did your meetings not go well?" Catrin ventured. She felt his shoulders stiffen.

"As well as can be expected," he finally answered.

"What happened?"

"Where do I begin?"

"Did Matron Antonia agree to help you?" Catrin asked, becoming frustrated with his reluctance to talk.

Marcellus inhaled deeply, then revealed the dangerous political game Matron Antonia was playing with the emperor's second-in-command,

Sejanus. Though Catrin didn't completely understand the complexity of the imperial intrigue, she quietly listened until he finished, saying, "Matron Antonia has agreed to help me arrange a meeting with Tiberius. But I had to swear my allegiance to her. I will most likely need to leave Rome so I can plead my case to take command of the northern legion directly to Tiberius in Capri. I fear, though, I might be caught in a firestorm, with Antonia's ploys against Sejanus."

Catrin reflected on what Marcellus had said and decided she needed to stay in Rome until Ferrex and Negasi were freed. "Did you speak with Senator Frugi about managing the spring festivals?"

"Yes. Our meeting was tense, though," Marcellus disclosed. "Senator Frugi doesn't know about you, thank the gods, but he voiced his concerns about Eliana."

"Eliana?"

"My affair with her is more widely known than I had realized." Marcellus shook his head, as if he were again regretting his reckless actions with Eliana a few years back. "I had to promise Senator Frugi that I would remain faithful to his daughter. And I had to pledge my allegiance to him. I've told so many lies to cover up the truth about you, I can't keep track of what I've said to everyone."

Catrin pressed her fingertips to Marcellus's head and began massaging it, trying to meld with his thoughts. She sensed something was repressing her ability to commune.

"Why can't I hear your thoughts anymore?" Marcellus asked, as if he knew what she was trying to do. "I felt so close to you when you had this ability in Gaul."

"I don't why," Catrin admitted. "Since my raven flew away after my match with Ferrex in the arena in Lugdunum, I can't connect with the Otherworld as I once could. It is as though a dark force has taken hold of me, and I can't shake it loose."

"What do you mean?"

"When I was enslaved, Decimus stripped away my humanity piece by piece. It was only in the depths of my despair that I could summon the forces of nature to destroy him. But now, that burning hate is melting away whenever I am with you."

"When you secretly met with me in Gaul, you had the ability to transform into a raven. Why would that be different now?"

"I don't feel that rage anymore. I just want to be with you."

"Could you truly be happy as my mistress in Rome? What about your people? What about your destiny?" Marcellus asked pointedly.

The prospect of abandoning those who believed in her claim to the throne—Trystan, Cynwrig, Negasi, Ferrex—gripped at Catrin's heart. The image of Marrock holding the three skulls in her nightmares made her shudder. "You're right. I could never forsake them. But I don't want to lose you, either."

"And I don't want to lose you," Marcellus said quietly. "Let's not think about that now. Let's cherish this moment together."

He turned to Catrin, scooped her up in his arms, and carried her to the dimly lit bedchamber. A candle flame flickered, and a warm breeze swirled around them as he laid her on the bed beside him. She touched his face, and he embraced her. Past memories and future quests dissolved into the present as his hands lovingly caressed her, eliciting the bliss of two souls joining as one. The translucent curtains surrounding the bed waved in synchrony with their ragged breathing throughout the night.

By early morning, the flame had blown out with the night's cool breeze, and they had fallen asleep in each other's arms.

21

SELENA'S SECRET

Rome, 22 March, 28 AD

Catrin awoke that morning without having had the reoccurring dream of Marrock in a dark room drawing flashes of lightning from the skulls of her father, mother, and sister—the bolts zigzagging from the eye sockets. For the first time since her enslavement, she was humming a tune, a glow radiating inside her as she remembered each time Marcellus had taken her last night. The first time, he'd touched her as though he were gently strumming a harp. The second, he'd overpowered her as his hand roamed freely over her body. And the third time was the best. She held her breath, sensing the throbs resonating deep inside her when he'd extended the late night into dawn.

Wrapping her arms around herself, she imagined the pleasure he had elicited. Though they had only lived together as husband and wife for two days, it felt like an eternity that would never end. How many times had he kissed her before reluctantly leaving to start his new position that morning? Five times? Ten times? She closed her eyes and inhaled his intoxicating, musky scent, which was still suffusing the bedchamber. His every breath filled her lungs with new life; his heartbeats still pulsed in her veins.

A whimper from outside drew her out of the daydream. She ambled out of the sultry bedchamber and into the atrium, where the soft beat of raindrops falling from the open roof onto the surface of the pool could be heard. Looking around, she didn't see either Cynwrig or Selena.

Strange, she thought.

Perhaps she had been so focused on Marcellus that she hadn't paid attention to what they said their tasks would be that day. Had they already left to shop at the forum?

Hushed voices emanating from the chamber in which Cynwrig slept at night piqued her curiosity. She tiptoed to the curtain that closed off what was happening in the room and slowly pulled the fabric back to peek in.

Cynwrig was kneeling beside Selena. "Why are you so sad?" he asked her in Celtic.

Neither of them seemed aware of Catrin's presence as he gently pulled a strand of hair away from her eyes. This gentle side was not one Cynwrig often displayed. Catrin recalled the sunny day when she'd seen him give his wife flowers. He'd pulled back a strand of her hair the same way before kissing her. But this appeared to be an awkward moment between the scarred-faced warrior and the dark-skinned attendant. Neither of them could understand each other's language. Instead, their gestures spoke for them.

Not having the heart to interrupt their privacy, Catrin released the heavy curtain from her hand and stepped away. She halted when Cynwrig's voice called, "Catrin. Come in."

She pulled the curtain open to enter and found both of them standing a few feet apart from each other.

"Help me speak to her," Cynwrig requested, keeping his good eye fixed on Selena. "Ask her why she is crying."

Catrin nodded and looked at Selena. "Cynwrig wants to know if you are all right."

Selena's face froze. "Domina, tell him it is nothing."

"Nothing? He won't accept that as an answer."

Selena's eyes lowered, as though she was ashamed. "Please, domina. Tell him I am fine."

"Do you prefer to speak with me alone?" Catrin offered.

"Do I?"

Catrin realized she would have to coax the truth from her. She turned to Cynwrig and commanded, "Leave us. We need to speak alone as women."

Cynwrig regarded Selena, then stared at Catrin. She raised an eyebrow

174 ✿ Linnea Tanner

to emphasize he needed to leave. He slowly walked to the curtained door, glancing back a couple of times before exiting.

After he left the chamber, Catrin said to Selena, "I can see you've been crying. Tell me what has happened."

"It is best I say nothing."

Noting Selena's wide, fearful eyes, Catrin tried to reassure her by saying, "I was once a slave. Whatever you say, I will keep it secret."

"Were you Marcellus's slave?"

"He bought me from another Roman commander and then freed me. As we told you, we married in Britannia. Yet, I suffered at the hands of my first master."

"Did he force himself on you?"

"No. But he hurt me in other ways," Catrin said, cringing from the memory of his rough hands violating her below.

"I must do what my dominus orders. He puts a baby inside me, then forces me to eat an herb to get rid of it. Each time I do this, I bleed, sometimes very heavy. Once, I almost died from losing too much blood. But this time, when I took it"—Selena placed Catrin's hand on her belly—"the baby is still in there. I am afraid of what he could do to me and the baby."

Catrin pressed her palms more firmly against Selena's belly, which felt like a hard ball below her naval. "How far along are you?"

"My last bleeding was before the winter solstice. In November. I told dominus, 'Baby gone.'" Selena choked back a sob. "But it's still in me."

"You have nothing to be ashamed of. You carry the child of a nobleman. The baby is brother or sister to Marcellus."

"In Roman eyes, baby slave just like me—property to be disposed like garbage or sold," Selena said bitterly.

The horror of what Selena had to endure each time she was forced to get rid of her unborn baby tore at Catrin's heart. She knew Marcellus's father had the right to cut the baby out of her womb to get rid of it or to kill it after it was born. A shiver of dread ran down her spine from the prospect that he could do the same to her if she conceived a child with Marcellus.

Catrin's voice trembled. "Do you want the child?"

"No, but it is too late to get rid of it . . . unless . . ." Selena covered her face with both hands. "What am I to do?"

"You will not go back. I will protect you," Catrin said fervently. "Our people would welcome your child as one of their own once we get to Britannia."

"Why would you risk this for me?" Selena asked, tears streaming down her face.

"Because you are more than a man's property. This is a noble child— the brother or sister to Marcellus. Trust me." Catrin handed Selena a linen cloth. "Here. Dry your tears."

Selena wiped her eyes. "Please do not tell Cynwrig."

"He might already suspect. Besides, he needs to guard you with his life," Catrin said, wondering how she should reveal the situation to Marcellus. How could she promise to keep Selena safe when her own life could be jeopardized if Marcellus's father discovered she was still alive? She shrugged off the danger and raised Selena's chin. "Let us get this off our minds. I'll help you shop today for dinner. We can buy something for the baby."

"No, domina. Marcellus will be angry if I do not do my tasks."

"You are not a slave in our home," Catrin said firmly. "We share household duties, do you understand?"

Selena meekly nodded, and her grimace turned into a smile.

"Cynwrig can escort us," Catrin added. "Where do you shop?"

"At the forum."

Catrin stared at the ceiling as doubts about going there flooded her mind. Marcellus was meeting with Senator Frugi at the Basilica Julia to discuss the duties of his new position. What if she bumped into Senator Frugi? Would he recognize her?

"Is it close to the Basilica Julia?" Catrin asked.

"Yes."

"Then we'll need to be careful," Catrin said, taking Selena's arm into hers as they walked from the chamber to the atrium, where Cynwrig was waiting for them.

Catrin felt as though her emotions were waves crashing on a beach and sweeping into a turbulent sea. The danger of the political machinations Marcellus faced hit her in the stomach like a fist. And now this. Selena's revelation that she was with child.

What if I become pregnant with Marcellus?

Why had she thrown out caution whenever she made love with Marcellus? Foremost, she should have a warrior's mien and rein in her emotions. She'd only survived Decimus's brutality because she had confronted each situation with a cool, steady head.

These questions whirled in her mind until Cynwrig broke her thoughts when he asked in Celtic, "Is everything fine?"

"We'll talk about this on our stroll to the forum," Catrin answered. "I want you to guard us as we shop."

"Didn't Marcellus order you to stay here?" Cynwrig asked.

"I don't take orders from him," Catrin snapped. "I am the queen."

Cynwrig lowered his eyes and shuffled his feet, as if chastising himself for openly questioning her.

"What are you two saying?" Selena interjected.

Catrin turned to her and smiled. "I told him we are all shopping today."

With that, they left the domus and walked into the gloom of dark clouds shadowing the city. As they walked through a narrow alley between the two-story buildings, Catrin disclosed the circumstances of Selena's pregnancy to Cynwrig. At first, he was quiet, stone-faced quiet, then his face flushed crimson, and he kicked a loose pebble from the cobblestones.

"That Roman is worse than an animal eating its young! Tell Selena I will marry her."

Not sure she'd heard him correctly, Catrin stopped and looked at him. "What?"

"You heard me. I want her as my wife," Cynwrig said, his one eye fixed on Selena, whose eyebrows were raised in confusion.

Catrin hesitated, not sure how to react to Cynwrig's demand. "Why don't you give her a chance to know you better?"

"My mind is made up."

"Does she not have a choice?"

"She will accept my offer. Ask her."

"Let's wait until we have a private moment at our domus," Catrin advised.

Cynwrig grimaced. "If not now, then when?"

Catrin glared at him. "Careful how you speak to me."

"My apologies," Cynwrig said flatly. "Let me walk behind you and keep guard."

He stepped back and followed Catrin and Selena to a more congested thoroughfare that led to the forum. Remaining quiet, Selena glanced back at Cynwrig a couple of times as they made their way to the storefronts where local farmers had set up their vegetables in carts— cabbages, parsnips, lettuce, asparagus, and onions.

Enticed by the aroma of freshly baked bread, Catrin stopped at a bakery close to the two-tiered, colonnaded Basilica Julia to purchase a small loaf sweetened with honey. She handed a warm piece to Cynwrig, who shoveled it into his mouth. His cheeks puffed out like a squirrel's as he chewed the bread. Selena covered her mouth with two fingertips to hide her amused smile, then took a piece that Catrin offered.

The sun finally broke through the storm clouds, the afternoon growing warmer. Selena helped Catrin select fabric for a tunica, stola, and accessories befitting a noblewoman. They also visited other shops, purchasing a sundry of items for dinner: olives, cabbages, raw oysters, porridge grains, and eggs. The final stop was an open storefront where Catrin bought a plaid, woven blanket for Selena's unborn child. Cynwrig, holding a basket laden with the purchased goods, spoke to the Gallic shopkeeper in the Celtic tongue. With people of all nationalities conversing in various languages, Catrin became distracted, eyeing jewelry in the adjacent storefront.

The crash of a cart toppling on the cobblestones startled Catrin out of the festive atmosphere. She turned around and found Cynwrig wrestling with a man on the ground. Their grappling drew undue attention from a crowd of spectators circling to watch the men wrestle each other on the ground.

Catrin suddenly realized Selena was not at her side. She frantically scanned the area and caught sight of a brawny man with a grip on Selena's arm, pulling her through a growing mob of onlookers on the other side from where Cynwrig was punching the man in the face. Her heart leapt into her throat, spurring her to chase down the abductor. She bulled her way through the spectators but lost sight of Selena.

She turned her focus to Cynwrig, who had been flipped on his back. Recognizing he needed her aid, she rammed through some spectators, then quickly unsheathed the knife from her belt.

One quick thrust into the neck of Cynwrig's opponent abruptly ended the fight. Catrin offered her hand to Cynwrig to help him up.

With fight instincts pulsing through her veins, Catrin brandished her knife as a warning for anyone foolish enough to confront her. Joining her, Cynwrig pulled an axe from beneath his cloak.

Miraculously, the crowd parted like a wave as Catrin and Cynwrig dashed through, swinging their weapons wildly to clear the way.

In front of them was a vegetable cart blocking their way.

Cynwrig forged ahead of Catrin and pushed the cart into two soldiers, whose swords flew out of their hands. He gestured for her to escape through an alley that ran alongside the massive Basilica Julia.

She rushed through the alley, then slowed to merge with a group of worshippers climbing the marble stairs to a massive temple. At the top, she hid behind one of the columns to catch her breath. Hearing ragged breathing behind her, she pivoted on her heels to find Cynwrig, sweat streaming over his sealed eyelid.

"Where is Selena?" he gasped.

"I don't know," Catrin said between pants.

"The soldier at the Red Chariot Inn, he was there with two other men," Cynwrig rasped, bending over.

"What happened?"

"One of them grabbed Selena while another tackled me," Cynwrig said, the wheezing in his heavy breathing easing.

The dangerous implications of what had just happened began to sink into Catrin's mind. "Do you think they followed us from the domus?"

Cynwrig leaned his head against the column in frustration. "All I know is we need to get Selena back, then leave Rome."

Possibilities of where Selena might have been taken raked through Catrin's mind. "Perhaps Marcellus will know where they took her. Let's go back to the domus. We can hide there and wait for him."

22

INVITATION TO DINNER

Rome, 22 March, 28 AD

Marcellus's muscles cramped from sitting so long at the stone top table in the windowless, unheated office that had been temporarily set up for him to greet clients, vendors, and agents at the northern end of the Basilica Julia. The chill in the dank room made his hands stiff as he dipped the tip of a quill pen into black ink, scribbled a message on a piece of papyrus paper, and rolled it up. He pressed his ring signet to imprint his family seal on its edges and handed it to Orvius—the Greek freeman loaned by Senator Frugi to help him make headway in the preparations for the upcoming Ludi Cerealia festivities in late April.

"Give this to Senator Frugi," Marcellus instructed. Noting the assistant's sour expression, Marcellus doubted the Greek had smiled a day in his life. The crowfeet etched at the corners of his eye and a perpetual scowl added to his disagreeable nature. His pale-brown eyes hovered over Marcellus like an eagle monitoring its prey.

"It's almost midafternoon," Orvius said sharply. "He won't likely be there."

"Fine. Deliver the message tomorrow," Marcellus muttered, becoming annoyed. "Make sure you schedule a meeting with Verus. He is a lanista originally from Lugdunum who has set up a new gladiator training center in Rome."

Orvius began to argue, "Senator Frugi works with Numerius—"

"Not this year!" Marcellus cut him off.

"What about the senator's gratuities?"

"He'll still profit from my negotiations," Marcellus assured him. "I've bartered with Verus before in Gaul. He's eager to compete his gladiators in Rome for the first time."

"What about my share?" Orvius demanded.

Marcellus gave Orvius a piercing stare. *Greedy man!*

"Doesn't Senator Frugi pay you for your services?" he snapped.

Not answering, Orvius's glare shot daggers at him. Ignoring the annoying assistant, Marcellus read an invitation from his father to join him for dinner that night. He paused to consider Matron Antonia's advice not to defy him.

"Tell Lucius Antonius I accept his invitation for dinner," Marcellus ordered. Then, he considered stealing an intimate moment with Catrin before attending the event. "But I'll be late."

"Do I have to walk to his household to tell him this?" Orvius asked.

Marcellus jerked his head back. "Yes. Is there a problem?"

"No," Orvius grumbled, slamming a wax tablet on an oval brass table near the entryway and muttering a curse.

Finally fed up with the ill-natured man, Marcellus waved him off. "Leave me now. Deliver the message."

Orvius huffed and stomped out.

Finally enjoying a moment of precious silence without Orvius's whiny voice, Marcellus sat back in his chair. He pressed his hands on the table's edge and rose from his chair. After only one day as a quaestor burdened with administrative tasks, he could feel his muscles complain from inaction. He'd rather take a vigorous ride with Catrin, who was more than his match on horseback, on the Via Apia outside of Rome. He rolled up the invitation from his father and tucked it into his belt. He stretched both arms above his head and inhaled the odor of rat droppings. He chuckled inwardly.

Rome nests all kinds of vermin—rodents and politicians.

Adjusting the toga on his arm, he left the chamber and wove into the throng of people roaming the three-story, roofed hall. Based on the sun's angle in the sky as he exited through the archways, he surmised it was late afternoon. Descending the stairs, he noticed Roman guards pushing shoppers away from a storefront in the forum. With his curiosity piqued, he joined the spectators to determine what was causing the commotion.

Two loin-clothed slaves were carrying a lifeless body through the crowd. Marcellus turned to an elderly woman. "What happened here?"

The woman's pale-gray eyes glinted with excitement as she relayed, "That man was stabbed to death."

"He was in a scrap with a one-eyed brute," a man nearby exclaimed.

Marcellus felt the hairs on his arm prickle. Only one man he knew fit that description. "Did the *Vigiles Urbani* catch the murderer?"

"It was a woman," someone declared.

That was all Marcellus needed to hear. An uneasy feeling gripped the pit of his stomach. He scanned the area for potential spies and then shoved through the crowd to an alleyway he could take to Capitoline Hill instead of the main road.

After reaching his domus, he knocked on the door.

Nobody answered.

He pounded harder. A panel in the door pulled away to reveal Herta's eyes peering through the open slit. The door slowly creaked open so Marcellus could enter. A foreboding shiver crawled down his spine when neither Selena nor Catrin greeted him in the darkened atrium. Most of the oil lamps had been extinguished, and the curtains were drawn across the entranceways of all chambers.

Marcellus asked Herta in a hushed tone, "Where is everyone?"

"In the back. Follow me," Herta replied.

Marcellus trailed the large-framed housekeeper to the garden outside. As they approached the cucina, Marcellus felt his skin crawl with the trepidation that something had happened to Catrin.

Entering the oven-heated cooking area, he found Catrin and Cynwrig coming out of the storage area used for food and cooking vessels. Relieved to see Catrin, he embraced her tightly and inhaled her sweet fragrance. From the corner of his eye, he caught a glimpse of Cynwrig's eyes boring into him.

Unnerved, he released Catrin and asked, "Why are you hiding in here? Has something happened?"

Catrin told him Cynwrig had been attacked at the forum. She emphasized that the disheveled soldier who had confronted Cynwrig at the Red Chariot Inn had kidnapped Selena in the midst of the shoppers. She killed the attacker as Cynwrig wrestled with him on the ground.

Shaking his head, Marcellus tried to digest what she was telling him.

Catrin's voice cracked. "We barely escaped. We could not save Selena."

Marcellus could barely utter, "Sweet Juno," as he grappled with the possible repercussions.

The urgency in Catrin's voice as she said, "Selena is pregnant with your father's child. We have to find her," jolted Marcellus out of his shocked disbelief.

The consequences of Catrin's actions bubbled to the surface. Any hope of them staying together in Rome had vanished in the blink of an eye. He had to help Catrin escape, of course. He was her husband, her soul mate. Yet, in the eyes of Rome, she was a criminal—a truth that cut his heart like broken glass. They no longer controlled their fates. The heat of irrational anger directed at Catrin pulsated in his face. His blazing eyes pierced her.

How could you be so stupid?

"I told you not to leave here!" Marcellus lashed out. "Why did you not stay put?"

The abrupt sound of Cynwrig's footsteps and the sight of his hand reaching for the hilt of his sheathed dagger alarmed Marcellus. Catrin blocked Cynwrig and spoke to him with a calm voice in Celtic. Even so, the one-eyed warrior glared, leaving no doubt what he would do if Marcellus dared rebuke his queen again.

"Tell your man to stand down," Marcellus demanded.

"I already have," Catrin said firmly.

Struggling to temper his voice and compose himself, Marcellus said, "Don't you understand? You have to leave Rome. Now! They will hunt you both down and crucify you."

Catrin blew out a deep breath. "What about Selena?"

Frustrated Catrin didn't seem to understand the futility in Selena's predicament, he explained, "She's most likely been taken by one of my father's men. Or Brutius's men, gods forbid. They'll torture her until she tells them everything she knows about me. They will find out about you and where we are staying. If the authorities don't find you first, my family will. Either way, you will be killed."

"I understand the risks, Marcellus. But Cynwrig won't leave without Selena." Catrin stepped up to Marcellus. "And neither will I."

"Catrin, you can't save her. Be reasonable. Let me help you escape."

"Can't you confront your father about Selena? Tell him you want her back."

"He is the paterfamilias. If pushed, he has the right to kill me."

"Give him something else he wants in exchange," Catrin suggested in a softer tone.

"He wants my total obedience and my promise to marry Licinia. Is that what you want?"

"If it will save her, then give it to him. I now know it was a fool's journey for me to come here. Only I can confront Marrock. Not you," Catrin said adamantly.

The hard reality that Marcellus could lose her trust and love again tore at his heart. He couldn't think clearly, grasping for ways to stay with Catrin. He could still free Ferrex and Negasi. His plan to request command of the northern legion could still succeed. He thought back to his time in the legion and the lessons he'd learned. In war, you must sometimes retreat from battle to regroup for conquest.

Marcellus closed his eyes and sighed deeply. They could not be together in Rome. Not now. But perhaps in Gaul.

Finally, he conceded to helping Catrin—the ruler over his heart. "I'll try to find Selena, but she could be held anywhere. Possibly at my father's home. More likely, she's at Brutius's villa just outside of Rome. It is rumored he keeps slaves there to sell to Tiberius."

"Take us there," Catrin said. "I could meld with a rodent's mind and search for Selena in the villa."

Marcellus had witnessed Catrin enter the mind of a raven or shape-shift into its form, but he had not considered her ability to use her magical powers with other animals until now. "And if you see her?"

"We'll find a way to rescue her," Catrin proposed.

An idea seeded in Marcellus's mind. "I have a plan that might work. I have an invitation from my father to dine with him tonight. I'll send a courier to Brutius's villa with an urgent message that our father has summoned him also. He'll run to my father like the trained dog he is. He'll probably have his bodyguard, Adonis, with him and leave his villa unprotected. If you can find a way to sneak in and get Selena out of there, do it. But make sure you do this so nobody sees you."

Catrin turned to Cynwrig and spoke to him in Celtic excitedly. The one-eyed warrior seemed to relax and pulled his hand away from his weapon.

Catrin smiled at Marcellus. "We will make this work."

"I'll have my horse trainer, Falco, stay with you," Marcellus said, grasping for a quick plan for them to escape. "While I'm at my father's home, Falco can show you the way to Ostia. There, you can take a ship back to Massilia in Gaul. I can't leave with you, though. My family will trail me like bloodhounds. I'll risk your life if I try to contact you. I'll give you all the coins I have to pay for passage."

"Oh, Marcellus." Catrin embraced him. "Will we ever see each other again in Gaul?"

Marcellus hesitated, his heart almost stopping with the thought that they could both be caught. He erased that prospect from his mind as another plan began to take form.

"Go to Lugdunum. I'll write a message ordering the steward to house you at my family's farm. Falco can deliver the message to emphasize the importance. Wait for me there."

Catrin pulled away from Marcellus. "When will you be able to come?"

"It could be a few months . . . possibly a year. However long it takes for everything to settle down in Rome. It will give me time to free your gladiators. I will convince Tiberius to give me command of the northern legion in Gaul. And together, you and I, we will destroy Marrock. Do you trust me?"

"I trust you, Marcellus." Catrin paused and averted her eyes from his gaze. "What if Tiberius doesn't agree?"

"He will," Marcellus said, conviction in his voice. "We must make this work, Catrin. There is no other choice. Go, arm yourself and get ready."

While Catrin and Cynwrig armed themselves and gathered some supplies, Marcellus went to his bedchamber to don his military attire: a knee-length red tunic, braccae, and a weapons belt. He retrieved all the coins he had hidden in a locked metal box and placed them into a leather pouch he attached to his belt. Taking the risk that Brutius would believe his father's summons was written by a scribe, Marcellus carefully wrote on a piece of parchment:

I urgently summon you to meet me at my villa tonight to speak about a delicate matter concerning your half brother, Marcellus. —Lucius Antonius

After rolling the parchment into a scroll, he pressed his signet ring into the melted wax to imprint the family seal.

Marcellus met everyone at the back of the garden, where they could escape over the wall into the alley, in case spies had positioned themselves near the front entrance. Their biggest challenge, he realized, was to hoist Herta, who could barely walk on her elephantine legs, over the seven-foot wall. He clasped hands with Cynwrig for Herta to step on. At the count of three, they boosted her up. Herta managed to get her arms over the wall, but she looked like a turtle flailing her legs to flip her body over the ledge.

Cynwrig boosted Marcellus up so he could get on the other side of the wall. At the count of three again, Cynwrig pushed Herta's legs up with his shoulders as Marcellus pulled her down by her arms. Their efforts finally succeeding, Marcellus took all of Herta's weight when she toppled on him.

Momentarily dazed, Marcellus saw brightly colored dots dancing before his eyes. When Cynwrig and Catrin, who were hovering over him, both came into focus, the lung-squeezing mass lifted off him. Cynwrig offered his hand to Marcellus to help him up.

They made slow progress down the alley to the main road. Even with the short distance, Herta's breathing was ragged, and she lumbered at the pace of a tortoise. They didn't have time to dawdle, so Marcellus made the decision to give Herta enough money to stay at a local inn until he could contact her the next day.

The three rushed to the horse stables near the Circus Maximus, where Marcellus instructed Falco to saddle horses and accompany them. On the way to Brutius's villa, Marcellus instructed Falco to cloak his head and serve as a courier to give Brutius the false message.

Marcellus trusted Falco implicitly to carry out his orders, but he prayed Brutius would take the bait and immediately ride with Adonis to their father's villa.

There, he would be waiting for them.

After that, he would throw his fate to the wind when he confronted them about Selena.

23

TRUTH BY TORTURE

Brutius's Villa, Rome, 22 March, 28 AD

Hearing footsteps from the vestibule, Brutius turned to find Adonis escorting Gaius Septimus into the atrium. He was taken aback when he recognized the slave in their custody as his father's.

"Urgent news from Legionary Gaius Septimus," Adonis announced as he gestured to the retired legionary. Unlike before, Gaius was clean-shaven, and his hair was freshly shorn. It was a relief the soldier had dressed in a fresh, gray tunic and didn't stink like a public latrine.

Brutius conveyed with his eyes for Adonis to stay as he greeted, "*Salve,* Gaius. What do we have here?"

Gaius's eyes appeared to dance with delight. "I thought this slave might interest you. I found her with the one-eyed Celtic warrior I told you about."

Brutius clenched his fingertips around the slave's jaw and pulled her face toward his. "My father misses you in his bed. You know what happens to runaway slaves, don't you?"

Selena's lips began to quiver. "I didn't run away."

"Then why are you here?"

Selena's almond-brown eyes went blank, as if fear had immobilized her.

Brutius tightened his grip around her jaw. "No answer. Perhaps if I crucify you?"

"Please . . . I beg—"

"You beg for my mercy." Brutius cut off her words like a sword. "Why would I do that?"

Tears welled in the slave's eyes as Brutius dug his fingernails into

Selena's face, her pained grimace arousing him—raw emotions of what a lion must feel before a kill surging through his veins.

Be patient, he reminded himself.

Don't lose control.

Not yet.

Brutius's upper lip curled as he ordered, "Adonis, punish this slave in the stalls while I talk with Gaius."

Adonis clenched her arm.

"Have mercy. Have mercy," Selena cried out as he yanked her to the back of the atrium, where her pleas faded when Brutius stepped into the peristyle with Gaius.

"Where did you find my father's slave?" Brutius asked.

"At the forum," Gaius said. "She was shopping with the one-eyed warrior."

"Was anyone else with them?"

Gaius scratched his head. "Not that I'm aware. While I was waiting for Marcellus to leave the Basilica Julia, I had guards positioned at the top of the stairs to signal me when they spotted them. I noticed the one-eyed warrior holding a basket into which the dark-skinned woman was placing items."

"Did anyone follow Marcellus when he left?"

"Uh . . . no," Gaius stammered.

"Careless of you, don't you think?" Brutius said sharply. "Tell me what happened, then."

"I ordered one of my men to block the Celtic warrior so I could abduct the woman for questioning. I handed her off to another guard so I could also seize the warrior for interrogation. But"—Gaius swallowed hard—"my man was killed."

"The one-eyed man killed him?" Brutius inquired.

"No. A woman from the crowd."

"A woman? Did you get a clear view of her?"

"I caught a glimpse of her through the crowd. She knew how to use her weapon."

Brutius's heartbeats quickened as he recalled the tales of a warrior sorceress seducing Marcellus in Britannia. "Did you recognize her as Vibius from Gaul?"

"It could be . . . she was fair-haired. But it was hard to see her clearly," Gaius answered.

Brutius clenched his hands. "Idiot! Always excuses. You didn't follow Marcellus. You didn't capture the one-eyed fighter. And you didn't recognize the mystery woman!"

Gaius nervously shifted his feet. "But we have your father's slave. We could torture her for the truth."

"Imbecile, I know that! That is why Adonis has taken her to my torture chamber in the back."

"Sir, I didn't mean to insult you. I just thought you'd be pleased we apprehended her to get the information you want."

"Let me do the thinking," Brutius snapped. "I need to know as much information about Marcellus as possible to put into my arsenal of tricks as I torture her. Have you learned anything else?"

"Yesterday, Marcellus visited Matron Antonia's villa before meeting with Senator Frugi," Gaius revealed.

"Matron Antonia? Curious."

"That is what I thought," Gaius said. "Give me another chance to find out more about where Marcellus is staying and why he visited the matron."

Brutius rubbed his chin, wondering if Marcellus was scheming to discredit him with the influence of the imperial matriarch. It was no secret she believed Sejanus was a threat to her grandsons' claims to the throne. What if there was a conspiracy between Marcellus and Matron Antonia to target him because of his allegiance to Sejanus?

I must strike him first, Brutius vowed.

Gaius's voice pleading, "Give me another chance," jolted Brutius out of his troubled thoughts. He gave the soldier a hard stare. "You have but one chance. Don't fail me again."

Gaius blew out a deep breath. "I will not fail you."

"Now show yourself out."

After Gaius left, Brutius strode to the back of the atrium and stepped onto the pebbled pathway in the peristyle. Images of the pain he could inflict on Selena—branding her with a hot iron, lashing her until her skin peeled off, cutting pieces of her face away, watching Adonis ravish her— flashed in his head, eliciting salacious euphoria. Still, she was his father's property. His father had the right to beat her to death, but if he spoiled her beauty, that would devalue her as property.

Take this as a challenge, he told himself, *to extract the truth. There are other ways to inflict pain without damaging the goods.*

Brutius, finally reaching the end of the narrow pathway to the enclosed stable, unlatched the wooden door to enter. Inside, he found Adonis with Selena, whose stare froze on him like a rabbit caught in a snare as he entered the structure. He gave her a wicked smile and then perused the instruments of torture on the wood plank walls: skewers, knives, clamps, branding irons, hooks, whips, braided cords, pincers, and mallets.

"Selena. Is that what my father called you?" he asked evenly.

After selecting a thin knife with a serpent handle, Brutius slowly stepped toward Selena as Adonis restrained her arms from the back. With sadistic glee, he waved the blade before her fearful eyes. She lowered her gaze like a helpless doe cornered by a bloodthirsty wolf.

"Oh," Brutius chuckled. "Has father used this on you before?" With the palm of his unarmed hand, he brushed her face, which shimmered like a black diamond in the illumination of a sconced torch on the wall. Breathing in her jasmine scent, he whispered, "Such beautiful skin."

Every muscle on Selena's face tensed as he softly caressed her skin, triggering a perverse pleasure inside him. One he preferred with men. He lowered his forefinger and rubbed her thick, wet lips.

"I can feel you tremble under my touch." He licked his fingertip and moaned. "Luscious."

Sensing her repulsion, Brutius stepped back and gave her an evil smile. "My bodyguard is skilled with the tools of torture on the wall. It would be a pity to mar your beauty. Besides, my father would not be pleased." He paused, relishing the terror in her eyes. "Why don't we forego the torture? All you need to do is answer my questions truthfully."

He looked at Adonis. "Shackle the slave against the wall."

As Adonis manacled Selena's wrists and ankles, Brutius thinly sliced his thumb with the razor-sharp blade of the serpent-handled dagger. When the blood dribbled from the cut, he bit his lower lip as he smeared a crimson line across Selena's forehead.

"Tell me, where do you stay with Marcellus at night?" he demanded.

Selena's voice cracked. "I don't know."

Brutius raised the blood-tinged blade before her face. "You don't know?"

Selena's eyes widened. "It's a different place each night."

Brutius noticed she was as motionless as a rock as she answered his questions. *Is it from fear? Or deception?*

"Besides you," he continued, "who else stays with Marcellus?"

"No one," Selena said, her voice shaking.

"Selena, you aren't lying to me, are you?" Brutius said evenly, though he felt the rapid heartbeats in his neck increase with the anticipation of luring Selena into his web. "We know about the one-eyed warrior. And we know about his foreign mistress."

Brutius's ears perked up after Selena gasped—so slightly but loud enough to know he was stripping away at Marcellus's secret. He sliced through one of the tunic strips to reveal her bare shoulder. Stroking the base of her neck, he felt her cringe as his fingertips wiped warm sweat from her skin. He stepped back and handed the knife to Adonis, then picked up a linen cloth to wipe the slave's musky odor from his hand.

"It's quite simple, Selena," Brutius pressed on. "You need only confirm what I already know. Does Marcellus bed you at night?"

Selena slightly shook her head.

"Does he have a mistress for that?"

"I don't know," she whispered.

Brutius paused, paced back and forth, and then lifted Selena's chin, noting the sweat beading on her forehead. "Reconsider your answer. Adonis takes pleasure in hurting slaves who lie. He can rearrange a woman's in-sides until she screams and screams for mercy."

Selena kept her eyes fixed on Brutius, her lips pursed, as if she was resolved to remain silent. Yet, her trembling body betrayed her terror.

"You want to remain loyal to Marcellus, don't you?" Brutius said evenly. "He helped you escape my father's brutality, didn't he?"

"I'm doomed no matter what I say," Selena uttered.

"Perhaps so. Or perhaps not." Brutius cupped Selena's face between his hands like a lover. "You have no choice but to beg for my mercy."

Selena jerked her head forward and spat in his face.

Shocked, Brutius wiped the vile sputum from his eyes. Then, anger struck him like a viper, and his rage uncoiled. He backhanded her across the face so hard she fell limp, unconscious, only the shackles holding her up.

"Throw water on that fucking bitch!" Brutius roared.

Adonis rushed out of the stable and returned with a bucket brimming with water. After he threw the water on Selena's face, she gasped for air and spurted water from her mouth. When she opened her eyes, Brutius pressed the tip of his dagger against her brow until blood dribbled down her nose.

"If you spit at me again, I'll cut out both your eyes and hang them over your neck," Brutius threatened. "You have but one chance to save yourself. Tell me where Marcellus keeps his sorceress whore."

Selena pressed her lips into a firm line.

"Tell me!" Brutius yelled in her face. "Or I'll unleash Adonis on you."

Streaming tears coated Selena's face as she stared at Adonis, who removed his loincloth to reveal his erection. Brutius admired the ridged scars etched on the ex-gladiator's massive chest and back—tokens earned from his conquests in the games. In private moments together, when they were entwined in each other's legs, Brutius had counted twenty-one tattoos covering his lover from head to toe.

"Such awesome size," Brutius remarked with admiration. "After he's done with you, I'll poke you inside with rods and skewers."

As Adonis approached Selena, Brutius turned his back to retrieve a skewer but halted when he heard Selena cry out, "Please don't! Don't do this! Everything you've said is true! Marcellus is married to a foreigner."

Clasping a foot-long skewer, Brutius felt a smile twisting on his face as he turned and waved Adonis away.

"Good girl."

"You . . . you won't hurt me, will you?" Selena pleaded between sobs.

"No. Not as long as you tell me the whole truth," Brutius said evenly, even though his blood boiled from the indignation of this bitch spitting in his face—an assault on his integrity as a Roman aristocrat.

A man's husky voice announcing, "There is a courier at the entrance," interrupted Brutius's plan to teach the bitch a lesson. Turning, he found his guard—an ex-gladiator charged with overseeing the handpicked slaves for Tiberius—standing in the doorway.

"I'm busy here," Brutius grumbled. "Can't my steward take the message?"

"The courier insists he gives you the summons from your father directly," the guard replied.

Taken aback, Brutius handed the skewer to Adonis. "Dig out as much information as you can from her."

Shrieks split the early evening silence as Brutius walked through the garden fragranced with jasmine to the atrium.

24

ESCAPE

Brutius's Villa, Rome, 22 March, 28 AD

The plan was set into motion. Falco was at the entrance of Brutius's villa, waiting to deliver the false message to Brutius. Marcellus had ridden off to his father's home with the hope that Brutius would take the bait and ride there with Adonis. Cynwrig and Falco were next to Catrin, on the hilltop overlooking the villa, as she scanned the area for a small animal that could easily enter undetected as soon as Brutius opened the door to take the summons.

Since Catrin's last gladiatorial contest in Lugdunum, at which time she had summoned lightning from the sky to destroy Decimus in the stands, she had hesitated to use her druidic powers. The ramifications of using these forces were unpredictable. She had decided it was too risky to shape-shift into an animal's form. Previously, she had lost consciousness during the transition from one form to another and often felt drained afterward, both physically and mentally. Seeing through the eyes of a small animal might be easier, though she had only previously done so with a raven.

She had difficulty concentrating, a sudden sadness weighing her heart down as she worried that Marcellus's farewell kiss could be their last. Struggling to rein in the shroud of gloom, she spotted a yellow-necked mouse scampering nearby. She focused her eyes on the rodent. Her thoughts floated in and out of the creature's mind until, finally, a flash of light blinded her—a signal she had entered its mind. Seeing through the mouse's eyes disoriented her at first. She had anticipated that a mouse would have sharp visual acuity, but everything was a blur around her. The wooded landscape appeared as black shadows with hues of blue and purple. Even so, her other senses were heightened. Various odors of moss, pine needles, and urine assaulted her nostrils. Any light touch on her whiskers and fur, she discovered, helped orient her to her immediate surroundings. She directed the mouse to jump on its hind legs and squeak to alert Falco and Cynwrig that she had successfully entered the rodent's mind. She saw her human form leaning against a tree, motionless as a corpse. As long as she was in the mouse's mind, she knew her human form would be vulnerable. There was no time to practice the mouse's movements. She had to scurry now!

Catrin leapt from rock to rock until she felt the cobblestone beneath her paws. Seeing only the shadow of the villa straight ahead, she scurried on the open road, despite her instincts to hide. Finally, she saw a bleary human figure and surmised it was Falco. Her heart jumped into her throat when she saw the door closing. With a burst of speed, she slid through the narrow opening before the door slammed.

She heard a man shout, "What just came in?" Then, she ran close to the vestibule's wall, the touch on her whiskers helping her to maneuver down the hallway to the main quarters. Though her vision was blurry, she could look in different directions for a housecat that might pounce on her.

Scrambling from chamber to chamber on the side of the atrium, she searched for Selena. Most of the rooms were empty except for a handful of slaves scrubbing the floors. Near the back of the atrium, she heard footsteps and a man yelling, "Get my horse ready."

Catrin's heart raced with anticipation that Brutius had taken the bait.

Staying in the shadows along the wall, she sniffed at the man's slight urine odor and followed him outside into the colonnaded peristyle. Gut-wrenching screams from the far end of the central garden blasted into her ears. She felt the mouse's rapid heartbeats roll like a drum as she scurried behind the man's sandaled feet through the garden. Her paws hurt from pounding on the sharp, pebbled pathway as she tried to keep up. The man halted in front of what looked like an enclosed stall. In the adjacent corral were two skittish horses prancing back and forth, snorting. To her right, she glimpsed a shadowy man's figure coming out of a back room onto the portico. A blurry stableman pulling the reins of a horse came into her right eye's view.

"Is Adonis going with you?" the man standing under the peristyle's roof called out.

"No. You can be my escort," the sandaled man, whom Catrin surmised to be Brutius, replied. "Adonis is busy punishing a slave."

"Who will transport the slaves tomorrow?"

"Gaius will transport them by wagon to Capri. I may need to stay the night at my father's house."

The sound of the stall unlatching drew Catrin's attention. She turned and saw the shadowy figure of a woman against the wall through a doorway. Liquid was flowing down her legs. Unable to discern the red color, she nonetheless smelled the metallic odor of blood. The pit of her stomach dropped like an executioner's axe. She closely watched the two fuzzy men, astride their horses, riding through an open gateway. After they left, the stableman latched it shut.

With the urgency to save Selena, Catrin forced herself out of the mouse's mind. A flash later, she found herself in her human body, but she felt woozy from the quick transition.

"What did you see?" Cynwrig asked, lifting her to a sitting position with his powerful arms.

Trying to clear her head, Catrin said, "Selena is in there."

"Where, exactly?" Falco asked in Celtic.

"At the back of the villa. In an enclosed stall," Catrin answered.

"Is there a way we can get in?" Cynwrig asked.

"A gate at the back. But it's latched," Catrin said, picturing what she had seen through the mouse's eye.

"Any guards?" Falco asked.

"One guard, for sure. A handful of house slaves." Catrin closed her eyes, trying to recall what the guard had said about other slaves. "There may be others I didn't see that are to be transported tomorrow."

"I'll boost you over the wall," Cynwrig told Catrin, "so you can let Falco and me in. Everyone ready?"

198 ☼ Linnea Tanner

Catrin and Falco nodded.

In the shadows of the tree, they furtively descended the hilltop to the back of the villa. When they reached the wood-spiked gate, Cynwrig clasped his hands together to boost Catrin up the wall. Gripping the wooden spikes, she swung her legs upward as she pulled herself up over the top and jumped off, her feet pounding on the ground.

Screams split the twilight's silence.

Panic gripping her chest, Catrin quickly unlatched the gate. Cynwrig and Falco quietly rushed through the opening and joined her. She pointed to the stall from where the tortured screams were emanating.

Cynwrig kicked the door open to reveal a naked, heavily tattooed man thrusting into a woman from the back, grunting like a wild animal devouring its prey. Only the wrist shackles kept Selena upright as the force of his weight jerked her violently.

The broad-shouldered man glanced back and quickly pulled away from Selena, pushing her face into the wall. Before he could fetch a weapon from the wall, Cynwrig's iron fist punched into his face with a horrific, bone-cracking crunch. The blow hardly stunned the bull of a man.

Catrin, unsheathing her *gladius*, burst through the open doorway to assist Cynwrig. She lunged and thrust her blade at the man's heart. He stepped back, the tip nicking him in the chest. With his back against the wall, he reached back with one hand and retrieved a spear. He thrust the weapon's tip at her head. She leaned back, the sharp tip barely missing its target.

Falco, at her back, cramped Catrin's mobility. One-eyed Cynwrig, to her right, was blinded in the left eye.

Three on one seemed like favorable odds. But the tattooed man skillfully jabbed his spear back and forth between Catrin and Cynwrig, keeping them off-balance.

Anticipating their opponent's maneuvers, Catrin barked in Celtic, "Falco, defend the doorway. Cynwrig, to my left."

She readied herself for their opponent's next strike, keeping her legs slightly apart and bent. Cynwrig and Falco whirled around her like dancers.

The tattooed man thrust his spear as quick as a lightning bolt, but she blocked it with her sword blade.

Cynwrig leapt and clasped the wooden shaft of the man's spear with both hands. Each of them gripped the spear with both hands and pulled, grunting, struggling to overpower the other.

Taking advantage of the deadlock, Catrin swept around the two men and sliced her blade across the back of their tattooed opponent.

But that did not stop the bull. Eyes ablaze with rage, he overpowered Cynwrig and threw him back. He pivoted, clasping the spear's shaft with both hands to block her blade with it, then surprised Catrin with a headbutt.

Dazed, she found herself flat on her back, stars dancing before her eyes. Just as her head was clearing, she felt a sharp, metal tip press into her chest the same instant she saw a battle-axe above her cleave off the man's head.

The headless body crumpled onto her, reawakening her senses to the danger. She frantically struggled to push the bleeding mass off her. The weight suddenly lifted from her chest, and Cynwrig appeared overhead, offering his hand. Taking it, she pulled herself up and quickly assessed the situation.

Outside the open doorway, Falco was fighting for his life with another burly guard. She spotted the spear lying on the straw-covered floor and ordered Cynwrig, "Look after Selena."

Taking the spear on the ground, she gripped it and rushed outside to assist Falco.

"What do we have here?" the gigantic guard growled as he thrust his sword, which Falco countered with his.

"Move away," Catrin ordered Falco in Celtic. He dropped to the ground and rolled on his shoulders, giving Catrin a clean shot at their opponent. She hurled the spear like a catapult. The metal tip rammed through the man's throat and exited out the back side of the neck. Blood spurted everywhere as the massive body toppled backward.

Hearing a faint gurgling sound, Catrin pushed the motionless body with her foot for any signs of life. The fingers clasping his throat twitched erratically as a crimson pool spread out from under his head.

Falco jumped to his feet and joined Catrin at her back, brandishing his sword. He said in a hushed tone, "See movement near the columns?"

She discerned a shadowy figure moving behind a column under the portico roof. A woman's voice called out, "Please don't hurt us."

"Are any guards with you?" Catrin demanded.

"Only household slaves are left."

"Come closer with a torch so I can see you," Catrin ordered, warily scanning the area for other figures.

The woman stepped away from the column with a burning torch in hand. As she approached Catrin, her olive face came into focus in the illumination of the torch flame. Dark eyebrows arched over her predominate feature, a bulbous nose that looked like it had been broken. She dropped her gaze to the slain guard.

"I am called Gabriella," she introduced herself, her voice nasal. "I supervise the housekeeping slaves. What do you want here? Coins? Jewels?"

"We've only come for the slave called Selena. Nothing else," Catrin replied.

Gabriella crouched and waved the torch over the body. The corpse's glassy eyes were open wide in a frozen stare. His hands were clasped around the shaft where it had entered his throat.

"Did you kill the Greek gladiator, Adonis?" Gabriella asked.

"The guard in the torture chamber?"

"Yes. That one."

"My man killed him. He's in there with Selena now."

Gabriella looked at Catrin with fear in her eyes. "You might as well take us, too. All surviving slaves will be condemned for the murder of these men."

The consequences of what would happen to the remaining slaves in the villa slowly dawned on Catrin. Roman justice was one-sided, with no mercy for human property. She put her hand on Gabriella's shoulder and offered, "You can go with us."

"What are you doing?" Falco argued. "You can't take—"

"I will take any slave who wants to escape with us," Catrin interrupted. She turned to Gabriella and asked, "How many other slaves are here?"

"Six serve the dominus. A stableman. About fifteen slaves chained in the back chambers," Gabrielle answered.

"Is there a latchkey to unlock the chains?" Catrin asked.

Gabriella handed the torch to Catrin. "Take this while I search the body." She fingered around the belt until she retrieved a latchkey.

Catrin and Falco followed Gabriella into a dimly lit chamber where six loin-clothed boys were chained together. After Gabriella unlocked the chain from each ankle shackle, Catrin inspected each boy, ranging in age from seven to twelve years old. Though they were slim, their muscles were toned, and their backs did not show any signs of scarring from lashings.

In the adjoining room, they found five naked, prepubescent girls, each chained to the wall. Seeing the fear in the girls' eyes as Falco knelt down to unchain them, Catrin told him to leave and watch over the boys. Gabriella helped Catrin unlock the manacles around each girl's ankle. Their eyes were glazed as Catrin inspected them. The sight of their bruised bodies and blood-smeared inner thighs—signs of recent rape—made Catrin's skin crawl. Flashbacks of Decimus stripping her in front of the male gladiators assaulted her mind. He'd harshly thrust his fingers inside her, threatening to have each gladiator rape her if she ever lost in the games. What he did to her was as degrading as rape—an assault on her body and soul.

This is what a Roman is. Cruel. Heartless. Demeaning.

Yet, she had given her heart to a Roman. Had she deluded herself into thinking he was not like other Roman men?

The burning rage she suddenly felt for Marcellus shook her to the core. This was the same hate she had felt for him to help her survive as a slave. She had to remind herself that Marcellus was different than his half brother, than his father. Quickly casting away her doubts about her Roman husband, she focused on saving the slaves in the villa. Clenching her trembling hands, she vowed to rescue every slave in the villa. She turned to Gabriella and ordered her to find garments for the girls. Meanwhile, she would check on Cynwrig and Selena.

In the stall, Catrin choked back sobs when she found Cynwrig cradling Selena's blood-soaked body in his powerful arms. He looked at her with a misty eye, as if seeking her assistance.

"Lay her down so I can treat her," Catrin said.

Cynwrig gently set Selena down on the straw-covered floor. Catrin knelt beside Selena's motionless body and pressed her fingers against her neck for a pulse. It was stronger than she had anticipated. Yet, her face was pale, and some of her wounds were still bleeding.

"It looks like she was lashed and cut with a knife," Catrin commented, noting only pieces of cloth clinging to her body. Afraid Selena might have miscarried during the ordeal, Catrin checked between her legs. There was bleeding, most likely from the tattooed man's rough, forced entry, but no large blood clots. Noticing a fair-haired slave peeking around the door-jamb, she ordered for her to fetch some clean water, vinegar, and fresh linen.

After the slave returned with the supplies, Catrin inspected Selena's body for open wounds, rinsing the blood away with vinegary water. The most serious cut was on Selena's left shoulder. Catrin pressed down hard with a piece of linen until the fabric was saturated with blood, then replaced it with another and pressed down even harder. A piece of skin flapping from Selena's cheekbone needed stitching, but there was no time. They needed to escape before Brutius returned and discovered the carnage.

Unfortunately, their escape would be complicated by Selena's injuries and the walking time it would take for the villa's slaves to travel to Ostia for boarding ships to Gaul. Yet, she had no choice. She would be damned by the Mother Goddess for leaving innocent people to be lashed and crucified.

After finishing treating Selena, Catrin told Cynwrig, "Cover her with your cloak and let her ride your horse. We're taking the remaining slaves with us."

"But they'll slow us down," he argued.

"They are witnesses and will be tortured and killed. Is that what you want?"

Cynwrig rolled his eyes in exasperation. "Hurry, then. I'll finish in here."

Catrin gathered all of the surviving slaves in the garden, including the stableman, and enjoined them to leave with her. Though a couple of the slaves protested, she said bluntly, "You have but two choices. Stay and be condemned as a criminal to die. Or escape for a chance to live."

Though there was still grumbling, all of them ultimately chose to escape. Falco helped them pack food, belongings, jewelry, and coins from the villa into satchels for their journey.

Catrin, realizing Cynwrig had not yet joined them in the garden, went into the stall to fetch him. To her shock, she was greeted with the spiked head of the tattooed guard on the wall. Stuffed into his mouth were the castrated parts that had ravaged Selena. Though she could understand Cynwrig's need for vengeance, a chill spliced down her spine, and she worried the act would beget more vengeance.

"We need to go," Catrin urged the one-eyed warrior, who seemed to be in a trance.

Tears filled his eye as he nodded his acknowledgement of her order. He gently picked up Selena as he would a child, cradling her head next to his shoulder, and whispered to her in Latin, "No one will hurt you again."

With that, they began their twenty-mile journey, under the cover of trees and night skies shrouding the landscape alongside the main cobblestone road to Ostia.

25

MOTHER'S WARNING

Antonii Villa, Rome, 22 March, 28 AD

Marcellus warily rode his horse to the front entrance of his father's domus. It felt as if he were going into battle blind, not knowing his enemies' strategy for attack. The political game of outmaneuvering his opponents behind battle lines was more disconcerting than fighting his foes in open warfare.

Questions tumbled in his mind about Selena's kidnapping. Had Brutius and their father joined forces to get her back? Was it possible Senator Frugi was part of his family's plot to kidnap Selena?

Am I overthinking this?

The only person who wanted Selena back was his father, whose pride Marcellus had pricked by stealing her. Doubts began gnawing at him about his decision to leave Catrin, Cynwrig, and Falco behind at the villa without first determining whether Brutius had taken the bait to meet their father that evening. What would Catrin do if she discovered Selena was in the villa?

Feeling queasy from the uncertainty of the situation, Marcellus tasted bile in his mouth. He looked all around, then jumped off the night-black stallion he used for chariot racing. Holding the reins in one hand, he clapped the lion-headed knocker with the other.

A wooden panel on the door slid open to reveal the steward's beady, acorn-brown eyes. "Why are you armed?" he asked, his voice quavering.

"Tell my father I want to speak with him. Out here," Marcellus demanded.

"I don't understand," Linos muttered. "You were invited to dinner, not a battle."

"You heard me," Marcellus said, raising his voice. "I want to speak with Father. Now!"

The panel clicked shut. A few moments later, Lucius stomped out, attired in his senatorial, purple-striped toga. His thick eyebrows furled together as his hard stare shifted to Marcellus's belted *gladius*.

"What is this?" Lucius asked, a sharp bite to his voice. "I invited you to dinner to settle our differences, and here you are, armed for war."

Marcellus responded likewise. "Resolve our differences? Explain this, then. Why was my bodyguard attacked and Selena kidnapped at the forum today?"

"What?"

"You heard me," Marcellus growled.

"Are you accusing me?" Lucius shook his head in disbelief. "Ridiculous. I was home all day."

Marcellus's mother momentarily broke the tension by shrilly inquiring, "Lucius, what's wrong?"

Lucius turned to his wife, who was standing in the doorway. "We'll be in soon. Wait for us inside."

Drusilla grimaced. "Why have you raised your voices?"

"Go inside. Now!" Lucius barked.

The door slammed shut, and sobs could be heard from inside the villa.

"Look what you've done," Lucius chided. "Do you plan to use that weapon on me and make your mother a widow?"

Marcellus felt a tinge of regret that he had alarmed his mother. Nonetheless, he met his father's hard stare and said bluntly, "What am I to think? You've had me followed since I left your house."

"Of course, I had you followed. What did you expect?" Lucius huffed, his face turning red, his eyes ablaze. "You stole my favorite slave and stormed out of my house. And you didn't have the stones to talk with me man-to-man to settle your grievance. What bothers me most, though, is that you went behind my back, speaking with Matron Antonia."

Marcellus jerked his head back. "Who told you this? Your spies?"

"You impudent ass!" Lucius rebuked. "Matron Antonia visited me this afternoon, pleading for me to postpone your wedding. That is why I invited you to dinner, to find out what you told her."

Marcellus rubbed his brow, reconsidering whether he had jumped to the wrong conclusion about his father kidnapping Selena. Before he could reply to his father, Brutius approached them on horseback. Strangely, Adonis was not with Brutius. Rather, another barrel-chested man with chestnut hair, whom Marcellus didn't recognize, was escorting his half brother.

Lucius gave Brutius a bewildered look. "Why are you here?"

Brutius's stare shifted from Marcellus to Lucius. "Didn't you summon me?"

"I summoned you on behalf of Father," Marcellus chimed in. "Did you take Selena?"

Brutius smirked and replied evenly, "Yes, I did."

The sight of Brutius's bulging, insect eyes lighting up with cruel joy enraged Marcellus. He dropped his horse's reins and stomped toward his half brother with the intent of unhorsing him.

Lucius interceded, blocking Marcellus with both arms as he ordered, "Brutius, get off your horse and explain yourself."

Brutius gingerly climbed off his horse and stumbled on the cobblestone roadway. He straightened his shoulders and wiped off his tunic. His lips twisted into a sly smile. "Father, I thought you'd be pleased with what I did."

Infuriated with his half brother's hubris, Marcellus jerked away from his father and shoved Brutius hard in the chest. "Where is Selena now?"

"Keep your filthy hands off me!" Brutius demanded, stepping back.

Suddenly, Marcellus's arms were restrained by someone behind him. Instinctively, he thrust his right elbow into the muscular ribcage and whirled on his heels to punch Brutius's guard in the jaw.

The brawny man, a head taller than Marcellus, staggered back, loosening his grip.

Marcellus pulled away and unsheathed his *gladius*. "Tell your mad dog to stand down, or I'll cut him to pieces."

Lucius barked, "Enough," which immobilized everyone. He pointed to Brutius's guard. "You, over there. Take everyone's horses to the back."

The burly man looked at Brutius, as if seeking his consent.

"Do what my father says," Brutius growled.

Taking the reins of everyone's horses one by one, the guard led the animals to the back of the domus, where the stables were located.

Still wary, Marcellus closely watched Brutius as he put his sword away.

Lucius gestured toward the front entrance. "Both of you follow me to the tablinum, where we can speak as rational men."

Following his father and Brutius into the vestibule, Marcellus noted the unfamiliar face of a striking, fair-haired female slave polishing the marble bust of Tiberius—a political addition to the household. As he entered the atrium, he glimpsed his mother peeking around a marble column near her bedchamber. He smiled at her, but she didn't respond in kind. Instead, her grimace deepened. He sensed she wanted to speak with him but was afraid to do so.

A deep sense of regret swirled inside him that he had unintentionally hurt his mother with his estrangement from the family. Even so, he had to continue deceiving everyone around him to keep Catrin safe. But, by doing so, he was tearing his family and Roman heritage apart. A foreboding chill crawled down his back as they approached the tablinum. Inside the chamber were wall paintings of bloodlust—Roman legionaries slaughtering Celtic warriors in battle. He inhaled deeply, sweeping the image of a headless body out of his mind.

Lucius unlocked the door and swung it open for everyone to enter. Once inside the lamplit room, Marcellus could feel Brutius's eyes burn into him, and their father vigorously rubbed the bust of Marcus Antonius, as if trying to erase their past.

Lucius began by asking, "Brutius, why did you take Selena?"

Brutius's dark eyebrows furled together. "Isn't that what you wanted, Father? Your favorite slave back?"

Not answering, Lucius stared coldly at Brutius, whose smirk quickly disappeared.

"Don't you at least want to know what the slave confessed?" Brutius offered.

"Tell me," Lucius snapped.

Brutius's lip curled up again. "Marcellus is living with a foreign whore. A whore he regards as a wife."

Marcellus felt as if his chest had been impaled with a spike. The only defense now was to go on the offense and deny everything.

"Liar!" Marcellus shot out.

"It's true," Brutius insisted. "We tortured Selena for the truth."

"She told you that because it was what you wanted to hear," Marcellus countered. "Everyone knows you've tried to discredit me ever since I returned to Rome."

"Then why the secrecy, little brother, about where you stay at night?" Brutius asked in a sardonic tone.

"Because Selena fulfills my needs while I wait to marry. I didn't want our arrangement trumpeted to Senator Frugi," Marcellus said firmly, hoping the answer would satisfy his licentious father.

Brutius smiled. "Adonis is with her now. By Roman law, she is not considered a credible witness unless she is tortured."

Clenching his hands, Marcellus stepped up to Brutius. "What am I on trial for?"

"For abandoning your pledge to marry Licinia. For lying to us about your sorceress wife," Brutius lashed out.

Marcellus turned to his father. "I have never broken my pledge to marry. Your spies at the basilica should have confirmed that I have fulfilled my duties to Senator Frugi."

"It's only a facade. Your true intent is to get out of the marriage," Brutius accused.

Marcellus glared. "I've never hidden my ambitions to take command of the northern legion."

"If so, let us return to my villa to hear Selena's confession," Brutius said, shifting his stare to their father.

"It's nightfall. A time when murderers and thieves are on the roads," Lucius cautioned.

"Isn't my little brother a battle-hardened soldier who can handle rabble like that?"

Marcellus was tempted to accept Brutius's challenge, but Catrin and the others could still be there. If he waited until morning, it would give him more time to contemplate how to counter everything Selena had confessed under torture.

"Let's do what Father says," Marcellus said, tempering his voice. "At dawn, we leave. Pray to the god of death that we find Selena alive."

After a tense dinner, where silence sliced like a sword, Marcellus excused himself to get some fresh air. Outside, he gazed at the starlit sky, wondering what he would find at Brutius's villa. The pattering of light footsteps drew him out of his contemplation. He turned to find his mother approaching him under the illumination of burning torches in the peristyle. He exhaled slowly. His mother looked deeply troubled, her eyes filled with tears. She held out her arms, and he embraced her, slightly lifting her off the ground. After he kissed her on each cheek, he could taste the salt on his lips.

"Oh, Marcellus. Why must you defy your father?" Drusilla asked, choking down sobs. "Please come back home."

Marcellus sighed deeply, feeling the weight of regret in his heart that he had caused his mother so much pain. "Please don't ask this of me. I'm a man now and must find my own way."

"The estrangement between your father and you is tearing our family apart. Though he might not show it, he cares for you."

Marcellus held back a chuckle. *Unlikely.*

Drusilla slowly shook her head. "Why does this always have to be about a woman? First, it was Eliana, and now, it's your father's slave. A slave!"

"You don't know what Father did to Selena, do you?"

"What does it matter?" Drusilla said sharply. "She is property. He can do whatever he wants with her. I look the other way whenever he sates his basic needs with her. As I do with you."

Marcellus's throat tightened. "I didn't take Selena for that reason."

Drusilla's deep-blue eyes bored into him. "Then why did you take her with you?"

"So Father wouldn't beat and rape her."

"When did you start caring for a slave over your family?" Drusilla asked sharply.

Marcellus hesitated, wondering if there was more to her questions. "Have I not done what Father demands? Pledge to marry Licinia to elevate our family?"

"I also want this," Drusilla said, clasping his hands. "I want you to marry a young woman who will bear your children. This marriage will help you rise politically."

"But I don't . . ." Marcellus bit his lower lip.

"But what?"

"I don't love her," Marcellus confessed. "She is but twelve years old and more like a sister to me."

"She just turned thirteen," Drusilla reminded him. "Is there another woman?"

Marcellus looked away.

Drusilla clasped Marcellus's face between her hands. "You love someone else, don't you?"

"No," Marcellus whispered.

"I can tell when you're lying. Is it the barbarian princess you met in Britannia?" she asked pointedly.

Marcellus's heart jumped into his throat. He rasped, "Who told you this?"

"I overheard your father and Brutius talking about her the other day," Drusilla revealed. "Tell me it's not true."

Marcellus hesitated, wondering who could have told his family that Catrin was alive. There would be no reason for Decimus to confess. He had disobeyed Lucius's order to kill her, instead sparing her so she could be his slave.

Someone else told them. But who?

"How could I possibly be in love with a Briton?" he finally said, struggling to keep a stone face. "I can't remember a thing that happened to me in Britannia. Explain how I would recognize this phantom princess?"

"Perhaps she found you and—"

"Rumors. Lies." Marcellus cut off his mother's words.

Drusilla did not back down. She gripped his arm, as if she were scolding a naughty boy. "Listen to me, Marcellus Antonius. If the rumors are true, Lucius won't stop until he has hunted down and killed this woman. You know what he is capable of. He won't let anyone stand in the way of his ambitions. Not anyone. Not even you."

"This is all nonsense," Marcellus tried to reassure his mother, even though his heart was hammering like a mallet against his chest.

How much does Father know about Catrin?

"If this foreign princess exists, break off the relationship," Drusilla demanded. "Do it to save her. To save you from the shame. Ask for your father's forgiveness. Don't throw your birthright away."

Marcellus swallowed back his emotions as he regarded her. Always the fierce mother, she was a lioness protecting her cub from the crunching jaws of other predators. "Let's see what tomorrow brings."

"You'll come home, then?" Drusilla asked, a hopeful glint in her eyes.

Marcellus kissed her forehead. "Perhaps. Let's get some sleep."

Drusilla exhaled and nodded slightly.

Though Marcellus had sworn not to return home, his mother's warning haunted him as he envisioned what he would find at Brutius's villa.

26

CARNAGE

Brutius's Villa, Rome, 23 March, 28 AD

At dawn, a sense of dread shrouded over Marcellus as he left on horseback with his father, Brutius, and their guards. They merged into a stream of service wagons leaving Rome after their nightly rounds, their wooden wheels clacking on the cobblestone road. A short distance south of the city, the group veered onto a dirt road lined with lush woods of cypress and oak trees. The clapping of the horses' hooves broke the forest's silence like clashing swords as they traversed a bridge over a meandering stream.

Glancing all around, Marcellus didn't see any signs of Catrin and the others. After they rode through an archway to the front gardens of Brutius's villa, the statue of an adolescent boy in the throes of passion with a satyr greeted them. Another bronze sculpture of a satyr flaunting an oversized phallus was next to the entrance door. He noticed a driverless, metal-barred wagon used to haul slaves at the far end of the circular driveway. Then, a man walked out of the shaded corner of the structure.

"*Salve*, Gaius," Brutius called out. "Is something wrong?"

Marcellus tensed, recognizing Gaius Septimus, the retired legionary he'd met at the Red Chariot Inn.

Gaius eyed Marcellus, then replied, "Nobody answered. I knocked on the door several times. I was checking around for any household slaves."

"Strange," Brutius muttered. "Check in back. Perhaps someone is waiting there to load the wagon."

Wondering if Catrin and the others were hiding nearby, Marcellus jumped off his horse and scanned the area while Gaius checked the back.

A couple of foxes leaping between two cypress trees startled him. He reached for his *gladius*.

"Why so jumpy?" Lucius shouted.

Marcellus pointed to the red foxes frolicking with each other.

"You gave me a fright. Put that damn weapon away," Lucius ordered.

Marcellus sheathed his *gladius* but continued glancing around for any movement. Gaius's voice yelling, "The gate is open at the back," drew his attention.

"Is the stableman there?" Brutius shouted.

"No. I don't see anyone."

Lucius's brow creased. "Let's stay together and check it out."

Marcellus mounted his horse again and rode with the others to the back of the villa, where they entered through an unlocked gate. Each of them spread out to check various areas in the villa.

Marcellus inspected the loading dock, where food supplies and household wares had been left. He caught a waft of what smelled like a dead animal. He dismounted, tethered the horse's reins to a post, and ventured into the cucina, expecting the kitchen scullions. Instead, a hissing, gray-striped cat met him at the doorway. He nudged it away and searched the nearby storage room.

A man's voice shouted from outside, "A body over here."

Marcellus poked his head through the doorway. Brutius's guard was kneeling over a motionless body. Unsheathing his *gladius,* he felt his heart drum in his chest as he stepped out onto the portico-roofed peristyle to get a closer look. He caught a whiff of a strong rotten egg odor in the stiff breeze. The sound of a slamming door made his ears perk up. Turning in the direction of the noise, he saw a stable door opening and shutting. With weapon still in hand, he slowly approached the structure and opened the door.

To his shock, Marcellus beheld the bloody, spiked head of Adonis on the wall. The overpowering stench made him gag and his stomach lurch. He stepped back, repelled by the scene of the desecrated head and the gaping wound in the headless body's groin where he'd been castrated. Swirling emotions gripped him as he surmised that Cynwrig had most likely done the vile deed. Adonis's headless shade would bear the mark of shame in the Underworld for all eternity.

Struggling to calm himself, Marcellus hesitated to announce what he'd found to the others. There would likely be a confrontation with his half brother, who would assume he had been responsible for ordering the dastardly act.

"Another body in the stall," Marcellus finally called out.

When Brutius approached the doorway, Marcellus stepped away to reveal the gruesome scene.

Brutius froze, and his face paled. His widened eyes shifted slowly from Adonis's spiked head to his headless body. For a few moments, Marcellus only heard his brother's ragged breathing. Then, suddenly, Brutius's eyes blazed at Marcellus.

"You did this to spite me!" he roared, charging headfirst into Marcellus's chest, knocking him against the wall.

Momentarily dazed, Marcellus barely recognized the danger of Brutius's dagger descending on him. First, he blocked Brutius's arm while popping his fingers into his half brother's eyes. Then, after hearing the dagger clink on the ground, Marcellus maneuvered around Brutius and refrained him in a headlock.

Lucius rushed toward them, shouting, "Stop that fighting now!"

"Marcellus butchered Adonis like a boar!" Brutius accused, struggling against the restraint. "And he stole your whore!"

"I had nothing to do with this!" Marcellus countered, cranking his arm tighter behind Brutius's head.

"He is lying!" Brutius roared, his face reddening from anger. "He is trying to conceal his sorceress wife from Britannia. His obsession with that bitch could jeopardize his marriage to Licinia and bring down our family!"

"Get control of yourself!" Marcellus growled through clenched teeth.

Then, Gaius appeared in the doorway. "All of the slaves procured for Tiberius are missing," he said. "And I don't see any house slaves."

The announcement made Brutius even more agitated; he clawed at Marcellus's wrists and savagely bit his hand to escape.

Heaving with rage, Marcellus hurled Brutius facedown on the ground with a skull-cracking crunch. Noting the blood seeping from Brutius's forehead, Marcellus checked for a pulse and then glanced at his father. "He's unconscious."

All the color in Lucius's face faded as he knelt next to Brutius's motionless body and placed a hand on his forehead. "I don't understand what happened here. Why would Brutius accuse you of such a heinous deed?"

"He is crazed, out of his mind. Only murderous thieves could have done this," Marcellus offered as a possibility to divert blame from Catrin and himself. "Let me carry Brutius away from here, to his bedchamber."

Lucius nodded slightly.

Marcellus lifted Brutius into his shaking arms. Looking down on him, Marcellus couldn't fault Brutius for lashing out after seeing his lover murdered. He would have reacted the same way if he had found Catrin brutally murdered. Yet, Cynwrig's desecration of Adonis's body sank into his gut like sludge in a cesspool. And he couldn't explain why all the slaves had disappeared.

After laying Brutius on a couch in his bedchamber, Marcellus ordered a slave to watch over him while he spoke privately with his father in the tablinum.

Lucius remained silent as he walked with Marcellus to the office chamber. After they entered the room, Lucius locked the door and turned to Marcellus. "Did you know Brutius was involved in the slave market?"

"I'd heard rumors that he was acquiring sex slaves for Tiberius, but I had discounted them," Marcellus answered, thinking back to what Matron Antonia had revealed.

"I don't want to report what happened here to the urban watchmen," Lucius said. "I'll deal with the matter myself."

"Let me assure you, Father, I had no hand in this," Marcellus tried to persuade his father, though Cynwrig's savage act began to gnaw at him.

Lucius exhaled. "After thinking about this more, I believe unscrupulous slave traders had a hand in this. Nasty business. What else could explain why all the slaves are missing? They must have taken them and Selena to sell."

Somewhat relieved his father gave no hint of suspecting him, Marcellus nodded in agreement. His mother's words resonated in his mind.

Break off the relationship. Do it to save Catrin.

If only he could find a way to speak with Catrin before she sailed away. Undoubtedly, spies would monitor his every move. Any attempt to find Catrin in Ostia could jeopardize her life, as his mother had warned. He decided the best course of action would be to make amends with his father and half brother to divert their attention from Catrin.

"Let's have slaves sprinkle salt over the areas where the bodies are," Marcellus suggested. "We can then arrange for a priest to remove all evil spirits."

"Still . . ."

"Still what?"

"I am still troubled by Brutius's accusation that Selena confessed you had a foreign wife." The corners of Lucius's lips turned down into a stern frown. "And now, we'll never find out from her."

"Believe me, Father, I don't have a foreign wife. But, if it would help alleviate the tension in our family, I'll return home," Marcellus offered.

"Your mother will be pleased." Lucius furrowed his shaggy eyebrows. "Is there something you want to say to me about the trouble you've caused me?"

Marcellus couldn't take the next step of apologizing. He walked out of the chamber without answering, his resolve to reunite with Catrin in Gaul only hardening.

27

A GRANDFATHER'S REVENGE

Southeast Britannia, 24 March, 28 AD

The pile of heads slowly shrunk as Marrock watched enslaved girls and boys toil away on each one, scraping off decaying flesh and digging out brain matter. Despite the winter winds gusting across the channel, the stench was so foul it made the young captives cough and gag, some vomiting. This was the price of preserving the power of the souls trapped in the skulls of his fallen enemies. Each skull had a special place on the Wall of Skulls being constructed on top of the sheer white cliffs overlooking the frothing, crashing waves below. The skulls of his most fierce enemies were placed in carved-out compartments on the highest tier to protect his kingdom from foreign invasion.

His pregnant wife, Ariene, diverted Marrock's attention by asking, "How many more heads must you place in the wall?" Looking askance, he noted her scrunched nose as she pressed a piece of linen cloth against it.

"Until I have enough strength to defend the coast and forge all the tribes into a nation to match Rome," he answered with assurance. "You cannot lead until you possess the essence of everyone beneath you."

Ariene pulled the cloth away from her face and grimaced. "Could we go back to the castle?" she requested. "There are a couple of things I would like done there."

"In a moment," Marrock said. "I need to make sure each skull is correctly purified before being put in its proper place."

"The skulls all look alike to me," Ariene commented. "How can you tell them apart?"

Marrock turned to his wife, heavy-laden with child, and noted the slight tinge of pink on her face from what had once been a purplish birth-mark, before their adopted daughter, Boudicca, had healed it. "Let me show you," he offered, taking her arm into his.

Marrock escorted her a short distance on the hilltop's pathway to the Wall of Skulls. There, he reached up to retrieve one of the skulls from the top tier. "See here"— he pointed to the fissure and hole in the bony crown—"This is Brennus, a fierce warrior who fought for King Epaticcus. I tore off his helmet and smashed his head in with a battle-axe."

Ariene gazed at the fog-laden channel. "I know of your reputation as a warrior."

Though his wife showed little interest in his battle stories, Marrock had to remind himself that she had always remained loyal to him. She was the epitome of a good wife and mother, sacrificing everything to care for him and the children. With such a good heart, she was naïve to the evil lurking around their family. And he wanted to keep it that way.

Sensing his wife's discomfort in the presence of the skulls, Marrock suggested, "Let us go back to castle. I haven't had a chance to be with the boys in a while."

Ariene smiled and took his hand.

At the stone fortress and lighthouse under construction, they found local craftsmen chipping away with stones and chisels, while brawny slaves meticulously placed stones on the inner wall under construction. An engineer and architect from the Roman legion had been recently commissioned by Governor Decimus Flavius to oversee the project. Though Decimus had recently refused to pay full price for slaves Marrock had procured, the governor had nonetheless fulfilled their treaty to provide skilled crafts-men to oversee the construction of a fortified castle and lighthouse, where Marrock could rule as Rome's client king.

Marrock turned to his wife. "What would you like done?"

"I want a place to plant herbs within the inner wall," Ariene requested, a tinge of excitement in her voice. "I can make potions to ease your burdens."

"Of course, my dear," Marrock said, smiling. "You have a mother's heart with a need to plant and nourish seedlings. I'll speak with the Roman engineer about this."

Ariene gave a coquettish smile and looked like she wanted to kiss him. "Thank you, my king."

Charmed by his wife, Marrock smiled in return and pointed to his face. He leaned over so she could give him a peck on his cheek.

After further inspection of the site, Marrock looked around for his two sons and adopted daughter. "Where are the children?" he asked his wife.

"Boudicca is with the nursemaid. I left Jago and Lud with your body-guard, Finn," Ariene said, pointing to the tower in its final stages of con-struction, where the two boys were playing.

Marrock howled three times as a signal for his sons to join the family pack. The stocky, chestnut-haired boys—mirror images of Marrock as a boy—loped jovially up to him and yipped like wolf pups. He picked up his eldest lad, Lud, and threw him up high. Howls of laughter broke through the cacophony of clacking wagon wheels, craftsmen chiseling stones, and men grunting from lifting stone. Jago—a robust boy of four summers—took his turn and squealed twice as loudly as his older brother.

After they finished playing, Marrock asked his sons, "Do you want to see the ancestral skulls?" They yipped their excitement. He motioned for the workers to move away from the tower that was almost built.

Next to the tower's inner wall was a padlocked, grilled doorway, which he unlocked and opened. He told Ariene to wait, concerned she may fall with her burgeoning belly. After lighting a torch, he waved for his sons to follow him. They descended a narrow staircase to an underground cave, where the four family skulls were stored. He put the torch in a sconce at-tached to the wall. To the right of the chamber was a tunnel that had been discovered during excavation. The narrow passageway had been widened and supported with timbers to serve as an escape route if the fortress came under attack. A stone archway with seven carved out compartments to set skulls in was at the back wall.

"This is the shrine where I keep my family's skulls," Marrock explained to his sons. "Only my family and trusted guards are allowed to see them."

He gestured to each skull, starting at the top and moving downward on the left side of the archway as he identified them.

"The uppermost skull is my father, King Amren," he pointed out. "He was a bad pa and banished me."

"What does banish mean?" Lud asked.

"Pa sent me away. No one from my village was allowed to speak to me," Marrock said, bitterness burning in his chest.

Lud and Jago exchanged terrified glances.

"I would never do this to my sons," Marcellus reassured them, patting each boy on the head. "Below my father's skull is my mother's—Queen Rhan. She was an evil ma, unlike yours. The bottom two skulls belong to Rhiannon, the false queen, and her bastard daughter, Vala."

"Pa, what is a bastard?" Jago asked, eyes wide with curiosity.

"A common warrior seeded her. Not the king," Marrock declared with contempt. "Only I and you are the true heirs to the kingdom."

"Who goes into the empty spots?" Lud ventured, stealing a glance with Jago.

"The remaining empty spots are for the skulls of a dark sorceress, an ancient druid, and my evil half sister, Catrin."

When Lud extended his hand to touch Vala's skull, Marrock jerked it away. "Only I should hold the family skulls. So they atone for what they did to me, I now use powerful forces from their skulls for the good of my kingdom."

"What does atone mean?" Lud asked.

Marrock leaned over and growled, "To make up for being bad."

Both Jago and Lud gasped, then, seeing their father's smile, they laughed.

Marrock pulled out his mother's skull to let his sons inspect it. He did not bother to explain that his mother's soul no longer resided in the skull because she possessed Agrona, a mute girl. Though the skull was powerless without his mother's soul, it brought back memories of when she'd treasured him and had been willing to sacrifice everything for him to be king.

With bitterness again sizzling to the surface, he spat contemptuously on the crown and put it back it its designated spot.

So much for a mother's love—she betrayed me!

Just then, a loud rumble from above unexpectedly shook the ground. Alarmed, Marrock told the boys to wait in case there was danger above. He scurried up the stairs, his shoulders bumping against the walls.

At the top of the stairs, Marrock was greeted by his wife and Finn, who extended a helping hand as he stepped outside. Before Marrock could ask what had happened, a flash of bright light from the top of the tower blinded him, followed by a deafening boom of thunder, making the ground shake.

Feeling chips of stone raining on him, Marrock protectively hovered over his wife as bolts of lightning, one after another, struck all around, until the billowing clouds suddenly lifted and vanished. Shaken, he glanced around the construction site to find a handful of motionless bodies lying on the ground.

Fearing the gods' wrath, he gawked at Finn. "What just happened?"

"I've never seen a storm like this," Finn exclaimed. "When you were below, black clouds appeared out of nowhere, and a bolt of lightning struck the tower."

With images of Lud and Jago flashing in his mind, Marrock diverted his eyes to the grated doorway. Ariene also looked in that direction and clasped his arm. "The boys are still down there!" she shrieked.

Galvanized into action, Marrock hurriedly lifted the grated cover to the circular staircase, stepped down, and bumped his broad shoulders against the wall as he descended the stairs, his feet slipping on its slick surface. On the final level of steps, an amber glow from the chamber eerily enveloped him. As he entered the space, his eyes focused on strands of amber light weaving in and out of the eye sockets of Vala's and Rhiannon's skulls, then crawling on the floor into the tunnel. A chill ran down his back as he saw the empty compartment at the top of the Archway of Skulls.

His father's skull was gone!

Gasping for air, he frantically looked around the chamber for his sons. He did not see them. "Jago. Lud. Where are you?" he called out.

All he heard was an annoying buzzing sound from the brightening tunnel. Was it possible they'd taken the skull? If so, were they hiding, afraid of what he might do to them if he found them with the skull?

"Quit playing games with me!" he shouted, his heart quickening with panic. "Come out now!"

Startled by heavy footsteps descending the staircases, Marrock pivoted on his heels to find Finn stepping into the chamber.

"Did you find your sons?" Finn gasped, breathing heavily.

Marrock widened his eyes. "They're gone."

Suddenly, loud screams of terror from the tunnel made them both jump.

"Where does that light go?" Finn asked, pointing to the tunnel.

A shudder sliced down Marrock's spine. Without thought, he forced himself through the narrow passageway until he reached a smaller chamber that was mysteriously lit by burning torches on the wall. To his utter shock, he found the motionless bodies of his sons on the chalky floor. He took a burning torch from the wall to illuminate the bodies but found no evidence of trauma except for their blackened, burned hands. He pressed two fingers on each of his sons' necks to detect a pulse. The youngest, Jago, had a slight pulse, while Lud's pulse throbbed strongly beneath his cold, damp skin.

Marrock lifted Lud to a sitting position and shook him to wake him. The boy slowly opened his eyes, confusion on his face. Marrock embraced his son, who began to weep. It felt as if his guts were being ripped out of him upon finding his sons had been mysteriously harmed.

"Jago needs to be moved," Marrock rasped. "I'm too big to carry him out. Can you pull him partway through the tunnel? Finn is on the other side."

Lud looked at Marrock with pathetic, tear-filled eyes. "I think so."

"Good boy," Marrock whispered, struggling to comprehend what could have happened to his sons. He would question Lud later. But first, they had to get Jago out of the underground chamber.

Marrock steadied Lud as they walked to the tunnel, then carried Jago to where Lud was waiting. While Lud pulled Jago by the arms through the tunnel, Marrock scanned the chamber for any evidence of what might have harmed his sons. Detecting an amber glow emanating from a crevice in the wall, he peeked in and found his father's skull lodged inside. He hesitated to dislodge the skull, fearing the power of the light threading in and out of its empty eye sockets.

Overcoming his trepidation, Marrock unsheathed a dagger from his belt and gripped the hilt tightly as he pried the skull out of the wall with the blade. The skull finally loosened and fell onto the floor, the strand of amber light fading from its eye sockets.

Bewildered, Marrock lightly touched the bony crown, which felt hot to the touch. Both anger and anguish burned through him like a firestorm at the possibility that his father's spirit had done something to his sons. These were the same emotions he had suffered as a young boy when he had been forced to watch his father strike off his mother's head. Only later had he learned the mute girl beside him at the execution had been possessed by his mother.

Had his father's skull taken Jago's soul? Had Lud somehow managed to escape?

Shaking his head, Marrock mulled over the possibility, then found the strength to regain his wits. Out of caution, he would leave his father's skull there until he could consult with other druids to interpret what had happened.

He squeezed his massive shoulders through the narrow channel, as if being born again, until he reached the chamber with the shrine of family skulls. There, he found Finn holding Jago's body, as Lud clung to the guard's leg, sobbing uncontrollably.

Durovernum, Southeast Britannia, 28 March, 28 AD

Marrock's hope that Jago had escaped King Amren's grasp faded as Ariene cared for him at their residence in the capital. She chanted and prayed daily and nightly.

Mother of Earth, I beseech you,

Embrace my son with life forces.
Father of Sky, I call upon you,
Fill my son with life-giving breath.
Brother of Seas, Sister of streams,
Flow life-sustaining blood in my son's veins.

Marrock told his wife, who was showing early signs of labor, to go to bed to rest. Grief finally overwhelmed him as he observed that his son's once ruddy face was almost white. His glassy, blue-green eyes stared vacantly at the ceiling. He kissed his son's forehead and wept. For the first time since his father had banished him, Marrock felt he didn't have control over his destiny.

With the hope that Boudicca could heal Jago, he brought her into the musky room. The chubby-cheeked girl, not quite four summers old, laid the palms of her hands on Jago's chest. Her blue-green eyes transformed to an amber glow as she chanted indecipherably. Her face paled as a rosy glow returned to Jago's cheeks. For a few moments, his body twitched with renewed life, but then, it stiffened again.

The color of Boudicca's eyes returned to blue-green as she uttered, "Jago with Papa Amren."

Alarmed, Marrock consulted with other druids about the meaning of what had happened in the underground chamber that cradled his family's skulls. Every druid advised, "It is best you seal off the passageway to prevent evil spirits from wandering into the physical world. Make a human sacrifice and wipe the sealed area with the blood to restrain their dead souls. It is best Jago's spirit stay with his grandfather's to assuage his wrath."

Though Marrock was at first hesitant to heed their advice, he finally accepted their counsel when Jago failed to recover. His eyes, which had previously glinted with mischief, were dull. The once vibrant boy continued to stare vacantly, and his breaths faded before finally ceasing.

"Jago with Papa Amren. Jago wants to play with Lud," Boudicca declared, alarming Marrock further.

At the funeral rites held outside the fortress, Ariene was inconsolable, blaming Marrock for his dead father's wrath. She threw herself onto the

SKULL'S VENGEANCE ❖ 225

burning pyre beside her son, but he pulled her off, rolled her in a blanket, and quickly extinguished the flames lapping at her dress. Inspecting her, he was relieved to see she had only suffered a few minor burns.

Misty-eyed, he cradled Ariene and whispered, "Soon, you will have another son."

Ariene's throat clutched with emotion, and her voice cracked. "No one can replace Jago."

Still holding Ariene in his arms, Marrock felt a sudden gush of liquid soaking into his tunic, taking him by surprise.

"My water has broken!" she wailed. "The baby is coming."

Marrock carried Ariene to her bedchamber for the midwife to manage the childbirth. A few hours later, the midwife came out and announced, "You have a healthy boy."

However, the joy of a newborn son could not overcome Ariene's grief for the death of another. She languished in bed, unwilling to nurse the newborn.

Marrock tasked the midwife to find a mother from the village who had recently lost her child to nurse and care for his newborn son. Overcome with grief, he plunged into an abyss of emptiness in which his fire for vengeance numbed.

And his newborn son remained nameless.

28

DRAGON SKULL

Durovernum, Southeast Britannia, 6 April, 28 AD

A fortnight after the funeral, Marrock was like the living dead, struggling to cope with the grief of the loss of his son and a wife who curled in her bed like a corpse in a crypt, too melancholic to care for any of her children. Lud clung to him like a lost wolf pup.

That was the day Gawain returned to the Cantiaci capital and stoked fuel into Marrock's fire for vengeance. Noting the blanketed object in the ox-drawn cart his assassin had driven into the forecourt, Marrock asked, "What do you have in here?"

Instead of answering the question, Gawain shifted nervously. "Can we speak in private?" he requested.

Suspecting Gawain had not brought back Catrin's head, Marrock gestured for two guards to watch the cart as he talked with the assassin in the great hall. Inside the high-beamed receiving chamber, he sat on a pedestaled, high-back chair and looked down at his assassin, who was standing before the dais.

"What did you bring me?" Marrock asked.

"I have brought back what you most desire. I have also learned of plots against you," Gawain answered, remaining stone-faced.

"Tell me more," Marrock snapped, noting the omission of Catrin's assassination in Gawain's reply.

Gawain's lips twisted into a smile, and he closely regarded Marrock as he spoke. "There is a massive skull in the cart. Local thieves in Gaul uncovered it in a cave. They told me, 'It is the skull of a dragon.' After they refused to sell it to me, I cut off their heads to add to your wall of skulls."

For the first time since his son's funeral, Marrock smiled thinly. "After we speak further, I would like to inspect this skull."

Gawain slightly bowed. "I would be delighted to show you, my king."

Marrock detected a glint of fear in Gawain's eyes. "What about the plots against me?" he inquired.

"In Lugdunum, I visited local inns and taverns. I learned Adminius was also in the city."

"Cunobelin's son?"

"That is the one," Gawain said. "A Roman soldier at a local tavern confirmed he was the prince from the Catuvellauni tribe."

"You speak the Roman tongue, then?" Marrock asked, taken by surprise that his assassin spoke the foreign language.

"A Roman merchant taught me when I was a boy," Gawain said with a smug smile. "And further, I learned Adminius met with Governor Decimus Flavius."

Marrock flung his head back in surprise. "When did this happen?"

"At the start of winter," Gawain replied.

"Why would Adminius meet with Decimus in Lugdunum in winter?" Marrock probed.

"I asked the Roman soldier the same question."

"And?"

"Adminius requested military support to defend their territory against your attacks. And, well . . ." Gawain paused and looked warily at Marrock.

"And what?" Marrock demanded.

Gawain lowered his eyes. "Decimus agreed."

Angered, Marrock abruptly rose from his chair. "What? Our treaty says I provide him slaves in exchange for keeping his nose out of my affairs."

"Some of the legionaries refer to the governor as a two-faced Janus," Gawain said, stealing a glance at Marrock. "He offers and breaks deals whenever it suits his ambitions."

Marrock stomped down the two steps of the dais and scowled at Gawain. "Why would Roman soldiers loosen their tongues with you?"

Gawain smirked. "Roll a coin, they spill their guts."

Marrock stroked his chin. "I wonder if Decimus found out about my secret dealings with Brutius Antonius."

Gawain's brow raised. "I know nothing about this."

Marrock mulled over the possibility, then turned his thoughts to other threats from his family. "Did you find Catrin?" he asked sharply.

Gawain averted his eyes from Marrock's hard stare. "I did, in Lugdunum. But fierce warriors were protecting her."

"And this stopped you?" Marrock growled.

Gawain hesitated. "On the contrary. I took this as a challenge. I slipped inside her living quarters . . . but, as you said, she knows how to fight."

"So, is she dead?" Marrock asked, knowing the answer from the glint of fear in Gawain's widened eyes.

"I was ready to slit her neck"—Gawain sliced his hand through the air—"but she sensed me and knocked my arm away. It felt as if flames were burning up my arm. You did say she is a sorceress with the gift of foresight. Her magic is stronger than that."

"So, you failed, then?" Marrock asked evenly, although he wanted to slice the assassin's throat open.

"Sometimes, it takes more than one attempt to get to know the target." Gawain's voice shook. "I just need another chance."

Marrock stepped up to Gawain, almost touching his face. "And why did you not take that chance?"

Gawain's jaw tensed. "She and her warriors vanished from the city. I didn't know where to find her."

"You did not know where to find her?" Marrock repeated through clenched teeth, while in his mind, he was conjuring ways to punish Gawain for his failure. "Did you not think of Rome?"

Gawain scratched his head. "Why would she be there?"

"As I told you, she has a Roman lover—Marcellus Antonius," Marrock said brusquely. "Show me the skull in the cart, and we can discuss this further."

"Right away, my king. As I said, you will be pleased," Gawain said, backing away and lowering his head.

Marrock strode with Gawain into the forecourt. The assassin eagerly pulled off the woolen blanket to reveal a massive skull that resembled a lizard with jagged teeth. Beside the dragon skull were four rotting human heads.

Rubbing the skull's jaw, Marrock could sense its raw power emboldening him. Though he should execute Gawain for his failure to kill Catrin, the assassin had brought back a trophy that could elevate Marrock's power to a higher level of black magic.

"For the dragon skull," Marrock said, turning to Gawain, "you will be rewarded with your life. For your failure to kill Catrin, you will be punished by the dragon's fire."

Gawain stepped back, panic striking his eyes. The two guards quickly restrained his arms as he attempted to bolt.

Marrock unsheathed his sword and handed it to another guard. "Have the blacksmith put the blade in the furnace until it is red hot."

As they waited for the guard's return, and as his assassin begged for mercy, Marrock's grief transformed into a fiery rage bent on vengeance. When the guard returned with the sword, Marrock inspected the red glow of the blade and spat on it. The spit sizzled and popped on the hot surface. He gave Gawain an evil smile. As another guard held the assassin's head still, Marrock pressed the blade against the left side of his face until he cried out in agony. Satisfied Gawain now understood what was expected, Marrock pulled the metal away and studied the blistered, reddened shape of the blade on his face.

The brand would forever mark the assassin's failure.

"Now, you won't forget," Marrock mocked. "Take a ship to Rome and bring back Catrin's head. Do not fail me again!"

29

NORTH STAR

Shoreline near Massilia, Gaul, 7 April, 28 AD

Catrin gripped the ship's rail and relished the breeze awakening her senses. She had begun her journey to an impossible dream—to take the Cantiaci throne that was rightfully hers. Yet, she had never led her people into battle or ruled over them. For the last four years, her only purpose had been to survive against all odds.

But that had all changed in the blink of an eye.

Her destiny was now as steadfast as the north star. All the slaves she had rescued from Brutius's villa were on the ship with her. Each of them embraced her as their queen. The freed girls were like daughters, seeking her strength, guidance, and comfort.

Though it seemed only days since the horrific night at Brutius's villa, the dangerous escape still replaying in her mind, three weeks had passed.

Their group of twenty people had traveled all night to avoid capture by the urban cohorts. Astride his horse, Cynwrig led the procession, with Selena nestled in his arms. Catrin, holding the reins of Lugus, followed him afoot with the freed female slaves, each of them taking turns riding her white stallion whenever they tired. Falco, the boys, and the stableman trailed at the back. Thieves, lurking by the stretch of cobblestone road from Rome to the coastal town of Ostia, posed the greatest danger to unsuspecting travelers foolish enough to venture at night.

Fortunately, the motley group had blended in with the criminal fringes on their twenty-mile trek.

After reaching Ostia, they'd split up into six groups and lodged at different inns. Luckily, Gabriella had stolen enough gold coins from a ceramic pot buried in the villa's garden to pay for lodging and food.

Catrin and Cynwrig, the latter of whom carried Selena in his arms, found a *hospitium* that advertised medical services. A gray-eyed innkeeper who had an eagle-beaked nose greeted them with suspicion in his voice. "What can I do for you?"

"We would like a room and a place to stable our horses until we can arrange passage on a ship from here," Catrin requested.

The innkeeper's gaze shifted to Selena. "What happened to her?"

"We were attacked by thieves." Catrin handed a pouch of coins to the innkeeper. "Can you summon a medicus to treat her . . . no questions asked?"

The innkeeper untied the pouch, looked inside, and fingered the silver coins. His lips upturned into a crooked smile. "You can be assured. We discreetly offer what you need."

They followed the innkeeper into an atrium, where porridge, bread, and figs were being served to guests seated at tables around a white-tiled pool. At the back of the atrium was an open courtyard lined with rooms for lodging. The innkeeper unlocked one of the doors in the center and gestured for them to enter.

Selena groaned as Cynwrig set her on a bed in the musty room that was sparsely furnished with a couple of chairs and a splintered, wooden table. The innkeeper motioned for one of the slaves in the courtyard to retrieve whatever Catrin required to treat Selena's injuries.

Sitting next to Selena on the bed, Catrin moistened some cloth with diluted vinegar and gently wiped away crusted blood from Selena's swollen and discolored face. When Selena began to gag, Catrin told Cynwrig to get a chamber pot. After handing the pot to Catrin, he helped Selena sit up so she could vomit in it.

Shortly after, a wiry Greek medicus entered the room, carrying a wood-handled box containing herbal medicines and instruments. The medicus set jars of powder, liquids, and surgical materials on the table near the bed and prepared a mixture of powder and water in a brass cup.

Holding Selena's head up, he brought the cup to Selena's mouth, from which she took a couple of sips.

"What's in the mixture?" Catrin inquired.

"Willow bark extract for swelling and pain," the medicus answered. "Clean her face with acetum to prevent pus while I prepare my instruments for treatment."

As Catrin cleansed Selena's face, she watched the medicus wave a scalpel over a candle flame, followed by a thin metal rod and needle. The strong odors of vinegar and burning metal made everyone in the room cough.

The medicus, holding a thin copper rod, told Catrin, "Tell that brute to hold her still as I realign her nose." He then rammed the rod up her nostril with one hand while jerking the side of her nose with the other. Selena cried out in agony, tears streaming down her face.

Cynwrig held her tighter as the medicus commenced with his next task of cutting some jagged skin from Selena's cheek and suturing the deep cut with flax fiber threaded into a copper needle. After he sutured the facial cut, he pushed some linen packs up her nose and rubbed a moistened paste on the sutured facial wound.

Selena snorted, struggling to breathe through her mouth. Thankfully, she lost consciousness before they removed her tunic for the medicus to inspect the rest of her body for serious injuries. As he pressed the palms of his hands on Selena's rounded stomach, the medicus commented, "It is a miracle she still carries the child."

After he finished suturing the wound on Selena's shoulder, he packed his instruments and medicinal herbs into the wooden carrier and reassured them, "The woman should be fine. Rub the ointment that I will leave on her face to help with the swelling. Remove the nose packs tonight."

"How soon can she travel by ship?" Catrin asked.

"Give her a few days to rest and to heal," the medicus advised. "As long as she can lie down, she should be fine after that."

After the medicus said goodbye and left, Catrin threw away Selena's bloodstained tunic, which smelled like metallic urine. She lightly anointed Selena with lavender-scented oil, the fragrance replacing the stench of vinegar and urine. Throughout the days and nights, Cynwrig and Catrin took turns caring for Selena, encouraging her to eat and drink.

It took almost two weeks before Falco could arrange passage for all of them on a merchant ship headed to Massilia. The extra time allowed Selena to rest and heal. Her face would be permanently scarred, but that didn't seem to matter to Cynwrig. He'd hardly left her side.

Yet, as the ship escaped the coastline, melancholy gripped Catrin. She'd had only a brief time with Marcellus, but now, the telltale signs of pregnancy—fatigue, nausea, and swollen breasts—had set in. Deep down inside, she'd known this would happen if Marcellus held her in his arms. She wondered whether she had succumbed to her underlying need to re-place the daughter she had lost.

Also, more concerning, she could no longer conjure the magic to mind travel to the Wall of Lives, to foresee the future in the life threads, or to reconnect with Marcellus in his dreams. Once before, she had lost these abilities, when she'd carried her stillborn daughter. All of her powers had been redirected toward creating the new life in her belly. Just as she had resolved to claim her right to the throne and rule over her people as their queen, fate had played a cruel trick on her. She now faced an uncertain fu-ture, with new life growing in her belly. The prospect of seeing Marcellus again faded from her thoughts as the distant coastline disappeared in a fog.

How can I now confront Marrock with his unspeakable powers if I can-not counter him with my magic?

With the up-and-down motion of the ship on the rough waves, Catrin became nauseated and leaned over the ship's edge to dry heave. The gray, overcast sky whirling around her, she sat on the deck and laid her head on her bent knees, hoping her stomach would settle.

Cynwrig broke into her thoughts by lightly touching her arm and asking, "Are you all right?"

"I am seasick," Catrin muttered, keeping her head down.

"I've been told that with good winds, we will land at Massilia in five days," Cynwrig informed her.

"Good. We can rest a few days there."

"Then what?"

"We'll get some wagons to transport everyone," Catrin said weakly, feeling sick to her stomach again. She rose quickly and leaned over the ship's edge.

With Cynwrig supporting her, Catrin retched, then belched loudly to alleviate the bloating in her belly.

"I'm worried about you," he said tentatively as he helped her lean against the side of the ship.

"I'm fine," Catrin snapped, wiping the cold sweat from her brow before diverting the conversation away from her health. "How is Selena?"

Cynwrig's grimace softened into a smile. "She is strong. Her wounds are healing." He looked away, chewing on his lower lip, then took a deep breath. "May I ask you something about us?"

Catrin's brow furrowed. She couldn't remember a time when the fearless warrior had looked so anxious.

"What?" she asked him.

"Do you . . . do you think Selena is fond of me? I sometimes see her look at me in the same way my wife once did." Cynwrig swallowed hard, becoming misty-eyed. "Do you think that, by saving her, I've redeemed myself for failing to save my wife?"

Catrin gave a heavy sigh. "Sometimes, good things come out of dark moments."

Cynwrig knelt next to Catrin. "How do you say, 'I want to marry you' in the Roman tongue?"

"*Ego te maritare volo*," Catrin enunciated slowly.

Cynwrig repeated the phrase with a thick Celtic accent but understandably. Catrin smiled at him, nodding her approval.

"Do you think it is too soon to ask her?" Cynwrig muttered, though more to himself, as if building up the courage.

"If you don't, you may lose the chance," Catrin encouraged him.

A grin formed on Cynwrig's face. "Then I will do it. Do you need help before I go down below to ask her?"

"Could you help me up so I can see the sunset?"

Cynwrig took Catrin's hand and lifted her against the ship's side before going below deck. She closed her eyes and imagined herself in a forest listening to the birds chirping near a waterfall plunging into an aquamarine pool. She visualized Marcellus coming out of the water, but before he could embrace her, she heard the pattering of feet approaching her, drawing her out of her fantasy. She opened her eyes to find Peccia—one of the freed slaves from Brutius's villa—at her side. On the cusp of womanhood, Peccia had features similar to Catrin: athletic build, gold-blonde hair, and turquoise eyes.

Peccia regarded Catrin for a moment. "Cynwrig asked me to check on you."

"I feel better," Catrin said in a weak voice.

"I am so glad." Peccia clasped Catrin's hand and spoke in the familiar Celtic tongue. "I also want to thank you for freeing me. If you had not . . ."

Catrin felt Peccia's fingertips tighten around her hand as tears filled the girl's eyes. After a few moments of awkward silence, Catrin asked, "Where are you from?"

"The island the Romans call Britannia," Peccia answered.

"From what tribe?"

"The Atrebates." Peccia paused and looked at Catrin with a puzzled expression. "Cynwrig told me you are his queen from the Cantiaci tribe. But it was a Cantiaci king who made war on my village."

Catrin's jaw tightened. "Marrock is my half brother. But I am the rightful heir to the throne."

"Cynwrig said you were once a slave to a Roman commander."

"It is because of Marrock that the Romans enslaved me," Catrin confirmed. "He butchered my father, mother, and sister like cattle." Catrin choked down a sob as the image of Vala's headless body assaulted her mind. "Only Mor, my sister, survived, but a rival prince has imprisoned her. Now, I seek vengeance for what Marrock has done."

"I also seek vengeance," Peccia hissed. "Marrock killed or captured almost everyone in my village to be sold as slaves. I want to be a warrior like you."

Catrin regarded the determination on Peccia's face. "You understand the dangers a warrior faces?"

"I'd rather die fighting for you than live in shame," Peccia said fervently. "This is true for everyone you freed in Rome."

Catrin wrapped her arms around Peccia's shoulders and pulled her close for a hug. "I'd be honored to have you in my army. Cynwrig is a great warrior who can train you."

"Cynwrig says you can summon magic," Peccia remarked.

Catrin sighed heavily. "Yes, at times, I have that ability."

Peccia pulled away from Catrin and gazed into the distance. "Beware of Marrock's sorcery."

Catrin knew full well what Marrock was capable of. A chill crawled across her shoulders. The image of Marrock cutting off their father's head invaded her mind.

"Have you seen his sorcery?" she asked Peccia.

"Yes, on a hilltop, before battle . . ." Peccia's words faded like a whisper in the stiff breeze.

"You fought against Marrock?"

"No. I hid behind a tree and watched." Peccia lifted her eyes to the crimson clouds streaming over the setting sun. "Marrock's warriors formed a line on the other side of a harvested wheat field. He rode to the front of the front line on a massive warhorse with three human skulls hanging off its back. He set the skulls on the ground and waved his hands over them. He cried out like a god of thunder. Lightning slithered in and out of the skulls' eye sockets. Then, the ground rumbled beneath my feet. Storm clouds billowed overhead. A bolt of lightning struck down some of our warriors. And then . . ."

Peccia grew silent, and her eyes widened.

"Then what happened?" Catrin urged Peccia to finish the story.

"Marrock's warriors charged us like a crashing wave. Slave catchers surrounded us and collared us like dogs."

"Did you see Marrock up close?" Catrin asked.

Peccia nodded. "He was a head taller than most of our warriors. He had long, chestnut hair and a comely face with the amber eyes of a wolf."

Catrin jerked her head back, not sure if she had heard the girl correctly. "A comely face?"

"He had features similar to you."

Catrin stared incredulously at Peccia. "Are you sure about this?"

"My eyes do not lie," Peccia said firmly. "He is a cruel monster. After he captured me, he tried to force himself on me, but I bit his tongue. After that, he ordered his men to do unspeakable things to me." She swallowed hard. "No man will touch me again. I would rather die fighting for you."

Stunned, Catrin looked away and gripped the rail.

How can this be?

When Marrock had attempted to kill her as a nine-year-old girl, ravens had pecked out chunks of his face, protecting her. His scarred face was as cratered as a silvery moon.

As she gazed at the western horizon, the clouds took the shape of a dragon, and its fiery breath alighted the sky.

After four more days at sea, Catrin spotted four islands jutting above the crystalline water. A man's voice shouting, "Massilia ahead," confirmed they would soon dock at their destination. As the ship sailed into the harbor, columnar structures appeared to climb a steep hilltop. Along the coastline, blue water transformed into emerald diamonds. A warm breeze brushed over her skin.

A sense of hope lifted her spirits. She closed her eyes and envisioned Marcellus sauntering with her on the pebbled beach. She could sense the heaviness of her round belly promising new life. Just as Marcellus bent down to kiss her, the crimson sun descended behind her and set the horizon afire.

No matter how much she tried to erase Marcellus from her mind, he was her Apollo; he raised and set her sun every day. Yet, when she opened her eyes, she saw herself merge with a raven and soar over Britannia's white cliffs, beckoning her home.

Will I wake up with this dream?

30

QUEEN'S COMMANDERS

Basilica Julia, Rome, 24 April, 28 AD

For almost a week, Marcellus worked with financial backers to sponsor various events for the religious festival to honor Bellona. It seemed paradoxical to him that Romans still celebrated the original female divinity of war even though they had adopted the Greek god of Mars. He had already paid a hefty sum to the priests of Bellona to initiate festivities.

This year, the gladiator games were cosponsored by his father and Senator Frugi. With only a week to make final preparations, he had worked throughout the day with Orvius, whom he despised. The rotund Greek scribe announced supplicants and recorded amounts they paid as bribes to participate in the festival for Bellona. The remaining bribes would be split among Senator Frugi, the imperial coffers, and himself.

When Orvius announced Verus had arrived, Marcellus fought back the impulse to choke the scar-lipped lanista for his brutal treatment of Catrin when he trained her to be a gladiator. Instead, Marcellus gripped the edge of the table as Verus entered the chamber. He needed to maintain a cold demeanor as he impressed the need for Verus to hand over his two most reputed gladiators to win political favor to participate in the games.

Verus slightly bowed his head as he entered the chamber. "Quaestor Antonius, what an honor to see you again. How does the female gladiator I sold to you fare?"

Noting the Greek scribe's eyebrow perking up with curiosity, Marcellus gestured at him. "You can leave now."

Orvius began to protest. "Do you not need—?"

"I can handle the records myself," Marcellus snapped. "Leave us. Now!"

Orvius handed the wax tablet of transactions to Marcellus with a scorching glare, then pivoted on his heels and bumbled into a table. On his way out of the room, he muttered a curse beneath his breath.

Marcellus glowered at the lanista. "I warned you not to speak about our past transactions in front of anyone. Did I not make that clear?"

"Perfectly clear," Verus said, meeting Marcellus's stare. "My only purpose is to finalize arrangements for my gladiators to fight in the upcoming festivities."

Marcellus motioned for Verus to sit across the table from him.

After Verus sat down, he began. "In our last meeting, we agreed I would provide ten seasoned gladiators to fight in the festival dedicated to Bellona."

"Indeed," Marcellus concurred. "And now, we can settle on the terms. To gain my patronage, you must offer me the gladiator called Ferrex, also known as the Red Lion, as a gift."

Verus clasped his hands on top of the table. "Ferrex is my most prized gladiator. If I give him to you, I do so at great loss to my stock. Due to the leg wound Catrin inflicted, Ferrex had to change his fighting style to better suit his brute strength. He now competes as a *murmillo* and is one of the mob's favorites."

"If I don't sponsor any of your gladiators, that is a death blow to your *ludus*, is it not?" Marcellus said, a biting edge to his voice.

Verus gave a thin smile. "I am sure we can negotiate a fair price for my gladiators to fight in the upcoming games to offset my loss."

Marcellus leaned back in his chair. "What do you consider a fair price to fight ten of your gladiators in the games?"

"All of my gladiators are highly rated, as you are well aware." Verus regarded Marcellus for a moment, then proposed, "One hundred twenty thousand sestertii. And Ferrex must fight in the upcoming games before you take possession."

Marcellus narrowed his eyes. "Why would I agree to such highway robbery? If Ferrex were to die, I would be left empty-handed. The most I can pay is . . . eighty thousand sestertii. And you give Ferrex to me now as a gift for my patronage."

Stroking his chin, Verus eyed Marcellus. "I have three top-rated gladiators for which I normally charge at least fifteen thousand sestertii for each game. I offer you my top ten gladiators to fight in the games at one hundred ten thousand sestertii."

"No more than ninety thousand sestertii for all ten gladiators," Marcellus countered.

Verus's lips curled into a smile. "As a favor to you, I could accept the bargain rate of one hundred thousand sestertii. But only on one condition—Ferrex must fight in the upcoming festival before I give him to you."

Marcellus rubbed the edge of his lower lip with a forefinger. "Hmm . . . perhaps I could agree to your price of one hundred thousand sestertii in exchange for two gladiators as an offering for my patronage. I would like both the Red Lion and the Black Sphinx. And I want them both today."

"Two gladiators? I can't agree to that!" Verus protested.

"The only reason your gladiators will participate is because of my political influence," Marcellus pointed out. "Do you accept the terms of my patronage or not?"

Visibly shaken, Verus looked at his clasped hands on the table. "I have made heavy bets on Ferrex to win. Who will cover my gambling losses if he doesn't fight?"

"Audacious of you to make bets without first meeting my demands," Marcellus said sharply.

Verus swallowed hard. "If I meet your demands, you must donate to my gambling losses today."

"How much?"

Verus hesitated and regarded Marcellus. "Ten thousand sestertii."

Marcellus nodded his agreement.

Verus's lips quirked into a smile. "When do you want to take possession of the gladiators?"

"Today," Marcellus demanded.

"It will take me until tomorrow to get the paperwork for them ready."

"Then I'll pick them up at your *ludus* tomorrow afternoon," Marcellus offered, "and recompense you for your gambling costs."

"You must also pay me for the services of my gladiators at the Festival of Bellona when you pick them up," Verus demanded.

"You'll get paid after the games like everyone else," Marcellus said brusquely. "Do we have an agreement or not?"

Verus frowned. "Said that way, I accept. So, what do you plan to do with these gladiators?"

"They will be my bodyguards," Marcellus replied as he recorded the transaction on a wax tablet. Finally, they sealed the agreement by pressing their signet rings on the wax to leave their imprints.

The next day, Marcellus went to Verus's *ludus* to retrieve the gladiators. A porter escorted him to the atrium, where wall paintings depicted gladiatorial games. On one wall was a *murmillo*, heavily armed with a *gladius* and long shield, combatting a Thracian with a small round shield and curved sword. Another fresco depicted a lightly armed retiarius with a trident and net fighting a heavily armed *secutor*. A third wall rendered two equites, each mounted on a horse, charging each other with spears. He noted that the pool under the opening of the roof was in disrepair. There were cracks and missing tiles in the mosaic underneath the water.

A man's voice greeting, "Welcome, Quaestor Antonius, to my *ludus*," drew Marcellus's attention. He turned to see Verus and two muscular men scantily dressed in loincloths with gray capes over their shoulders at the back of the atrium. He recognized one of the gladiators as Negasi, also known as the Black Sphinx. Marcellus recalled his unsettling meeting with the Ethiopian in Lugdunum, Gaul.

As Catrin was being treated for her wounds after her combat with the Red Lion in the gladiatorial games, Negasi bluntly informed Marcellus that she had lost a stillborn daughter fathered by him a year earlier. The Ethiopian gladiator had tended to her when she almost bled to death after birthing the premature baby. Negasi challenged Marcellus to free Catrin if he loved her. His final words still stung in his mind.

Catrin's love for you has been nothing but a curse.

Marcellus sensed Negasi's cold stare freeze on him. A shudder ran down his back. He was freeing a gladiator who despised him and was trained to kill.

But then, Marcellus noticed the Red Lion's eyes blazing at him. He wondered if he had confronted the gladiator in Britannia, where a dark druidess had erased his memories of events there.

After Verus talked with two armed guards, he approached Marcellus, leaving the gladiators under watch at the back. Coming face-to-face with Marcellus, the lanista glanced around.

"Did you bring any guards to escort the gladiators?" Verus asked.

Marcellus shook his head. "I assume you received payment this morning as a gesture of my generosity to you?"

"Indeed," Verus replied. "I have documents transferring ownership of the gladiators to you. You need to imprint your seal on the wax tablet in my hand to acknowledge you received them." He opened the wax tablet, on which Marcellus imprinted the family seal with his signet ring.

Verus waved for the guards at the back to bring the gladiators forward, then turned to Marcellus. "Do you want my guards to escort the gladiators to their new quarters?"

"I can handle them myself," Marcellus said, regarding the scowl on each gladiator's face directed at him as they stood before him.

"Ankle chains, then," Verus offered.

"No. And you can unchain the gladiators' wrists," Marcellus demanded.

Verus scrunched his brows together. "Do you think that is wise?"

Marcellus eyed each gladiator. "Do I have reason to keep you chained?"

The gladiators exchanged confused looks and then shook their heads in unison.

Marcellus decided to risk that the gladiators would not try to escape once he told them Catrin desired them to be commanders in her army. "Unchain them."

Verus gestured at the guards. "You heard Quaestor Antonius. Unchain them."

Both gladiators smirked as they held out their hands. The guards unclicked the locks in their cuffed chains.

Marcellus waved both gladiators forward to inspect them. He focused on the Red Lion to jolt his memory if he had confronted the Briton before. The aptly named and ruddy-faced gladiator had lionlike features of widely spaced, hazel eyes, a flat-bridged nose, and a mane of chestnut, shoulder-length hair. Blue-tattooed paws ran down the length of his right arm, which Marcellus assumed was his fighting arm. A ridged scar on his thigh left evidence of where Catrin had wounded him during their match. The gladiator's pugnacious stare made Marcellus uneasy.

"What do you want me to call you?" Marcellus asked the Red Lion.

"You can call me Ferrex, Roman," the lion-maned gladiator growled in a thick Celtic accent.

Agitated by the gladiator's disrespect, Marcellus stepped up to him and glared. "Slave, you will call me dominus."

Ferrex stole a glance at Negasi, who cocked an eyebrow in warning.

"Apologies, dominus. I meant no slight," Ferrex replied in a tempered tone.

Marcellus turned his attention to the Black Sphinx. The Ethiopian appeared to be in his mid-thirties with cropped, gray-streaked hair and a creased brow forged by hardship. Past the prime age of most gladiators, Marcellus assumed Negasi had other attributes, such as cunning, which helped him to survive.

"As I recall, you are called Negasi," Marcellus commented.

"That is my Ethiopian name, dominus," Negasi answered with a stone face.

Marcellus nodded his approval to Verus and bid him farewell. Then, he ordered the gladiators to follow him.

After they left the *ludus*, both gladiators strode behind Marcellus. He waved them forward so he could explain why he had purchased them.

"I hope you don't have any intention of escaping," Marcellus began. "I purchased you at the behest of Catrin."

Both gladiators raised their brows in surprise.

"Did you free Catrin?" asked Negasi.

"Yes, I freed her," Marcellus said.

"Is she in Rome?"

"She was here in March but has since returned to Gaul to recruit other warriors for her army. She wants both of you as her commanders."

Negasi chuckled. "So, we are to report to the raven queen?"

"She is not yet queen. Marrock stands in her way. But I promised her Roman military support to overthrow him," Marcellus declared, although he still needed the emperor's final approval for his assignment to command the northern legion.

Ferrex spat. "Was it not your father's legion that aided Marrock?"

Marcellus halted and stared at Ferrex. "I don't like your impudence. Did we meet in Britannia?"

"Do you not remember?" Ferrex growled.

"I do not, but Catrin told me a dark druidess by the name of Rhan erased my memory of events there," Marcellus answered brusquely.

Ferrex frowned. "Then let me refresh your memory, Roman. I was there at the fertility rite. It was me who punched your face in when I found you coupling with Catrin."

Taken aback, Marcellus felt his jaw drop. "What?"

"King Amren promised Catrin to me," Ferrex proclaimed. "But Myrddin tricked the king. The druid declared that you had to marry Catrin and that she had to declare you as a king to break the curse."

Flummoxed, Marcellus struggled to reconcile what Catrin had previously told him about their marriage ceremony. They'd been married in a fertility ritual in which he'd dressed like a stag and she as a raven. Before they'd had a chance to finish the fertility rite, Marrock had kidnapped him, and the dark druidess named Rhan had forced him to swallow a potion called the drink of oblivion to erase his mind. But Catrin had said nothing about a rival suitor.

"Tell me about this curse," Marcellus finally said.

"Rhan foretold her son, Marrock, would strike off Amren's head," Ferrex answered.

"Gods above! Do you plan to do the same to me?" Marcellus asked.

Negasi chuckled. "It looks like we all have a claim on Catrin."

Marcellus gawked at the Ethiopian in disbelief. "What do you mean?"

"I also have affection for her," Negasi confessed.

"I can't believe this," Marcellus said, shaking his head. "I should give both of you back to Verus instead of taking you to Catrin."

"I never said she had feelings for me," Negasi interjected. "I accept her offer to be a commander."

"As do I," Ferrex added.

"I may regret this," Marcellus said as the image of his spiked head rose into his mind. Then, when his stomach began to grumble, he remembered he had not yet eaten that day and diverted the conversation to ease the tension. "Let us get something to eat."

"You'll get no argument from me," Negasi said enthusiastically.

"I would like something besides porridge," Ferrex added.

"That can be arranged," Marcellus said, still unsure whether to trust the Red Lion. He pivoted on his heels and strode to some open storefronts serving food.

Ferrex and Negasi ordered flatbread, cheese, and strong ale, while Marcellus requested olive oil to dip the bread in, smoked fish, and wine. After Marcellus paid for the food, they stood at a high counter to eat. Ferrex and Negasi exchanged glances as they ravenously ate and spoke to each other in Celtic, ignoring Marcellus. As a tribune in Gaul, he'd had to work in auxiliary forces with men from other countries. It was not easy to win their trust until they battled against a common enemy.

"I want both of you to know," Marcellus began, "that I wholeheartedly support Catrin's cause. You may view me as an adversary, but I want what you want—Catrin on the throne."

"And what do you want from her? To rule as her king?" Ferrex asked pointedly.

"I want nothing in return," Marcellus insisted.

Negasi's eyebrow cocked. "Is that so? Power is a strong aphrodisiac."

"I promised to aid her. My word is my honor," Marcellus proclaimed. "I have not always done right by her, but I will atone for any mistakes I have made."

"If that is so, how do you plan to aid Catrin?" Negasi asked bluntly.

Worried others may overhear their conversation, Marcellus looked around. "We need to talk about this elsewhere."

After they finished eating in silence, Marcellus took them to a one-room apartment at the bottom of Palatine Hill, which he had leased to serve as their temporary living quarters. Even though Marcellus still felt some trepidation about trusting the foreign gladiators, he revealed his plan to overstep Sejanus and speak directly to Tiberius.

"An influential noblewoman is arranging for me to meet with Emperor Tiberius so I can request his patronage to assign me as a military commander in northern Gaul. There, I can provide military assistance to Catrin to overthrow Marrock."

The gladiators exchanged bewildered glances. Negasi stared at Marcellus. "What does Rome have to gain?"

"Peace and open trade ways for merchants," Marcellus replied, not disclosing that he had to first convince Tiberius of the need.

"Rome has wanted to occupy us ever since Caesar invaded our land," Ferrex declared. "What is to stop them now?"

"As long as there are strong treaties to guarantee open trade, Rome has no interest in occupying Britannia," Marcellus reassured them.

"What do you want from us?" Negasi asked.

"I want you to be my bodyguards until we meet Catrin in Gaul," Marcellus demanded, studying each of their expressions. "I also have a problem with a half brother who would like to see me dead."

Ferrex chuckled. "So, you and Catrin have something in common."

"You could say that. Furthermore, my father and future father-in-law don't agree with my plan to return to military command. They may try to stop me from speaking with Tiberius."

Negasi shot Marcellus a nasty scowl. "Your father-in-law?"

"That is another matter I must deal with," Marcellus snapped. "Let us end the conversation there. Do I have your backing?"

Ferrex's lips quirked into a sneer. "Roman, take your father's advice and marry one of your own kind. In answer to your question, I will guard your arse until I meet up with my queen in Gaul for further orders."

"And so will I," Negasi concurred, but then, he warned, "But you better not break Catrin's heart again."

Sensing the heat of their blazing eyes, Marcellus hesitated. "Can I trust you to keep your word?"

"My word is my honor," both gladiators said in synchrony.

31

IMPERATOR TIBERIUS CAESAR

Island of Capri, 12 May, 28 AD

Marcellus gazed at the massive villa on top of the sheer cliffs as the ferry-boat approached the Island of Capri. Beside him were Ferrex and Negasi, who had accompanied him as his bodyguards on the three-day journey to Capua by horseback. Ferrex had talked nonstop, speaking in Celtic to Negasi, on the morning boat trip. The Ethiopian said very little but often chuckled. From the sarcastic tone of voice, Marcellus surmised they were mocking him. Though he still felt uneasy being with the gladiators, he had a greater appreciation for why Catrin had recruited them as her commanders.

On the Appian Way to Capua, they had rescued Marcellus from what appeared to be a kidnapping attempt. The skilled gladiators fought off four heavily armed men who accosted Marcellus in the middle of the day. Not sure who the assailants were, Marcellus felt unsettled. He didn't know if his stomach was queasy from the motion of the undulating ship or from his anticipation of meeting Tiberius.

"Are you ready to toss your morning meal?" Ferrex jested, wearing a lopsided smirk. "You look as white as those cliffs."

"No!" Marcellus snapped.

"Rough waves today," Negasi remarked. "Hope it is calmer on our way back."

"Nervous about the meeting?" Ferrex interjected with a smug grin. "I would be if I were you. The emperor lives in a palace fit for a god."

"He is a god in Rome. He personifies Jupiter," Marcellus admitted.

"Then you *are* ready to puke your guts out," Ferrex said, jabbing

Marcellus in the side. Marcellus gagged and leaned over the boat's rail to vomit the sour contents of the moldy cheese he had eaten for breakfast.

"Feel better now?" Ferrex quipped. "It always does, particularly before a battle."

Both bodyguards' laughter pounded into Marcellus's ears as he tried to balance himself against the rail. "*Futue te pisi,*" he cursed.

The gladiators chortled even harder.

Feeling dizzy, Marcellus stumbled into Negasi's broad chest, who steadied him as the boat docked in the harbor.

Still sick to his stomach, Marcellus disembarked on the ship's plank, with Negasi and Ferrex behind him. Waiting onshore were four armed members from the Praetorian Guard who greeted them.

Marcellus showed his credentials and the letter of introduction by Matron Antonia to the commanding officer. "I am Marcellus Antonius. Tiberius Caesar accepted my petition to speak with him today."

The stern-faced guard inspected the document, then wrote something on a wax tablet with a stylus. "All documents seem in order," he said, then regarded Negasi and Ferrex. "Who are the two men with you?"

"My bodyguards," Marcellus clarified.

"They can escort you to the Villa Jovis, but only you will be presented to Tiberius Caesar," the commanding officer demanded.

Marcellus nodded his agreement.

The praetorian officer pointed to the cliffside. "My guards will take you up those stairs to the main floor of the villa."

The stone stairs along the sheer cliff looked like those used by the gods to ascend to the heavens, isolating themselves from the mortals. Dreading the steep climb with an upset stomach, Marcellus took a deep breath and clutched his abdomen. Breathing hard, he struggled to keep pace with Ferrex, who bounded on the stairs like a lion after his prey. Negasi stayed a short distance behind Marcellus. As they ascended the stairs, the surrounding countryside transformed into a lush landscape of streams and woods.

"Look at that," Ferrex said, pointing at a meandering stream. "It looks like a man with goat legs."

Marcellus caught sight of what appeared to be a satyr chasing a nymph across a stream in the distance. He asked himself if this was where Roman power truly lay. On a mythical island away from Rome? Then, his mind suddenly shifted to the disturbing discussion he'd had with his father about how Augustus had forced him to witness Iullus Antonius's suicide before exiling him to Gaul. His father had hoped to gain Augustus's favor by rising politically in the imperial family, but he instead suffered the consequences of his father's sins throughout his life.

Will I suffer the same fate by appealing directly to Tiberius and over-stepping Sejanus?

Shaking off his sense of pending doom, Marcellus continued his ascent to the palatial villa atop the cliff, his breathing ragged and his muscles burning from the arduous climb. As they approached the first level of the multistoried residence, their footsteps crunched louder and louder.

At the villa's entrance, another praetorian guard escorted everyone inside. "Your men will need to wait here," he informed Marcellus. "They can eat in the dining hall where the other guards eat."

"Do you have stout ale?" Ferrex blurted, making Marcellus cringe from the Red Lion's lack of decorum. But then, to his relief, the praetorian guard smiled and responded warmly to Ferrex.

"Aren't you the gladiator known as the Red Lion?"

"That I am," Ferrex replied.

Another guard joined the conversation. "I saw you fight in the spring games. Your opponent's head flew off after one strike of your sword."

Ferrex spat. "He was an arrogant Germanian from the Rhineland."

"And you must be the Black Sphinx," another guard shouted, approaching Negasi.

"We can tell you all about our fights over food and drinks," Negasi offered.

Taking a deep breath to calm himself, Marcellus watched the gladiators walk away amid their admiring fans. Various aromas from the kitchens made him feel queasy again as he followed one of the emperor's guards up a wide stairway to the second floor. There, they entered a corridor and passed several closed-door rooms before entering an enormous reception hall, where Tiberius was seated atop a dais.

Marcellus was shocked to see how the princeps had aged over the last five years. He had last seen Tiberius speak in the Roman forum. Tiberius did not have a trace of hair on his head. Variegated veins marred his ulcerous face. The round-shouldered, gaunt ruler was the shadow of Augustus's famous general who had helped tame the outer frontiers of the Roman Empire.

Standing at the side of Tiberius was a loin-clothed boy who appeared to be about six years old. The elderly statesman lasciviously smiled as he slid his hand under the boy's loincloth to pat his buttocks while whispering something into his ear. The old man's sexual palette for young males was in open display, leaving a sour taste in Marcellus's mouth. Yet, he was not there to judge the emperor's foibles; he was a supplicant beseeching the emperor to advance his military career in northern Gaul over the objections of his father and Senator Frugi.

"Tribune Marcellus Antonius, son of Senator Lucius Antonius, is here to meet with you," the guard announced.

"Take my minnow to the bath," Tiberius ordered a loin-clothed adolescent slave standing behind him. The older boy took the child's hand and disappeared into another chamber behind the dais.

The stern-faced imperator leaned forward in his chair and peered down at Marcellus with piercing brown eyes. He waved for Marcellus to approach him.

Humbly bowing his head, Marcellus stepped to the bottom of the four-step dais and acknowledged Tiberius. "Imperator Caesar."

"It is a shame Matron Antonia is not with you," Tiberius began. "She spoke highly of your military accolades when I dined at her villa in Neopolis last week."

"It is a career I hope is as illustrious as yours," Marcellus flattered.

Noting Tiberius's glare, Marcellus recalled Matron Antonia's advice not to overpraise Tiberius, who had the mindset of a soldier. Disconcerted, he felt warm sweat bead on his forehead as dead silence filled the room.

Wearing what seemed a perpetual frown, Tiberius continued, "I find it odd that Matron Antonia supports your ambitions to be a commander in northern Gaul. Why did you not talk to Sejanus about this request? The senate usually handles assignments such as yours."

Marcellus hesitated, wondering if his decision to overstep Sejanus might backfire, but he was determined to move forward with his plan to aid Catrin. "I thought it best to speak with you directly about the discord in Britannia that could disrupt Rome's trade there."

"Sejanus keeps me apprised of events in Britannia," Tiberius said sharply. "Cunobelin recently petitioned Sejanus to send legionary forces to Camulodunum to defend his territory against King Marrock's invasions. He told me some Roman merchants had been killed during some of the attacks."

Marcellus swallowed a lump in his throat. "That is why I am here. I believe I can capably handle the political unrest between the tribes. As you may be aware, I accompanied my father to Britannia on a diplomatic mission four years ago. At that time, I was held as a hostage as he negotiated terms with Marrock's father and Cunobelin."

Tiberius's stare swooped down on Marcellus. "Why did you seek Antonia's patronage instead of your future father-in-law's, Senator Frugi? She told me you are betrothed to his eldest daughter, are you not?"

Marcellus's heart skipped a beat. "Yes, I am. I am deeply honored that our families will be joined in this marriage. Nonetheless, I have Matron Antonia's ardent support to quell hostilities in Britannia."

"Careful about depending on a woman to laud your laurels. My mother constantly reminds me that my stepfather would not have adopted me as his son if it were not for her. She is the reason I am in power. Or so she says," Tiberius said, a sharp edge to his voice. "Women are like gnats, constantly biting at you with their snide remarks. Men rule—not women who foolishly aspire to rule. They bring nothing but misery to an old man."

Marcellus widened his eyes at the aging statesman. The rumors that Tiberius had isolated himself on the island to escape his mother's control must be true. Marcellus had heard stories that Julia Augusta often circumvented her son's authority to serve as a patron to various dignitaries.

Tiberius stiffened, as if realizing he had been too loose with his tongue. "I commend Antonia, though, for being a loyal companion to my mother during her feeble years. Antonia has shown me utmost loyalty, and I respect her advice."

"Do I have your support to command a peacekeeping force in Britannia to protect our merchants?" Marcellus ventured.

Tiberius's stare pierced through Marcellus. "To receive a favor, you must grant a favor in return."

"What do you have in mind?" Marcellus asked, recognizing his request could have a steep price.

Tiberius lips twitched into a thin smile. "The empire is a difficult beast to tame. You must be on the watch for my enemies in the senate. It is like holding a wolf by the ears. Do you understand my meaning?"

"I believe so," Marcellus said, understanding Tiberius wanted him to spy on any rivals who may be a threat to his power. He wondered if Matron Antonia had insinuated to Tiberius that he would be willing to do so.

Tiberius regarded Marcellus for a moment. "Then you have my patronage. I will recommend to the senate that you be assigned as commander of the Gesoriacum garrison in northern Gaul. Then, you will report to the governor in Lugdunum. There, Decimus Flavius will have your final orders on how to stop the political turmoil in Britannia."

Marcellus felt as though his stomach had dived off a cliff at Tiberius's mention of Decimus—a long-standing nemesis who had enslaved and abused Catrin. Decimus had served under Tiberius in Germania. Had they maintained their friendship since then?

Tiberius cast a glance at his scribe. "Prepare a document with my recommendation for Marcellus Antonius's promotion that we just discussed. Then, arrange for my herald to present it to the senate."

Dreading what his father might do after hearing about his military assignment, Marcellus felt his stomach clench. "I am deeply grateful you have granted my request," he said, bowing his head.

"Do not disappoint me," Tiberius demanded—a phrase Decimus had often said to Marcellus to keep him in line.

32

DANCE WITH AN ASSASSIN

Rome, 6 June, 28 AD

When Brutius opened the door to the tablinum, he found his father with his back turned, slowly rubbing the head of Iullus Antonius. It was as if Lucius had traveled back in time, reliving the moment he had witnessed his father fall on his sword. The soft sobs pervading the chamber disquieted Brutius. His father was a man of steel, seldom expressing any emotion. Yet now, he appeared as vulnerable and dangerous as a wounded lion.

Brutius felt his chest heave with burning rage. He blamed Marcellus for wounding their father, bringing back bitter memories. Why did his worthless half brother continue to draw out their father's raw emotions from the past? Perhaps this time, the tenuous bond between father and wayward son had finally severed.

To alert his father he was entering, Brutius walked heavily on the marble floor into the dimly lit chamber. "Father," he called out.

Lucius's back jerked, and his voice cracked. "Shut the door."

"There is someone outside I want you to meet," Brutius said in a hushed tone.

The candle flickered, and shadows lowered on the walls like dark ghosts in a crypt. Lucius straightened his shoulders, as if taking rein of his emotions. "I told you to shut the door," he repeated brusquely, not turning.

Brutius tiptoed to the door, shut it partway, and spoke to the cloaked man through the cracked opening. "Wait outside until I summon you."

The man pulled the hood down lower over his face and stepped beside the doorjamb.

Taking a deep breath, Brutius clicked the massive door shut.

"What did Sejanus say?" Lucius asked in a stronger voice before turning to face Brutius.

Unable to discern if his father had been weeping in the dim candle-light, Brutius answered. "Sejanus is enraged that Marcellus overstepped his authority and directly approached Tiberius. He confirmed that Matron Antonia made the arrangements."

"Did you know Marcellus just left my home?" Lucius asked, his voice growling louder. "No explanation. Just a cold farewell. See you in a few years."

Brutius knew to stay quiet as Lucius put a clenched hand against his chest and spewed out his words. "Marcellus told me that he had fulfilled his duty to Senator Frugi and me by hosting the Festival of Bellona. He then told me to postpone the wedding because Tiberius had ordered him to serve as his commander in Gaul. When I asked him how long he would be gone, Marcellus did not answer."

Brutius placed a hand on his father's shoulder. "Did he speak with Senator Frugi about postponing the wedding plans?"

Lucius gave a dark chuckle. "Apparently not. Invitations for the wedding celebration were sent out last week. Why would Marcellus consider my feelings or the embarrassment he has caused? He only shrugged, leaving me to clean up the political mess. There is nothing I can do to stop him. It is an imperial order that he take command of the northern legion."

"Is there anything I can do to assuage the situation?"

Lucius exhaled loudly. "This time, Marcellus has crossed the Rubicon and declared civil war on me. But something—or someone—is compelling him to return to Gaul."

"Perhaps I can shed light on the truth," Brutius offered.

Lucius met Brutius's eyes. "Does the truthbearer stand outside our door?"

"He is an assassin sent by Marrock," Brutius disclosed in a whisper.

Lucius eyes widened. "For what purpose?"

Brutius gave a grim chuckle. "You are not the target, Father. Marrock's intended target has fled to Gaul. And the assassin needs our help to find the woman."

Lucius's mouth dropped. "Woman?"

"Can I bring the truthbearer in here to explain?"

Lucius nodded. "Let us see what options Janus has opened to divert the political windstorm."

Brutius stepped to the door and yanked it open. A cloaked man entered and looked around at the walls painted with Roman soldiers battling Celtic warriors.

"Father, this is Gawain," Brutius introduced, pointing to the cloaked man. "An assassin sent by King Marrock from Britannia."

Appearing uneasy, Lucius acknowledged the man with a slight nod.

Brutius cast a glance at Gawain. "This is my father, Senator Lucius Antonius. And the busts near the platform are those of my great ancestors."

Gawain lifted his head, his eyes glinting from the flame of the lamp near him. "I sense their spirits are here to advise us."

"Tell Father what you told me," Brutius demanded.

Gawain studied Lucius for a moment and smiled—an evil smile that cut to the bone.

"Last winter, in Gaul, my king ordered me to assassinate his half sister, Catrin. But alas, she escaped my attempt to slice off her head." Gawain pulled back the cowl of his cloak to reveal a blue tattoo dancing across his forehead and one side of his face layered with splotched, reptilian skin. "Marrock burned half of my face with a hot blade, then threatened to burn me alive if I failed to bring back Catrin's head. That is why I am here."

Lucius shook his head in disbelief. "I do not understand. I ordered my military commander, Decimus, to execute Catrin before the final battle to overthrow King Amren. He assured me later he had followed my orders."

"I know nothing about this," Gawain said, his slit eyes fixed on Lucius. "King Marrock told me I could find Catrin in Rome. He assumed she had escaped to the safety of her Roman husband."

Lucius's stare was riveted to Gawain. "Roman husband? You mean Marcellus?"

"Your youngest son, I believe," Gawain answered with a thin smile.

Brutius interjected, "Marrock told Gawain to approach me first with this information. As you know, Father, I have direct ties with the king to negotiate for slaves instead of using Decimus as our broker."

"Are you telling me Decimus lied to me?" Lucius's face flushed with anger. "And that what the retired soldier—the one you hired to trail Marcellus—said is true? What was his name?"

"Septimus," Brutius reminded his father.

Lucius's eyes lit up, as if the truth had finally dawned on him. "Decimus must have kept Catrin for himself instead of killing her. Marcellus must have then reunited with her when he reported to him in Gaul, as Septimus surmised." Lucius stared at Gawain. "That sorceress, Catrin, bewitched Marcellus, but I never knew he'd married her."

A corner of Gawain's mouth curled into a smirk. "King Marrock told me they married in a fertility rite—"

Brutius cut in. "When Gawain told me this, I then suspected Catrin and her ruffians slaughtered my guards and helped Selena and my slaves escape. It also answers the question of why Marcellus begged Tiberius to grant him command of the northern legion. He wants to help that evil sorceress overthrow Marrock!"

Brutius paused to regard his father's shocked expression before taking the next bold step. "Gawain has agreed to strike off Catrin's head and assassinate everyone who betrayed you."

"Are you saying we should kill both Decimus and Marcellus?" Lucius's face contorted into an anguished grimace.

Brutius's burning resolve to destroy his half brother forged into cold steel. "Yes. They must both suffer for what they have done to you."

A lump formed in Lucius's throat. "Perchance, we can kill Decimus—but not Marcellus. Not my son. He must marry Licinia to forge a political alliance with Marcus Frugi."

"Did you not swear your utmost loyalty to your father, Iullus Antonius?" Brutius pressed his father. "Did you not say the only way to avenge him is to restore our family name? Both Marcellus and Decimus stand to discredit our family's name."

"But I cannot destroy my own flesh and blood," Lucius moaned, clutching his chest. "It is that Celtic witch who cast a spell on him. Kill her, not Marcellus."

Frustrated with his father's stubbornness, Brutius stepped closer to him and looked him straight in the eyes. "What if Marcellus helps that Celtic sorceress take Marrock's throne? She is a bold-blooded murderer who hacked my guards to pieces like swine. What if Marcellus decides to stay with that barbarian bitch and refuses to marry Licinia? He had no compunction about postponing the marriage, did he?"

The corners of Lucius's eyes creased with angst. "I have tried to reason with Marcellus. What more can I say to him to make him understand the importance of restoring our family name?"

"Break him down," Brutius said coldly. "Break down his resistance. Break down his spirit. Make him obey you. Make him marry Licinia. Make him fulfill your promise to restore the Antonii name."

"How do I do that without him hating me?" Lucius asked, his voice cracking with emotion.

"He can hate me instead," Brutius growled.

Lucius inhaled a sharp breath. "If I allow you to break Marcellus down, you cannot mar his face or emasculate him. He needs to sire my grandsons. Make him understand his duty to me. His duty to our family. His duty to Rome. We cannot risk our political alliance with Senator Frugi."

"No one understands that more than I do. Gawain can help me convince Marcellus," Brutius said, feigning empathy, as images of what he could do with tools of torture danced in his head.

Gawain's gruff voice saying, "I do not torture," jolted Brutius out of his gleeful fantasy of ripping out his half brother's fingertips with forceps. He felt his pulse pound in his temples as Gawain continued, "I have more scruples than that. I only do clean kills."

Brutius glared at Gawain, struggling to temper his voice. "What? Torture is against your moral code but slicing someone's throat open isn't?

That does not make sense! You will do as I command, or you will not get my aid in tracking down Catrin. Is that what you want? To fail King Marrock a second time?"

Gawain's lips quirked into a thin smile, unnerving Brutius. "We all have our moral code, do we not? My first rule is to live and be rewarded. Let me consider your plans."

Brutius felt rage burn in his chest as his steely stare bored into Gawain. *You cross me, swine, and I will slash your throat.* Clenching his hands to compose himself, he looked back and forth between his father and the weaselly, mouthy assassin as he disclosed his scheme.

"I have asked Sejanus for imperial authority to supersede Decimus Flavius. Decimus has a role to play in our plan to convince Marcellus he must return to Rome for his marriage."

"Remember what I said. No long-term harm can come to Marcellus," Lucius reiterated as his stare stabbed into Brutius.

Brutius nodded his agreement, but Gawain's wry smile made him uneasy.

33

SEARCH FOR HAVEN

Antonii Villa near Lugdunum, 25 July, 28 AD

Catrin furtively hid behind the trees to study the Antonii villa from a distance for any signs of Falco near the corralled horses. The morning mist made it difficult to see clearly. The main residence was eerily quiet, showing no signs of bustling slaves doing tasks. A foreboding sense of doom loomed over her as she tethered Lugus to a beech tree. Falco had not returned to their campsite as promised to confirm it was safe for them to stay at the villa for a respite after an arduous, two-month trip on foot and horseback from Massilia.

The escape to Lugdunum had begun with hope when Cynwrig and Selena exchanged marriage vows in a forest full of wildlife and a bubbling stream. But, as the group traversed northward on foot, in a wagon or on horseback, their initial excitement of escaping into Gaul waned. They often traveled at night or off the main road in deep woods during the day to avoid Roman legionaries patrolling the main road. Perpetual nausea and fatigue from her pregnancy plagued Catrin. Selena, approaching full term, faded more and more each day from the strain of travel. Others in their group had fallen ill with fever, including Cynwrig, with the onslaught of recent torrential rainfall. A twelve-year-old boy and an older household slave had died the previous night.

Catrin was desperate to find a haven where they could rest and recover, but she was not sure if Marcellus had notified the *major domus* about his arrangements for her to stay at the villa. Not knowing if any ramifications had unleashed after their deadly act in Rome, Falco volunteered to assess the situation, assuring her everyone at the villa would expect him to return from Rome after transferring freshly trained horses for chariot racing. He would covertly investigate whether Marcellus had sent any instructions to the overseer of the villa.

But when Falco did not return after three days, Catrin decided to slip out of the camp without telling anyone and survey the villa grounds herself. She was the only one in the group familiar with the villa's setup and could secretly search for Falco or speak with one of the trusted slaves.

A gravelly voice saying, "Do not go there," startled Catrin out of her muse. She looked all around but could not find the source of the voice in the dense trees.

From above, another ominous voice croaked, "Do not go there."

Alarmed, Catrin snapped her head up and recognized the Raven perched on an upper branch as the one she had left at the amphitheater in Lugdunum to haunt Decimus. It bobbed its ruffled head and gurgled, as if warning her.

The sound of nearby crackling twigs galvanized her senses. Holding her breath, she crouched behind some scrubby bushes and observed what looked like a shadow moving slowly in the dense pines.

"Do not go there," the Raven warned again.

Catrin froze in trepidation and scrutinized the shadowy figure lumbering in and out of the dark woods. Sunlight escaping dark clouds suddenly illuminated a hunched man with a staff in his hand. She recognized the serpent-headed handle with the pearl-white orb in its mouth.

Is it Myrddin?

That I am. Myrddin's voice connected with her thoughts.

How did you find me?

Your raven led me here, Myrddin communed.

The Raven suddenly swooped down and landed on Myrddin's shoulder. The centuries-old druid mumbled some incomprehensible gibberish to the Raven, its eyes aglow under the shadows of leaves trembling from a warm breeze. The druid's stare froze on Catrin as his croaky voice resonated in her mind.

You must travel another path.

"What path?" she whispered.

The one that leads to your destiny, Myrddin's voice whispered in her head. He motioned for her to join him at an oak that towered over the other trees in the woods.

A shudder spliced down Catrin's spine. *Should I trust him?*

The first time Catrin had met the wandering druid, he'd appeared to her as an owl but shape-shifted into his decrepit human shape. Later, he'd tricked her into transforming into a white raven, while Rhan shape-shifted into Catrin's human form to seduce Marcellus. Worried the dark druidess was nearby, Catrin grasped the pommel of her sheathed sword and glanced around.

"Where is Rhan?" she murmured.

Nearby, on hollowed grounds, Myrddin said.

"Hollowed grounds?"

Where dark secrets are buried.

"What dark secrets?" Catrin asked, suddenly queasy.

"My eyes are too weak to see below, but souls of the dead haunt these grounds," Myrddin said in an audible voice as he limped toward her, using the staff for support.

Catrin's stomach clenched, and she leaned over to spew acrid contents. Once her stomach settled, she inhaled deeply, but her lips quivered as cold sweat flooded her face. Light-headed, she gingerly sat against the tree trunk and placed her head on bent knees.

"Are you here to meet your twin flame?" Myrddin inquired.

"My twin flame?" Catrin repeated, raising her gaze to meet Myrddin's opaque, gray eyes.

"Marcellus," Myrddin replied. "Is that not his family's villa down there?"

"Yes," Catrin said weakly. "What do you mean by twin flame?"

"His soul is the mirror of yours. Only his love can burn your soul forever," Myrddin explained. "You have the raven's darkness, whereas his soul radiates like a flame. Together, you are one soul—darkness and light balancing each other. But you cannot see light until you understand the shadow he casts on you."

Unnerved by the druid's words, Catrin asked, "Why are you here?"

"You know why I am here," Myrddin said as he removed an egg from his nest-like, white beard. "Only I can anoint you as the raven queen of the Cantiaci kingdom."

"Did you not declare my half brother the rightful king after he cut off my father's head?" Catrin said sharply.

"I never declared Marrock as king. Only you can speak for the earth goddess and proclaim the next king," Myrddin retorted. "Do you recall declaring your twin flame as king in the fertility ritual in Britannia?"

"Even so, Marrock declares himself as king," Catrin said, growing frustrated with Myrddin, who often spoke in riddles. "Besides, you tricked my father into believing he could break Rhan's curse by marrying me to Marcellus."

Myrddin pressed his forefinger to his lips. "Shhh. Keep your voice down. An enemy is hiding in the villa."

Catrin shuddered. "What enemy?"

"As I told you, my eyes are too weak to see that far." Myrddin shuffled closer, leaned over with the support of his staff, and squinted at her belly. "But you could see the enemy if you were not so blinded by the brightness of your twin flame."

Unnerved, Catrin clasped her rounded belly, which was clearly visible through her tunic.

Myrddin shifted his eyes to the Raven and talked to it as though she was not there. "No wonder she cannot connect with you. It appears her twin flame has seeded a child in her womb," he declared. "What are we to do? The Roman shades the light to her destiny."

The Raven bobbed its head and croaked, "Unwise. Unwise."

Catrin angrily rose to her feet. "Speak directly to me as your queen. It was my choice to lie with my Roman husband."

Myrddin shook his head and sighed. "All your energy goes into creating life when you most need it to defeat Marrock."

"Marcellus promised me military aid," Catrin asserted.

Myrddin's gray eyes narrowed. "Only you can unleash the dark forces of the ancient druids to defeat Marrock. Not Roman forces. Trystan, who is now at our campsite, has told tales of how Marrock destroyed Adminius's army in battle. Roman troops have been sent to Britannia to help defend his kingdom."

"That must mean Marcellus is in command, yes?" Catrin asked, assuming the news about her Roman husband meant he had kept his promise to aid her.

"The commander is Tribune Arius Petronis," Myrddin clarified.

The tribune's name sounded familiar to Catrin. "The only reason Roman troops are in Britannia must be because Marcellus ordered them there. So, he must command the northern legion in Gaul."

"What does it matter? Marrock will also destroy the Roman army," Myrddin said, emphasizing with a stomp of his staff on the ground. "He harnesses dark forces from souls of children he has murdered and transformed into his wolves. By adding the combined powers of your family's souls imprisoned in their skulls, he can summon dark forces of nature from the bowels of the Otherworld."

Catrin recalled what Peccia had recounted about Marrock's dark magic. "A slave I freed described these forces as earthquakes and lightning."

"It is much more than that," Myrddin exclaimed. "He can shape-shift into a dragon and exhale poisonous gases and fire. You only have the power of one soul. And, as long as the babe is in your womb, your magic is diminished. That needs to change if you are to fulfill your destiny."

Catrin protectively rubbed her hardened belly. "What are you asking me to do? Get rid of my baby?"

"Innocent babies grow up to be Roman conquerors," Myrddin said, shaking the staff until the orb began to glow.

Catrin gaped at Myrddin in horror as she felt the unborn baby kick aggressively inside her belly. "You cannot make me sacrifice my child," she said firmly.

"For the slightest chance of defeating Marrock, you must fuse with other souls," Myrddin said emphatically.

Catrin stared at Myrddin in disbelief. "How can I do that?"

"Let me show you." Myrddin pulled his long tunic over his head to reveal naked folds of skin sagging from his skeletal, gaunt body, then he pointed to the pasture at the edge of the forest. "Look at Rhan over there."

Armed in chain mail and a helmet, the dark druidess walked out of a grove of beech trees to the wild-flowered meadow. Myrddin thumped his serpent-headed staff on the ground three times.

A flash of bright light from the serpent's orb momentarily blinded Catrin as a blast of heat singed her face. Opening her eyes, she saw a brown-spotted owl fly directly at the Raven like an arrow. She cringed, anticipating the birds would collide. Instead, the owl vanished into the Raven's body. Dumbfounded, she gaped at the Raven as it flew away.

Sudden crackling sounds from the serpent-headed staff on the ground diverted her attention. To her amazement, filaments of light were emitting from the serpent's orb to Rhan, who was in the midst of a lightning storm. She waved her mail-gloved hand, as though directing the charged light, which was blaring like trumpets announcing a chariot race, to twist and turn around her.

Gasping in disbelief, Catrin fell to her knees, barely able to catch her breath. A shudder raced down her spine when she saw the dark druidess kneel and lift a skull from the ground. Charged light weaved in and out of each eye socket. As Rhan rose, the light and the cacophonous sounds faded.

The phenomenon was similar to what Catrin had conjured at her last gladiatorial game, when she'd used a spear to channel the force of a lightning bolt to strike the stands. The godlike ability had been fueled by her burning rage to destroy Decimus—a fleeting, uncontrollable force.

Yet, Rhan had controlled the charged light like a spider spinning its web.

Catrin staggered to her feet, her mind trying to understand the supernatural forces she had witnessed Rhan harnessing and directing. The dark druidess had somehow generated lightning from a skull and controlled its motion—an awesome ability Catrin feared. She now felt as helpless as the child growing in her belly and feared Rhan's ability to destroy her and the baby.

34

HIDEAWAY

Shaken, Catrin looked up and gazed at the Raven soaring overhead, cawing at her. Myrddin's owl form could no longer be seen. It was as though the owl had dissolved into the Raven to become a part of it.

Rhan called out to Catrin in a deep, smoky voice. "Did you see where Myrddin disappeared to?"

"I don't know," Catrin replied nervously. "He shape-shifted into an owl but then appeared to merge into the Raven."

"He can be a trickster," Rhan remarked, then she inspected the skull in her hands. "I wonder who this is?"

Unnerved, Catrin felt her heart hammer against her ribcage at the possibility it was Falco's skull. Her voice cracked. "Did you kill him?"

"Of course not, my love. Why would I do that?" Rhan rubbed her finger around the edge of the bony eye socket. "I only harnessed the power from the soul trapped in the skull."

The dark druidess shifted her stare beyond Catrin and pointed. "The killing fields behind you hide more dark secrets. You will find what you are looking for there."

Trembling with trepidation of what she would find, Catrin turned and spotted a dirt mound. She crouched and scooped away the loose dirt until a bluish forehead appeared. She frantically dug away the remaining loose dirt with her hands to reveal a severed head. Rivulets of cold sweat burned her eyes as she gawked in horror at blood-tinged foam leaking from the mouth and nose. Repulsed, she fell on her hands and retched.

Rhan leaned over on her hands and knees and crawled up to the head like a wolf ready to sniff its dead prey. "Is this the one you seek? Falco?

I sense a dark force lurking at the villa. We need to go, or we will meet Falco's fate."

"What do we do with his head?" Catrin asked, her nerves on edge.

"Leave it," Rhan snapped, pressing her hand on the ground to get up. "The souls of the dead haunt these grounds."

"What about Myrddin?"

Rhan picked up the serpent-headed staff from the ground and studied it. "We will take his staff with us. I have never experienced such a force as when his soul merged with the Raven."

"What force?" Catrin asked, still confounded that the serpent's orb appeared to be a conduit for the charged light emitting from the skull. Or, possibly, the orb generated the light and the skull served as the conduit?

A corner of Rhan's lips twisted up. "You will soon learn how to forge the power of your soul with others. Until then, you will stay at a safe haven until you give birth to your child and your magical abilities return. Help me onto your horse so I can take you to our encampment Warriors await your arrival there."

Catrin was hesitant to go with Rhan, but what other choice did she have? If she sought refuge at the villa, she could meet Falco's fate. Her sickly group, now in the custody of Rhan, needed time to rest and recover. Shaking off her uneasiness, she intertwined her fingers for Rhan to step on to mount Lugus. Still, questions rolled in Catrin's mind about whether she could trust the dark druidess as she climbed onto Lugus and positioned herself in front of Rhan. Following Rhan's directions, she reined her horse in a northerly direction. They rode alongside a meandering stream deep into dense woods. The loud cracks of tree branches splitting in the hot sun resonated all around them.

Catrin kept a watchful eye for falling trees as the horse's hooves trampled on twigs, branches, and leaves on the forest floor. As the sun was reaching its zenith, the bouncing motion made Catrin feel queasy. Feeling sick, she quickly dismounted and leaned over to dry heave until her stomach spasmed in pain. Breathing hard and sweating profusely, she felt Rhan lightly touch her arm. Looking up, she saw the dark druidess kneel next to the stream, scoop water into the palm of her hand, and take a couple of sips.

"The water is sweet here and will settle your stomach," Rhan remarked.

After Catrin belched to relieve some gas, she also bent over to scoop the water into her hand and drink. The cold liquid surprisingly eased her queasiness.

"The water has healing properties," Rhan commented. "It will ease the discomfort of the life growing inside you." The dark druidess closed her eyes and jerked her head back, as if she were listening to the wind. "I can hear your baby's heartbeats, your thoughts. Do not fret about your child. No one will harm your unborn son. His fate is sealed along with yours on the dagger."

Catrin tried to block Rhan from probing her mind but was powerless to do so. She breathed deeply to clear such thoughts from her mind. "Why did you bring me here?"

"To tell you that Myrddin now believes your fate is annealed in the dagger's metal."

"And what is my fate?"

Rhan gave a wolfish smile. "If I reveal your fate, you might choose another path. We cannot let that happen, can we? Your father sealed your fate when his soul melted into the dagger's blade. Remnants of his soul are still there."

"How can you know this?"

Rhan chuckled darkly. "It is Amren's revenge on me to assure your victory. Once you draw the dagger out of the serpent stone, you doom Marrock. Amren is forcing me to destroy our son so you become queen. In return, I give you my daughter sired by Marcellus to raise. It is also her destiny to become a warrior queen."

Catrin felt the sting of bitterness in her heart. "I will never forgive you for seducing Marcellus. I will never forgive you for scheming with Marrock to destroy my father and my family. And I will never forgive you for the Romans enslaving me!"

"I do not seek your forgiveness, my dear." Rhan's eyes blazed at Catrin.

"I only seek atonement from the gods for creating a monster out of the depths of my hatred. Only I can destroy what I create. And you must also sacrifice what is most precious to you to balance these creative and destructive forces."

A shudder spliced down Catrin's spine at the thought that her unborn son would have to be sacrificed in her quest to destroy the monster. She would never let that happen.

Sensing Rhan's essence probing her mind, Catrin shut down her thoughts and spoke plainly. "Do not speak to me in riddles. Tell me what I need to sacrifice."

Rhan paused and regarded Catrin for a moment. "You will discover the truth of what you must do at the moment it happens. Make no mistake, though. The wheel has been set in motion and is turning toward your destiny. The Roman emperor has assigned Marcellus to stop our warriors' attacks in Gaul. You cannot stop what happens next."

Catrin jerked her head back. "What attacks?"

"We are plundering Roman estates to fund our war against Marrock and to pay mercenaries."

"Did you just plunder Marcellus's estate?" Catrin asked apprehensively.

Rhan answered with a grim smile. "A few horses only . . . a burned barn. Nobody was killed. Nonetheless, the ramifications from the raid will force you to choose: Marcellus or the Cantiaci kingdom."

Growing suspicious that Rhan was spinning a web to force Marcellus to view her as his enemy, Catrin probed deeper. "What are you saying? I must risk my child to lead these attacks?"

Rhan chuckled. "Of course not. You will not go on these raids. Instead, you will be kept in a large cave—a safe hideaway—until your son is born. Our encampment moves there in the next couple of days." The dark druidess paused and looked up. Following the direction of her gaze, Catrin found the Raven circling overhead.

"Your warriors tell tales of how your spear transformed into lightning," Rhan said, "as you threw it at the stands in the arena. In their eyes, you are unbeatable—a raven goddess who will overpower a tyrant and bless your followers with victory. All you need to do is perform war rituals to embolden your warriors before they embark on each raid. I have told your warriors that the baby in your womb was sired by the thunder god. You must continue to make your people believe you are immortal."

Struggling to accept Rhan's scheme to present her as a goddess to the warriors, Catrin walked slowly back to Lugus and leaned her head against his neck.

I am none of these.

"You are if you believe it," Rhan declared, as if reading her mind.

The affirmation did not ease Catrin's suspicions about Rhan's true intent, but she remained quiet as they both mounted Lugus and rode about a mile to an encampment where several tents had been set up.

For the first time since being enslaved, Catrin again entered the domain of Celtic warriors with blue tattoos of fierce-looking animals, whorls, and tendrils covering most of their bodies. Knotted patterns, which spiraled down their arms and legs, represented the never-ending cycle of rebirth and death. Images of wolves running, ravens flying, and salmon jumping endowed warriors with strength, swiftness, and courage. As Catrin rode through the camp, Rhan wrapped her arms around her swollen waist, while bare-chested warriors danced in crazed excitement and chanted, "*Cobranoriga,* raven queen."

Other warriors reached out their hands toward her and hailed, "*Belloriga*, war queen."

Some reverently touched her legs as she rode through their midst.

For the last four years, she had primarily spoken the Roman tongue. Today, the guttural Celtic language sounded foreign, almost threatening. Her heart quickened as the warriors continued swarming around her and spooking her horse.

When Lugus finally reared, ready to buck, a shudder ran down Catrin's back. She pulled tight on one rein to pull the horse's head around to get him under control.

She recognized Trystan as he rushed to the horse and waved everyone away, shouting, "Move back!"

After Catrin finally calmed the stallion, Trystan helped both Rhan and her off the horse.

Rhan pointed to the Raven circling above and thundered, "It is an omen from the gods!"

Awestruck, the warriors quieted as the Raven descended from the heavens into the nearby woods. Through the trees, a brilliant light flashed, its glare so bright that Catrin had to cover her eyes with her left arm. A few heartbeats later, she opened her eyes to find a naked Myrddin lumbering out of the forest. One of the warriors unclipped his blue plaid cape and placed it around the druid's hunched shoulders. The centuries-old druid shuffled through the warriors, who stepped back to allow him through.

After Myrddin joined Rhan and Catrin, the dark druidess declared, "An ancient prophecy foretold a warrior queen would come to us in a time of strife. And that queen is here with us now." Rhan pointed to Catrin. "Queen Catrin will embrace the dagger's destiny. The Raven will bestow her with the fury of the thunder god. She will unleash vengeance on Blood Wolf and lead us to victory!"

All of Catrin's senses heightened as warriors beat weapons on their shields like one beating heart. She inhaled the scent of heavy air, signaling a thunderstorm.

Thunder rumbled through the air.

Unexpectedly, the Raven flew out of the forest and landed on Rhan's extended arm.

Emboldened, Catrin waved her arms like wings over her head, visualizing herself as a raven. Recognizing she had to forge an alliance with the formidable dark druidess to fulfill the prophecy, she was now ready to face the specters from her past—Marrock, Adminius, Decimus, and Marcellus's family.

35

FINAL ORDERS

Governor's Headquarters, Lugdunum, 6 August, 28 AD

Marcellus, climbing the steep cobblestone road to the forum, felt his pulse race with the anticipation of meeting with Governor Decimus Flavius at his headquarters. The forum was adjacent to the coliseum where he had watched Catrin fight as a gladiator. Ironically, her opponent, Ferrex, was walking alongside him, on his left, while to his right was Negasi. He recalled the Ethiopian's rebuke for not being there for Catrin when she had given birth to their stillborn daughter. On their journey from Rome to Lugdunum, the gladiators had had ample opportunity to slit his throat, but they had remained loyal.

Or so it seemed.

More likely, they would only serve him until they reunited with their queen—an unsettling likelihood that their loyalty was thread thin.

As they approached the forum on the hilltop between the Saône and Rhône rivers, Marcellus noted a temple with a massive altar flanked with statues of two-winged women set on columns. A raven suddenly swooped over his head, startling him, and landed on the shoulder of one of the temple's statues.

An omen from Catrin?

The imperial mandate that he would receive his final orders from Decimus left a bitter taste in his mouth. Every bone in his body mistrusted the unscrupulous governor, who drank from the trough of influential statesmen to elevate his political standing. Not knowing the extent of the friendship between Tiberius and Decimus put Marcellus at a disadvantage.

Furthermore, his former commander had blackmailed him into paving the way for his political ambitions.

To this day, Marcellus regretted deserting his post in northern Gaul to help Catrin escape enslavement from Decimus—an impetuous and treasonous act punishable by death. To save both their lives, Marcellus had to concede to Decimus's demand of convincing his father to support the commander's ambition of assuming governorship of Gallia Lugdunensis. To gain possession of Catrin, Marcellus had threatened to expose Decimus's criminal act of syphoning imperial funds from the legion to line his pockets. The threat might come back to bite him.

Decimus now held the upper hand.

With unknown factors at play, Marcellus felt his stomach clench. He also had to consider his father a threat. He remembered how his father's pierced stare had cut through him before he'd left for Gaul. Would Decimus know about the mayhem at Brutius's villa?

What acts of vengeance could twist my father's mind? Would he pit Decimus against me?

Marcellus took a deep breath to steady his nerves as he strode into the interior of the forum. At the arched entranceway of the governor's quarters, he presented his credentials to a centurion standing alongside five armed guards.

"I am Praetor Marcellus Antonius," he declared. "I am here to meet with Proconsul Decimus Flavius."

The grim-faced centurion studied Marcellus for a moment, then shifted his gaze back and forth between Ferrex and Negasi. "Identify the men with you," he demanded.

"Ferrex and Negasi, my bodyguards," Marcellus introduced, gesturing to each.

The guard's stare lit on Negasi. "Are you not . . . the Black Sphinx? I saw you—"

A gruff voice from inside the chamber ordering, "Bring them in," cut off the centurion's words. Marcellus thanked the gods that another fanatic spewing praises for one of his freed gladiators did not delay the meeting.

The centurion snapped to attention and shouted, "Right away. I am checking for weapons."

Ferrex and Negasi unsheathed the swords hidden beneath their cloaks and handed them to a guard. Marcellus, attired in formal military uniform, offered his *gladius* and *pugio* to another guard, then took off his red-crowned helmet.

The centurion escorted them into a dimly lit chamber, where Decimus sat behind a large table on which scrolls were strewn. At his back were cubicles jammed with additional scrolls. A pudgy assistant dressed in an oversized, white linen tunic and toga hunched next to Decimus—like a dog waiting for orders.

The centurion announced Marcellus and handed the sealed scroll to the assistant to unseal and open. Decimus greeted Marcellus with an ice-cold stare. Marcellus nervously acknowledged Decimus with a slight nod and waited for him to read the imperial orders.

Decimus's eyes shifted downward as he read the parchment. "Impressive," he repeated, occasionally stealing a glance at Marcellus.

The anticipation of what Decimus's final orders would be made Marcellus's heart beat as rapidly as a war drum. The deathly silence finally broke with the clap of Decimus's hand on the tabletop, signaling he was ready to begin.

"Leave us," Decimus barked, exchanging glances with his assistant and the centurion. They both left the chamber and shut the massive door with a bang on their way out.

Decimus rubbed the corner of his eyelid as he studied Marcellus and the two ex-gladiators. "I find it unsettling, Marcellus, that you have brought two fierce gladiators with you."

"Do you want them to wait outside?" Marcellus asked.

Decimus shook his head. "No. I want them to hear what I have to say. They can stand at the entry door."

The governor's unexpected response took Marcellus by surprise. He gestured for Negasi and Ferrex to do as Decimus ordered.

For a moment, Decimus rubbed the facial scar at the corner of his mouth. "So, you have an imperial order decreeing that you are the praetor of the northern garrison?"

"Yes, but Tiberius mandated that I report to you for final orders," Marcellus said, still questioning why Decimus had asked the gladiators to stay in the chamber.

"You must be on friendly terms with Tiberius, then," Decimus commented.

Marcellus nodded. "I met him at his palace on Capri."

Decimus breathed in deeply. The blue vein in the crescent-shaped facial scar stretching from his left eye to his mouth pulsated as he spoke evenly. "Did you know your father threatened to cut off his patronage of me? He knows Catrin is alive and accuses me of being a liar. How did he find out?"

"I never told him," Marcellus replied. "But it is hard to keep a dark secret like that."

Decimus regarded Marcellus with probing eyes. "What is clear, though, is that you had a falling-out with your father."

"I am not here to discuss my personal life. I am here for final orders," Marcellus said firmly, to divert the conversation.

Decimus leaned back in his chair but kept his eyes riveted on Marcellus as he spoke. "Well, then, let me give you an update on military operations. I ordered expeditionary forces to Britannia to defend the Catuvellauni territory from Marrock's raids. I advised Tiberius of this."

"Wise move," Marcellus said without any inflection in his voice, despite Decimus's contemptuous scowl.

"I made the decision because Adminius, a son of Cunobelin, petitioned for military support in late fall of last year. Did you know the prince is betrothed to Catrin?"

"I was not aware," Marcellus said flatly, although he could feel his pulse pounding in his neck.

Decimus studied Marcellus for a moment. "I find it highly irregular to petition Tiberius directly to assign you as a commander of the northern legion."

Marcellus met Decimus's piercing stare. "That said, I assume my final order is to take immediate command of the fortress at Gesoriacum."

Decimus rose from his chair, and his voice grew louder. "Subordinates do not assume. Subordinates do not overstep. Subordinates obey. Only I, as governor, understand the regional issues. I speak the native tongue, which you never bothered to learn. I am in charge of military operations here. Not you—a boy who needs to think with his head! Do you understand?"

Marcellus averted his gaze from Decimus's glazed eyes and looked at the cubicles. "I understand. Would you enlighten me about my assignment?"

Decimus leaned forward, both hands firmly planted on the tabletop. "You are to remain in Lugdunum and hunt down rebels plundering Roman estates. Centurion Priscus Dius will report to you. You remember him?"

Marcellus clenched his hands in anger, recalling how the centurion had abused Catrin during training in the legion.

That slimy guard dog!

"What about the expedition to Britannia that Tiberius promised I would lead?" Marcellus asked, more bluntly than he intended, noting the frown on Decimus's face.

"Tribune Arius Petronis is the commander for military operations in Britannia. Not you," Decimus declared. "His forces are set to sail back to northern Gaul in September. After that, Tiberius will reassess the situation to decide whether we need to commit more troops to Britannia. Meanwhile, you will stay in Lugdunum."

Marcellus cocked an eyebrow. "To do what?"

"Do you recall the raven at the gladiatorial game last year?" Decimus asked unexpectedly.

Marcellus's stomach dropped. Catrin had used the raven as a stage prop to incite fear in the mob during the games.

Decimus continued. "Remember, it flew out of the arena after Catrin's fight? Alas, it has returned to haunt me. Every day, the black demon perches on a column at the coliseum, ready to swoop down on me. It has clawed the top of my head and made it bleed." He inhaled sharply. "But it suddenly vanished about a month ago."

"A good thing it is gone," Marcellus said, thinking of the raven that had swept over him just before this meeting.

"Strange. The raids at Roman estates began around the same time the raven disappeared. The only explanation I can think of is that Catrin has returned to Lugdunum. As we both know, she speaks directly with Apollo and can summon her magic from his messenger, the Raven." Decimus's eyes narrowed. "Do you know where Catrin is?"

Marcellus nervously shifted his feet. "How would I know? She left my villa almost a year ago, after I freed her."

A nasty scowl contorted Decimus's face as he walked around the table and stepped up to Marcellus. "Now that you are here, it is strange the raven has vanished. That seems more than a coincidence."

Marcellus gave a nervous chuckle. "Most likely, the raven found a mate outside the city."

"Or perhaps the mate found the raven," Decimus said, a biting sarcasm to his voice. "I've been told a woman leads the raids on the estates. And a raven is always with her."

Marcellus swallowed down a sense of panic. He kept his eyes fixed on Decimus, though his heart raced with the thought that Catrin was spear-heading the raids. It made sense. She'd freed Brutius's slaves in Rome and had stolen coins.

"One of the plundered estates is yours," Decimus added. "The thieves stole most of the horses. Some of the slaves went missing—possibly dead or kidnapped to be sold as slaves. A barn was burned down."

Stunned, Marcellus felt his mouth gape open. "Catrin would never attack my villa."

"Did I say it was Catrin?" Decimus suddenly took a step back, and his eyes widened in the direction of the doorway. "Control your gladiators. They look like they are ready to cut out my guts. Be warned. The guards outside will crucify anyone who tries to harm me."

Marcellus pivoted on his heels to find both Negasi and Ferrex with fire in their eyes. He shook his head and mouthed, "Stand down."

"Fulfill your duty to Rome and to your father," Decimus demanded as Marcellus's back was turned. "And do not complicate my life further."

Marcellus turned and met Decimus's burning glare. "I will do what Rome demands," he said firmly.

"Make sure you do," Decimus growled. "Dismissed."

As Marcellus strode out of the chamber to the forum, with Negasi and Ferrex on each side, every muscle in his body contracted like a coiled serpent ready to strike. Had Decimus tricked him into believing Catrin had spearheaded the raids? If she had led the raids, how could he stop her if he did not know where she was?

Negasi's deep voice drew Marcellus out of his contemplation. "What do you plan to do?"

Marcellus caught a glimpse of a man staring at them from a distance. "Keep your voice down. Someone may be following us. I have no choice now but to do my duty and investigate what happened at my family's villa."

Ferrex stepped up to Marcellus. "So much for your promise to aid Catrin," he growled.

Negasi gripped the Red Lion by the arm. "Hold that temper until we learn more. One thing is clear, though. Catrin is in danger. We need to work together to protect her."

"Exactly," Marcellus snapped. "Did you not wonder why Decimus had both of you at the meeting?"

Ferrex snarled. "A good reason to slice your neck."

Negasi tightened his grip on Ferrex. "That is exactly what Decimus wants. He wants us to turn on Marcellus. For once, think with your head."

Suddenly, a raven's screech drew their attention to the top of a column in front of the amphitheater.

Negasi smiled. "It looks like we have a way to find our queen."

A strange feeling that someone else was watching them gripped Marcellus's chest. He looked askance. A heavily tattooed man was staring at them.

"Quiet. Spies everywhere," Marcellus said in a hushed tone. "Let's get settled in the barracks and come up with a plan."

Marcellus checked in at the stone-built garrison on the outskirts of town and summoned Centurion Priscus Dius to the main headquarters. He told Ferrex and Negasi to stand next to the entrance door so they could listen to the conversation and assess the situation.

As Priscus entered the chamber and announced himself, the red-edged scar slicing down his face triggered an image in Marcellus's mind of the centurion brutally whacking Catrin across the face with the back of his sword and knocking her senseless. Marcellus had challenged Priscus to spar with him, then cut his face with the tip of his sword in retribution.

"Proconsul Decimus Flavius has given me strict orders to escort you everywhere and report directly back to him," Priscus arrogantly declared.

Marcellus felt the same intense rage as when Priscus had brutalized Catrin. Restraining his impulse to bash the centurion's head into the wall, he rebuked, "You will strictly follow the chain of command. You are only to obey my direct orders and report to me as we brush these rebels out." He glared and stepped up to Priscus. "Do not forget our fight in Gesoriacum."

Priscus lowered his eyes. "I understand," he grunted.

"Good. Then it's settled," Marcellus said, keeping his eyes on Priscus. "Tomorrow, you will gather twenty of your best legionaries to scour the grounds at my estate for clues about the raid. We leave at sunrise."

With his jaw clenched, Priscus nodded and turned on his heels to leave. Ferrex bumped hard into the centurion's shoulder as he left.

Marcellus smirked and gestured Ferrex and Negasi forward so he could speak privately with them. "What do you think of the centurion's comments?" he asked.

"He should be lashed for insubordination," Ferrex answered.

Negasi chuckled. "Indeed. But who is in command here?"

"Good question," Marcellus interjected. "That is why I want you both to enlist in the Roman auxiliary. I need other eyes and ears to make sure nothing happens behind my back. You both speak the local language. Possibly, you can learn from the natives where the rebels are hiding. Then, we can find out if Catrin is involved in the raids."

"The last thing I want to do is report to you in the Roman legion," Ferrex said with fire in his eyes.

"Neither do I," Marcellus said sharply. "But here we are, both fighting for your queen. Today, I will expedite the documents to enlist you, then get you settled in the barracks."

Ferrex shot him a nasty scowl. "I only fight in her army."

"That you will," Marcellus agreed. "But first, we need to find her and tell her to stop the raids. Once the situation improves, I will find a way to take command of the northern legion."

Ferrex and Negasi nodded their agreement.

At dawn the next day, Marcellus, Ferrex, and Negasi saddled their horses and joined Priscus and twenty infantrymen in a formation of four men in each line. After Marcellus inspected the contingents, he gestured for Priscus to give the order to move out. They rode behind the marching legionaries through the main watchtower and to the main cobblestone road.

After traveling a half mile north of the city, they veered right onto a dirt road through the woods. Ghostly fog hovering in the treetops filtered out most of the sunlight. The sound of songbirds chirping and animals chattering resonated around them. A raven croaking, "Fall in line," could occasionally be heard as they traveled deeper and deeper into the gloom.

As the infantrymen continued marching ahead, Marcellus slowed his horse and gestured for Ferrex to come closer. "Follow the raven above and report what you find," Marcellus ordered in a hushed tone. "Do you know how to find my villa?"

"Do not worry, Roman. Barbarians always find their way back," Ferrex replied haughtily.

"All right, then," Marcellus said, doubtful the Red Lion would return if he found Catrin.

Ferrex reined his horse off the pathway and disappeared into the trees as Marcellus continued riding alongside Negasi, keeping an earshot distance from the marching legionaries.

"Catrin told me many things about you," Negasi commented.

Taken aback, Marcellus looked at Negasi. "She did?"

Negasi paused, as if considering his next words. "She said you were a great commander in the legion. Tell me—how can you defeat enemies from four different fronts?"

Marcellus cocked an eyebrow. "Is this a trick question?"

"Think about what Decimus said," Negasi said. "I see four factions trying to block Catrin from ruling as queen. Marrock with his dark magic. Decimus with his political clout. Adminius with his desire to be her king. Yet, I fear the fourth enemy the most."

Marcellus looked askance at Negasi. "Who is that?"

"Your father," Negasi answered bluntly. "You went behind his back and spoke directly with the emperor. Your fight with him puts Catrin at risk."

The truth opened a gaping wound Marcellus had failed to mend with his father. Since meeting with Decimus, he had mulled over possible ways to assuage his father's ire.

"Were you in the army?" Marcellus asked, curious to learn more about the military background of the even-tempered Negasi, who often wore a stone face.

"I served in the cavalry for the Kush king. After I won a hard-fought battle, he assigned me to his royal guard to protect his queen." Negasi sighed heavily. "But I did not do my duty."

"How is that?"

"The king found me in bed with his queen, Aminitore," Negasi confessed.

"I would not have expected that from you," Marcellus jested.

"Love makes a man lose reason. The king sentenced me to death, but Aminitore helped me escape. The last time we embraced, she revealed she carried my child."

"What happened to her?" Marcellus asked, suspecting this was a tale of caution directed at him.

"Alas, I do not know. I sailed the seas as a pirate and never saw her again." Becoming misty-eyed, Negasi swallowed hard. "Enough about me. You never answered my question. How can you defeat four enemies?"

"You tell me," Marcellus challenged.

"Do what Decimus says," Negasi said bluntly. "Take away your father's anger. Do your duty and marry the woman he chose for you."

The answer cut into Marcellus's heart. He glared at Negasi. "Do you say this because you hold affection for Catrin?"

"I cannot deny this," Negasi said with a wry smile, "but I am wise enough not to act on my feelings. I accept Catrin's charge, though, to serve as a commander in her army. This is my advice to you. To win a war, you must eliminate each enemy one by one. But first, take away your father's fire."

"It may be too late," Marcellus muttered.

He kicked his horse into a gallop, leaving Negasi at the rear, while taking the lead of the formation. The Ethiopian's words pervaded his mind as he continued to ride through the mist-filled forest he had once explored as a boy on his black stallion, which he'd named Bucephalus after Alexander the Great's warhorse. At the time, the stillness of the deep woods had calmed him, unlike the noise-filled streets of Rome and Lugdunum. But now, his muscles were as tense as a catapult ready to release its weapon. This was no longer his cherished boyhood homestead but a crime scene. To his disappointment, he would not lead an expeditionary force to aid Catrin in her quest to overthrow Marrock. Instead, he had to patrol the area to hunt down rebels. Even though he did not want to believe Decimus's accusation that Catrin had led the raid on his family's villa, she had undoubtedly plundered Brutius's villa, released the slaves, and murdered the guards. His mind whirled with conflicting emotions, wondering if his true love had turned everything on its head. He glanced up to find the sun breaking through the dark clouds.

Is this a sign about where Catrin truly is?

At the point where the narrow road diverged into two smaller pathways, Marcellus barked out the order, "To the right."

Shortly, the lush garden in front of the villa came into view. He passed two empty, fenced corrals that could hold up to ten chariot race horses. Approaching the third corral, which had three horses inside, Marcellus noted a man sitting atop the upper rail of the fence. Thinking it was Falco, he reined his horse toward the man but was surprised to discover a fierce-looking stranger. The right side of his face had a red-edged scar from what looked like a burn from a hot blade. The red insignia of a dragon on the man's black cape put Marcellus on edge.

"Who are you?" he asked sharply.

The man's pale-blue eyes pierced him like cold ice. "Who asks?"

"Praetor Marcellus Antonius. I own this estate."

The man gave him a half smile and jumped off the fence. "Forgive me, dominus. I am Gawain, the horse trainer," he said with a thick Celtic accent.

"How long have you served here?" Marcellus asked, wondering if Falco ever returned to the estate with Catrin.

"Less than a moon," Gawain answered. "Lucius Antonius—your father, I believe—hired me in Rome."

Marcellus probed further. "Did you witness the raid on the estate?"

"No. I came after," Gawain said. "Do you want me to take you to the villa?"

"I know the way," Marcellus said, eyeing the sheathed dagger at Gawain's side. "But follow me. I would like to question you further at the villa."

36

UNREQUITED LOVE

North of Lugdunum, Gaul, 6 August, 28 AD

The raven swooped down, landed on Ferrex's extended arm, and gawked. Had it recognized him? At first, Ferrex wondered if the creature was Catrin in her shape-shifted form, but then, he reconsidered. Previously, she had always changed into a pristine, white raven. The ruffled, iridescent black plumage on the thick-necked bird changed color under the shadow cast by a cloud overhead. Catrin had told him that the Raven—a magical guide from the Otherworld—shed light on the past to illuminate the future. It felt as if its amber eyes pierced him to the soul. Emerald-green leaves wavering above him entranced him as he rode. He could hear the breeze whispering in his mind, *For almost four summers, you have prayed to the gods for a chance to pour out your heart to Catrin. You cut your hand and offered your blood to make it so.*

With a sensation of floating in a haze, Ferrex communed to the wind. *No man is as loyal or can love the queen as much as I do.*

A twinge of remorse tugged at Ferrex's heart as he recalled his final days in Britannia, where the Romans captured and enslaved him. Through mishap, he had not been able to protect Catrin—a princess who was barely fifteen summers at the time—in the final battle led by Catrin's mother, Queen Rhiannon. Instead, Roman soldiers brought him down like a wild beast as he defended the Cantiaci capital against a Roman ambush. To his shame, he was captured and sold as a gladiator to showcase in their blood sport. Deeply seeded anger coursed through his blood as he envisioned the lanista lashing him and beating him almost daily to make him yield to his command. It was only when he resolved to survive and to reunite with Catrin that he finally obeyed their commands.

For a fleeting moment after each fight, the mob crowned him as their hero, but then, they condemned him to be a caged lion in his stark quarters at night. Sometimes, Roman aristocrats paraded him like a prize bull at lavish banquets held before each spectacle. Once, he overheard a richly dressed noble say, "The gladiators know how to die, barbarians they are." Both noblewomen and noblemen forced him to satiate their sexual pleasures in secret hideaways. He carried the weight of shame for how he'd longed for Catrin's touch during these times he was debased. Each time, he lost a piece of his dignity and his soul to them.

Is that what the Romans crave? To lick the sweat off my wounds as an aphrodisiac? To revel in the blood I spill?

Though he had suffered, his greatest fear was that Catrin had endured a worse fate in the brothels. His prayers that they would reunite had been answered when they'd faced each other in the Amphitheater of the Three Gauls. But alas, their hope of escaping was dashed like a wave on a rock when Catrin misdirected the lightning strike to the lower stands, injuring both of them in the mayhem. When he briefly spoke with her before being transported to Rome to fight, he learned Marcellus had purchased her. He swore then that he would find her, fall on his knees, and swear his fealty and love. He would protect her with his body and soul and never leave her side.

A sob caught in his throat as his memories shifted farther back in time, to Catrin's trial, when King Amren accused her of treason for aiding Marcellus at the prisoner exchange. The king's final judgment on Catrin resonated in his mind to this day.

The repercussions of what you did will haunt you for the rest of your life. Today, I banish you from my sight. Ferrex will train you at his family's farm until I deem you ready for my final judgment. Before I take you back, you must first prove you are worthy of my respect and love.

King Amren had promised Ferrex that Catrin would be his bride as a reward for training her to be a warrior and for teaching her the importance of duty during banishment. He clung to the king's promise, hoping against all odds that he would one day capture Catrin's heart. His dream shattered, though, when the smooth-talking Roman snake offered a truce to King Amren to stop a pending war by brokering a political marriage between Catrin and the rival prince, Adminius. Myrddin had tricked Amren into believing that if Marcellus was made king for a day, Rhan's curse foretelling his destruction would be broken.

Ferrex could still feel the stabbing pain as he watched the Roman lecher publicly rut his promised bride, imitating a stag in a fertility ritual.

A mockery! A public disgrace!

It did not matter that this was the tribal tradition for proclaiming a new king. If he had only known that the mock marriage was intended to distract King Amren from the real danger—Marrock and Romans secretly gathering forces to destroy their kingdom—he would have struck the Roman king down.

Sensing the raven's thoughts melding with his, Ferrex inwardly shouted. *That Roman cur stole my bride!*

The Raven communed in his mind. *Negasi advised you not to show anger toward Marcellus. Rather, be a lion. Let him make the first move. Patiently stalk him. Then, when he least expects it, pounce on him for the kill.*

Ferrex jerked his head back, suddenly cognizant that the mystical creature was speaking in his father's voice, thus breaking his trance. His mind floated into a thick fog, lulling him back into a dreamlike state. He explained to the Raven that he'd studied the Roman as Negasi had advised.

"He is an enigma—bold to the point of recklessness. He has steel balls to speak with the Roman emperor and win command of the northern legion. What disarms me, though, is his affection for Catrin. I thought he only lusted after her. Yet, her quest to overthrow Marrock has become his quest. To be sure, the Roman could be a powerful ally. And his plan almost worked. The might of Rome was on the verge of aiding Catrin to overtake Marrock. But then, Decimus unraveled the plans. I am so angry he failed that I want to slice his neck open for his hubris."

The Raven's voice audibly whispered in Ferrex's ears. "Your hatred of the Roman stems from your love of the queen. She does not belong to you. She belongs to her warriors, to her people. She is a war goddess with powers to destroy all enemies. You cannot hold on to such a love as this. And neither can Marcellus."

"What about Adminius and his betrothal to Catrin?" Ferrex asked, frustrated another rival suitor was vying for Catrin. "And there is the Roman's family to reckon with. How can we defeat enemies such as these?"

"You will know at the time." Then, the Raven's voice faded.

A sudden jerk on his arm roused Ferrex out of his dreamlike state. Disoriented, he frantically glanced around for the Raven. A sense of panic sliced through him when he did not recognize the landscape and could not get his bearings. He must have ridden several miles while entranced.

"*Ubi est corvus maledictus*," he cursed. Annoyed at himself for instinctively speaking the Roman tongue, he raised a fist and shouted in Celtic, "Cursed raven, where have you gone?"

The Raven's croaky voice answered from above. "*Ut in acie!*"

Ferrex chuckled. "Even you get the tongues confused."

The Raven mimicked his laugh and swooped over his head in the direction of the late afternoon sun filtering through the trees. Finally clear-headed, he reined his horse in the direction of the bird's flight.

After a while, he heard the faint beating of drums. He dismounted and led his horse by the reins in the direction of what sounded like hearts beating as one. Through the trees, a steep, verdant hillside came into his view. As he cautiously walked closer, he scoured the hillside and spotted what appeared to be a stone archway of a cave. Two horsemen, with the distinctive Cantiaci blue-and-white plaid capes wrapped around their shoulders, were riding up a steep pathway to the entrance.

Dressed in a Roman auxiliary uniform and his hair freshly shorn, Ferrex hesitated to announce himself. The armed warriors from his tribe might take him for an enemy and strike him down. With an idea seeding in his head, he extended his arm and whistled to the Raven soaring overhead.

The creature abruptly flipped upside down in midair and shot headlong toward Ferrex. Anticipating a hard landing, he braced his left arm with his right. As the Raven descended into the treetops, it leveled its wings and landed on his arm.

"Cursed raven," he grumbled, trying to hold his arm steady as the bird settled on his chain mail sleeve. The Raven bobbed its head, as if signaling him to do something.

"Here goes nothing," Ferrex mumbled, and he strode out of the woods with the Raven perched on his left arm and the horse's reins in his right hand.

One of the horsemen saw him and waved to the other. They abruptly veered their horses and galloped toward him at full charge. Recognizing one of the warriors, who was brandishing a longsword for the attack, he shouted, "Trystan, it's Ferrex from the Cantiaci!"

Both men slowed their horses and lowered their swords as they approached Ferrex.

"That looks like Catrin's raven from the amphitheater on your arm," Trystan called out. "How did you find us?"

"The Raven led me here," Ferrex answered, wondering if Catrin had connected with the creature to lure him there.

"Were you followed?"

Ferrex shook his head. "Only this bird and me."

"Drop your weapon, then we'll talk," Trystan demanded.

Ferrex released the reins and fumbled for the sword at his side. Off-balance with the Raven still on his arm, he fumbled for the pommel of his *gladius* and dropped it on the ground.

Trystan and the other man, whom Ferrex did not recognize, dismounted and stepped up to him. Trystan picked up the sword while keeping his eyes fixed on Ferrex.

Ferrex exhaled the breath he had been holding. "Not the warm greeting I expected."

"You're not dead," Trystan replied sharply. "Why are you dressed like a Roman soldier?"

Ferrex took off his helmet to reveal his face. "I report to Praetor Marcellus Antonius. He freed me in Rome so I could join Catrin's cause."

A grin flashed across Trystan's face. "I hardly recognize your ugly face with the cropped hair. So, Marcellus is here?"

"Right now, he is at his family's villa investigating a raid purportedly led by Catrin," Ferrex replied with disdain.

"A raid led by me," Trystan admitted. "We need to be careful, though. Enemies lurk everywhere. Let us talk further in the cave."

"Is Catrin there?" Ferrex asked.

"She and more than one hundred of her warriors are there. You'll be glad to know Cynwrig is not dead. He is with us."

Shocked his cousin was still alive, Ferrex felt his mouth gape. "I saw him fall in battle."

"Battle-scarred but not dead," Trystan said grimly as he and the other warrior jumped on their horses. They turned their mounts around and waited for Ferrex to join them. He tried to wave the Raven off his arm to mount his horse, but the stubborn creature clawed into his chain mail to hang on and threatened to peck him.

Exasperated, Ferrex looked at Trystan and shrugged.

Trystan gave an amused smile. "You can follow us on foot."

Annoyed with the pesky raven on his arm, Ferrex clasped the reins of his horse and walked behind the two horsemen. Thankfully, a boy greeted Ferrex at the cave's entrance and offered to take the horse. Ferrex handed him the reins, then followed Trystan into a vast, labyrinthine cavern. The moss-covered ceiling sloped down toward tunnels leading to more dark places below. A handful of tents were along the walls.

Inquisitive warriors swarmed around them as Trystan escorted Ferrex toward the back. A one-eyed man with a grotesque facial scar stomped up to Ferrex and spread his arms like the wings of an eagle. Not sure who he was, Ferrex leaned back to avoid the one-eyed warrior's embrace.

"What is wrong with you?" Cynwrig's gruff voice blared. "Do you not you recognize me, cousin?"

Flashing a grin, Ferrex gave Cynwrig a bear hug and slapped him on the back. "I thought the Roman devils left you for the ravens to feast upon."

"As you can see, I am the walking dead, cursed with half of a face," Cynwrig said in a lighthearted tone.

Ferrex grabbed both sides of Cynwrig's head with the palms of his hands. "Much better looking, I think. The women must love you."

Cynwrig flashed a lopsided grin. "That they do. I want you to meet my new wife." He walked over to a nearby goat skin tent and pulled the flap aside to peek inside. A moment later, a dark-skinned woman cradling a swathed newborn came out.

"This is my wife, Selena. And she holds my son, Bladud, named after my father," Cynwrig proudly introduced.

Ferrex noted several thick-ridged scars marring Selena's face, but her almond-shaped eyes sparkled with hints of past beauty. He bent over to look at Bladud. The newborn's features were dissimilar to his parents. His olive skin contrasted with Cynwrig's ruddy complexion and Selena's dark-brown skin.

Feeling a tap on his shoulder, Ferrex turned around to meet the exquisite, turquoise eyes of Catrin. His heart skipped a beat as he beheld her beauty. Her ivory skin glowed in the light of a nearby torch, and her golden, plaited hair lay gently on her shoulder. With a gasp caught in his throat, he fell to his knees and reverently bowed his head.

"My queen."

"Rise," she commanded

As Ferrex rose to his feet, he was surprised to see a rounded belly beneath Catrin's tunic. Grasping for words, he gawked at her expanded belly, trying to comprehend what was obvious. Then, the words, "You are pregnant," shot out of his mouth.

A tinge of red blossomed on Catrin's face. "I am with child."

Ferrex stammered, his tongue twisted with shock. "How can . . . this be? Who?"

A sudden grip of his forearm tore Ferrex's stare away from Catrin to the dark-haired druidess he recognized as Rhan. She tightened her hold and proclaimed, "The thunder god sired the child!"

"A bastard of a god? I think not," Ferrex blurted, his mind reeling from the hard truth that Catrin must have copulated with Marcellus during the short time they were together in Rome. It felt as if the cave's walls were collapsing on him. Intense emotions of unrequited love, anger, and jealously sliced through his heart.

"Listen to me," Rhan demanded, gripping Ferrex by the arm to take him aside. "Everyone here knows the thunder god blessed Catrin with his child and immortality. She is the raven goddess I prophesied would bring us victory against Marrock. You must also believe this."

Fighting for composure, Ferrex looked at the heavily tattooed warriors in the cave. They gazed at Catrin with awestruck eyes, while others threatened him like a pack of wolves ready to devour him. He felt like a foreigner reentering the Celtic world of sorcery and rituals. He grappled with the truth, which hit him like a brick to his gut. The Raven was right. Catrin did not belong to him. She was the savior promised by Rhan. Their hopes, their dreams, were latched to their queen, who could wield the power of the gods to put an end to Marrock's tyranny. Did he, a mere mortal, have the right to dash their hopes?

Rhan's voice warning, "Control your emotions, warrior," brought Ferrex out of his disjointed thoughts. "The Cantiaci follow her because she speaks to the gods."

Ferrex pried Rhan's hand from his arm and stared at her wolfish, close-set, amber eyes. "She may have divine powers, but she is in mortal danger. That is why her raven led me here."

Catrin interceded and clasped his hand. "Let me speak with Ferrex alone in my headquarters."

Rhan's gaze shifted to the warriors gathering around them. "What will they think?"

"It does not matter. Am I not their queen?" Catrin said in a hushed but commanding tone.

Ferrex's first impulse was to smirk at Rhan after Catrin's unexpected, steel-edged demeanor, but he grew apprehensive as he followed her to a palatial tent. Inside, he found two heavily tattooed men dumping silver vases, jewelry, and coins into an open box near the entrance. Other locked, wooden chests lined both sides of the tent. In the middle, maps were spread out on a tabletop. He assumed the curtained off area in the back was her sleeping quarters.

Catrin gestured for the two warriors to leave. After they left, she stepped up to Ferrex, and he felt her eyes burn through him. "Can you not sheath that tongue of yours?" she asked harshly. "What would make you accuse my baby of being a bastard?"

Taken aback by her temper, Ferrex lowered his eyes. "Forgive me, my queen. You know me. I speak without thinking. But we both know the Roman is the father."

Catrin inhaled sharply. "You still begrudge Marcellus, don't you?"

Ferrex's jaw clenched. How could she still love a Roman who was once her master?

You should be with a man from your tribe. Like me!

Struggling to contain his emotions, he stared at her feet. "You have always known my hatred for the Roman," he said candidly, but then, his voice cracked with deep emotion. "And you know I love you."

There was a long pause, and Catrin lightly touched his hand, taking him by surprise. Unable to look at her, Ferrex swallowed hard to contain the emotions burning inside him.

"Let us talk about this," she suggested in a softer voice. "You have always had a special place in my heart, Ferrex. But not in the way you want. Marcellus is my husband. And you must accept this."

Ferrex met her gaze with a fierce stare. *I will never accept this!*

"But Myrddin tricked—" he began, but Catrin cut off his words.

"It does not matter. He is my husband and king," she said firmly.

"What about Roman law?" Ferrex asked, his rapid breaths burning with fire.

Eyes ablaze, Catrin stepped closer and gave him a stern rise of her brow. "What? You accept Roman law when it suits you—that a noble cannot marry a barbarian?"

Ferrex tensed and floundered for words. "A fish cannot fly with a raven!"

Catrin chuckled. "Yet, here you are, dressed as a Roman soldier. That can only mean Marcellus freed you."

"I report to him in the Roman auxiliary," Ferrex begrudgingly admitted.

Catrin tore her eyes away. "I was so afraid he would not come. Not after what I did in Rome."

The abrupt switch from her confidence to vulnerability unsettled Ferrex. He inquired further. "Then it is true. You raided his brother's villa in Rome?"

"His half brother, Brutius," Catrin clarified. "We went there to rescue Selena—Cynwrig's new wife. She was almost tortured to death. We found other slaves, starved and beaten. What else could we do but rescue them and seek vengeance on their brutal guards? Brutius is a monster like Marrock."

"Your actions have incited a swarm of angry hornets," Ferrex warned.

"How is that?"

"Governor Decimus Flavius mentioned that Marcellus's father knows you are alive and has threatened to cut his patronage. Decimus reassigned Marcellus to hunt down rebels in the area instead of taking command of the northern legion. Decimus accuses you of leading raids in the area."

"Rhan plans the raids," Catrin said firmly. "I am only here because she offered me shelter. I am at my weakest when I am pregnant. The slaves I freed were sickly and dying. Though I fear Rhan's dark magic, she has promised to keep me safe in the cave until I give birth. Yet, she remains silent about her next steps to destroy Marrock. She tells me our souls must forge into steel to destroy Marrock. Remember when Rhan isolated me in her cottage to remove evil spirits that supposedly possessed me?"

Ferrex nodded. "I regret to this day that I did not help you escape when your mother assigned me to guard you there," Ferrex said somberly.

Catrin's eyes widened. "I sense Rhan is spinning a web to join my soul with hers, just like she did with Agrona's. You must take me with you so I can speak with Marcellus."

Ferrex hesitated. "It's too dangerous. Decimus watches Marcellus closely to make sure he carries out his duty to stop the raids."

"I must tell Marcellus I carry his child," Catrin stubbornly pressed. "He will find a safe place for me to give birth. After that, we can plan the attack on Marrock."

"What about the warriors in this cave who pledged their fealty?"

"Before I can lead, I must survive childbirth." A sob caught in Catrin's throat, and her voice cracked. "You profess your love for me. I am begging you to take me to Marcellus."

"You know I would do anything for you," Ferrex said adamantly. "But it is best you stay here for now. Decimus has spies watching Marcellus. If they found you with him, I fear what they would do to you and the baby. To calm everything down, you need to convince Rhan and the others to stop their raids."

"I will stop the raids. But promise me, Ferrex, you will tell Marcellus about our unborn child," Catrin said with pleading eyes. "Find a way for us to reunite."

Ferrex was silent for a few moments, then said, "I will do as you command. First, show me the tunnels and escape routes, in case we need another way to escape from here."

37

KILLING FIELDS

Antonii Villa, Gaul, 8 August, 28 AD

Marcellus sat on the bed, reminiscing about the bittersweet moment when he'd been with Catrin the previous fall, before leaving for Rome. He picked up a cushion on which she'd laid her head while recovering from her wounds. The whiff of stale odor dispirited him. Before, he had always sensed her essence, even when they were far apart. But now, he felt empty, not knowing what had happened to her since she escaped Rome. It was as if the world, the fates, and the gods were against their love. Negasi's advice for Marcellus to assuage his father's anger and remove the threat on Catrin's life weighed heavily on his mind.

A husky voice from outside saying, "Praetor Antonius, Eques Ferrex has returned," took Marcellus by surprise. He'd believed the brash Red Lion had deserted after not reporting back the previous day. Taking a deep breath, he rose from the bed and told the soldier behind the closed door, "Tell both Ferrex and Negasi to meet me in the tablinum."

For two days, Marcellus had lingered, detaining the legionaries so he could further question the house slaves about the raid. His ultimate hope was to find a clue about Catrin's whereabouts. Depending on what Ferrex had found, he may need to make the most difficult decision of his life.

Betray Rome or forsake his heart.

Marcellus ambled through the peristyle garden redolent with the fragrance of roses, the pink-blushed ivory blooms reminding him of Catrin's satiny skin. When he stepped inside the atrium, he found Ferrex and Negasi standing at attention outside the tablinum. He motioned for his steward,

Celadus, to unlock the door to the chamber used to secure important business documents and funds to pay for the estate's expenses.

A fresco painting of Apollo abducting Daphne greeted Marcellus as he entered, followed by the ex-gladiators. After Celadus closed the doors, Marcellus turned to Ferrex and frowned.

"Where have you been? It has been two days," he chided.

Ferrex gave his usual annoying smirk, and Marcellus barely refrained from slapping it off. "I am only here because my queen ordered me to return."

Marcellus's heart pounded against his chest, his grim mood lifting with the anticipation that he would soon learn what had happened to his wife. "So, Catrin is nearby?"

"She is in a safe place with her warriors," Ferrex said curtly, offering no more information.

"Is she well?" Marcellus probed, sensing the Red Lion's hesitancy to reveal any details.

Ferrex pressed his lips into a firm line. "Well enough."

"'Well enough.' Is that all you have to say?" Marcellus said, growing irritated.

"What else do you need to know?" Ferrex said in a dismissive tone.

Negasi knocked his shoulder against Ferrex, which Marcellus recognized as a cautionary gesture for the Red Lion to tone down his roar.

"Can you take me to her?" Marcellus demanded.

Ferrex exchanged glances with Negasi. "There is a small problem. Catrin's warriors raided your villa. And you have been ordered to bring them to justice."

Marcellus stepped up to Ferrex and met his stare. "I am not the enemy!"

"Decimus considers my queen a criminal for leading the raids. You cannot have it both ways—loyalty to both my queen and to Rome," Ferrex said, the contempt evident in his voice.

"The only way I can assure her safety is to divert my legionaries from her," Marcellus insisted.

Negasi interceded. "Listen to yourself, Marcellus. If your duplicity comes to light, Rome will execute both you and Catrin."

The urgency of making the choice punched Marcellus like a fist to his gut. For days, he had wrestled with ways he could provide military aid to Catrin despite his orders to track down the rebels, which Ferrex confirmed she led.

"Tell him, Ferrex," Negasi said.

Ferrex did not answer but pressed his lips into a firm line.

"Tell me what?" Marcellus snapped, becoming increasingly agitated with the Red Lion's defiance.

"My queen is pregnant," oozed out of Ferrex's mouth.

Taken aback, Marcellus was not sure he had heard Ferrex correctly. "With my child?" he asked.

"Your bastard!" Ferrex hissed, his face turning as red as burning embers.

Marcellus clutched his chest, his heart hammering from mixed emotions of anger at Ferrex and concern for his wife and unborn baby. "I need to see her," he insisted.

"Over my dead body," Ferrex challenged, his hand grasping the hilt of his *gladius*.

Negasi gripped Ferrex by the arm and pulled his hand away from the weapon.

"I told you to pour cold water on that fire of yours," he berated Ferrex, as though Ferrex were a child. "For once, think! We are all in agreement here. We need to devise a plan on how to protect Catrin and support her claims for the throne."

Ferrex's eyes flared at Marcellus despite Negasi's grip on his arm. To avoid any further conflict, Marcellus stepped back to allow space and time for both Ferrex and him to regain their composure. He had to think clearly. Thus far, his decisions of defying his father and overstepping the chain of command to speak directly with Tiberius had unleashed a cascade of dire consequences. From now on, he needed to make deliberate decisions to safeguard what was most precious to him. He held the lives of Catrin and their unborn baby in his hands.

298 ✿ LINNEA TANNER

Finally, Negasi commanded, "Catrin or Rome? You must choose."

"Catrin," Marcellus said without hesitation.

With his eyes fixed on Marcellus, Ferrex asked, "What about your duty as a Roman commander?"

The potential ramifications of deserting the legion hurled into Marcellus's mind. *Decimus could try me for treason . . . sentence me to death—crucify me. Father could seek vengeance on Catrin ... track her down—burn her alive!*

"I need to think on this," Marcellus finally muttered, still grappling with how he could counter these threats.

"I know this is a big step," Negasi said, as if he were a father talking to his son. "You need to be smart about what you do next."

The first idea that came to Marcellus's mind was that he needed funds to pay for bribes and to cover expenses if he was forced to escape with Catrin and their baby from Roman retribution. He recalled Celadus had said that the thieves did not steal the cache of coins hidden under the flooring of the tablinum in the villa.

Marcellus scoured the floorboards for any gaps under which a secret compartment had been built. His gaze landed on the vibrantly painted statue of his father near a wall. At his family's villa in Rome, jewels, coins, and secret documents were hidden under the feet of the paterfamilias statue. He gestured for the two ex-gladiators to help him move his father's statue.

Ferrex leaned his back into the limestone base as Negasi and Marcellus maneuvered it away from the wall. The statue caught on something, stopping their effort. Negasi and Ferrex exchanged glances, and with one big heave, they lifted the statue over what appeared to be a metal object on the floor.

Marcellus knelt to inspect the metal ring latched to the floor. He pulled on the ring and opened a trapdoor. Negasi grabbed a torch from a sconce and illuminated the secret compartment from above as Marcellus surveyed the contents consisting of filled linen bags and a wooden chest.

"This is where my family's treasures are kept," Marcellus said with a pang of guilt for what he planned to do. "We need to order Priscus and his men back to the villa so we can take this without them knowing."

Negasi and Ferrex exchanged surprised glances.

"And then what?" Negasi asked.

"Devise a strategy on how to lead Roman forces away—"

A loud knock on the chamber door abruptly ended the discourse. The three men stared at the closed door as Priscus's distinctive, grating voice shouted, "Come quick. We have found something you need to look at."

Worried the centurion might have overheard their conversation, Marcellus closed the trapdoor to the hidden compartment and gestured for Ferrex to stand on the metal ring to conceal it. Then, he hurried to the closed door and abruptly opened it outward. Outside, he found Priscus on his rear. The centurion shot him a nasty scowl, staggered to his feet, and stood at attention.

"What did you find?" Marcellus asked, wiping sweat from his flushed forehead.

"A severed head," Priscus grunted. "It might be the missing horse trainer."

"Take me there," Marcellus ordered, then strode with Priscus, Negasi, and Ferrex to a wildflower meadow near the edge of the forest. There, legionaries were digging with shovels and mattocks. One of men wildly waved his arms at a raven pecking at a decomposing head to scare it off.

The black creature flew to a high oak branch and bobbed its head as it screeched, "Killing fields. Killing fields."

Marcellus, wary of what other dark secrets might be discovered, felt a chill crawl around his neck. He ordered everyone around him—Priscus, Ferrex, Negasi, the legionaries, and some field slaves—to search for other human remains. He also joined in the effort of digging up thick sod and dirt.

After a backbreaking morning at the task, they uncovered two more rotting heads and corpses, accounting for the missing house slaves from the villa.

But Marcellus had not anticipated finding the other human bones and skulls scattered all about.

There were no vestiges of remaining tissue on what appeared to be older bones, suggesting the bodies had been buried several years ago. Of particular interest was an intact skeleton of what appeared to be a woman with strands of long, gold-blonde hair still on her skull. Buried beside the skeleton was a wooden chest.

Family treasures, perhaps?

Marcellus gestured for Negasi to pry the lid of the chest open with a pickaxe. After it was opened, he was shocked to find a skeleton of a baby shrouded in faded, purple cloth only a wealthy noble could afford. The mass graves confounded Marcellus; Romans usually burned their dead on pyres.

Priscus, holding one of the skulls they found, showed Marcellus the cracks and hole in the middle of the crown. "This person was bludgeoned to death. Other skulls we found show similar head wounds. Do you know what happened here?"

Baffled, Marcellus shook his head. He remembered, as a boy, the house slaves often told tales that the area was haunted by evil spirits from the forest. On a dare from Brutius, he had slept alone there one night. At midnight, he'd been awoken by the sound of a whimpering baby. When he'd opened his eyes, he'd glimpsed a ghostly woman carrying a bundle into the nearby woods under the illumination of a full moon. When he'd ordered her to stop, she'd vanished into a thick fog behind some trees.

Frightened he had observed a lost soul searching for its body, Marcellus had never spoken of what he saw to anyone. He wondered if there was a connection between the apparition and the skeletons of the woman and baby. Kneeling down, he observed no signs of trauma to their skulls. An amulet draped over the baby's ribcage drew his curiosity. He lifted the leather strap and inspected the tiny, marble figure of Apollo. Though smaller, it was similar to the amulet he had given to Catrin as a gift to show his love.

A chill sliced down his spine.

Is this a presage of what could happen to Catrin and our baby?

Marcellus was roused out of his grim reflections when a man asked,

"What do you plan to do with these remains?" Glancing up, he found Gawain standing over him.

"You know, souls that dance on graves tell dark secrets," Gawain added.

"Why are you not at the stables?" Marcellus demanded, unnerved by how the newly hired horse trainer seemed to read his thoughts.

"I came here to help you dig up those secrets," Gawain said with a smug smile. "You didn't answer me. What do you plan to do with the remains?"

Marcellus rose to his feet. "It is of no concern to you," he snapped. "Get back to the stables."

Priscus, still with the skull in hand, stepped over to Marcellus. "Why don't you answer his question? These desecrated grounds could be haunted by evil spirits."

"Have the men bury the bones in a mass grave," Marcellus ordered.

Priscus shot him a burning glare. "You have slaves who can do that. Our duty is to find rebels."

Marcellus realized then that dismissing Priscus and his legionaries from the area would buy him time to strategize his next steps privately with Negasi and Ferrex and remove the family's treasures from the villa. He called Priscus back.

"On second thought, take the men back to the garrison," he said, noting the relief on the centurion's face. "I'll stay here with my two auxiliaries to oversee the burial and have priests remove the evil spirits. I will return to the headquarters in a couple of days."

Priscus nodded and turned on his heels to gather the men for the march back to Lugdunum. As the soldiers packed up, the raven swooped over Marcellus and flew in a northeast direction. Noting Gawain's cold, gray eyes aimed at him like the tip of an arrow, Marcellus hesitated to follow the raven's flight and possibly find Catrin. First, he needed to find a safe haven where he could covertly meet with her and arrange for a midwife to deliver their child.

38

NEW AUTHORITY

Governor's Headquarters, Lugdunum, 3 September, 28 AD

Armed in a newly crafted *lorica musculata*, Brutius puffed out his chest and swaggered down the corridor of the forum. Etched on the metal pectoral plates was the image of Apollo's face with wings spreading from the god's head—a symbol of Brutius's newfound political power. As he mentally prepared for the meeting with Governor Decimus Flavius, he vaguely remembered meeting him, as an adolescent, during a banquet at their family estate in Lugdunum. A tribune then, Decimus had bragged that he considered the crescent scar descending from the corner of his eye to his mouth as a trophy for fighting with Tiberius in Germania.

The uncivilized area around Lugdunum still left a sour taste in Brutius's mouth. As a boy, he had always felt out of place in the Roman province that bred barbarians like rats. Conversely, his unsophisticated half brother, Marcellus, thrived like a crazed barbarian horseman in the wilds of the backwoods. It was not until their family moved to Rome that Brutius found his talent for playing deadly political games in the imperial city. And now, he was eager to test his skills in his next moves against Decimus and Marcellus and fulfill his pledge to his father to elevate their family legacy.

"Decimus is a man of steel you can bend with enough heat," his father had advised before he'd left for Rome.

Brutius was confident he could forge the former commander into a two-edged sword to bring Marcellus to his knees. He smiled at the thought that he could cut a fine line between life and death and force his half brother to beg for mercy.

Finally reaching the doorway to the governor's headquarters, Brutius presented his credentials to an armed guard posted there. "I am Legatus Brutius Antonius, here to see Proconsul Decimus Flavius."

The thin-lipped guard glanced at a wax tablet on an oval table next to him. "I don't see you on the list to meet with the governor."

Insulted, Brutius lifted the scroll in his hand and shot the guard a nasty scowl. "Do you not recognize the imperial seal? This is a mandate from Imperator Tiberius Caesar Augustus himself. Consider your next words carefully. You may end up reporting to me."

The guard stole a nervous glance at a nearby centurion who was speaking with another nobleman. The grim-faced centurion, wearing the distinctive rooster-crowned helmet, excused himself and stepped over to Brutius. "Can I assist you?" he asked evenly.

"As I told your man here, I have urgent imperial orders to give to the governor," Brutius demanded.

"Let me see the seal?" the centurion asked, extending his hand for the scroll. Brutius slapped it into the officer's hand. After inspecting the seal, the centurion glanced at Brutius. "Give me a moment to inform the governor you are here. He is currently speaking with the city magistrate."

Brutius frowned and waited at the doorway until he saw a richly attired nobleman stride out of the chamber. Impatient, he burst in and found Decimus seated at a table, with the sealed scroll in hand, speaking with the centurion.

Decimus abruptly rose from his chair. "What is the meaning of this?"

Seeing the centurion clasp his sheathed *gladius*, Brutius did likewise. "I am Brutius Antonius, son of Senator Lucius Antonius. Tell your man to stand down," he demanded.

Decimus gestured for the centurion to step back, then regarded Brutius with a steel-edged stare. "No one notified me you were coming."

"That is why I am here, to notify you of imperial orders that my military authority supplants yours," Brutius said brusquely.

Decimus's brow creased. "I don't understand. I have military operations well in hand."

Brutius met the governor's hazel eyes, which appeared to shift from brown to green in the lamplight. "Imperator Tiberius Caesar and the senate have lost confidence in your ability to handle rebels in Gaul and anti-Roman factions in Britannia," he bluntly informed Decimus.

Decimus's jaw tensed. "I explained to your father that Marcellus reports directly to me and must obey all my orders."

"Indeed. That was the arrangement." Brutius paused to savor the governor's alarm but was taken aback when Decimus calmly gestured for him to sit at the table.

"Why don't we relax with some wine while we discuss the imperial orders?" he offered, lifting the sealed scroll in his hand.

"Do you have Caecuban wine?" Brutius asked, keenly aware the astute governor was masking his apprehension and plying him with wine to dull his senses.

"Indeed," Decimus said and turned to the centurion. "Priscus, tell my assistant to bring in the finest vintage. Then, wait outside unless I call for you."

After Priscus left, Brutius sat across the table from Decimus, while a gaunt slave with wisps of gray hair entered with a flagon of wine. He poured the red liquid into translucent-blue, glass goblets—the newest trend in Rome.

Decimus raised his filled goblet. "To Minerva and cooler heads."

"To Mars and martial peace," Brutius toasted back. He tasted the full-bodied wine that was barely diluted with water. "Why don't you read the imperial mandate? Then, we can discuss."

Decimus broke the wax seal and opened it with a flat-edged knife, then he spread the parchment on the tabletop. His jaw slowly dropped as his eyes shifted over the document. He took a deep breath and looked at Brutius. "This is a mandate from Praetorian Prefect Lucius Aelius Sejanus."

"The real power in Rome, as you know," Brutius said with a sharp bite in his voice.

Decimus's eyes narrowed. "This contradicts orders from Tiberius that Marcellus is to report to me for further orders in the northern region."

"Not at all," Brutius said with a wave of a hand. "It clarifies that I supersede your authority in military matters. Marcellus still reports to you. And he is to take command of the northern forces in Gaul, as Tiberius decreed. That has not changed."

Decimus rubbed his temple, as if trying to relieve a headache. "I don't understand. I loyally served Tiberius during the Germanian campaign and have his complete trust. Why would Sejanus override his directive in this matter?"

Unable to contain his delight at seeing a crack in Decimus's steel-edged demeanor, Brutius did not answer, but he smirked.

How does it feel to be emasculated?

Keeping his eyes fixed on Decimus, Brutius sipped some wine to extend the awkward moment. "Of course, you delude yourself as to what constitutes loyalty to my father," Brutius finally commented.

Decimus opened his mouth, ready to speak, but then pressed his lips into a firm line when Brutius rose threateningly from his chair.

"The ugly truth, Decimus, is that you betrayed my father," Brutius snarled. "He was a most generous patron to you. That is, until you deceived him about killing everyone in King Amren's family. Two of his daughters still live: Mor and Catrin."

Decimus's voice cracked. "I thought they died in battle."

Brutius planted his hands firmly on the tabletop and leaned toward Decimus. "Do you think my father a fool? We have informants who swear you disguised Catrin as a boy to serve you in the Roman legion—as a slave called Vibius."

Decimus swallowed hard. "If I had not spared her, the gods would have cursed me. You and your father do not understand the divine powers she wields."

Brutius jerked his head back. "What powers?"

"The power to strike lightning at her enemies," Decimus exclaimed.

Amused with the ludicrous claim, Brutius stepped back from the table and laughed. "Father warned me about your superstitions."

"I honor the gods," Decimus said adamantly. "And so should you."

"I revere the power of Rome. And so must you," Brutius countered.

Decimus downed the rest of his wine and waved off the assistant from pouring more. "Tell me, what must I do to receive Rome's favor again?"

Brutius noted Decimus's creased brow furrowing deeper. "There is a way, but . . . we must work in the shadows. I've been told you ordered Marcellus to track down rebels who are raiding Roman estates in the area. I've also been told of rumors that his Briton lover, Catrin, leads these attacks. If Marcellus shields her from being captured, this constitutes treason. It is up to us to seek justice against criminals who plunder Rome."

Decimus's eyebrows lifted. "What do you want of me? To execute Marcellus and Catrin?"

"It depends on what we find," Brutius said, refraining from smirking. "To catch a wolf, you must first lure it into a trap. Marcellus is not aware of the new imperial orders. And it should stay that way. Change his orders back to what Tiberius originally mandated. As you are aware, informants say his true intent for seeking military command in Gaul was to aid Catrin's quest to overthrow Marrock. Marcellus will become careless, thinking he can again focus on his original plans."

"Any further instructions?" Decimus asked.

"Select six of your most trusted legionaries who know of his relationship with the Celtic sorceress and could identify her," Brutius continued. "Have them spy on Marcellus and report back to you. Make them swear their loyalty to you under pain of death if they fail to keep this secret. When Marcellus tries to unite with Catrin—and he will—I want them both incarcerated. I will deal with them both then. Let me warn you. Anyone who betrays my father will not receive mercy."

Decimus stared nervously at Brutius. "Does that include me?"

Brutius smiled thinly. "It depends on how you answer my next questions and what you do."

"What are your questions?"

"How can we break the spell Catrin has put on Marcellus?"

Decimus gave a dark chuckle. "You could torture him to death, but he would never betray her. He deserted his post to help her escape my enslavement."

Brutius stepped around the table and looked down on Decimus. "Why did you not execute him for this?"

Decimus rose from his chair and met Brutius's hard stare. "How would I explain to the powerful Senator Lucius Antonius that I executed his son?"

Though Brutius suspected there were other reasons Decimus had not carried out the death sentence, his ultimate goal was to burn Catrin at the stake and strike at Marcellus's heart. "Tell me more about this sorceress," he said. "What does she look like?"

"A striking woman, a few years younger than Marcellus She has golden hair and turquoise eyes that can bewitch you. Don't let her innocent looks fool you. She is both a seer and fierce warrior. She can shift into other life forms and has fought as a gladiator. That is why her half brother, Marrock, wants her dead."

Though Brutius's first impulse was to shake off the governor's comments as nothing more than his overly active superstition, a shudder unexpectedly sliced through him. He decided to err on the side of caution and glean more information about Catrin from Gawain, who awaited him at his family's villa. Together, they could devise a scheme to apprehend both Marcellus and his Celtic whore.

Assured Decimus would fall in line, Brutius straightened his shoulders and informed Decimus of his next step. "I will investigate the aftermath of the raid on our family's villa. Based on what I find there. I will give you further instructions on what you must do next with Marcellus. Do we have an understanding?"

Decimus pressed his lips into a firm line. "Understood. Are we done here?"

"For the moment," Brutius said. He pivoted on his heels, struggling to hide his smirk, and strode out of the chamber.

39

EXECUTIONS

Antonii Villa, Gaul, 10 September, 28 AD

Astride a thick-maned, black Maremmano stallion from the Lazio region, Brutius rode in front of a contingency of six infantrymen led by Centurion Priscus Dius. The only thing Brutius liked about the gritty, tattooed centurion was that he detested Marcellus as much as he did. Brutius recalled their discussion at his quarters earlier in the week, when Priscus revealed he had trained a boy slave called Vibius while he served under Decimus in northern Gaul.

"Tell me more about this slave," Brutius had probed.

"I am sworn to secrecy," Priscus answered, yet his eyes lifted, as if searching for an incentive to say more.

Brutius tossed Priscus a shiny gold coin. As is true with most greedy men, Priscus gladly took it. Obviously, he held no loyalty to Decimus. Brutius restrained from showing his disdain for the centurion as he readily spilled out the information.

"When Decimus first enslaved Vibius, he stripped her in front of me to humiliate her, then ordered that I train her like a gladiator." Priscus frowned and shook his head. "He never explained why."

"How soon after that did Marcellus report to Decimus?"

"A few years after," Priscus answered. "I could tell by the way he looked at Vibius that he was stricken by her. Further, he attacked me during one of our training sessions, accusing me of mistreating Vibius."

"Did Marcellus know Vibius was a woman?" Brutius asked, recalling that his father had told him his half brother's memory had been erased by a dark druidess while in Britannia.

"It did not seem so, at least not at the start . . ." Priscus hesitated, as if deep in thought. "But he soon knew."

Brutius cocked an eyebrow. "How do you know that?"

"Decimus ordered me and a handful of guards to accompany him to find Vibius, who had escaped." Priscus gave a dark chuckle. "We found Marcellus near a waterfall, on top of Vibius, rutting her like a bull. The men were shocked to discover the boy was a woman. Some thought the boy had shape-shifted into a woman to seduce Marcellus. Though I knew the truth, I nonetheless found it disturbing to find her with long hair. She'd kept it short."

"She must have been wearing a wig," Brutius interjected.

"No. Strangely, it was . . ." Priscus muttered, his words fading. "It was as if her hair grew to her waist overnight."

"What did Decimus do then?"

Priscus grimaced. "He made us swear to keep the incident a secret."

"You can trust me," Brutius told Priscus disingenuously. "There are more rewards for your loyalty."

Priscus's eyebrows raised. "Gold coins?"

Brutius flipped the greedy centurion a silver coin. "Possibly. It depends on what you say and do."

Priscus's eyes widened with a gleam of greed. "After we found them, Decimus ordered me to spar with Vibius in an exhibition for a lanista to see her skills. He sold her as a gladiator, then assigned Marcellus on a dangerous mission. He had to put an end to rebels plundering and murdering Roman citizens—like he is doing now."

He tossed the centurion another gold coin. "For your loyalty in the future."

Now, Brutius drew out of his thoughts about his discussion with Priscus. The chill from a fog crawling up around him made him shiver. As he rode on the dirt road leading to his family villa, he tied up the pieces of information he had learned in his mind and concluded Decimus had lied to his father about killing Catrin. Marcellus must have reunited with Catrin in Gaul and deserted the legion to help her escape. Decimus should have executed them both, yet he had not. Was that the reason, to save both of them, that Marcellus had persuaded their father to support Decimus's political ambitions?

Passing a fenced corral, Brutius caught a waft of horse defecation. The stench reminded him of Marcellus shoveling horseshit out of the barn as a boy—a slave's task his half brother didn't mind doing when caring for the horses. Images danced in Brutius's head of how he could torture Marcellus. Not even flaying him alive would satiate his bloodlust to avenge the desecration of his lover's body. No doubt Marcellus had connived with his witch to murder Adonis and steal Selena for his sexual pleasure.

Bitterness about his father's order not to destroy his scum half brother who had infested their family's legacy gnawed at Brutius. As the eldest son, he deserved his father's love and respect. Instead, his father blamed him for the death of his mother in childbirth, while his stepmother, Drusilla, championed her own son. She accused him of unfettered cruelty. But really, it was nothing more than his curiosity to test how quickly he could snap a pup's neck or skin a barnyard cat alive. Brutius smirked. She knew nothing about the boy slave he had raped and buried with the other human remains he'd discovered at the villa—past secrets buried in the killing fields, he assumed, that must be part of his father's legacy. Brutius was, after all, the embodiment of a Roman conqueror and always followed his father's advice.

"Dominate your enemy with a two-edged sword. Know when to strike. Know when to retreat to fight another day. But most of all, make sure the war ends in victory."

Approaching the villa's forecourt, Brutius roused out of his thoughts and studied the estate. It has been almost twelve years since he'd left his boyhood home to live in Rome. Little had changed, except the statue of Cupid abducting Psyche near the entrance door was gone. It reminded him of the tale of Cupid, who secretly protected Psyche and then became her husband. Invisible to her by day, he visited her at night— an allegory of Marcellus and Catrin.

Brutius was determined to alter their fate to unite and instead destroy them both.

A silver-haired man, whom Brutius did not recognize, met them in the courtyard. "Greetings. I am Celadus, the overseer of the estate. What brings you here?"

"I am Legatus Brutius Antonius, son of Lucius Antonius."

"You look splendid in your armor," Celadus flattered. "Your brother, Marcellus, was also here, about a month ago, in military uniform."

"My half brother," Brutius corrected. "Did he stay long?"

Celadus gave him a perplexed look. "Did he not tell you? He was here to investigate the raid on your estate."

"No. I just arrived in Lugdunum a few days ago," Brutius answered. "What did he find?"

"His soldiers dug up the severed heads of the horse trainer and two other missing slaves," Celadus said. "More troubling, they unearthed older human bones. One was a skeleton of a baby inside a wooden box."

The unearthing of a baby's skeleton— a dark secret he knew nothing about—aroused Brutius's curiosity, but his main objective was to find out more information from his spy.

"Is Gawain here?" Brutius asked.

"He's inside eating."

"Tell him to come out," Brutius demanded, then he dismounted from his horse.

Celadus disappeared into the residence and came back with Gawain, who was eating flatbread. Brutius motioned for the assassin to speak with him away from the earshot of Priscus and his infantrymen.

"What did you find out?" Brutius asked in a hushed tone.

Gawain picked at some food particles stuck in his teeth, repulsing Brutius, and answered, "Last fall, Marcellus ordered the slaves to tend to a woman called Catrin. She left in November. Nobody knows where or why she left. I pressed a dagger to the neck of a horse trainer, who had just returned from Rome, and asked if he knew about the assault on your villa in Rome. He confessed, with coaxing from my blade, that he escaped with Catrin after the attack. Your slaves are with her; many of them are ill or dead. Falco came here to see if Marcellus had left word with Celadus to give her shelter."

"And did Marcellus leave word?" Brutius asked.

"No. Falco was leaving to tell Catrin when I confronted him," Gawain said. "Before I removed his head, he told me Catrin was with child."

Surprised, Brutius jerked his head back. "Pregnant?"

"Yes," Gawain affirmed.

"Father will want to know this," Brutius said, anticipating his father's arrival in Gaul with Drusilla. "Did Falco tell you where Catrin was?"

Gawain nodded, stealing a glance at Priscus, who was staring at them. "I checked the area out but did not find her," he said in a quieter voice. "I also had to cut off the heads of two slaves who saw me kill Falco. As a wise man told me, 'The dead tell no secrets.'"

"And who is the wise man?" Brutius asked, noting the assassin's smirk.

"Me."

"Wise counsel," Brutius said sarcastically. "Have you sharpened your skills today?"

Gawain's eyebrows furrowed. "Your meaning?"

Without answering, Brutius motioned for Priscus to come forward. "Have the soldiers gather all the estate slaves and bring them here."

As instructed, Priscus had his men collect about forty men, women, and children of all ages and line them up in the courtyard.

Brutius walked up to Celadus. "Point out any slave who arrived after the woman called Catrin left the estate last fall."

The overseer's hand shook as he pointed out five male and three female slaves.

"They can leave, but everyone else, on your knees," Brutius demanded. "And that includes you, Celadus."

The remaining slaves stole glances at each other as they fell on their knees.

Brutius looked sideways at Priscus. "Position the soldiers behind the slaves and strike down anyone who tries to escape."

The legionaries marched behind the slaves and gripped the hilt of their sheathed swords as Brutius spoke.

"You are accused of treason. You chose to remain silent and not inform my father, Senator Lucius Antonius, that the rebel and murderer called Catrin was staying at his estate. She has been identified as the leader who has plundered Roman homes. If you tell me where she is, I will spare your life. If not, you are condemned to death."

"Dominus, Marcellus commanded us to keep Catrin," Celadus said, his eyes pleading as he raised his folded hands for mercy. "We assumed your father knew. A heavily tattooed woman with dark hair led the raid. Not Catrin. We did not realize the thieves had killed Falco and two of the slaves until Marcellus dug their heads up."

"You are a liar," Brutius accused. "Tell me where Catrin and her rebels are."

"We are all victims of the raid," Celadus doggedly insisted. "We do not know where any of them are."

Brutius's voice thundered with rage. "You are not victims! You should have fought the thieves off with your lives."

Celadus's voice trembled. "How could we do that? Slaves are not allowed to be armed."

"You defend this estate with whatever weapon you find or your bare hands," Brutius lashed out. "Cleavers and knives from the kitchen, mallets and pitchforks from the barn. You defend this property with your lives or forfeit your lives for your inaction."

The sound of wailing women and children brought a cruel smile to Brutius's face. Still, despite his threat, no one answered. He nodded at Gawain. "Do your duty," he ordered.

Gawain glared at Brutius in defiance. In turn, Brutius shot him a nasty scowl. "You heard me. Do your duty."

Gawain unsheathed the dagger from his belt, and with one swipe of the blade, he cut Celadus's throat. The overseer clutched the fatal wound, blood spurting through his hands. His body collapsed on the ground and convulsed, blood pooling around his head.

"Now are you ready to talk?" Brutius yelled at the other slaves.

A couple of young male slaves tried to bolt, but Brutius cut them down with his sword. He glowered at Gawain. "Do it again until someone talks!"

Gawain walked down the line of slaves and systematically sliced open the throats of three field laborers and a houseslave as Roman soldiers threatened the others with their swords. The shrill sound of women's wailing filled the air as the bodies, in the throes of death, convulsed in pools of blood.

Brutius's heart raced as he savored the power he held over the trembling lowlifes. "Where are they?" he shouted again, but the exhilaration of watching the executions faded when he met the deadly stare of Gawain, who was wiping blood off his dagger with a piece of cloth.

"Enough! No one knows," the assassin snarled.

Taken aback by the open defiance, Brutius was at a loss for words. The thought that he should have Priscus cut Gawain down crossed his mind, but the assassin's feral eyes made him hesitate.

"We will find other ways to track down the rebels," Brutius finally conceded, backing away from a confrontation that could leave him dead. He would deal with Gawain later.

Brutius gestured to Priscus. "Burn these bodies with the other human remains you found."

"Who will oversee the estate, then?" Priscus asked.

"Slaves are easily replaced," Brutius said coldly. "I will stay here until my father arrives."

40

NEW ORDERS

Lugdunum, Gaul, 15 September, 28 AD

"You've been summoned by Governor Decimus Flavius," Centurion Priscus grunted as Marcellus wrote on a wax tablet that there had been no attacks on Roman estates during the previous week.

Marcellus looked at Priscus. "For what reason?"

"The governor did not tell me why."

Uneasy that Decimus had sent Priscus instead of one of his own messengers, Marcellus snapped the wax tablet shut. He retrieved his helmet from a shelf and strapped it on. After he exited the headquarters with Priscus, six guards met them. Their presence further unnerved Marcellus. He looked warily at Priscus.

"What is this?" asked Marcellus.

"They have been assigned to escort you."

"Is that necessary?"

"Orders from the governor," Priscus said.

To avoid a confrontation, Marcellus nodded and marched in the middle of the six guards—one in front, another in back, and two on each of his sides—from the garrison to the city gate. When they went through the city gate, the main road was congested with townspeople celebrating the weeklong *Ludi Romani* festival. Today, the celebration culminated with gladiator games in the newly renovated coliseum that Catrin had damaged the previous year when she summoned lightning to strike its stands—a divine power of hers he had disregarded in his mind.

"Make way for the praetor," Priscus shouted at the celebrants, pushing a couple of them back.

316 ✿ LINNEA TANNER

They continued marching through the congestion up the steep cobblestone road until they reached the forum. By then, sweat beaded on Marcellus's face. His helmet felt too tight, and his head pounded. Possibilities of why Decimus had summoned him assaulted his mind. Had Catrin's hideaway been discovered? Would he be ordered to attack them and crucify any survivors?

When they reached the entrance to the governor's chamber, Priscus dismissed the guards, then announced to Decimus, "Praetor Antonius is here to see you."

Marcellus clenched his sweaty hands as he entered the chamber. Sitting behind a table, Decimus was reading a parchment. He looked up, smiled, and waved for Marcellus to sit across from him. Wary of the uncharacteristically warm invitation for him to sit instead of stand, Marcellus unstrapped his helmet and placed it on the corner of the table before sitting down.

Decimus offered him some wine—another unexpected, amiable gesture. Marcellus kept his eyes fixed on Decimus as he took a sip of wine and commented, "Fine vintage."

Decimus set his half-filled goblet on the table. "We started on bad footing, which I hope to rectify," he began.

Marcellus suspiciously studied the governor's face for any hint of deception as he continued speaking. "I have received direct orders from Tiberius. You are to be placed in immediate command of the fortress at Gesoriacum. We have received reports that King Marrock ambushed Roman forces defending the Catuvellauni capital. There have been strange accounts that a dragon burned some of the soldiers alive. Others died when the air filled with a noxious odor . . . presumably from the dragon's breath."

Mystified, Marcellus jerked his head back. "Could it have been a siege tower that looked like a dragon?"

Decimus tapped a couple of fingers on his mouth, then inhaled sharply. "These were accounts by Tribune Arius Petronius—your friend."

"You will find no one more credible," Marcellus said, though he wondered if Decimus was fabricating the tale. "What about my assignment to hunt down the criminals plundering Roman estates?"

Decimus furrowed his thick eyebrows. "Assaults that mysteriously ceased after you arrived. Nonetheless, Centurion Priscus has been assigned that duty."

Marcellus was taken aback by the sudden change in orders. He had just made arrangements for Catrin to stay in a cottage outside the city, where he could meet her privately and have a midwife assist in the childbirth.

"When am I to take command?" Marcellus inquired.

"Immediately."

"How many men will accompany me?"

"You can choose twenty to accompany you."

The cold expression on the governor's face reminded Marcellus of a death mask. "Give me a week or two to gather my forces, pack, and prepare for the journey."

Decimus nodded.

"What are your directives when I get there?" Marcellus asked.

"Wait for further orders," Decimus demanded. "Arius can bring you up to speed on anti-Roman factions in Britannia that are threatening Roman trade ways."

"I assume Marrock is considered one of them?" Marcellus ventured.

"He is," Decimus said, a tinge of irritation in his voice. "Most troubling, Cunobelin's rogue son, Caratacus, has allied with Marrock and caused a family feud with his father and brothers."

In the back of his mind, Marcellus questioned how much leeway he could be given to support Catrin's quest to overthrow Marrock. However, now was not the time to explore that possibility. Instead, he would make plans with his friend Arius, who was currently commander of the garrison, when he arrived at the city.

"Is there anything else?" Marcellus asked.

Decimus's stare pierced Marcellus. "Have you reunited with Catrin?"

Unnerved by the question, Marcellus inhaled sharply. "I have not seen her since last year. I am committed to my betrothal to Senator Frugi's daughter."

Decimus rubbed his mouth, as if hiding a smirk. "Your father must be relieved."

"I never gave him doubt to believe otherwise," Marcellus retorted.

Decimus's eyebrows arched up. "Indeed. Then we have nothing further to discuss. You can take your leave."

Marcellus scooted his chair back, stood up, and put on his helmet. Every bone in his body mistrusted Decimus, but he remained stone-faced as he left the chamber. To his surprise, Priscus and the six guards were not in the forum to escort him back. He glanced all around but did not see them. Were they hidden, spying on him?

The questioning by Decimus regarding Catrin troubled him. How could he assure her safety?

Rushing through the forum, he mulled over the various options of what their next steps could be. Would it be safer for her to stay at the abandoned farmhouse until she delivered the baby?

As he descended the steps of the forum, a loud screech drew him out of his thoughts. Looking around, he found Catrin's raven gawking at him from atop a column at the amphitheater. Believing this was an omen, he watched the raven fly off and descend to the roof of the Red Cock tavern—a favorite hangout for soldiers known for its strong drinks and the lively brothel in the back. As he approached the tavern, he observed the raven fly down the alleyway. He peered through the narrow alleyway and saw the raven on the ground, waddling close to a veiled woman in a short tunic, most likely a prostitute from the tavern.

She waved for him to come closer.

If the raven had not landed next to the woman, Marcellus would have ignored her. Intrigued yet wary, he glanced around for a possible trap, then walked closer, keeping a hand on the hilt of his *gladius*.

The woman pulled the lower end of the black veil cross her face. "Are you Marcellus Antonius?" she asked in a hushed tone.

Marcellus nodded slightly, his eyes shifting all around for any unexpected movement.

"Deidre wants to speak with you tonight."

"Deidre?"

"A slave from your family's villa. She has a warning for you," the woman whispered.

Marcellus raised an eyebrow. "What is this about?"

"Meet me in the tavern and ask for a mare that can ride you tonight. Then, you will find out." The woman's voice faded as she walked away, the raven waddling alongside her, into the shadows of the narrow alley.

The hairs on the back of Marcellus's neck stood up. If it weren't for the unexpected appearance of the raven, he would not have considered the woman's invitation. But now, he was concerned. Deidre had been Catrin's personal attendant when she'd stayed at his family's villa the previous year. Why would she risk speaking with him?

Seeing the raven fly overhead in the direction where the two rivers merged, he pushed through a stream of spectators ascending the hilltop to watch the gladiatorial games. Losing sight of the raven, he returned to the garrison.

As he entered through the main gate, he found the raven perched on top of his portico-roofed headquarters—an omen of pending danger? Should he risk having Catrin travel with him to Gesoriacum? But if she prematurely gave birth and lost their child as a result of the long trip, would he ever forgive himself?

He extended his arm for the raven to land on. Its eyes glowed a brilliant amber—a sign of its mystical abilities.

Marcellus looked into its eyes and thought, *You must deliver a message to Catrin today.*

41

BLIND TO THE FUTURE

Cave Northwest of Lugdunum, Gaul, 15 September, 28 AD

Catrin dreamed she was in the throes of unspeakable pain as Marcellus delivered their baby, with warriors battling around her. He lifted the newborn. To her dismay, it looked like a blood-soaked eaglet with outstretched talons.

"We were joined in love but have been separated by an evil hand," he said somberly.

Alarmed, Catrin roused from her nightmare. Soaked with cold sweat, she trembled from the damp air in the cave. Or perhaps it was from her fear that both she and her baby could die in childbirth. Up to that moment, with her condition, she had been blind to the future, her gift of foresight diminished.

Was my dream a rare glimpse of the future?

Suddenly, a shadow of a dragon appeared on the tent's wall, taking her breath away. The image of the tattooed dagger on Gawain's forehead flashed in her mind. It was the same image that had projected on her father's shadow as it faded away in his skull.

Was it a warning, as it was then, that he would try to kill her?

Shaking, she closed her eyes, then forced them open. To her relief, the shadowy figure had disappeared from the tent's wall. Struggling to a sitting position, she moaned, looking down at her burgeoning belly.

How did I get so big?

Constant fatigue from sleepless nights had compelled her to rest that afternoon to maintain her strength for the long ride that night with Marcellus. Though excited about seeing her Roman husband again, she nonetheless felt miserable from unrelenting nausea, leg cramps, and painful kicks from her baby. Drinking goat's milk, meat broth, and potions, which Selena suggested, had not eased her discomfort. Eating meat from the game the warriors had hunted or berries, edible roots, and nuts the others had gathered also did not help.

The unborn child had stolen most of her energy, making it difficult for her to focus on the spring campaign to challenge Marrock. Even so, she would not let her pregnancy be an excuse. By November, after giving birth, her druidic powers should be restored.

Nonetheless, she should heed the vision. It could be a portent that the etched destiny on the dagger could play a cruel trick on her. Could she still die in childbirth or be assassinated?

She shuddered. Who would lead her army then?

Suddenly clammy and nauseated, she spewed bile into a bowl kept near her bedding. She forced herself to drink an herbal mixture that Selena had left to ease the nausea, but the pressure of the rapidly growing baby played havoc on her stomach. This was not a promising start to the day she would finally reunite with the baby's father.

Will he feel the same love for me when he beholds my misshapen body?

Hearing Trystan's voice, Catrin rose and pulled aside the curtain separating her sleeping area from the main headquarters. Her trusted commander was instructing two brawny men on where to move a chest filled with coins, silver utensils and dishes, and gem-studded jewelry plundered during the raids.

Since Ferrex's warning a month earlier that Romans were actively searching for their group, her warriors had begun transporting treasure-filled containers in wagons to another cavern close to the northern coast. Rhan and Myrddin were already there, recruiting more mercenaries and buying ships and supplies for the expedition in Britannia. Over the next couple of weeks, the remaining warriors would leave for the new hideaway, traveling in smaller groups to avoid detection.

Catrin gestured for Trystan to speak with her. He ordered the two men to carry the chest out of the tent and presented himself to Catrin with a slight bow.

"What is your pleasure, my queen?"

"Escort me to the pool below so I can leave a votive for Mother Goddess to bless me before Marcellus arrives," she ordered.

They stepped outside the tented headquarters near the back of the cave. He retrieved a burning torch from the stone wall, and she followed him into a narrow passageway. With her bulging belly, she felt like a baby being born, awkwardly maneuvering the narrow channel that descended into the depth of the earth's womb. The rhythmic dripping of water from the cave's ceiling echoed all around.

The tunnel darkened whenever Trystan turned a corner with the flaming torch in hand—the only source of light.

It was difficult to breathe in the stagnant air, making her breathing ragged.

Trystan glanced back. "Just a little farther," he assured her.

Shortly, they entered another massive cavern, with structures hanging like icicles from the ceiling. A beam of light from an overhead opening shone on a thin, white column extending to the floor.

"I call that the witch's finger," Trystan commented, hooking Catrin's arm into his. He assisted her down what looked like an undulating staircase that had been carved by nature over the centuries.

When they reached the base of the pool, Trystan set the torch in a sconce attached to the wall and turned to Catrin, lifting his brow. "I sensed you wanted to talk with me in private."

Catrin nodded. "What I say must stay here. My father implicitly trusted you as his second-in-command. As I do."

Trystan regarded Catrin for a moment. "Agreed."

Catrin took a deep breath. "Tell me truly. Do you trust Rhan?"

Trystan lifted his eyes, as if hesitant to answer her question. "At first . . . I didn't trust her. I feared her magic. But she helped me escape from Marrock's prison. Her drive to destroy Marrock rings true. It makes sense. What is a more hideous crime than a son killing his mother? Furthermore, Rhan grieves for the daughter Marrock stole. He uses the little girl's healing powers for no good. Rhan has never wavered on her prophecy that you are destined to be the raven queen of the Cantiaci people."

"What if I were to die in childbirth? Would Rhan not claim the kingdom?" Catrin probed.

"You will not die," Trystan said fervently. "Your destiny to overthrow Marrock is written on your father's dagger."

"I had a vision that I deliver a baby eaglet on a battlefield." Catrin swallowed down a sense of foreboding. "I fear this is an omen that I must sacrifice my life to assure victory over Marrock."

Trystan grimaced. "You will not die. You will fulfill Rhan's prophecy."

"How can you be so sure?" Catrin questioned. "We are both blind to the future. What if the spinners weave a different fate—that I die? Who would rule then?"

Trystan inhaled sharply. "Marcellus?"

The bite in his voice jarred Catrin. Until then, she had not detected any underlying hostility toward her Roman husband.

"I want Mor to rule with me," she demanded, closely studying Trystan's reaction.

He swallowed hard, and his voice cracked. "But she is not your father's true daughter."

"I know. You are the father," Catrin said, noting the surprise on Trystan's face.

"You know, then?" he asked.

"I always suspected," Catrin confirmed. "But my father recognized Mor as his daughter—an heir to his throne. And so do I."

Trystan shook his head, perhaps in disbelief of her proposal. "What about Adminius? He won't release Mor unless you to marry him."

"No Catuvellauni king will rule over my people!" Catrin proclaimed.

"You've pledged to marry him, though. If you renege, he could use that as a reason to declare war on you."

"Does he know I am pregnant?"

"I do not know"—Trystan scratched his head—"and I'm not sure how he would react if he knew."

"That is why we need to rescue her," Catrin insisted. "Adminius has negotiated with Decimus to gain his military support. But I don't know what agreement was made. That is why it is important I speak with Marcellus to coordinate our military operations."

Trystan's brow creased. "What about seeking Rhan's counsel?"

"I don't trust her," Catrin snapped. "And I am troubled that you do."

Trystan jerked his head back. "I only serve you, my queen. With your condition, I just thought—"

Catrin cut off his words. "I never transferred my duties to Rhan. I am the queen, and I will be treated as such. Do you understand?"

Trystan bristled. "I understand. What are your orders?"

"I designate you as my general," Catrin said, noting Trystan's shoulders relaxing and the obvious pride on his face as she continued, "Move everyone else up north in small groups before winter sets in. Assign drivers to transfer the plunder up north in wagons throughout winter, if necessary. Marcellus has freed Ferrex and Negasi, who will report to you as your new commanders. They can help you arrange for ships to convey our army to Britannia or to recruit mercenaries."

"Tell me more about Negasi. I've only heard of his reputation as a gladiator," Trystan said.

"He was a pirate on the high seas before Marrock captured and sold him as a gladiator. He would know how to recruit crews for our ships," Catrin answered.

Trystan cocked an eyebrow. "When will you travel north?"

Catrin paused, hesitant to broach the topic of Marcellus. "I will stay with Marcellus until the birth of our child."

Trystan pressed his lips into a firm line, as if restraining his words, but then spoke bluntly. "You asked if I trust Rhan. You should ask yourself the same question about Marcellus."

"Of course, I trust him," Catrin snapped. "He is my husband."

"What role will he play in your kingdom?"

"He will be my king," Catrin proclaimed.

Trystan looked away for a moment. When he met her eyes again, she could feel the heat of his blazing gaze. "You have a hard decision to make, my queen. Rome will not acknowledge you as his wife. And the Cantiaci people will not accept Marcellus as your king."

"Yes, they will," Catrin said, raising her voice.

Trystan remained stone-faced, but his eyes pierced into hers, making Catrin reconsider her hard stance. Perhaps her people would accept Marcellus after he offered his Roman military aid. "The people will accept our child as the rightful heir to the kingdom," she retorted.

Trystan smirked. "The child was sired by a god. Or so Rhan proclaims."

Catrin stiffened. "I will deal with that myth later. Right now, it is imperative that Marcellus and I plan how to move forward with his forces."

"We are to trust Marcellus instead of Rhan—the druidess who rallied support for you to be the next queen?" Trystan said sharply.

Catrin felt as if she were balancing on a fence post. She now realized that the loyalty of her warriors was tenuous. *Power is the ability to influence the actions of others,* her father had often said. And that influence depended on her fulfilling the prophecy to overthrow Marrock, as foretold by Rhan.

"She and Myrddin will remain my spiritual advisers," Catrin conceded, but then, she abruptly ended the discourse by saying, "Let me pray to the Mother Goddess now, before Marcellus arrives."

"Should you not also speak to the goddess of war?" Trystan said with a tinge of sarcasm.

Catrin shot a scathing scowl at him as a warning not to say another word. Trystan flinched, then lowered his eyes and stepped back.

"Forgive me, my queen," he apologized in a softer voice.

In preparation for prayer, Catrin closed her eyes and focused on the rhythmic music of the water dripping from the ceiling or rippling in the pool. The weight of any lingering anger at Trystan lifted; she felt as light as a feather floating in the cold, damp air. Opening her eyes, she took her amulet off and stroked the white marble figurine of Apollo. Her father's words again came to mind. *True love comes with sacrifice.*

What more must I sacrifice?

She had lost her family, her freedom, and her kingdom because of her unconditional love for Marcellus. She had sworn vengeance against the Romans for enslaving and dehumanizing her.

And yet, she could not break her bond with her Roman husband. Perhaps Trystan was right. Why would her warriors be willing to die to take back her kingdom if her love revolved around one man? Whenever she was in his arms, her resolve to leave him always melted away. Was she fooling herself in thinking he could aid her?

Holding the amulet in her hand, she placed it in the cold water, seeking the blessing of Mother Goddess to survive childbirth. A ripple of water tugged on the amulet, but she held onto the leather strap.

Then, she prayed to the war goddess.

Mighty Andraste, I beseech you. Give me the courage to face the blood of childbirth and battle. Do not let my resolve to fulfill my destiny falter. Embolden me with your wrath.

The unborn baby kicked hard inside her belly, making her flinch.

Misty-eyed, she let the amulet slip out of her hand and drop to the bottom of the shallow pool. She could easily retrieve the amulet, if only she took one step into the water.

"This is my votive, my sacrifice, to you. I accept the dagger's fate," she finally whispered. She took a deep breath and turned to Trystan. "I am ready to go."

Trystan gave her a concerned look. "Are you ill? You look pale."

"I am fine," she said somberly.

Taking her arm, he escorted her up the stairs, past the witch's finger, and into another passageway. The dim light of the setting sun filtered through another entrance to the caves, where they were to wait for Marcellus.

Walking outside with Trystan, she found her horse, Lugus, tethered to a sapling near the cave. She lifted her eyes to the crimson clouds and inhaled the fresh autumn air. With winter coming, the trees would soon shed their life-sustaining foliage in hues of brilliant red, orange, and yellow. When the Raven, soaring overhead, called out to her, she closed her eyes but could not sense the creature's essence. Instead, she felt the dusk's cool breeze brush across her face, luring her into the silence of darkness.

Suddenly hearing the rhythmic clip-clop of horses' hooves and heavy breathing, she opened her eyes to find two horsemen approaching. To her consternation, Marcellus was not with them, though she was excited to see her loyal companions, Negasi and Ferrex.

After they dismounted, she hugged Negasi excitedly. In turn, his powerful, brick-hard arms pulled her in for a tight embrace. "You are safe with us," he whispered in her ear.

Negasi held a special place with her. The Ethiopian gladiator had been at her side during the premature birth of her daughter. Defying the lanista's order to let her die from loss of blood, he'd tended to her and saved her life. He had been her true friend at the gladiatorial training center. As he was now.

The sound of Ferrex clearing his throat drew Catrin's attention. Looking sideways, she noticed the dejected look on his face as he slightly bowed his head.

"Do I get a greeting?"

Stepping away from Negasi, she exuberantly wrapped her arms around Ferrex's neck, her belly bumping into him.

Ferrex chuckled. "There is so much more of you."

Catrin feigned an angry scowl. "You have not changed. Your tongue still cuts sharp."

Ferrex shrugged and gave a wry smile.

Catrin glanced in the distance behind them to see if her Roman husband might still ride in. "Where is Marcellus? I thought he was coming."

"He suspects spies in his ranks. He will meet you at the farmhouse tonight," Ferrex said.

Catrin's pulse raced. "Is he in danger?"

"Just a precaution," Negasi reassured her, though his eyes hinted she did have reason to worry. He added, "Marcellus is anxious to see you again. Can you manage the ride tonight?"

"Of course," Catrin replied, though it had been a month since she had ridden.

Trystan joined the group, introducing himself to Negasi, and then spoke plainly. "I will not let Catrin go with you unless you can assure her safety."

"You risk her life if she stays here," Ferrex said bluntly. "For that matter, everyone needs to leave here. The Romans may have picked up your scent."

"We are in the process of doing so now," Trystan assured them. "We need to plan our next steps with Marcellus."

"He has been ordered to take command of the Roman fortress at Gesoriacum. We leave in a few days and can meet you there," Ferrex suggested.

A sense of foreboding gnawed at Catrin as she recalled her vision of delivering her baby in the midst of a battle. "I thought his order was to track us down. Is there a reason for the sudden change?"

"Let us take this as a good sign, the first step to your destiny," Negasi said, looking reassuringly at Catrin.

"Then let my destiny begin."

42

MESSENGER'S WARNING

Lugdunum, Gaul, 15 September, 28 AD

Marcellus lifted his mug in toast as he closely scrutinized the legionaries sitting around him at a table in the Red Cock tavern. Suspecting spies in his midst, he glanced to his right.

Centurion Priscus was in a corner with an infantryman from the garrison, their eyes fixed on him.

Shifting his gaze to the left, Marcellus noted a man nursing his drink, sitting alone, staring at him. The cowl of the man's cloak was pulled over his head, making it difficult to recognize him.

Marcellus pretended to sip his ale as the rowdy soldiers surrounding him at the long table in the middle of the tavern drained theirs. He had to keep his wits sharp to minimize the risk of leading spies to Catrin. The tavern's servers came around with more pitchers of ale and jars of wine. He slipped one of the servers some silver coins to pay for everyone's drinks and then waved him off. This would be a long night—first meeting with the slave, Deidre, then assuring a solid alibi of why he would not return to the garrison until the next morning, so he could spend the night with Catrin.

"Is there any mare who can ride me tonight?" Marcellus raised his voice above the clamor—a signal for Deidre's friend to present herself.

"I can ride you, stallion," a woman's sultry voice said from behind him.

Marcellus turned on the bench and found the golden-haired woman he had met earlier in the alleyway. Ample breasts spilled out of her low-cut dress as she gave him a wet kiss, thrusting her tongue into his mouth, and swung one leg around his. She kept her mouth locked on his as she pressed her pelvic bone against his unexpected erection.

Continuing the facade, Marcellus gripped her buttocks. "Give me a taste of how hard you can ride me," he moaned. He had a sudden urge to hump her after so many months without a woman's touch. To contain his lust, he coaxed the harlot off his lap and stood up beside her.

"Take me to your stables," he jested.

The fair-skinned woman grinned broadly when he publicly slipped a silver coin into her hand so everyone could witness the transaction. The soldiers around the table hooted and cheered, raising their cups in toast.

"See you in the morning, boys," Marcellus shouted above the drunken clamor. "Drinks are on me for the rest of the night."

That announcement drew even more cheers from the patrons in the tavern. In their drunken, Bacchanalian state, Marcellus felt assured most of them would not remember the night, except possibly for his generosity or for leaving with a high-priced prostitute.

As the fair-skinned harlot led him by the hand, weaving around the tables to the back, he stole a glance at her big, blue-green eyes, which reminded him of Catrin's. She pulled the curtain aside at the back and led him down the corridor with makeshift rooms separated by sheer fabric panels on each side. The grunts and moans of men and women in coitus could be heard from all directions.

"What is your name?" he asked.

"Iberdees," she said in her sultry voice.

"Unique name. Where is your friend?" Marcellus inquired, careful not to mention the runaway slave's name in public.

Iberdees gave him a lusty smile. "Waiting to join us for fun in a locked room."

"Perfect," Marcellus commented as he looked for possible spies peeking through the cracks in the fabric panels.

At the end of the corridor was an innkeeper waiting in front of a sleeping room. Marcellus handed him a newly minted silver coin. "For your discretion."

The innkeeper grinned broadly, revealing gaps in his mouth where teeth used to be, the remaining decaying ones of little use. He unlocked the door.

After Marcellus entered, Iberdees shut the door and latched it. The room was sparsely furnished with a couch bed in front of a shuttered window, a three-legged table to the side, and built-in shelves on the wall.

From the back corner of the room, a young woman, not more than sixteen years old, stepped into the illumination of a burning candle on the tabletop. He vaguely remembered the dark-haired, ivory-skinned slave who had attended to Catrin's and his personal needs.

"You have a message for me?" he inquired.

"My life is in danger. And so is yours. I ran away and need your protection." Deidre's voice trembled.

Though wary, Marcellus could see the fear in her wide eyes. "What danger?" he asked.

Deidre took a deep breath, then words flew out of her mouth. "Just before the last full moon . . . or maybe it was waning—a few weeks after you left, anyway—your brother, Brutius, arrived at the villa with Roman soldiers."

Deidre paused and regarded Marcellus, as if seeking permission to tell him more.

"Continue," he urged.

"Brutius made all the slaves stand in a line. He ordered us to tell him where Catrin and her rebels were hiding. How could we know? She left the villa almost a year ago. The overseer told him that."

"Celadus?"

Deidre nodded. "But Brutius did not believe him. He ordered the horse trainer to slit our throats until someone confessed."

"Gawain, the newly hired trainer?"

"Falco disappeared shortly after he arrived from Rome. Gawain was hired the next day," Deidre said, then added, "He had the marking of a blue dagger on his forehead. He . . . he . . ." She looked down, tears welling in her eyes.

"What happened next?" Marcellus asked.

Deidre's lips quivered, and her eyes lifted as she retold the horrific moment. "Gawain killed Celadus . . . then one, two, three field hands and a houseslave. I was next. I prayed to Juno to save me. She did. Gawain refused to kill me."

Alarmed, Marcellus wondered if Brutius had worked behind the scenes to pressure Decimus to reassign him as commander of the garrison at Gesoriacum. But for what reason? It did not make sense.

"How many Roman soldiers were with Brutius?" he asked.

"Six, I think. And an officer"—Deidre sliced her hand sideways across the top of her head—"with a crest on his helmet."

Suspecting the commander was Priscus, Marcellus asked, "Was the officer's face horribly scarred."

Deidre nodded.

Marcellus inhaled sharply, fearing for Catrin's life. If Deidre was found, then she would likely be tortured and crucified as a runaway slave. She might confess she had secretly met with him. With the night slipping away, he still had to ride to the farmhouse under the dim lighting of a waning moon to meet Catrin. He had to discuss with her the best way to protect her and their baby.

He looked at Iberdees. "I need to go. Will you be safe here?"

"I will be fine," she said, though a glint of panic in her eyes indicated otherwise.

Marcellus had to make a quick decision about what to do with each woman. Iberdees was his alibi, whereas Deidre's life was in immediate danger. He moved the couch bed away from the window, pulled the shutters back, and gripped Deidre's arm.

"You are coming with me," he ordered, pushing her through the open window.

After following Deidre outside into the alley, Marcellus glanced around to get his bearings. The only source of light came from the distant torches burning in the main street. He pulled the cowl of his cloak over his head and took Deidre's hand as they scurried down the alleyway to the main street. There, he found a couple of drunken soldiers staggering on the cobblestone road.

No threat.

But the hairs on the back of his neck stood at attention when he heard rapid footsteps approaching him from the alley behind him.

Marcellus motioned for Deidre to run to the stables across the street. He withdrew his dagger from his belt and pivoted to find a Roman soldier leaping at him.

With fight instincts taking over, Marcellus drove his dagger into the man's chest. In the illumination of the torchlight, the soldier's eyes widened, then glazed over as he slumped to the ground.

Recognizing the man who was with Centurion Priscus in the tavern, Marcellus clamped his mouth shut to muffle his ragged breathing. He glanced all around.

Where is Priscus?

Not seeing the centurion, Marcellus sheathed his dagger, grabbed both arms of the dead soldier, and dragged him back into the shadows of the alley. He leaned over and rolled the limp body against the wall. The stench of urine and feces from the soldier's soiled clothing made him gag.

Feeling woozy, Marcellus abruptly rose. Cold sweat beading on his body made him shiver. Anxious to escape, he staggered down the alley to the main road. There, he glanced up and down the storefronts.

Seeing no one, he sprinted across the street to the stable, where he had previously saddled a different horse to ride. Leaving his cavalry horse there all night would strengthen his alibi that he had spent the entire night with a lively strumpet.

Pulling the stable door open, he found, to his horror, that Priscus was inside, his knife pressed against Deidre's throat.

"Is this one of Catrin's rebels?" the centurion growled.

"I don't know her," Marcellus said, stepping sideways to get a better view of his cavalry horse, which had somehow gotten loose from its stall. Anticipating his next strike against Priscus, Marcellus threw up his arms. The stallion reared on his command.

334 ✿ Linnea Tanner

The instant Priscus glanced back at the horse, Marcellus unsheathed his dagger and leapt at the centurion, knocking his elbow while thrusting the dagger deep into his chest.

To Marcellus's dismay, Priscus kept a tight hold of Deidre, taking her down with him as they fell to the straw-covered floor. Grunting loudly, Priscus stabbed her in the chest with his knife. She shrieked in pain and terror, spooking the horse. It reared again and almost stomped on her as she fought to get away.

Heart pounding hard, Marcellus withdrew his *gladius* and brought the hilt down on the back of Priscus's head with a bone-crushing blow to get him to release Deidre.

The battled-hardened centurion—once a gladiator who had won his freedom—did not let go of Deidre. Just as Marcellus readied his *gladius* to strike Priscus again with the hilt, the centurion stabbed Deidre in the chest once more. This time, the blade stilled her.

Enraged, Marcellus yanked Deidre from Priscus's grip, then swung his blade. The centurion's head cut clean from his shoulders.

But the deadly blow did not calm the raging storm inside Marcellus. He knelt next to the headless body and hacked it over and over with the blade of his weapon. To avenge the cruelty Priscus had inflicted on Catrin. To avenge his treachery with Brutius. To avenge his brutal murder of an innocent slave.

Finally, all his energy was spent. He sat back on the blood-soaked straw and took in the carnage. Two bloody bodies. One headless. Another with a knife embedded in her chest. Blood was splattered all over the walls. Blood was dripping off the muzzle of his calvary horse, who was staring at him, its ears alert.

Shocked, he felt paralyzed with inaction. How would the vigilantes from the city view the crime scene? A headless centurion lying close to a runaway slave's body. Another bloodied body in the alley. Would they connect their deaths to him?

No time to ponder. Leave now.

Gathering his steel resolve, he inhaled deeply, then rose to his feet and stepped over the bodies to pat the stallion's neck to calm him . . . and to calm himself. Spotting the swayback mare he had saddled earlier, he grabbed its reins and led it through the back doorway, leaving his cavalry horse behind with the bodies.

Outside, he climbed on the mare's back and rode slowly through the narrow alleyway to avoid undue attention. When he reached the city gate, he waited in the shadow of the fortress wall until the guards pulled over a man in an oxen-driven wagon to question. The city guards barely noticed him when he slipped by.

Once outside the city gate, Marcellus pressed his legs against the horse to make it go faster. The lazy horse did not respond to his command. Frustrated with the nag, he kicked it harder. This time, the mare accelerated to a cantor, albeit about half the speed of his cavalry horse.

Though he had familiarized himself with the landscape between the city and to the farmhouse during the day, the dim light of the waning moon made it difficult for him to discern the mile markers. After riding a while, he realized he had passed the nine-mile signpost, close to the path he should have taken. He backtracked until he located the signpost and took the path to the farmhouse.

As Marcellus rode through the dark woods, the only sound he could hear was his rapid heartbeats in his ears. Both dread and anticipation of seeing Catrin again heightened his senses. He focused his eyes on the pathway to make sure he did not veer off. Nerves on edge, he flinched when he heard a twig crackle, followed by the growl of a creature hidden in the trees.

After a distance of about two miles, the shadowy structure of the farmhouse appeared in the distance. His rumbling stomach reminded him that he had not eaten yet that night. Furthermore, he had not brought anything to eat, either.

The anticipation of seeing Catrin after so many months took hold of his thoughts. Swallowing down a sob, he imagined her with a swollen belly with their son, who was waiting to be born. That was what the priestess of Minerva had predicted a few years back, when his memory of Catrin had been erased, before he had reunited with her in Gaul. The priestess told him that his soul must reunite with a female warrior who haunted his dreams. In a previous life, he had met this woman. For him to be whole, he must again join her soul in this lifetime.

However, the priestess had also warned, *Your union with this woman will set catastrophic events in motion, in which you and your son play major roles.*

The warning unsettled Marcellus as he finally reached the darkened cottage. He dismounted, tied the reins of his nag to a post, and then looked around.

There was no sign that Catrin had arrived with Ferrex and Negasi.

Wary someone might have followed him, he walked to the back of the cottage, where the door had been left unlocked. A sconce with an unlit torch had been placed on the outer wall, as he had instructed Ferrex to do. He took the torch and struck a piece of iron on the flint stone to ignite a spark. The sudden brilliance of the lit torch momentarily blinded him, and two squeaky field mice scurried over his feet, startling him.

He jumped away and waved the torchlight back and forth to make sure no one was lurking in the dark. Seeing nothing out of the ordinary, he inhaled deeply but still felt the weight of the need to protect Catrin. Who could he trust?

Perhaps Negasi.

Ferrex had a score to settle—his claim on Catrin. At least he never hid his hate.

Decimus, on the other hand, embraced him like a friend while stabbing him in the back for political gain.

Undoubtedly, his father wanted to kill Catrin. His stomach lurched. And likely their baby, too, if his father knew. That must be why Brutius was at the villa: to carry out their father's deadly plans.

Marcellus held his breath as he cracked the door open and peered inside the cottage for any movements. Seeing none, he exhaled and cautiously entered the dusty, one-room structure. He found a toppled table and a couple of stools near the central hearth. A basket full of loose twigs and logs was set against the wall.

Retrieving a fire log and some tinder, he threw them in the hearth and started a fire. He stretched out his hands to warm them over the flames. He tried to imagine Catrin's naked body with a swollen belly. Did he dare make love to her to fill the emptiness he had suffered so many months?

Glancing down, he shuddered at the sight of his blood-spattered cloak. He unwrapped the garment from his shoulders and tossed it into the corner. When he inspected his tunic and braccae, he found darkened spots of crusted blood.

What else can go wrong?

With everything that had happened—the slaughter at Brutius's villa, the raid and execution of slaves at his family's villa, the brutal killing of Priscus and a soldier—had the catastrophic events the priestess had foreseen begun to unleash as a result of his relationship with Catrin? She was a warrior queen with a clear vision of her destiny, which intertwined with his?

Must I forfeit my identity as a Roman to join her cause?

He knew killing Priscus and one of his soldiers could jeopardize his military career if anyone found out he had done the deed. The estrangement from his father had already widened to the point of no return. The image of the heavily armed Catrin, standing across a fiery pool from him, had haunted his nightmares the previous two nights. It was the same as his drug-induced vision, which the priestess of Minerva had interpreted—except this time, his grown son was not standing beside him. Was this an omen that his newborn son would not survive? As before, in his vision, he dreamed he stepped into the fiery pool to meet Catrin halfway, only to be consumed in flames as he embraced her.

Marcellus vowed he would not let Catrin or their son die, that he would choose his destiny to protect Catrin and their son, even if it meant sacrificing his life.

43

TWO SOULS REUNITED

**Abandoned Farmhouse, North of Lugdunum,
Midnight, 16 September, 28 AD**

Fatigued from the arduous journey in darkness, Catrin sighed in relief at
the sight of the illuminated farmhouse. She assumed Marcellus had already
arrived, but Negasi questioned why a nag was tethered to the post in front
of the structure instead of his calvary horse. He asked her to wait in front
while he and Ferrex checked the surrounding area before entering.

The cool night air hinted at the change of season from summer to autumn. To keep warm, she tightened her shawl around her shoulders. Her
stomach was aflutter with the anticipation of seeing Marcellus again. Or
perhaps it was the new life inside it.

As Negasi and Ferrex covertly walked to the back of the cottage, peeking through the shuttered windows, Marcellus suddenly opened the door
and rushed out to assist her off the horse. Although it was dim under the
waning moon's silvery light, she could tell he was gazing into her eyes and
sensed her strong bond to him as he gently rubbed the side of her arm.

"Are you all right from the ride?" he asked.

"Tired. But happy to see you," she answered, trying to discern the
expression on his face.

Marcellus leaned over and kissed her lightly on the lips, as if trying
to figure out how to maneuver around her burgeoning belly. At first, he
tentatively drew her into his arms, then his strong embrace made her gasp
as he hungrily pressed his lips on hers. Their bodies shook with pent-up
desire as they kissed each other. Though she had sworn not to allow her

overwhelming love for him to override her decisions as queen, she felt as helpless as a moth to his flame.

His heartfelt words, "I missed you so much," made Catrin's eyes fill with tears.

She swallowed down her swelling emotions. "I missed you, too."

"Let us go inside, where it is warmer," he suggested. "Where are Negasi and Ferrex?"

"In the back, searching for anyone who might steal me," she said lightheartedly.

Marcellus picked Catrin up and carried her over the threshold of the cottage, as if she were a bride he had kidnapped. Yet, when Negasi and Ferrex suddenly rushed through the back doorway with weapons in hand, Marcellus, wide-eyed with alarm, abruptly set Catrin on the floor.

Negasi inhaled sharply and sheathed his sword. "Did anyone follow you?"

"No, I was careful," Marcellus replied, taken aback by the brusque tone in Negasi's voice and Ferrex's glare.

"Whose wretched mare is outside?" Ferrex asked.

"It is mine. Let me explain." Marcellus paused and looked at Catrin, as if hesitant to continue. "I ran into a bit of trouble in the city."

Catrin shuddered, seeing the angst on Marcellus's face.

"What trouble?" she asked.

Marcellus conveyed how he'd arranged with a prostitute to meet a female runaway slave from his family's villa. The chance encounter with a harlot unsettled Catrin, but she remained silent as he continued.

"A runaway slave called Deidre warned me that Brutius interrogated slaves at my family's villa about the location of Catrin and her rebels. On Brutius's orders, the newly hired horse trainer, Gawain, executed some of the slaves when they couldn't tell Brutius where Catrin was."

The mention of the executioner's name sent a shiver down Catrin's spine. "Gawain is the name of the man who tried to murder me. He could be one of Marrock's assassins."

"I remember you telling me that in Rome," Marcellus affirmed. "When

I was at my villa to investigate the raid, he was there. My father hired him, so I could not dismiss him. I asked the overseer to keep me apprised about him. But alas, Deidre told me Gawain executed him."

A sick feeling churned in Catrin's stomach at the possibility that Marrock was scheming with Brutius to assassinate her. She kept that thought to herself as Marcellus finished his story.

"As I was leaving the city with Deidre to assure her safety, Priscus and another soldier confronted me. I killed them both. Priscus killed Deidre in the conflict."

Noting the bloodstains on Marcellus's clothing, Catrin asked with concern, "Are you hurt?"

"Nothing serious. A few cuts and bruises."

Ferrex blurted, "Where was the stableman when you killed Priscus?"

The blood drained from Marcellus's face, as if he had not considered that possibility. "I did not see anyone, but he could have been there, hiding."

"Then we must assume he witnessed the fight with Priscus. Who saw you leave with the prostitute?" Negasi asked tersely.

Marcellus shrugged. "Everyone in the tavern. I thought it would be a good alibi in case anyone questioned why I did not return to the garrison that night."

"Stupid!" Ferrex spat.

Marcellus shot the Red Lion a scathing scowl. "What did you say?"

Ferrex's close-set eyes pierced Marcellus. "Stupid, I said! You have wax in your ears."

Negasi gripped Ferrex's arm. "Hold that tongue of yours. The question we should be asking is if anyone saw Marcellus try to escape with the runaway slave."

"I only saw the soldier I killed," Marcellus said.

Ferrex jerked away from Negasi's grip and puffed out his chest. "What if Priscus circled to the front of the tavern and saw you kill the soldier?"

"What does it matter? He is dead!" Marcellus snapped.

Still bothered that Marcellus had had a chance encounter with a whore,

Catrin asked bluntly, "Why would you trust a prostitute to arrange a meeting at the brothel? Were you set up?"

Negasi blurted, "The queen has a good point."

Marcellus's face flushed crimson as he shifted his eyes between Catrin and Negasi. "I was not set up! I believe what Deidre said, that Brutius is hunting down Catrin."

Hesitant to display her irritation with Marcellus in front of her commanders, Catrin tempered her voice. "Have you been back to your family's villa to verify her story?"

Marcellus gave Catrin a burning stare. "There was no reason to go back after I investigated the raid. I had other duties at the garrison."

Catrin softened her stance. "From what I gather, then, there is no way of knowing if there are witnesses who can pin you to the crime. After all, it is a nobleman's word against that of a stableman or a prostitute."

The tension in Marcellus's face began to ease. "True enough. The courts will not believe a stableman or prostitute unless they were first tortured."

"Before making any final decisions, we should determine if there are any potential ramifications for what you have done," Catrin suggested. "What concerns me, though, is that both Marrock and Brutius may be working together to kill me."

"We should check out the villa and verify if Brutius is there with any soldiers or henchmen," Negasi suggested. "Possibly, he made demands of Decimus at the behest of his father. That could explain why the governor suddenly changed orders for Marcellus's assignment."

"It doesn't make sense that Father would want me assigned to northern Gaul. He wants me back in Rome to marry," Marcellus countered.

"What if he is using you as a decoy to find Catrin?" Negasi proposed. "And it might have worked if Priscus had followed you here."

Marcellus gave Negasi a steely stare. "What are you saying? That I should abandon my position in the Roman legion?"

Negasi bristled. "I never said that. But you have a decision to make."

Noting the growing tension between Marcellus and her commanders, Catrin held his hand to demonstrate her loyalty to him—her chosen king.

With the delicate situation of carrying a foreigner's child, she was dancing on shards of glass to gain her commanders' respect and that of her gathering army in the north.

"I want you to know," Catrin said firmly, "I implicitly trust that Marcellus will make the right decision. I will travel north with him."

"That is not a good idea, my queen," Ferrex argued. "I will stay here and guard you until the birth of your child."

Marcellus glared at Ferrex. "My wife travels with me. It is my duty to protect my queen and our child with my life."

"And I recognize you as my king," Catrin affirmed, taking both of Marcellus's hands in hers.

For a moment, a deadly silence hung in the air. Negasi knelt on one knee and slightly bowed his head. "I swear my fealty to you, my queen, and to your chosen king. I also swear to protect you both, and your child, with my life."

Ferrex flinched when Negasi shot him a glare. He looked away, then reluctantly knelt beside Negasi. "I also swear my allegiance to you, my queen, and pledge to protect you and the rightful heir with my life."

Though Ferrex's vague meaning of the "the rightful heir" slightly irritated Catrin, she motioned for them to rise and declared, "I will hold you both to your pledges."

"I would now like to be alone with my wife," Marcellus demanded. "We can further discuss our next steps tomorrow."

Negasi, who seemed to anticipate a derisive comment from Ferrex, shook his head at the red-maned warrior. "Ferrex and I will gladly sleep in the pens. As there are no pigs to share our space, we should rest comfortably," Negasi jested, then pushed his arm into Ferrex's back, shoving him in the direction of the front door.

44

FLEETING RESPITE

"How can I work with your commanders?" Marcellus asked, latching the front door. Catrin stepped up to him.

"They have pledged their loyalty to us both," she reassured him.

"Ferrex butts me like a ram. Negasi patronizes me. Furthermore, they have both confessed . . ." He bit his lower lip and looked away.

"Confessed what?" Catrin asked, taking his hand.

Marcellus gave her a hard look. "Their affection for you. Not only am I battling my father, but I am battling them, too."

"I chose you. They both know I only hold you in my heart," Catrin said. "Can we not just enjoy our time together? It has been so long since we've held each other."

Marcellus's frown softened. "I would like that. And I would like to become acquainted with my son."

Catrin chuckled. "Son? What if it is a daughter?"

Marcellus knelt and placed his face against her swollen belly. "He is my son. A part of you . . . a part of me."

Catrin placed a hand on his head, overwhelmed by the bond she shared with Marcellus. Her eyes welled with tears, which she quickly wiped away. The mercurial emotions were so unlike her; she had to remain strong. She lovingly stroked the curls of his dark hair with her fingertips.

Marcellus's voice cracked as he caressed her belly like it was a rare jewel. "I could not bear to lose you . . . or my son. Wait. I feel something." He leaned back on his heels and pressed both of his palms on her belly. "Such strong kicks."

The baby squirmed again. At the baby's next powerful kick, Catrin gasped with the unexpected pain.

Marcellus laughed. "Our son needs to be gentler."

"He is like his father—a general, demanding to get out," Catrin jested.

"He is a warrior, like his mother." With the baby's next punch, Marcellus chuckled. "That boy of mine needs to let you rest."

"Yes, I would like that," Catrin said, fatigued from the long ride.

Marcellus rose to his feet and picked her up in his arms.

"Why must you pick me up like this?" she asked, gazing into his deep-blue eyes, which had a glint of purple in the light of the flaming torches.

Carrying her to the straw bedding, Marcellus said lightheartedly, "I must serve the queen."

"And you will do what I command?" Catrin asked, her voice velvety.

Marcellus gave her a wry smile. "Which is?"

"I want you to lie with me," she said, closely regarding his befuddled expression, which soon turned sullen.

Marcellus sighed and set her down on the bedding, then sat down next to her. "You want to do this after what I did tonight? I feel so unclean," he finally confessed, looking down. "I have put you at great risk, though it was never my intent. It tears at my heart that my own family wants to harm you . . . the baby, too. And possibly me, if I do not comply with my father's wishes."

Catrin caressed the side of his face. "We are both blind to what will happen in the future. But what is certain is that we are together now. Let us embrace tonight. Tomorrow, we can face our fate."

Marcellus cupped Catrin's face and drew her into a feathery kiss. His warm breaths caressed her lips as he said softly, "Every time we part, I forget how beautiful you are. That is, until we meet again. You are more beautiful today—your body rounded with my child. But you seem so fragile."

"I won't break," Catrin said with an amused smile.

"What if I hurt the baby?"

"I have enough love for both of you," Catrin said, sensing the desire in his eyes.

"Well, then." Marcellus swallowed a lump forming in his throat. "Can I remove your clothes?"

"Do you need to ask?"

With a lopsided smile, Marcellus fumbled to pull the dress over her round belly and up her shoulders. Catrin took over the task, pulling the garment over her head and dropping it on the bedding. His gaze shifted over her body, as if he had never seen her naked. To ease his trepidation of touching her, she placed his right hand over her swollen breast.

"Sweet Juno," he groaned, cupping the tissue with his hand.

When his face flushed to a bright crimson from what suddenly felt like an awkward moment, she could feel the heat of his hand radiate into her skin. She leaned over and gently bit him on the neck. Startled, he jerked his head back, then a corner of his mouth lifted into a smirk.

"You are still a vixen," he growled.

"You bring that out in me." Catrin tugged at the corners of his tunic to pull it up. "Now, it is my turn to strip you."

He helped her remove the tunic and dropped it on top of her garments. She slowly caressed his bare chest; it was more muscular than she'd remembered. As she lowered her hand over his abdomen, she released his loincloth. He closed his eyes, delight on his face as she stroked him.

His breaths becoming ragged, Marcellus drew Catrin down on the bedding beside him. She pulled up a wool blanket to cover them. Feeling warm and secure in his arms, she felt like she was in a euphoric dance as his hand explored her rounded body. Flesh and souls joined as one. Calmness infused them, and the dark cloud of danger lurking over them then dissolved in a dreamless sleep.

Catrin's nightmare of giving birth in the midst of battle resurrected in the morning's darkness just before dawn. The baby's strong kick in her lower abdomen startled Catrin awake. The blanket had come off her during the night. Chilled from cold sweat, she cuddled closer to Marcellus and deeply inhaled his musky scent.

The baby squirmed, and she flinched from its next kick.

Marcellus stirred. "Doesn't that baby know when to rest?" he grumbled.

"It's not the baby who keeps me awake."

"Then what does?" he whispered.

"I had a foreboding dream." Catrin's voice quavered.

"What did you see?" Marcellus asked, turning to face her.

"Your father and Brutius were speaking to each other in the midst of a battle with Britons," she disclosed.

"Was it a battle scene painted on a fresco?" he asked.

Catrin envisioned the murals in the chamber. "How did you know?"

Marcellus shrugged. "The frescos of painted battles on the walls of Father's tablinum came to mind. What else did you see?"

"Your father then pointed to an image of me giving birth in the battle." Catrin could feel the blood drain from her face as she spoke. "The next thing I saw was Brutius opening a prison door . . ."

Marcellus looked concerned. "Go on. What was behind the door?"

Catrin trembled. "It was our son, in the shape of a baby eaglet. He was clasped in the talons of a vulture!"

He embraced her. "Don't let your dreams trouble you. Your pregnancy is playing tricks on your mind."

"No. These are omens," she insisted.

"You have always had the mettle of a warrior, but now . . ." His voice faded.

Catrin abruptly sat up. "I am still the same?"

Marcellus also sat up and rubbed his temple. "Sorry. I meant no offense."

The first light of dawn filtered through the shuttered window, making his skin glow. The shadows of Negasi and Ferrex bustling outside could be seen through the thin blinds.

Suddenly overwhelmed with sadness that Marcellus would soon leave, Catrin fought back tears. "We have spent so little time together as husband and wife."

"More than anything, I want to stay with you now, but I need to get back to the garrison to assess the situation after last night."

Catrin saw the tension in Marcellus's jaw—not from their disagreement but from the heavy burden of trying to protect her. Perhaps the potential loss of his heritage, his birthright, and his political power weighed heavily on his mind. Yet, she had also suffered. And now, she had to move from her past to her present.

After a few moments of silence, Marcellus hugged Catrin and stood up, offering his hand to help her up. They both dressed as the men outside noisily walked around the cottage and knocked on the front door.

Marcellus unlatched the door and let Negasi and Ferrex in. Both bowed their heads at Catrin as they entered and said in unison, "My queen."

Ferrex had some crusty bread and dried meat in his knapsack, which he gave to her and the others as they made their plans on how to evaluate the repercussions from Marcellus's actions. They all agreed that Marcellus should investigate the potential ramifications of his actions in Lugdunum.

Concerned for Catrin's safety, Marcellus balked at the plan that Negasi would ride that morning to the garrison and oversee trusted auxiliary cavalrymen as they prepared to travel north. Negasi agreed to stay with Catrin instead, while Marcellus initiated preparations.

Meanwhile, Ferrex volunteered to ride to the cave and solicit Trystan's assistance in protecting Catrin with more of his warriors. Possibly, other noncombatants still left in the cave could be safeguarded as part of the caravan.

Before riding away, Marcellus kissed Catrin. When he glanced back at her, she pressed her lips against her hand and released a kiss into the soft breeze. He gave her a boyish smile.

Negasi wrapped his arm around Catrin's shoulders as fresh tears rolled down her cheeks. Her soul again felt empty as she watched Marcellus disappear into the glare of the rising sun. Closing her eyes, she recalled the first time he'd kissed her in Britannia, nearly four years earlier. His first kiss had felt like butterfly wings on her lips, as his kiss had the previous night.

A fleeting moment etched in her memory.

Yet now, a sense of doom lurked over her. She and her baby could ultimately die at the hands of her husband's family.

45

POTENTIAL WITNESS

Lugdunum, Morning, 16 September, 28 AD

Marcellus stopped at the garrison gate, feigning that nothing had happened the previous night. A guard commented, "Why are you on that bag of bones?"

Marcellus chuckled. "Long night. I'll be picking up my cavalry horse later. Could you have someone summon Centurion Priscus Dius for me?"

The guard looked down at a wax tablet. "According to my records, he is on assignment with thirty other legionaries. It is unclear when he will return."

The revelation both perplexed and unsettled Marcellus; Priscus should have been with his men last night. And where were his men? Nonetheless, the guard seemed unaware of what had happened to the centurion. It would be best to make arrangements to leave the city soon, before Decimus became aware of the killings.

"Oh, now I remember. Summon Centurion Gaius Justus to my headquarters instead," Marcellus ordered. "Have a stableman feed my horse. And have it ready for me to ride by midday."

At the headquarters, Centurion Gaius Justus reported to him as a slave was assisting Marcellus with his armor. Marcellus showed the new orders by Decimus—that he would take command at Gesoriacum—to the centurion.

"Have supply wagons packed with provisions for one hundred people. We leave in two days," Marcellus ordered.

Gaius Justus raised an eyebrow. "It says only twenty legionaries will escort you."

Marcellus leveled a hard stare at the centurion. "I make the final orders."

The centurion lowered his eyes and remained silent.

After recording further instructions, Marcellus imprinted the family seal with his signet ring and handed it to the centurion. "Any questions?"

"None whatsoever."

"Then get to it," Marcellus commanded, then he followed the centurion outside to retrieve the swayback nag and ride to the stables.

As Marcellus approached the stables in Lugdunum, he noted a noble-man, garishly dressed in a clashing rose-colored toga over a bright gold tunic, talking to a stooped, elderly slave. His gemstone rings flashed in the midday sun as the noble gesticulated as he spoke.

The silver-haired noble's order, "Go to the garrison and report to the governor what has happened here," gave Marcellus the opportunity to intrude.

"Is something wrong here?" he asked, dismounting his horse.

The noble nervously glanced at the stooped man. Seeing their anxious looks, Marcellus introduced himself. "I am Marcellus Antonius, a praetor from the city garrison. There have been reports that thieves have stolen cavalry horses from this stable."

The patrician adjusted the silver-haired wig on his head, then intro-duced himself. "I am Titus Ennius, a city magistrate. I own the Red Cock tavern and this stable. We cannot find the stableman."

"Is that so?" Marcellus said, thinking it odd how the magistrate an-swered his question. "Can I take a look inside and account for the horses from the garrison?"

Titus's voice quavered. "I had nothing to do with this."

Marcellus feigned ignorance of the bloody carnage inside. "Have to do with what?"

Titus handed him a gold coin with a shaky hand. "You need to be dis-creet about what you find here. Bad for business."

Marcellus rolled the coin between his fingertips. "I can be discreet."

"Good. I am glad we have an understanding." Titus gestured at the stooped man to open the stable door.

Marcellus followed Titus into the stable. He acted shocked to find the mutilated, headless corpse he'd hacked like butchered meat. He rolled the cut-off head close to the woman's body.

"This looks like a centurion from the garrison."

"A curse from Mars!" Titus grumbled.

"Do you know the woman?" Marcellus asked as he leaned over to get a closer look at the knife embedded in her breast. "This is a standard *pugio* issued in the legion."

Titus's bloodshot eyes widened. "I have never seen her before."

"One of your prostitutes, perhaps?"

"I am not in charge of the brothel," Titus quickly replied.

Marcellus narrowed his eyes at the magistrate. "Are there any other bodies?"

Titus rubbed his jaw. "One more in the alley . . . a Roman soldier."

"Show me," Marcellus demanded.

"I had it moved. Bad for business," Titus said again.

Losing patience, Marcellus snapped, "Where did you move it?"

Titus did not answer but had a question of his own. "What am I to do? I cannot dispose corpses of soldiers—"

"Bad for business, I know. I'll arrange for funerary services," Marcellus offered. "Now, show me the other body."

Titus again adjusted the silver-haired wig on his head and wiped the sweat dripping down his face with a corner of his toga. "I hope you remove these bodies soon. Horses do not like the smell of blood."

"Have your slave take the horses and tether them out front so owners can claim them," Marcellus suggested, then glanced around for his horse. It was loose outside a stall containing a gray mare. Pointing to his horse, he said, "I claim the black stallion over there. You can keep my nag."

Titus instructed the stooped slave where to take the horses. Marcellus bridled his calvary horse and led it by the reins as Titus escorted him through the alley to the back of the Red Cock tavern. A different innkeeper from the previous night escorted them to a room down the corridor, where the body had been dumped on the floor.

Marcellus lifted the blanket off the corpse but did not recognize the soldier. The cause of death was obvious. A stab wound to the heart.

"Clean death," Marcellus commented to Titus. "This may not be associated with the deaths in the stable. Do you know who discovered the body?"

The innkeeper grimaced. "One of the women working here."

Wondering if she had seen him and Deidre beforehand, Marcellus told Titus, "I would like to speak with her."

Titus's face contorted. "Is that necessary?"

"It won't take long."

Titus exhaled in exasperation, then whispered in the innkeeper's ear. Turning to Marcellus, he agreed. "The innkeeper will make the arrangements. Are we done here?"

Marcellus nodded.

Titus pulled the end of the toga over his arm and stepped out of the room. After he left, the innkeeper informed Marcellus, "The woman is in the next room. She is a high-priced healer who offers lots of services to our patrons."

Marcellus smirked.

Iberdees.

He followed the innkeeper to the adjacent room, which he had to unlock. Opening the door, Marcellus found her massaging rolls of fat on a naked, flabby man.

"Iberdees, this is Praetor Marcellus Antonius from the garrison," the innkeeper introduced.

"I am almost done," Iberdees said, stealing a glance at Marcellus. "Then, we can talk in here."

The man grumbled incomprehensibly as Iberdees leaned over. Her ample breasts fell out of her low-cut dress. Marcellus flushed with embarrassment as he found himself gawking at her hardened nipples. She gave him an amused smile.

Discomfited, he went outside the room and into the corridor. Hot and sweaty, he felt like a stupid adolescent experiencing involuntary arousal. When the door opened, the disheveled man was fumbling to wrap a toga around the folds of his hanging belly. His fleshy jowl bounced with every heavy step he took as he left the room.

Peeking in, Marcellus could not help but stare as Iberdees provocatively put her breasts back into her dress, barely covering the nipples.

She waved him in. "Stop gawking and come in."

Entering the room, he looked around to familiarize himself with the room again. He had not noticed the bottles and jars of ointments on the table the previous night. He slowly closed the door. "When did you find the body of the soldier?"

Iberdees stepped back and nervously stared at his belted weapons. "I peeked out the window and saw you kill him. I did not say anything until this morning."

Keenly aware that, under torture, she could identify him as the murderer, Marcellus impulsively gripped her arm. "You will come with me."

Iberdees planted her feet and refused to move. "I am a free woman and can go as I please," she protested.

Marcellus cocked an eyebrow. "Is that so? Why are you in a brothel, then?"

"I treat men for what ails them. I am a healer," Iberdees insisted.

Not wanting to argue the point, Marcellus said bluntly, "Deidre is dead. And you could be next."

Iberdees's mouth dropped open. "How? When?"

"Stabbed. Last night. Can you ride?"

Iberdees's voice cracked. "A horse?"

"It doesn't matter. You can ride with me," Marcellus said, pulling the shuttered window back. He pushed Iberdees through the window and followed her into the alley. There, he hoisted her onto his horse and jumped on its back behind her.

"Could we have just walked out?" Iberdees asked as he wrapped his arm around her.

"Everyone can be left guessing," he retorted.

After they rode through the city gates, Marcellus decided not to take the main road to the juncture where he would take the dirt road to the farmhouse. Instead, he took an alternative route through forested hills along the Rhône River, familiar to him since boyhood. The pace was slow with Iberdees riding with him.

Deep in thought, his mind swam with options regarding what he would do next. No doubt, he would travel north with the caravan of Roman auxiliary and warriors from Catrin's band as quickly as possible. What concerned him most was what he could not anticipate. He recalled Catrin cautioning, *We are blind to the future.*

Iberdees asking, "Where are we going?"—a question she must have asked at least ten times—broke his contemplation.

He inhaled sharply. "To an abandoned cottage where you will be safe."

The next comments from Iberdees came in rapid succession.

"Who else will be there? Catrin?" she asked.

"Catrin and some of her warriors."

"Deidre said I looked like Catrin," she remarked.

"True enough," Marcellus said, visualizing a strand of Catrin's golden hair straying over one of her turquoise eyes. "Except she is heavy with child."

"Your child?"

"What do you think?" Marcellus said, unsettled that Iberdees knew more personal things about him than he realized.

"I sense a heavy weight on your shoulders." Her voice became monotone, as if she were falling into a trance. "You have had visions of your future. A fiery pool. Two bodies consumed in flames."

The revelation cut to the truth, disquieting Marcellus further. "So, you're a healer and can read people's minds?"

"I heal what ails people—both their minds and bodies," Iberdees proclaimed.

Has Apollo fated me to meet this woman? Marcellus wondered.

"Can you deliver babies?"

"That and other things," Iberdees said. "What do you plan to do with me?"

Suddenly hearing what sounded like horse hooves trampling on twigs and muffled voices from up the hill, Marcellus did not answer. With sunset approaching, it was difficult for him to see clearly through the sun's orange glare.

"Let us stop here." He dismounted and helped Iberdees off. Taking the reins of his horse, he hid with her behind some fir trees.

A raven shrieked from overhead.

A warning.

Cautiously peering around a tree trunk, he saw a group of Roman infantrymen marching on a rarely used pathway up the hill, which joined the main dirt road to his family villa. Approaching from the opposite direction of the infantrymen were armed, tattooed warriors on horseback. Surprisingly, the lead horseman with the warriors was armored with *lorica musculata*, the marking of a wealthy Roman patrician flashing his status with bronze pectoral muscles. The horseman was astride a tar-black stallion, similar to the thick-maned breed Marcellus rode. When he took off his helmet and scratched his vulturous nose, Marcellus immediately recognized him.

Brutius!

Shocked, Marcellus held his breath and waved for Iberdees to stay back with his horse near the river. He slowly exhaled and crouched to maneuver uphill toward the two groups of armed men to listen to their conversation. Peering around the trunk of an oak tree, Marcellus recognized the lead infantrymen at the front of the formation of six soldiers in five rows as he stepped forward to greet Brutius. He could barely hear the conversation.

"*Salve.* I am Optio Quintus Livius . . . orders."

Brutius leaned forward on his horse, his voice raised. "Where is Centurion Priscus Dius?"

"I'm not sure," Quintus Livius said, his voice fading in and out in a brisk breeze sweeping over the forest. ". . . went ahead without him . . . send someone back . . ."

Brutius dabbed a purple scarf to his mouth and gave an order Marcellus could not hear clearly. A lanky infantryman bent over on hands and knees beside the black stallion. Brutius stepped down on the soldier's back, using him like a footstool, then stepped to the ground.

Brutius handed a red leather cylinder to Quintus Livius. Quintus Livius took a scroll out, and as he read it, his mouth gaped open.

Brutius again dabbed his mouth with a purple cloth, then lifted a leather purse and walked back and forth in front of the infantrymen. Marcellus could only decipher a few of the words.

"Reward . . . Marcellus Antonius . . . trial."

Marcellus's heart catapulted into his throat when the infantrymen's cheers rose like a clap of thunder as Brutius strutted in front of them like a peacock showing off its tail feathers.

Brutius then waved one of the horsemen—a heavily armed, barbaric warrior with a sword sheathed on his back and belted weapons at his side—to move forward.

Marcellus recognized the triangular blue tattoo across the man's forehead.

Gawain!

Breathing hard, he tried to grasp the reality of the danger before his eyes: two deadly enemies made up of Roman soldiers and possibly Cantiaci horsemen. A gust of wind blew against Marcellus's face as he watched Brutius lift a different drawstring bag. Gawain rode back and forth in front of the infantrymen. The only words Marcellus could discern as Brutius spoke were, "Reward . . . head . . . Catrin."

Shadows of ravens soaring overhead suddenly shrouded the sky. Even for the most hardened soldier, this was an omen of pending death. A distraction under which Marcellus could hopefully leave the area without being detected.

He ran back to where Iberdees was hiding and vaulted onto his horse, pulling her up in front of him. He reined his horse toward the river and depended on his instincts and familiarity with the area to navigate back to the farmhouse.

46

UNEXPECTED GUEST

Isolated Farmhouse, Midnight, 17 September, 28 AD

Catrin stooped over to stroke the fur of a stray gray-striped cat that had unexpectedly wandered near the hearth late that night. Hearing the stomping of hooves outside, she eyed Negasi. He unsheathed his weapon and gestured for Ferrex and Trystan to do likewise.

Earlier in the afternoon, while picking berries, she had observed horsemen in the distance. She waved for Negasi, who was hunting for game, to go to the farmhouse. After they went inside, they latched the doors and waited for the others to return.

Shortly after, Ferrex and Trystan arrived with a horse laden with food. Ferrex told them that they had taken another route to avoid being detected by a group of Roman infantrymen marching on a seldom used pathway.

By nightfall, when Marcellus had not yet returned, everyone's nerves were on edge.

Now, Trystan peeked through the window shutters as Ferrex positioned himself next to the doorjamb at the front, and Negasi guarded the back entry. Catrin retrieved a dagger from under her straw bedding, the cat following and purring. She held her breath and peeked around the curtain separating her sleeping quarters from the main room for a signal from Trystan.

He raised his forefinger for one rider.

She exhaled slowly.

Perhaps it is Marcellus.

Catrin's heart quickened as Ferrex cracked the front door open to peer through the narrow opening. The instant Marcellus burst through the door, knocking Ferrex back, she sensed an outside force.

A woman dressed like a harlot in a low-cut dress appeared in the open doorway, stunning everyone. In the illumination of the hearth's flames, her features were eerily similar to Catrin's—almost like a reflection on polished metal. With her diminished gift of foresight, Catrin could not discern if the outside force was the woman's aura or something else.

Disturbed by the presence of the unknown woman, Catrin pulled the curtain away and walked up to Marcellus. Reaching for his hand, she felt a charge emit from her fingertips, making him flinch.

He shot a bewildered look at her.

She frowned and pointed to the gray-striped cat rubbing against the fabric around her legs.

Marcellus chuckled softly but then tensed as he eyed each commander. Their set jaws reflected her aggravation that he had brought a strange woman into their midst. He looked at Catrin with concern.

"Are you ill?" he asked. "You have a slightly yellow tint to your skin."

"I feel fine. Who is she?" Catrin asked, anger brewing at the sight of the prostitute's cleavage.

"Her name is Iberdees. She is a healer," Marcellus said, his eyes searching hers. "I believe Apollo sent her to help with the childbirth."

"Indeed," Catrin said in a biting tone. "What did you learn in Lugdunum?"

"None of the guards at the garrison are aware of what happened to Priscus," Marcellus said. "Titus Ennius, the proprietor of the stables and Red Cock tavern, wanted to get rid of the bodies. 'Bad for business,' he said. I found Iberdees and brought her here to protect her."

The fact that Marcellus had brought back Iberdees made Catrin steam with anger, though she remained silent as he continued.

"What I witnessed coming back here concerned me more. I saw Gawain and Brutius meet on a pathway that leads to my family's villa. They were with Roman infantrymen and tattooed warriors on horseback. I could not hear everything, but I believe they are working together to bring back your head," Marcellus said with a pained grimace.

Catrin's stomach lurched. "We also saw horsemen in the distance today."

"And we saw Roman troops on our way here," Trystan added.

"The sightings raise more questions than answers," Marcellus said.

With the late night, Catrin grew fatigued and queasy, dissociating from the conversation. It was as if a veil had been pulled around her mind, and the men's voices droned in heated discussion about the next steps. She sensed strands of threads slipping over her fingertips, as if weaving. Strange questions swam in her mind. Did expectant mothers go to a dark cave so a soul from a past life could resurrect into their babies? Did the soul resurrect in a baby at the moment it took its first breath? Or could the soul enter the baby prior to birth?

A man whispered in her ears, but she could not understand the words.

A woman's voice offering, "Let me put you to bed," momentarily broke Catrin's trance, and uncontrollable fear took hold. "But I won't wake up," she muttered.

She found herself in a dark cavern, where ghostly images in her mind spattered on the wall: a baby transforming into an eaglet; life threads weaving in and out of the Wall of Lives, then untangling; Marcellus reaching for her to pull her into his horse-driven chariot racing across starlit sky.

"Am I dreaming?" she whispered to Marcellus.

"You are in my skull," her father's voice said. "You can only unleash its vengeance when you are ready."

"Ready for what?" Catrin asked.

"The magic of the ancient druids," her father whispered. "When you most need it, the Raven will know."

47

NEXT STEPS OF ESCAPE

Isolated Farmhouse, Gaul, 17 September, 28 AD

Catrin's sudden collapse deeply concerned Marcellus. He watched over her as she languished with fever, in restless sleep, until dawn. Feeling helpless with the inability to cure what ailed her, he gently stroked her forehead. Her skin felt hot to the touch.

"Is Catrin dying?" he asked Iberdees.

The healer placed a hand on each side of Catrin's face and closed her eyes, as if in a trance. "What ails her is not from this world," she said.

Recalling Catrin's belief about the ability of souls to enter another body, Marcellus asked, "Does an evil spirit possess her?"

Iberdees opened her eyes. "A soul from her past."

Marcellus looked desperately at Iberdees with pleading eyes. "You said you can treat all ailments. Mental and physical. Please do not let Catrin and our baby die."

"I cannot treat what plagues her mind," Iberdees said gravely. "However, I can give her something to break the fever and help her condition. But I left the herbs in my room."

"I will get them," Marcellus said, then he rose to tell the other men his decision.

When Marcellus pulled away the curtain to enter the main room, he found Negasi with his back turned and Ferrex and Trystan across the hearth from him. They all turned to him with anxious looks as he stepped into the main room.

Marcellus sighed deeply. "She is not any better. Iberdees cannot treat her without certain herbs. She left them at the Red Cock Tavern. I'm going to Lugdunum to get them. While I am there, I need someone to help me dispose of the soldiers' bodies."

Negasi nodded. "I will do it."

Trystan shot a glare at Marcellus. "So, you plan to return to the garrison?"

Marcellus leveled his eyes at Trystan. "I considered your advice to desert, but I will not betray Rome. I will still keep my promise to aid Catrin."

Trystan's jaw tightened. "Despite the danger Brutius and Gawain pose?"

"I believe they are working together for a singular purpose. Marrock wants Catrin's head. And so does my father."

"And perhaps your head, too," Trystan retorted.

"Perhaps. But that is not what Rome wants," Marcellus said, closely studying Trystan's flushed face, which glowed even brighter from the hearth's flames. "Decimus made it clear that Marrock is a thorn in the imperial ass. That is why I'm going back. To get the auxiliary cavalrymen assigned to me and go north to take command of the garrison at Gesoriacum."

Trystan pressed his lips into a firm line. "Your loyalty is to Rome. My loyalty is to our queen."

"Mine, too," Ferrex chimed in.

"I am also loyal to my wife," Marcellus said, struggling to temper his voice from the frustration of working with commanders resistant to him. "As such, she should be moved elsewhere, where it is safer. That is why I propose that Catrin be immediately transported in a wagon to Durocortorum. As you told me, several of your warriors are already there, in hiding. She should leave tonight under the cover of darkness and take the less travelled roads in the forest."

"Should we not wait until she is better?" Ferrex asked.

"Gawain and Brutius might find her if she stays too long in the area. With the herbs, Iberdees can tend to her on the trip. Then, we pray," Marcellus said, the commanders' piercing stares making him doubt his plan.

"I agree," Trystan finally concurred. "I'll return to the cave today and assign my best warriors to guard the queen when she leaves tonight."

"After we dispose of the bodies in Lugdunum, Negasi can come back here with the herbs Catrin needs," Marcellus said. "I will prepare my forces to leave in the next couple of days and try to find out more information. My activities should distract Gawain and Brutius."

"It could take at least a month to get there. She might go into labor before then," Ferrex cautioned.

"I know. But we have to take the risk," Marcellus said, though he was uncertain.

"How will we find you once you've left?" Negasi asked.

"We'll take the main route," Marcellus replied, noting the thin smile on Ferrex's lips, as if he would not make any attempt to find him.

"Then we are in agreement," Trystan concluded.

Later that morning, at the Red Cock tavern, Marcellus introduced Negasi as a funerary worker to Titus Ennius. "He is here to collect the bodies."

"Do it quietly," Titus emphasized. Then, both he and Marcellus said in unison, "Bad for business."

Titus grimaced. "Will you clean up the blood and guts?"

"We are only here to collect the bodies," Marcellus said.

Titus's brow furrowed. "Any more issues about reporting the murders?"

"With no witnesses, the case is closed," Marcellus said, even though he did not know how widely the disappearances of Priscus and the other soldier were known at the garrison.

"Then I hope we do not meet again," Titus said with a grimace.

Marcellus gave a slight nod. "Have someone give us access to the bodies. Then, we will be out of your face."

Titus had the innkeeper escort Marcellus and Negasi to the room where the soldier's body was stored. When Marcellus entered, he observed that the body was starting to bloat and emit a foul odor. Negasi quickly wrapped the body in linen and hoisted it over his shoulders to put it in a cart waiting in the alley.

Meanwhile, Marcellus bribed the innkeeper to unlock the door to the next room, where Iberdees kept her medical supplies. In the corner, he found a wooden, handled container packed with trays of powders, capped jars and bottles, gauzes, and instruments. He also packed other containers he found in the room and met Negasi outside in the alley.

The next stop was the stable, where Titus's guards allowed them inside. A host of flies were buzzing around the mutilated body. The stench of horse manure and body parts was overwhelming. Negasi and Marcellus wrapped scarves around the bottom half of their faces to block the odor, then placed Priscus's body parts in a linen sack and wrapped a linen sheet around Deidre's body. Negasi hauled everything out to the horse-driven cart and drove off to burn the bodies on pyres outside the city, leaving Marcellus for the final task of reporting back to the garrison.

This time, the guards at the gates told him about rumors that Priscus and another soldier had deserted, also telling him that Decimus had summoned Marcellus.

When Marcellus entered the governor's headquarters, he struggled to mask his nervousness. Decimus was sitting behind a table with stacked scrolls. He looked up and stared silently at Marcellus.

"You summoned me?" Marcellus said, looking straight ahead at the fresco of Mars clasping the breast of Venus.

"It has come to my attention that Priscus and another soldier are missing. Some surmise he deserted," Decimus said gravely.

Marcellus's throat felt parched. He swallowed and stole a glance at Decimus, who appeared stressed. Decimus lowered his head into his hand, as if it were too great a weight to bear.

"I was told the other day that he had gone on a mission," Marcellus said. "Who told you he was missing?"

"Optio Quintus Livius. A direct report to Priscus," Decimus answered in a subdued voice.

"Since Priscus no longer reports directly to me, I was not made aware," Marcellus said evenly.

Decimus straightened and folded his hands on the table. "So, you have made preparations to leave?"

"I leave within the next few days with twenty auxiliary cavalrymen, as you approved."

"Before you leave, I want you to know that we are both caught in the same political crosswinds."

Suspicious of Decimus's candor, Marcellus looked him straight in the eye. "How so?"

Decimus gave him a nervous smile. "Are we not but players in a game, trying to anticipate our opponent's next move? To win, you must do the unexpected."

Marcellus felt his rapid heartbeats throbbing in his neck. "Your meaning?"

"That, you must figure out," Decimus said with a grim smile.

In the silence that followed, Marcellus understood Decimus had just warned him not to take the main route to Gesoriacum.

48

FOREBODING OMENS

One Month Later . . .

Midway to Durocortorum, 17 October, 28 AD

Catrin had languished on the arduous trip to Durocortorum. Mostly traveling by night, she found it difficult to rest on the wagon's hard bed. With the drop of her rapidly expanding belly, the rocking motion of the wagon made it hard to get comfortable. Her hands and legs were also swollen. Furthermore, the baby's relentless kicks often interrupted her rest. The wheels' click-click-click-clop rhythm and the pattering rain on the wood-covered wagon added to the drudgery throughout each day and night. With the length of daylight shortening, nightfall felt as it if would go on forever—as did her pregnancy.

Suffering with intermittent fevers, she was haunted by the same vision. It began with her soul floating out of her body and into the depths of a dark cavern. She huddled with other bats, like a cluster of grapes, watching images project on the stone wall.

A red wolf slowly comes into focus, followed by the image of a young boy with shoulder-length, bronze hair. Three human skulls roped together with a gigantic reptilian skull appear. The boy slices the rope with the blade of a dagger, detaches the largest human skull, and holds it up. Lightning webs across the sky, and Catrin finds herself inside the skull. Her father's voice tells her, "The time approaches. You will gain the power of the ancient druids when you most need it."

A sudden chill, making Catrin's body shake and her teeth clatter, awoke her. Her head spun as she tried to orient herself. Opening her eyes, she found a fair-skinned woman looking down on her. It took her a few moments to remember that it was Iberdees and that they were in a covered wagon.

Iberdees softly touched her forehead and pulled Catrin's eyelids back to inspect. "You had another fever, but it has broken."

"I was talking to my father in his skull," Catrin remarked, still bothered by what she had envisioned.

"No doubt," Iberdees said, as if she did not believe Catrin.

The strong arms of a man behind lifted her to a sitting position as Iberdees gave her a bitter liquid to drink.

"How far have we traveled?" Catrin asked.

"We are midway to Durocortorum."

"That cannot be," Catrin said weakly, vaguely remembering that she had been in a farmhouse. "How long have I been asleep?"

"A day and night," Iberdees said. "You were again stricken with fever. I gave you something to help."

"How long have we been traveling?" Catrin asked, disconcerted that she could not remember much of the trip.

"Almost a moon cycle," Iberdees said.

"Where is Marcellus?"

"Behind you," he answered.

Her husband's presence made Catrin feel better as she ate the porridge and berries Iberdees offered her. After she finished eating. Marcellus again reminded her that Negasi had gathered the bodies of Priscus and a soldier he had killed, burned them on a pyre, and scattered their ashes.

Marcellus had taken Decimus's advice not to take the main road. Traveling in the cover of dense woods had slowed them down. With the heavy rains, their arrival in Durocortorum could be delayed by as much as two weeks. Trystan had sent messengers north to relay to the various caravans of both warriors and noncombatants, traveling in wagons with plundered treasures, to rendezvous with them in Durocortorum. He had returned with ten of his most battle-hardened warriors to help protect Catrin.

Even though Marcellus assured Catrin that the scouts had not yet detected any threats, an uneasy feeling gnawed at her that Decimus had tricked him into taking a slower route.

Over the next fortnight, Catrin felt stronger as she rode in the wagon with Iberdees over various dirt paths through the deep forest. Initially, a handful of ravens followed the caravan, but the number grew to ten ravens the next day and to hundreds at the end of two weeks. Fearing the creatures were there to collect the souls of the dead, Catrin grew anxious that their slow-moving caravan could be ambushed.

Finally, when the wagon wheels mired in the mud from torrential rains, she convinced Marcellus that she and Iberdees should travel by horseback to quicken their journey. She wanted to deliver the baby in Durocortorum and not in the wildwoods. He reluctantly agreed and rode alongside her, and Ferrex, Trystan, Negasi, and other warriors led packhorses with supplies behind them. The auxiliary cavalrymen split in two, half of them as a vanguard, with the other half riding at the back. Iberdees, an inexperienced rider, awkwardly bounced on a mare not much more than the height of a pony. At times, she lagged at the back of the caravan.

Close to Durocortorum, Gaul, Eve of Samhain, 31 October, 28 AD

After a day of drizzling rain, the waxing moon finally escaped the shroud of black clouds on the eve of the Samhain. The constant rocking motion of the horse made Catrin feel queasy. She leaned over her horse to ease the pressure in her contracting belly. At first, it seemed to help, and she straightened after the discomfort eased.

However, the next series of contractions intensified as her belly hardened. She could not yet convince herself she was in labor. The baby was not due for another month. At least, that was what Iberdees estimated, counting the weeks since Catrin had had coitus with Marcellus in Rome. Her last bleeding had been in January, six weeks before sleeping with Marcellus. Before that, her bleedings had been irregular, sometimes stopping during intense training as a gladiator.

A blessing, she often told herself, with the leveling of her emotional ups and downs from monthly bleedings. But now, with her condition, her emotions were like a waterfall, cascading over a cliff and plunging into a turbulent river below. It felt as if she had been pregnant for years. The baby had stolen her life's energy, a sacrifice she had not anticipated.

And now, could it be possible her son was announcing he was ready to greet the world?

But why must it be here? In the wilderness, close to winter?

Seeing Marcellus slumped in sleep on his horse, Catrin wondered if she should wake him and tell him she was in labor.

Ferrex rode up to Marcellus and slapped him on the shoulder. "Stay awake!"

Marcellus jerked upright and rubbed the drowsiness out of his eyes. He halted his horse and poured water from a canteen over his head. Catrin also stopped and repositioned herself to brace for the next contraction. As her belly hardened like a rock, she felt something pop inside, and fluid gushed out. Nauseated, she spewed sour liquid from her stomach.

"I have to get off," she moaned loudly, in pain.

Marcellus jumped off his horse and helped her to dismount. "What happened? You are wet," he said, a tinge of panic in his voice.

The next contraction swept over Catrin like a wave. She leaned against Marcellus and clawed her fingernails into his shoulder as the contraction peaked. Flinching as he held her up, he cursed beneath his breath, "Damn! Damn! Damn!"

When she released her grip, he helped her to lie down on some tufts of grass by the road and knelt beside her.

Ferrex joined Marcellus and crouched next to him.

"What is wrong?" he asked.

"She could be in labor. Get me a cape to cover her," Marcellus ordered.

The next waves of contractions crashed on Catrin one right after the other. She could no longer control her bodily functions. Frantic, she looked wide-eyed at Marcellus and screamed, "Get me to the forest!"

But it was too late.

Runny stool streamed down her legs, the stench assaulting her nostrils. Her stomach cramped, and she curled over on the ground.

Ferrex discomfited Catrin by harshly commenting, "It smells like shit!"

"Keep your voice down," Marcellus cautioned.

"Is she having that baby?" Ferrex asked in a quieter voice.

Marcellus shrugged. "What should we do?"

"By the gods, how would I know?"

With the next contraction, Catrin groaned loudly, "Get me off the road and fetch Iberdees!"

For several moments, Marcellus and Ferrex stood frozen. Growing agitated, Catrin wondered what were they waiting for—a lightning bolt to strike them in the buttocks? They finally jolted into action when she screamed, "Get me to the forest!"

Marcellus barked at Ferrex, "Cross your arms with mine, and we can pick her up. Tell Negasi to hobble the horses and have Trystan tell the auxiliaries we are camping here."

Ferrex cried out orders to Negasi as he worked with Marcellus. When Catrin's next contraction ebbed, she draped her arms over their shoulders, and they lifted her up. Marcellus and Ferrex staggered with her to an oak with low-hanging branches deeper in the forest.

Catrin's jaw clenched as she groaned, "Put me against the tree." As Marcellus helped her lean against the trunk, she groaned, "Get me . . . oil . . . rags to clean myself."

Marcellus turned to Ferrex. "Get a packhorse with those supplies."

Freed from modesty, Catrin removed her soiled clothing, leaned naked against some branches, and squatted to ease the rectal pressure. When she began shivering, Marcellus wrapped a cloak around her. "What do you need?"

Catrin could not answer; she instead braced herself for the next contraction. Her lower back felt as though it might break when the contraction crested. As the pressure eased, the faint red light of the rising sun filtered through the trees. Out of the glare, Ferrex brought over a packhorse, tied its reins around a branch, and handed Marcellus a jar of oil and cloth strips. He told Marcellus, "Negasi started a fire near here While you tend to Catrin, I'll boil some water."

"Where is Iberdees?" Marcellus asked.

With a concerned look on his face, Ferrex leaned over and whispered something in his ear. Moaning from the crushing pressure, Catrin could not hear what they were saying, but a sense of panic struck her that Iberdees was still not there.

After Ferrex left, Marcellus poured oil onto some cloth and wiped Catrin's legs, which embarrassed her. She tried to grab the cloth from him. "I can do it."

"Let me do this," Marcellus said, continuing to clean her. "I have seen men soil themselves in battle."

Catrin loosened her grip on his hand, but the pain began building again. Blowing out air rapidly, she gripped a tree branch as her belly contracted. Pain stabbed throughout her tailbone as the baby's head pushed against her lower back.

"Rub my back," she snapped at Marcellus.

At first, he gently massaged her back and hips, but she needed his hand to counter the pressure of the baby's head driving against her lower spine.

"Harder!" she screamed.

This time, Marcellus pressed hard against her lower back, somewhat easing her pain.

Ferrex returned, and his brow creased as he knelt by Marcellus.

"Is everything under control?" Marcellus's voice trembled.

Ferrex muttered something incomprehensible, then said, "Stay with your wife." He jumped to his feet and rushed toward the road, unsheathing his sword.

Catrin knew then that something was terribly wrong, but she was in so much pain that she did not dare think about what it could be. She felt Marcellus's hand shake as he circled the oil-soaked cloth over her belly. He seemed distracted, frequently glancing over her head. At the next contraction, her legs trembled with the burning pressure of the baby's head bearing down on her pelvis. She gritted her teeth and began pushing.

Suddenly, a raven flew overhead and screeched.

Catrin's heart pounded when she saw the terror in her husband's eyes. He squeezed a dagger into her hand and drew his sword. "Don't cry out."

He pivoted around her and rushed away.

49

BIRTH IN BATTLE

South of Durocortorum, Gaul, Samhain, 1 November, 28 AD

A short distance from Catrin's hiding place, Marcellus observed a Roman centurion and five soldiers stepping out of the sun's glare in the east. Ferrex had warned him a contingency of possibly forty Roman soldiers had been marching on the main road nearby. It seemed more than a coincidence that Iberdees and a few men had disappeared. Marcellus looked for Ferrex or Negasi but could not see them. Not sure of the soldiers' intent, he walked toward them. The black raven circled overhead, its croaks echoing through the forest.

"Why are your swords drawn?" Marcellus asked them.

The brawny centurion said, "We are looking for a fugitive from the Roman legion."

Marcellus darted his eyes around. "What does he look like?"

"A Roman in his early twenties with dark hair and blue eyes."

Marcellus tightened his hand around his sword's hilt. "I have not seen anyone by that description."

The centurion narrowed his eyes. "You match the description."

"I am a Roman officer in command of nearby forces," Marcellus declared.

When a loud grunt sounded from the woods, the centurion jerked his head up. "Who is over there?"

Marcellus remained stone-faced. "A slave of mine."

Catrin's voice cried out.

"What is wrong with her?" the centurion asked.

372 ❖ Linnea Tanner

"She is sick. Do not get any closer. She has the flux," Marcellus warned, wondering where his men were.

The centurion looked suspiciously at Marcellus. "You look familiar. Drop your sword and come with us."

Looking around for Ferrex and Negasi, Marcellus saw two shadows flitting between the trees. Marcellus stepped forward and drew his sword. Though outnumbered, he prepared to pounce on the centurion first and then attack the other four soldiers.

The centurion shouted, "Apprehend the woman!"

As one soldier moved toward Catrin, Marcellus felt his blood raging through him as he evaded the centurion's spear thrust and ran after the fast-moving soldier.

"Bastard! Keep away from her!" Marcellus's cry echoed through the trees.

The soldier reached Catrin and grabbed her shoulders. Roaring like a lioness, she plunged her dagger into his belly. He staggered backward, clutched his stomach, and dropped his jaw in shock. Catrin crumpled on the ground beside him.

Crazed with bloodlust, Marcellus kicked the soldier in the balls and buried his sword in his chest. The soldier fell backward with the force.

Marcellus jerked the blade out and knelt beside his wife. He held his sword out, now ready for the centurion.

"The baby is coming!" she screamed.

Panicked, he leaned Catrin against a tree, jumped to his feet, and moved toward the centurion, who was now brandishing a sword. The centurion swung his blade; Marcellus countered with his sword but slipped in some mud. With his breath jarred out of him, Marcellus shuddered at the sight of the centurion's descending blade. He jerked sideways, barely avoiding the blow.

Suddenly, a raven swooped at the centurion, its claws drawing blood. The centurion screamed and waved his arm at the attacking bird. Behind the centurion was Ferrex, his arms flaming with tattoos as he whirled forward with his battle-axe. He smashed the axe into the centurion's back. For a moment, the centurion's eyes widened, then he fell forward. Breathing hard, Marcellus glimpsed Negasi pulling his spear from another Roman, lying among some tree roots, and prepared to fight another soldier.

Marcellus returned to Catrin and knelt in front of her. He could see the baby's head crowning. Paralyzed, he didn't know what to do. With adrenaline-heightened senses, he was shocked as blood splattered all over his face—Ferrex hacking off another soldier's head.

Marcellus shouted, "Gods beneath me! Stop that!"

Ferrex yanked the severed head away from the body and held it up by the hair. Marcellus felt sick to his stomach, but he managed to swallow the bitter bile. Ferrex yelled at Negasi in Celtic.

Marcellus turned back to Catrin and now saw the baby's head emerging. He gasped. His throat constricted. He turned to Ferrex. "What—what . . . should I do?" he stammered.

Ferrex opened his mouth, but words did not come out.

"Catch the baby!" Catrin screamed.

Seeing the baby's shoulders appear, Marcellus wrapped his red cape around the emerging newborn. After the baby gushed out, Marcellus inspected his bluish-faced child. A proud smile broke out on his face. The baby had a scrotum and a penis—a son!

By then, both Negasi and Ferrex had joined Marcellus in the joyous moment.

With tears welling in his eyes, Marcellus marveled at the sight of his son's wavy black hair and the tiny fingers curling into a fist. Dumbfounded, he couldn't find words to describe the miracle of delivering his own son. He held his boy out for Negasi to wipe the birth slime from around his face. The baby gasped and cried in protest at leaving his secure womb. Not sure how to calm his son, Marcellus looked anxiously at Catrin, who reached for the baby and cradled him in her arms. The newborn calmed and nuzzled against her breast, seeking the nipple.

Then, Marcellus saw blood stream down his wife's legs. His stomach knotted. It was like watching a warrior bleed to death. He grabbed a linen cloth to catch the liver-like afterbirth as it slid out of Catrin's womb.

Marcellus shifted his gaze between Ferrex and Negasi. "What do we do with this?"

"When in doubt, do nothing," Ferrex suggested.

Negasi took over the task, grumbling, "Idiots." He carefully wrapped the placenta in some cloth.

As Marcellus watched with a helpless feeling, Negasi helped Catrin lie down, with the baby in her arms. Seeing her shiver, Marcellus covered her with another cape offered by Ferrex and kissed her gently on the forehead.

"You are safe now. Rest while I talk with the men," he said softly.

Catrin smiled weakly and closed her eyes.

Marcellus beckoned for Ferrex and Negasi to follow him. Keeping his voice down, he asked, "What happened to the other soldiers Trystan spotted?"

"I told Trystan what was happening to Catrin," Negasi answered. "He said the formation of Roman soldiers continued to march away on the main road farther down. In the chaos, it is not clear what happened to Iberdees. Two of our men were found dead. It is not clear who attacked them."

"Do you think Brutius had a hand in this?" Ferrex asked.

Marcellus nodded. "Undoubtedly." His concern then shifted to Gawain, who had not been seen with his warriors and the Roman forces on the road.

Marcellus wiped the blood from his hands as he stepped over to the headless body to inspect it, then he glanced around the clearing. He told Negasi and Ferrex, "We will need to get rid of the bodies. But first, we need to find Iberdees and scout for any other potential danger. We should split the auxiliary forces. Negasi, you take command of the vanguard and have them protect Catrin. Ferrex, join me and the other men to search for Iberdees and scout for any other warriors."

50

AFTERMATH OF BATTLE

South of Durocortorum, Gaul, Samhain, 1 November, 28 AD

Catrin cuddled her newborn son, whose warmth flowed into her. As the baby vigorously suckled her breast, Catrin felt her womb cramp and discharge sticky blood. The forest was eerily silent—except for the shrieks of ravens circling overhead and the drone of men's voices in the distance. She could sense her raven protector's rage as it pecked at the eyes of a soldier's severed head. Beside her, a second raven gawked at the vacant eyes of the dead centurion.

She felt the strength of Marcellus's arms lifting her, with the baby still nursing. He carried her to a nearby cypress tree and laid a sword beside her.

"You need to stay hidden while we scout the area," Marcellus warned. "Negasi and some of the auxiliaries will guard you."

"Are there more soldiers nearby?" Catrin asked.

"No. They are all dead," Marcellus said evenly, but she could tell by a glint of fear in his eyes that there may be more.

Light-headed and weak, Catrin clasped his hand. "Please, no more running. I'm tired and dirty. Get Iberdees to help me clean up."

He replied, "Iberdees has disappeared," which disquieted Catrin, and she suspected something sinister had happened to her.

Marcellus kissed her. "Everything will be fine. Trystan is now riding to Durocortorum to get some additional warriors and a midwife to tend to you."

Weary, Catrin could not keep her eyes open and fell into a dreamless sleep with the baby in her arms.

Later in the morning, Catrin awoke when the baby began to fuss. The forest was eerily quiet as the auxiliary cavalrymen stalked around her, tending to their horses. Marcellus and the others had not returned. She could sense something strange happening, as if weak, electrical charges were sparking in the air. Ravens were swooping down and landing on corpses to peck and eat tissue from the heads. The eyes were their favorites. Empty eye sockets stared at her as ravens left patches of bony skull.

Turning her gaze away from the horrific sight, she offered her son a breast to suckle. Stroking her son's hair, she inhaled his earthy scent. The rhythmic motion of her son's feeding mesmerized her into drowsiness.

Suddenly, ravens shrieked overhead, the sound followed by the hiss of flying arrows, snaps of their impact, and thuds of dropping ravens and human bodies. Catrin opened her eyes and saw an arrow whizz by, just barely missing her head. She cuddled her baby tightly and turned her back to protect him from the arrows. Glancing sideways, she saw some Roman auxiliary lying on the ground.

And then, her recurring nightmare became reality.

Tattooed warriors, shrieking their war cries, rushed through the trees, on foot or on horseback, brandishing their weapons. The bloodlust of the enemy was stopped by the legionaries' shield wall circled around Catrin. Negasi and six other men formed a second inner circle, ready with shields and swords to strike any enemy who broke through the front line.

But how long could they drive back the assault?

The chaos of battle split the air. War cries, clashing steel, trampling feet, horse neighs, blaring horns, and raven shrieks resonated all around the forest.

Catrin's heart wrenched at the fierce fighting. Fearing for the safety of her newborn, she hid him in a den an animal had dug out in the fallen tree behind her. She retrieved a *gladius* and dagger Marcellus had set near the tree and positioned herself to rise quickly and defend herself. Light-headed, she felt more blood ooze down her inner thighs, which were already irritated from dried blood from childbirth.

A tattooed horseman jumped over the shields of the front line. He threw a spear at Negasi, who abruptly leaned sideways to avoid the hit. The near miss galvanized Negasi into action. With the skill cf a gladiator and the circular swing of his sword, he sliced the shoulders of the warhorse.

The warrior flew over the horse's head and rolled on the blood-splattered, mossy ground. The warrior jumped to his feet. The whites of his eyes popped open when Negasi charged him, his sword in hand, its steel blade glinting in the sun.

Horrified, Catrin watched the raging fight. This was no longer a vision. This was reality. This was not the destiny her father had promised. It could not end like this, in carnage. Her father had foretold she would withdraw the sword embedded in the serpent stone on the white hills in her homeland and destroy Marrock.

But now, she was in the midst of battle in Gaul and could be slain—and her precious son with her.

"Father!" she cried out. "Why have you betrayed me?"

Simultaneously . . .

White Cliffs, Southeast Britannia

The portals through which the dead could pass to wander with the living had now opened. The spiritual guide, the Raven, heard Catrin's cries and awoke King Amren's soul in his skull.

"Now is the time to unleash Catrin's fury," the Raven proclaimed. "She must begin the trials of the ancestral druids to overthrow Marrock."

After the Raven's essence merged with a physical raven, it circled above Lud—Marrock's eldest, seven-year-old son, whose red, shoulder-length hair was as lustrous as wolf fur. The boy was brandishing a wooden sword in the courtyard of the newly built stone fortress. He had a razor-sharp dagger, which he had stolen from his father—or borrowed, as a young boy would rationalize—hidden at his side. The Raven knew Lud's greatest desire was to be like his father, who could shape-shift into a dragon with the powers of the souls that resided in the skulls of a dragon and his family. To arrest these powers until needed, Marrock roped the skulls together, weaving the ends in and out of each eye socket.

The Raven knew it could easily trick the gullible boy. It waddled around Lud, watching the boy thrust back and forth, pivot, and swing his sword all around. The boy tried to strike the Raven with the wooden blade.

"Lud. Lud," the Raven gurgled, teasing the boy.

With a lopsided smile, Lug swung the wooden blade again to whack the Raven. The bird again dodged the strike.

The Raven continued to taunt the boy, hopping away every time the boy thrust his wooden blade at it. "Lud. Lud," it mocked, waddling to the recently finished chamber used to display the family skulls, roped together with the dragon's skull.

The Raven pecked at the chamber's door that Lud opened to let them both in. The bright golden glow from the room glinted in Lud's eyes.

South of Durocortorum

To Catrin's horror, four more warriors rushed at Negasi, two in front and one at each side. Negasi yanked his sword out of his last kill and held his shield up to defend himself from the warrior charging at him in front, then swiftly pivoted and slashed the thigh of another.

Terrified, Catrin's heart raced as she glanced around, hoping to see Marcellus and Ferrex return with other forces. Two auxiliaries in the outer circle were struck down, leaving a gap in the shield wall.

A blue-faced horseman broke through. An auxiliary threw a spear at him but missed.

Chaos erupted as the battle crept closer to Catrin. She cried out, "Father, don't let me die like this! Send me the battle raven!"

In the midst of the fighting, a raven landed in front of her; its amber eyes glowed—a sign the creature had connected with her spiritual Raven guide.

Shrine of Skulls, Britannia

The Raven hopped into the shrine of skulls, croaking, "Lud. Lud. Loose. Loose." Then, it flapped its wings and flew to the top of King Amren's skull.

The display of interconnected skulls was chest-high to Lud. The boy smirked and flipped out the dagger. He took a step forward but then hesitated.

The Raven continued to tease, "Loose. Loose," then connected with the boy's thoughts.

Lud bit his lip and appeared to be in a trance as he began to slice the rope connecting the dragon's skull to King Amren's skull.

"Lud. Loose!" the Raven shrieked.

Lud's blade sliced faster and faster.

"Lud, loose. Lud, loose!" the Raven screeched.

The blade cut through the outer strands of the rope.

"Let loose. Let loose," the Raven's voice thundered.

Lud cut the last strand of rope and pulled one end out of the eye sockets of King Amren's skull. When Lud reached out to grab the Raven, still perched on Amren's skull, it pecked his hand.

Lud let out a wail at the top of his lungs as flashes of light transferred from the Raven's amber-colored eyes to Amren's skull. The flashes of light webbed around the skull like a lightning storm.

South of Durocortorum

Catrin's mind connected with the Raven. Burning shocks surged through her veins, empowering her with the magic of the ancient druids. Sensing her father's essence, she stood with renewed strength as hot blood seeped down her inner thighs. Clearheaded, she brandished her sword, ready to face anyone who challenged her.

Horsemen trampled through the failing outer shield wall. A warrior with a hideously scarred face stepped over the body of an auxiliary. The blue-tattooed dagger on his forehead seemed to jump out at her.

Gawain!

Catrin's heart wrenched as the assassin walked directly toward her with deadly intent in his feral eyes.

Negasi interceded and met the steel blade of Gawain's sword with his own. Sparks flew off the metal. Negasi lunged, his sword aimed at Gawain's chest. The assassin abruptly stepped back as the steel of his sword struck Negasi's blade with lightning speed. It was clear to Catrin that Gawain's skill with the sword evenly matched Negasi's. The two men fought fiercely, each stepping back and forth, then sideways, as they clashed. No one had the advantage in the fight until . . .

Gawain pivoted quickly and surprised Negasi with a deep cut to his right ankle.

Catrin gasped, anticipating Gawain's next maneuver would be another crippling strike against Negasi—her closest friend from the gladiatorial school. He'd risked his life to help her deliver her premature, stillborn daughter despite the lanista's order that she be left to die.

Rage and thirst for vengeance raced through her veins. "Father! Father!" she screamed. "Loose the forces now!"

Morning sunlight suddenly transformed into darkness. Lightning bolts webbed across the sky as Gawain sliced Negasi's other ankle, bringing him down.

Shrieks, screeches, and caws rose like a thunderstorm. Out of a dark cloud, a tornado of flapping black wings descended. The funnel touched the forest floor, emitting Otherworld ravens with razor-sharp beaks and talons.

Catrin turned back toward the fight between Negasi and Gawain. Despite ravens swarming around Gawain and attacking him from all sides, he lowered his sword swiftly on Negasi's neck. She gaped in wide-eyed horror as Negasi's head was separated from his shoulders. It felt as if all the air had been punched from her lungs.

The ravens continued their aerial assault on the remaining enemy, but Gawain, holding an arm up to protect himself from the onslaught of ravens diving at his face, moved with an even, steadfast pace toward Catrin, his bloody sword in hand.

Negasi's blood.

Readying her weapon, she watched as three surviving auxiliaries intercepted Gawain from all sides. A cloud of ravens darted all around, attacking the enemy, obscuring her vision of the battle.

Shrine of Skulls

"What have you done?" Marrock bellowed into the chamber.

Lud's eyes widened as his father appeared in the open doorway.

Marrock's blue eyes changed to a deadly amber glow. The Raven sensed his rage as he rushed into the chamber, pushing Lud aside. Before the Raven could escape its physical form, Marrock's teeth sank into its neck and tore off its head, disconnecting the forces from King Amren's skull.

South of Durocortorum

Catrin could no longer sense the charged energy from her father's skull. The ravens stopped their aerial attack and scattered all over the blood-spattered ground, fighting each other to feast on the mutilated bodies. No one from the battle was left, except Gawain and her. Every man who had fought to protect her was dead. The same was true for Gawain's warriors. She could not tell if the warriors had fallen from mortal wounds in battle or from the raven attack.

The previous clamor of battle faded into the bone-chilling sound of ravens pecking and tearing away flesh, loosening it from the skulls to gulp down. Even though thick blood continued to flow down her legs, she felt the bloodlust of the souls of the fallen warriors transmitting into her as she stared at Gawain. Blood-smeared, he was about twenty feet from her, looking wide-eyed at the ravens gorging on corpses all around him. Then, her baby's cries drew his attention.

Gawain's eyes shifted in the direction of the fallen tree where Catrin had hidden her son. He stared at the spot for a moment, then turned his gaze to her.

Conflicting desires tugged at Catrin; she did not know whether to pick up her baby to comfort him or to stay in her position. The baby's cries turned into gasping screams, tearing at her heart.

"Are you wounded?" Gawain shouted over the baby's crying.

Catrin's heart leapt into her throat as she tightened her grip on the hilt of the sword. The strong love she had for her son transfixed her. If needed, she would fight to the death to protect him. With both hands, she lifted her sword, ready to kill.

"I know how to use this," she said.

Also with sword in hand, Gawain regarded Catrin for several moments, then surprised her with the question, "Can you slay the dragon?"

At first confused by what he meant, Catrin paused and studied his grim face. She felt a searing pain on her face, as if hot metal was burning her flesh, then envisioned Marrock's moon-cratered face the ravens had sculpted while defending her when she was a young girl. Like then, the ravens had come to her aid when she most needed them. Thinking back to the reptilian image she had seen in her father's skull, she knew Marrock was the dragon.

"I can slay the dragon," she declared. "And I will slay you."

Gawain gave a wry smile, but then, his eyes fixed on something in the distance behind Catrin. He sheathed his sword. "We will meet again, I am sure," he said, and then, he gingerly stepped around the ravens still feasting on the flesh of the fallen. He mounted a nearby horse that had survived the battle and galloped off.

Catrin, hearing men's voices and horse hooves trampling, turned to find Marcellus, Ferrex, and Trystan returning with their forces. Iberdees was riding with Marcellus on his horse.

The ravens flew off the heads of the fallen warriors and formed the shape of an arrow as they flew toward the sun escaping the dark clouds.

51

BIRTH AND DEATH

South of Durocortorum, Samhain, 1 November, 28 AD

Catrin leaned over to pick up and cradle her screaming baby in her arms. The distress on her son's face tore at her heart. She sat down and offered him a breast, which he frantically suckled. Tears streamed down her face, and both relief and grief overcame her as she looked at the carnage— mutilated bodies, some headless, and heads eaten away to skulls on the blood-soaked ground. She had never seen ravens so quickly strip the flesh from the heads after a battle. Among the dead was Negasi, who'd valiantly fought off Gawain.

Marcellus, Ferrex, Trystan, and other warriors stooped over the bodies to inspect the carnage, while Iberdees knelt down by Catrin and took charge of the situation.

"Bring me the basket of supplies," Iberdees ordered, waving at Ferrex.

As Ferrex scurried away, she motioned to Marcellus. "Boil some water."

Trystan stepped forward. "I can do that." He turned to pick up some dried tinder to start a fire.

Iberdees touched Catrin's forehead and looked at the baby in her arms. "You poor dear, giving birth alone. I will take care of you and the baby."

"What happened to you?" Catrin asked.

"I was taken by some Roman soldiers, but Marcellus and his men rescued me," Iberdees said. She peeled back Catrin's eyelids and shot a concerned look at Marcellus.

"Is something wrong?" Catrin asked.

"I am not sure if it is a trick of the light, but there is an amber glow to your eyes," Iberdees remarked. She smiled at Catrin and squeezed her hand. "What can I do for you?"

"Please clean me and the baby. Bless me and remove any evil thing inside me," Catrin requested.

"Before I begin, I need to ask you some questions. Did you deliver the afterbirth in one piece?"

"Yes, it's wrapped in the cloth beside me."

"Was the cord cut?"

"No."

"Do you feel light-headed, ready to pass out from bleeding?"

"I am clearheaded and feel better than I did," Catrin answered.

"Both you and baby have good color," Iberdees said with a smile. She looked at Marcellus. "Please bring me a hot, wet cloth."

Marcellus nodded and stepped over to Trystan, who was boiling water in a copper pot.

Meanwhile, Iberdees pulled out salt, honey, and olive oil and mixed them in a red, glossed bowl. She leaned over Catrin. "First, I will wash the baby and then clean you."

Iberdees ceremoniously lifted her arms and unveiled the umbilical cord and placenta from the cloth, allowing the tissue to dry in the open air beside Catrin. Iberdees nudged the baby away from the breast, but he protested with wails.

Catrin protectively clutched her son closer.

"Don't worry," Iberdees assured her. "He is eager to use his lungs."

Catrin reluctantly let go of her baby and watched Iberdees rub a grainy mixture all over his tender skin. Marcellus handed Iberdees a warm, wet cloth so she could wash away the residue. She repeated the process, and the baby's mouth quivered as he screamed in protest.

"He is a fighter," Iberdees chuckled as she dabbed a little oil around the baby's face. She wiped away the remaining mucus, cut the dried umbilical cord, swaddled the baby with linen cloth, and handed him to Marcellus. She then washed Catrin with a wet cloth smelling of vinegar and helped her into a clean, loose-fitting tunic.

After finishing, Iberdees beckoned Marcellus over. "Dig a hole to bury her afterbirth. There are evil spirits of dead warriors still fighting around her."

Marcellus dug a hole next to an oak tree, where Iberdees reverently placed the placenta in some linen cloth and set it into the hole as she chanted.

Druantia, Goddess of Oak,
Accept our sacrifice,
Renew life from decay,
Embrace new life in your branches.

Catrin sensed Iberdees's warm and calming aura as she intoned, "In birth and battle, blood drains from mother and warrior. Blood from the dead springs forth new life in the spring."

After the ceremonial cleansing, Marcellus carried Catrin to a bedding of blankets, where she lay down. Iberdees handed Catrin the screaming baby, who immediately quieted down in her arms as they rested and bonded throughout the day.

That night, Catrin was filled with sorrow as she watched the remaining auxiliaries pile bodies on the pyres. She wept when she observed that the ravens had left Negasi's severed head untouched. His arms were crossed over a sword on his chest. Negasi had been there when she'd lost her daughter. And he'd been here to save her son.

The price of battle weighed heavily on Catrin's heart—the loss of Negasi was almost too much to bear as she lit the pyre. The flames lapped at his body, turning it to ashes that floated into the night sky.

The gallant Ethiopian warrior, known as the Black Sphynx when he was a gladiator, was now among the stars. Perhaps Amanitore, the queen he had loved and lost from his kingdom, was with him.

As Marcellus wrapped his arms around Catrin to comfort her, she recalled what Negasi had told her. *Hate can be as blind as love. Don't let either control you.*

The following morning, when the dead no longer wandered with the living, Catrin caressed her son's soft face as he nursed. Overwhelming joy filled her as she gazed into his gray eyes while his tiny mouth suckled at her breast. Their son now had a name.

Marcus Antonius Primus.

She looked up at the proud father and smiled, cherishing the moment, before they set off on the final journey to her destiny.

As the cart carried Catrin and her baby away to Durocortorum, Marcellus rode proudly beside them. The forest again became alive with the music of songbirds chirping and cuckoos whistling a winged beat. The wind whispered through the swaying branches with few remaining leaves. A nearby stream babbled as water flowed over rounded rocks and through the forest before draining into the river and finally merging with the ocean to her homeland.

Though emboldened with her renewed magical abilities, she sensed that yesterday's deadly conflict portended what would be needed to slay the dragon. The day of Samhain marked the beginning of the darker half of the year as winter approached.

LIST OF CHARACTERS
(ALPHABETICAL ORDER BY FIRST NAME)

Major Celtic Characters

Amren—King of the Cantiaci; beheaded by his son, Marrock; biological father of Catrin and Marrock

Boudicca—Daughter of Rhan and Marcellus; Agrona's soul was transmigrated into Boudicca at her birth

Catrin—Cantiaci queen, druidess, warrior, and gladiator; daughter of Amren and Rhiannon; Celtic wife of Marcellus Antonius (marriage not recognized by Rome)

Cynwrig—One-eyed Cantiaci warrior known as the Red Executioner

Falco—Gallic Horse trainer employed at the Antonii estate in Lugdunum, Gaul

Ferrex—Cantiaci warrior and gladiator known as the Red Lion; former mentor and loyal friend of Catrin; auxiliary cavalryman serving under Marcellus Antonius

Gawain—Marrock's deadliest assassin with a blue tattoo of a dagger on his forehead

Iberdees—Gallic prostitute and healer

Lud—Eldest son of Marrock and Ariene

Marrock—King of the Cantiaci, known as Blood Wolf; druid, wolf shape-shifter, and dragon shape-shifter; half brother of Catrin; son of Rhan and Amren; son-in-law of Cunobelin through his marriage to Ariene

Myrddin—Ancient druid, also known as the Wild Druid and Wandering Druid

Rhan—First queen of King Amren; powerful druidess who possessed Agrona as a child; both of their souls resided in the same body until Agrona's soul transmigrated into Boudicca

The Raven—Spiritual guide that Catrin can access through a physical raven

Trystan—Amren's second-in-command; former lover of Rhiannon; father of Vala and Mor

Minor or Ancestral Celtic Characters

Agrona—Amren's druidess adviser who, as a child, was possessed by Rhan; both Agrona's and Rhan's souls resided in Agrona's body until Agrona's soul was transmigrated into Boudicca

Adminius—Pro-Roman Catuvellauni prince; eldest son of Cunobelin; formerly betrothed to Catrin

Ariene—Catuvellauni druidess; wife of Marrock; daughter of King Cunobelin

Bladud—Adopted son of Cynwrig (named after Cynwrig's father); bastard son of Lucius Antonius and his slave, Selena

Caratacus—Anti-Roman Catuvellauni prince; son of Cunobelin

Celadus—Gallic slave responsible for operations of the Antonii estate in Lugdunum, Gaul

Corvus—Roman stage name for Catrin when she was a female gladiator

Cunobelin—King of the Catuvellauni; father of Adminius, Caratacus, and Togodumnus

Epaticcus—Brother of Cunobelin; ruler of the Atrebates Tribe at Calleva Atrebatum (modern-day Silchester, United Kingdom)

Finn—Marrock's bodyguard

Jago—Youngest son of Marrock and Ariene

Malena—Wife of Cynwrig; killed by Romans in an assault

Mor—Middle bastard sister of Catrin; daughter of Rhiannon and Trystan

Peccia—Young girl from the Atrebates tribal kingdom; captured by Marrock and sold as a slave to the Romans

Rhiannon—Second wife of King Amren; beheaded by her stepson, Marrock; mother of Vala, Mor, and Catrin

Togodumnus—Anti-Roman Catuvellauni prince; son of Cunobelin

Vala—Eldest bastard sister of Catrin; beheaded by Marrock; daughter of Rhiannon and Trystan

Vibius—Roman name for Catrin (who was disguised as a boy in the Roman legion)

Major Roman Characters

Antonia Minor—Second daughter of Marcus Antonius (Mark Antony) and Octavia; wife of Nero Claudius Drusus; half sister of Iullus Antonius

Brutius Antonius—Half brother of Marcellus Antonius; oldest son of Lucius Antonius

Decimus Flavius—Roman military commander (ranks include tribune, praetor, legatus, and governor); Catrin's master; patronage sponsored by Lucius Antonius

Lucius Antonius—Roman senator; father of Marcellus Antonius and Brutius Antonius; son of Iullus Antonius and Claudia Marcella; grandson of General Marcus Antonius (Mark Antony)

Marcellus Antonius—Roman military commander (ranks include tribune and praetor) and nobleman; Roman husband of Catrin; great-grandson of Marcus Antonius (Mark Antony); grandson of Iullus Antonius; youngest son of Lucius Antonius and Drusilla

Priscus Dius—Roman centurion and former gladiator serving under Decimus Flavius

Verus—Lanista who trains gladiators; patronage sponsored by Marcellus Antonius and Decimus Flavius

Minor or Ancestral Roman Characters

Arius Petronius—Roman nobleman and tribune; best friend of Marcellus Antonius

Augustus Caesar—First Roman emperor from 27 BC–14 AD; defeated Marcus Antonius (Mark Antony) in the Battle of Actium in 31 BC

Claudia Marcella Major—Eldest daughter of Octavia and her first husband, Gaius Claudius Marcellus Minor; wife of Iullus Antonius; grandmother of Lucius Antonius

Cornelia—Divorced wife of Brutius Antonius; daughter of Cossus Cornelius Lentulus

Cossus Cornelius Lentulus—Consul of Rome in 25 AD; former father-in-law of Brutius Antonius

Drusilla—Second wife of Lucius Antonius; mother of Marcellus Antonius

Eliana—Former Roman lover of Marcellus; wife to Consul M. Asinius Agrippa

Fulvia—Third wife of Marcus Antonius (Mark Antony); mother of Iullus Antonius

Gaius Justus—Centurion serving under Marcellus Antonius

Gaius Septimus—Former Roman soldier serving under Marcellus Antonius

Gaius Julius Caesar (Caligula)—Son of Germanicus and Agrippa the Elder; grandson of Antonia Minor and Nero Claudius Drusus; third Roman emperor, ruling from 37 AD–41 AD

Iullus Antonius—Roman consul, senator, and poet; second son of Marcus Antonius (Mark Antony) and his third wife, Fulvia; executed for adultery with Julia, daughter of Augustus; father of Lucius Antonius; grandfather of Marcellus Antonius

Julia the Elder—Augustus's only daughter; second wife of Tiberius; banished for adulterous affair with Iullus Antonius in 2 BC

Julia Augusta (Livia Drusilla)—Influential wife of Augustus Caesar; mother of Tiberius; according to Roman historian Tacitus, Tiberius loathed his mother and sent Caligula to deliver the funeral oration while he remained on Capri

Licinia—Daughter of Marcus Licinius Crassus Frugi; betrothed to Marcellus Antonius

Linos—Household steward of the Antonii villa in Rome

Livilla (Claudia Livia)—Only daughter of Antonia Minor and Nero Claudius Drusus; lover of Lucius Aelius Sejanus

Lucius Aelius Sejanus—Influential prefect of the Roman imperial body-guard, known as the Praetorian Guard, which he commanded during the reign of Roman Emperor Tiberius

Lucius Calpurnius Piso—Roman consul; shared duties with Consul Marcus Licinius Crassus Frugi

Marcus Claudius Marcellus—Son of Octavia and her first husband, Gaius Claudius Marcellus

Marcus Licinius Crassus Frugi—Praetor, Roman consul, and senator; political ally of Lucius Antonius

Marcus Antonius (Mark Antony)—Roman consul, triumvir, and general; lover of Cleopatra (marriage not recognized by Rome); father of Iullus Antonius; grandfather of Lucius Antonius; great-grandfather of Marcellus Antonius

Marcus Antonius Primus—Son of Catrin and Marcellus Antonius (Note: historical parentage unknown but assumed to be grandson or son of Lucius Antonius)

Octavia—Fourth wife of Marcus Antonius (Mark Antony); sister of Augustus Caesar, the first emperor of Rome

Quintus Livius—An optio reporting and enforcing the orders of Centurion Priscus Dius

Rufus—Roman slave dealer working in conjunction with Marrock, Brutius Antonius, and Decimus Flavius

Titus Asinius—Roman magistrate and landlord

Scribonia—Wife of Marcus Licinius Crassus Frugi

Tiberius Caesar Augustus—Roman Emperor from 14 AD–37 AD, succeeding the first emperor, Augustus Caesar

Titus Ennius—Magistrate and proprietor of the Red Cock tavern and stable in Lugdunum

Vibius Gallius—Jewelry shopkeeper on Capitoline Hill

Other Major Characters from the Roman Empire

Negasi—Ethiopian gladiator; befriended Catrin when she was a gladiator; auxiliary cavalryman serving under Marcellus Antonius

Selena—Ethiopian slave serving the Antonii villa in Rome; wife of Cynwrig; mother of Lucius Antonius's bastard son

Other Minor or Ancestral Characters from the Roman Empire

Amanitore—Ethiopian queen; former lover of Negasi

Adonis—Greek enforcer; lover of Brutius Antonius

Brigata—Former Germanian slave mistress of Lucius Antonius when he was a young man

Cleopatra—Egyptian queen; former mistress of Julius Caesar; mistress and wife of Marcus Antonius (Mark Antony) (marriage not recognized by Rome)

Deidre—Runaway slave from the Antonii estate in Lugdunum, Gaul

Gabriella—Slave who supervised household slaves at Brutius's Roman villa

Hector—Boy slave at the Antonii villa in Gaul whom Brutius first seduced and killed to silence him

Herta—Germanian slave assigned to serve Marcellus and Catrin

Orvius—Greek freeman assigned by Consul Frugi to be an administrative assistant to Marcellus Antonius

Ranulf—Germanian slave serving as a steward to Antonia Minor

Servia—Germanic household slave serving at the Antonii Villa in Gaul, Lugdunum

Mythological Deity

Andaste—Celtic war goddess

Apollo—Roman god of the sun, healing, music, truth, and divination

Janus—Roman god of beginnings, passages, and change

Juno—Roman goddess and female counterpart of Jupiter; goddess of marriage

Jupiter—Supreme god in the Roman pantheon of gods

Lugus—Celtic deity in the pantheon of gods associated with Mercury and sometimes known as the storm god or sun god; associated with Lugh in Irish mythology

Mars—Roman god of war

Minerva—Roman goddess of wisdom and strategic warfare

Moirai—Three Roman goddesses that spin the fates of humankind. **Nona** spins the thread of each person's fate, **Decuma** dispenses it, and **Morta** cuts the strand, determining the moment a person dies

Mother Goddess—Goddess of nature, motherhood, fertility, creation, and destruction

Pluto—Roman god of the Underworld

Raven—Celtic goddesses of war are linked with ravens symbolizing death and war; messenger of the Roman god Apollo

Cities in Britannia (Modern-Day United Kingdom)

Camulodunon—Catuvellauni capital; modern-day Colchester, United Kingdom

Calleva Atrebatum—Modern-day Silchester, United Kingdom

Dubris—Modern-day Dover, United Kingdom

Durovernum—Cantiaci capital; modern-day Canterbury, United Kingdom

Cities in Gaul (Modern-Day France)

Durocortorum—Modern-day Reims, France

Gesoriacum—Modern-day Boulogne-Sur-Mer, France

Lugdunum—Modern-day Lyon, France

Massilia—Modern-day Marseille, France

ACKNOWLEDGMENTS

I'm indebted to several people who have supported me on my adventure to write *Skull's Vengeance* (Book 2 *Curse of Clansmen and Kingsmen*). My original draft went through major revisions, incorporating new plotlines and twists, based on valuable feedback I received from my critique partners and developmental editor. First of all, my heartfelt appreciation is extended to my critique partners—Kate Anderson, Tom Goodfellow, and Ryanne Buck—for keeping me on track with the storyline and for making sure my characters were consistent. My developmental editor, Julie Cameron, provided me valuable feedback to keep the tale more focused on Catrin rather than Marcellus. As a result, I added several new chapters at the beginning of *Skull's Vengeance* to expand Catrin's adventure. The series will now expand to six books to adequately tell the epic tale. Catrin's quest to overthrow Marrock will be highlighted in **Book 5: *Dragon's Anvil***, and the series will conclude in **Book 6: *Raven's Sacrifice*.** It is also my vision to write a stand-alone historical fiction novel about Marcellus's involvement in the downfall of Sejanus, Commander of the Praetorian Guard, and to finish the prequel, *King's Curse*, centering on King Amren.

I'd also like to acknowledge Bublish, Inc., for editing, designing, and distributing *Skull's Vengeance*. Most of all, I'd like to thank my family, fellow writers, and readers who have joined me on this journey and inspired me. And finally, to my husband, Tom—my soul mate and warrior who is the embodiment of Ferrex—thank you for your support of my dream of becoming an author and for your advice on how to counter an opponent in a life-threatening fight.

AUTHOR'S NOTE

The *Curse of Clansmen and Kings* series is a blend of fantasy woven into the historical backdrop of ancient Britannia and Rome before the invasion of Emperor Claudius in 43 AD. Researching ancient Celts, who left almost no written records, was the biggest challenge in this project. Historical events had to be supplanted by Greek and Roman historians and medieval writers who spun Celtic mythology into their Christian beliefs. Archaeological findings from this time period also help fill in some of the gaps.

The political background used in this series is based on my research of southeast Celtic tribes in Britain, which evolved differently than those in Wales, Scotland, and Ireland. After Julius Caesar's military expeditions to southeast Britannia in 55–54 BC, Rome had a strong influence over its politics and trade. Many of the first-century British rulers, who were educated as hostages in Rome, adopted the taste for Roman luxury goods. To support their extravagant lifestyles, kings warred with other tribal territories to supply the Roman Empire with slaves and expand their territories.

Although there are no written accounts of any Roman expeditionary forces sent to Britain before Claudius's invasion in 43 AD, there are recorded incidents of British kings pleading for Rome's help to intervene on their behalf. Client kings, paying tribute to Rome, could rule their kingdoms independently, similar to Cleopatra's reign in Egypt. Archaeological evidence now supports that Claudius's invasion was nothing more than a peace-keeping mission to halt the expansion of anti-Roman factions led by Cunobelin's sons—Caratacus and Togodumnus. There may have already been a Roman military presence that protected the areas of Britannia vital to trading with the empire—an assumption I've used for writing the series. The tribal names in this novel are based on Ptolemy's map of Celtic kingdoms generated in 150 AD.

The Celtic characters in this novel are fictional except for Cunobelin, King of the Catuvellauni (referred to as the King of Britannia by the

396 ○ Linnea Tanner

Romans), and his sons, Adminius and Caratacus. Based on coin distribution, Adminius ruled over the Cantiaci but was deposed in 39 or 40
AD. His fall may have been the result of a revolt of the Cantiaci people
against the Catuvellauni rule. He fled to continental Europe and surren-
dered to Emperor Caligula, who falsely heralded this as a great victory
over Britannia. Epaticcus, the brother of Cunobelin and the ruler of the
Atrebates Tribe at Calleva (modern-day Silchester), is another historical
figure introduced in this book.

Several of the Celtic characters in the series speak Latin because of
their formal education in Rome or through their interactions with Roman
merchants or masters. Although the Celtic society was becoming more pa-
ternalistic, women were still held in high regard and could rule. The Roman
historian Tacticus writes that the Britons were accustomed to women commanders in war. The warrior queen Boudicca united the Celtic tribes in
Britannia and almost expelled their Roman conquerors in 61 AD. She is
also known as a powerful druidess who sacrificed some of her victims to
the war goddess Andaste—or so the Romans claim.

Though many of the Roman characters in this book are fictional, there
are some based on historical figures during the tumultuous period when
the infamous Praetorian Prefect, Lucius Aelius Sejanus, over-reached to
gain power from Emperor Tiberius Caesar Augustus through murder, conspiracy, and betrayal. Tiberius was the second emperor of Rome. Though
he'd been an able general and diplomat, his final years as emperor were
tyrannical. Rumors abounded of his sexual perversity and child moles-
tation. At the pinnacle of Sejanus's power as consul in 31 AD, Tiberius
unexpectedly had him arrested and mercilessly executed. One of my goals
is to write a separate, stand-alone historical fiction novel that highlights
the fall of Sejanus through the perspective of Marcellus.

Antonia Minor was the daughter of Marcus Antonius (Mark Antony)
and Octavia, the sister-in-law of Tiberius and the half sister of Iullus
Antonius. As a confidant to Tiberius, Antonia Minor may have had a role
in the downfall of Sejanus, motivated by her fears that Caligula would meet
the fate of his older brothers who were arrested and died during their exile.

She was probably unaware that her daughter, Livilla, who was engaged to Sejanus, was involved in a murder conspiracy to poison Tiberius's son in 23 AD. Julia Augusta (Livia Drusilla) was the influential wife of Augustus Caesar and the mother of Tiberius. According to the Roman historian Tacitus, Tiberius loathed his mother and sent Caligula to deliver her funeral oration in 29 AD while he remained isolated on Capri. He later vetoed honors granted by the Roman Senate after her death and canceled the fulfillment of her will.

Lucius Antonius was the son of Iullus Antonius and the grandson of Marcus Antonius (Mark Antony). Little is known about Lucius Antonius except that he lived in Gaul after his father, Iullus Antonius, was accused of treason and forced to fall on his sword. It is unclear whether Lucius had any children, but it is speculated he may have been the father or grandfather of the famous Roman general Marcus Antonius Primus, who was born around 30 AD. I've taken historical liberty that Marcus Antonius Primus is the son of Marcellus and Catrin.

Marcus Licinius Crassus Frugi (ally of Lucius Antonius), a powerful politician who came into favor with Claudius, may have been involved in diplomatic negotiations with British rulers during the Roman invasion in 43 AD.

Most of the information about the druids came from the accounts of Julius Caesar (100 BC–44 BC), who had personal dealings with the Celts in his conquest of Gaul. The druids were the intelligentsia of the Celtic tribe who could have more power than kings in making decisions. The druids believed their religion forbade them from committing their teachings to writings as these could be made public. The most profound philosophy that Caesar highlighted about the druids was their belief that the soul does not perish but instead passes from one body to another after death. The bravery of the Celts sprang from their lack of fear of death—the result of their belief that the soul does not die but is reincarnated after death. The head served as the dwelling place for the immortal soul. The human head was venerated above all else since the head was considered by the Celts to be the temple of the soul—the center of emotions, as well as of life itself, and a symbol of divinity and the powers of the world of the spirits. To possess the enemy's head was to possess his soul. As with so many aspects of the warrior's life, the taking of an opponent's head in battle, preferably in single combat, had a mystical significance. The series expands on the concept that magical power can be harnessed from souls trapped in their severed heads.

The Roman historian Diodorus Siculus wrote: "When their enemies fall, they cut off their heads and fasten them to the bridles of their horses; and handing over to their retainers the arms of their opponents all covered with blood, they carry them off as booty, singing a song of victory. These first fruits of victory they nail to the sides of their houses just as men do in certain kinds of hunting with the heads of wild beasts they have killed. They embalm the heads of their most distinguished foes in cedar oil and carefully preserve them. They show them to visitors, proudly stating that they had refused a large sum of money for them."

The importance and extent of the cult of the severed head among the Celts is demonstrated by their display in shrines, either mounted in stonework at La Roquepertuse in southern Gaul or on wooden poles at the Bredon Hill Fort in western Britain. It is interesting to note that in both instances, the heads were set up at the entrances. Perhaps the souls of these unfortunate warriors protected their enemies' strongholds.

Pliny the Elder (23 AD–79 AD), who came from a family of Roman colonists in Gaul, described the druids as natural scientists, doctors of medicine, and magicians. He referred to the druids as the *magi*, saying: "Even today Britain is still spellbound by magic, and performs its rites with so much ritual that seemed to be a source of Persian customs." Perhaps it was his fascination with magic that explained why he recounted the "Druid's egg" or "serpent's egg." The eggs were reportedly made by hissing snakes put together, the foam from their mouths producing a viscous slime that became a ball when tossed in the air and caught by a druid, who then used it to counteract incantations. In the series, this concept was used to explain how the dagger was embedded in the serpent stone.

Most of the fantastical elements of the series are based on magical abilities of heroes and heroines from Irish and Welsh mythology and legends.

SKULL'S VENGEANCE ✿ 399

I've expanded on the abilities of Catrin and Marrock to shape-shift and to harness the forces of nature. In Celtic mythology, the dragon is a gatekeeper to other worlds and was believed to influence the land. Areas frequented by dragons were believed to possess special power.

ABOUT THE AUTHOR

Linnea Tanner, an award-winning author, weaves Celtic tales of love, magical adventure, and political intrigue in Ancient Rome and Britannia. Since childhood, she has passionately read about ancient civilizations and mythology. Of particular interest are the enigmatic Celts, who were reputed as fierce warriors and mystical druids.

Linnea has extensively researched ancient and medieval history, mythology, and archaeology and has traveled to sites described within each of her books in the ***Curse of Clansmen and Kings*** series. Books released in her series include ***Apollo's Raven*** (Book 1), ***Dagger's Destiny*** (Book 2), ***Amulet's Rapture*** (Book 3), and ***Skull's Vengeance*** (Book 4). She has also released the historical fiction short story "**Two Faces of Janus**."

A Colorado native, Linnea attended the University of Colorado and earned both her bachelor's and master's degrees in chemistry. She lives in Fort Collins with her husband and has two children and six grandchildren.

DRAGON'S ANVIL
BOOK 5 OF CURSE OF CLANSMEN AND KINGS SERIES

Follow Catrin and Marcellus in their epic Celtic tale of forbidden love, magical adventure, and political intrigue in Ancient Rome and Britannia. Don't miss the next installment of the **CURSE OF CLANSMEN AND KINGS** series, coming soon.

Linnea Tanner's
DRAGON'S ANVIL
A Celtic warrior queen must meet her destiny, which was etched on her father's dagger, and slay the dragon.

Queen Catrin has barely escaped an ambush from Marrock's deadliest assassin while giving birth to her son in the midst of battle. Still, she must meet her destiny that was etched on her father's dagger and strike vengeance against her half brother, King Marrock. An evil sorcerer, Marrock can shape-shift into a dragon and wreak havoc on the kingdoms of Britannia. Catrin's devoted Roman husband, Marcellus, and her commanders join in the quest to slay the dragon in the darker half of the year as winter approaches.

But other enemies from Rome and Britannia stand in her way. Family loyalties are tested. Warriors fall. Betrayed and torn from those she loves, Catrin must embrace her essence as a dark druidess to face her greatest challenge yet: battling the dragon and ruling the kingdom as its rightful heir.

I would greatly appreciate if you would leave a
review for *SKULL'S VENGEANCE*.

To keep up-to-date with the latest news on the upcoming books in the epic
Curse of Clansmen and Kings series, please visit and
sign up for the FREE e-Bulletin:
https://www.linneatanner.com/

www.ingramcontent.com/pod-product-compliance
Lightning Source LLC
Chambersburg PA
CBHW021754190726
48290CB00005B/1271